If I
Stay

If I Stay

GAYLE FORMAN

BLACK SWAN

TRANSWORLD PUBLISHERS
61–63 Uxbridge Road, London W5 5SA
A Random House Group Company
www.rbooks.co.uk

IF I STAY
A BLACK SWAN BOOK: 9780552775458

First published in the United States by Dutton Books, a member of
Penguin Group (USA) Inc.
First published in Great Britain
in 2009 by Doubleday
an imprint of Random House Children's Books
Black Swan edition published 2010

Addresses for Random House Group Ltd companies outside the UK
can be found at: www.randomhouse.co.uk
The Random House Group Ltd Reg. No. 954009

The Random House Group Limited supports the Forest Stewardship Council®
(FSC®), the leading international forest-certification organisation. Our books
carrying the FSC label are printed on FSC®-certified paper. FSC is the only
forest-certification scheme supported by the leading environmental organisations,
including Greenpeace. Our paper procurement policy can be found at
www.randomhouse.co.uk/environment

MIX
Paper from
responsible sources
FSC® C016897

Typeset in 11/16.25pt Giovanni Book by
Falcon Oast Graphic Art Ltd.
Printed and bound by CPI Group (UK) Ltd, Croydon, CR0 4YY.

8 10 9

For Nick
Finally . . . Always

Contents

7:09 a.m.

Everyone thinks it was because of the snow. And in a way, I suppose that's true.

I wake up this morning to a thin blanket of white covering our front lawn. It isn't even an inch, but in this part of Oregon a slight dusting brings everything to a standstill as the one snowplow in the county gets busy clearing the roads. It is wet water that drops from the sky – and drops and drops and drops – not the frozen kind.

It is enough snow to cancel school. My little brother, Teddy, lets out a war whoop when Mom's AM radio announces the closures. 'Snow day!' he bellows. 'Dad, let's go make a snowman.'

My dad smiles and taps on his pipe. He started smoking one recently as part of this whole 1950s, *Father Knows Best* retro kick he is on. He also wears bow ties. I am never quite clear on whether all this is sartorial or sardonic – Dad's way of announcing that he used to be a punker but is now a middle-school English teacher, or if becoming a teacher has actually turned my dad into this genuine throwback. But I like the smell of the pipe tobacco. It is sweet and smoky, and reminds me of winters and wood-stoves.

'You can make a valiant try,' Dad tells Teddy. 'But it's hardly sticking to the roads. Maybe you should consider a snow amoeba.'

I can tell Dad is happy. Barely an inch of snow means that all the schools in the county are closed, including my high school and the middle school where Dad works, so it's an unexpected day off for him, too. My mother, who works for a travel agent in town, clicks off the radio and pours herself a second cup of coffee. 'Well, if you lot are playing hooky today, no way I'm going to work. It's simply not right.' She picks up the telephone to call in. When she's done, she looks at us. 'Should I make breakfast?'

Dad and I guffaw at the same time. Mom makes cereal and toast. Dad's the cook in the family.

Pretending not to hear us, she reaches into the

cabinet for a box of Bisquick. 'Please. How hard can it be? Who wants pancakes?'

'I do! I do!' Teddy yells. 'Can we have chocolate chips in them?'

'I don't see why not,' Mom replies.

'Woo-hoo!' Teddy yelps, waving his arms in the air.

'You have far too much energy for this early in the morning,' I tease. I turn to Mom. 'Maybe you shouldn't let Teddy drink so much coffee.'

'I've switched him to decaf,' Mom volleys back. 'He's just naturally exuberant.'

'As long as you're not switching *me* to decaf,' I say.

'That would be child abuse,' Dad says.

Mom hands me a steaming mug and the newspaper.

'There's a nice picture of your young man in there,' she says.

'Really? A picture?'

'Yep. It's about the most we've seen of him since summer,' Mom says, giving me a sidelong glance with her eyebrow arched, her version of a soul-searching stare.

'I know,' I say, and then without meaning to, I sigh. Adam's band, Shooting Star, is on an upward spiral, which, is a great thing – mostly.

'Ah, fame, wasted on the youth,' Dad says, but he's smiling. I know he's excited for Adam. Proud even.

I leaf through the newspaper to the calendar section. There's a small blurb about Shooting Star, with an even smaller picture of the four of them, next to a big article about Bikini and a huge picture of the band's lead singer: punk-rock-diva Brooke Vega. The bit about them basically says that local band Shooting Star is opening for Bikini on the Portland leg of Bikini's national tour. It doesn't mention the even-bigger-to-me news that last night Shooting Star headlined at a club in Seattle and, according to the text Adam sent me at midnight, sold out the place.

'Are you going tonight?' Dad asks.

'I was planning to. It depends if they shut down the whole state on account of the snow.'

'It *is* approaching a blizzard,' Dad says, pointing to a single snowflake floating its way to the earth.

'I'm also supposed to rehearse with some pianist from the college that Professor Christie dug up.' Professor Christie, a retired music teacher at the university who I've been working with for the last few years, is always looking for victims for me to play with. 'Keep you sharp so you can show all those Juilliard snobs how it's really done,' she says.

I haven't gotten into Juilliard yet, but my audition went really well. The Bach suite and the Shostakovich had both flown out of me like never before, like my fingers were just an extension of the strings and bow. When I'd finished playing, panting, my legs shaking from pressing together so hard, one judge had clapped a little, which I guess doesn't happen very often. As I'd shuffled out, that same judge had told me that: 'it had been a long time since the school had seen an Oregon country girl'. Professor Christie had taken that to mean a guaranteed acceptance. I wasn't so sure that was true. And I wasn't 100 per cent sure that I wanted it to be true. Just like with Shooting Star's meteoric rise, my admission to Juilliard – if it happens – will create certain complications, or, more accurately, would compound the complications that have already cropped up in the last few months.

'I need more coffee. Anyone else?' Mom asks, hovering over me with the ancient percolator.

I sniff the coffee, the rich, black, oily French roast we all prefer. The smell alone perks me up. 'I'm pondering going back to bed,' I say. 'My cello's at school, so I can't even practice.'

'Not practice? For twenty-four hours? Be still, my broken heart,' Mom says. Though she has acquired a taste for classical music over the years – 'it's like learning to appreciate a stinky cheese' – she's been a not-always-delighted captive audience for many of my marathon rehearsals.

I hear a crash and a boom coming from upstairs. Teddy is pounding on his drum kit. It used to belong to Dad. Back when he'd played drums in a big-in-our-town, unknown-anywhere-else band, back when he'd worked at a record store.

Dad grins at Teddy's noise, and seeing that, I feel a familiar pang. I know it's silly but I have always wondered if Dad is disappointed that I didn't become a rock chick. I'd meant to. Then, in third grade, I'd wandered over to the cello in music class – it looked almost human to me. It looked like if you played it, it would tell you secrets, so I started playing. It's been almost ten years now and I haven't stopped.

'So much for going back to sleep,' Mom yells over Teddy's noise.

'What do you know, the snow's already melting.' Dad says, puffing on his pipe. I go to the back door and peek outside. A patch of sunlight has broken through the clouds, and I can hear the hiss of the ice melting. I close the door and go back to the table.

'I think the county overreacted,' I say.

'Maybe. But they can't un-cancel school. Horse is already out of the barn, and I already called in for the day off,' Mom says.

'Indeed. But we might take advantage of this unexpected boon and go somewhere,' Dad says. 'Take a drive. Visit Henry and Willow.' Henry and Willow are a couple of Mom and Dad's old music friends who'd also had a kid and decided to start behaving like grown-ups. They live in a big old farmhouse. Henry does Web stuff from the barn they converted into a home office and Willow works at a nearby hospital. They have a baby girl. That's the real reason Mom and Dad want to go out there. Teddy having just turned eight and me being seventeen means that we are long past giving off that sour-milk smell that makes adults melt.

'We can stop at BookBarn on the way back,' Mom says, as if to entice me. BookBarn is a giant, dusty old used-book store. In the back they keep a stash of twenty-five-cent classical records that nobody ever seems to buy except me. I keep a pile of them hidden under my bed. A collection of classical records is not the kind of thing you advertise.

I've shown them to Adam, but that was only after we'd already been together for five months. I'd expected him to laugh. He's such the cool guy with his pegged jeans and black low-tops, his effortlessly beat-up punk-rock tees and his subtle tattoos. He is so not the kind of guy to end up with someone like me. Which was why when I'd first spotted him watching me at the music studios at school two years ago, I'd been convinced he was making fun of me and I'd hidden from him. Anyhow, he hadn't laughed. It turned out he had a dusty collection of punk-rock records under his bed.

'We can also stop by Gran and Gramps for an early dinner,' Dad says, already reaching for the phone. 'We'll have you back in plenty of time to get to Portland,' he adds as he dials.

'I'm in,' I say. It isn't the lure of BookBarn, or the fact that Adam is on tour, or that my best friend, Kim, is busy doing yearbook stuff. It isn't even that my cello is at school or that I could stay home and watch TV or sleep. I'd actually rather go off with my family.

This is another thing you don't advertise about yourself, but Adam gets that, too.

'Teddy,' Dad calls. 'Get dressed. We're going on an adventure.'

Teddy finishes off his drum solo with a crash of cymbals. A moment later he's bounding into the kitchen fully dressed, as if he'd pulled on his clothes while careening down the steep wooden staircase of our drafty Victorian house. He started belting out the lines to 'School's Out'.

'Alice Cooper?' Dad asks. 'Have we no standards? At least sing the Ramones.'

Teddy carried on singing the tune over Dad's protests.

'Ever the optimist,' I say.

Mom laughs. She puts a plate of slightly charred pancakes down on the kitchen table. 'Eat up, family.'

8:17 a.m.

We pile into the car, a rusting Buick that was already old when Gran gave it to us after Teddy was born. Mom and Dad offer to let me drive, but I say no. Dad slips behind the wheel. He likes to drive now. He'd stubbornly refused to get a license for years, insisting on riding his bike everywhere. Back when he played music, his unwillingness to drive meant that his bandmates were the ones stuck behind the wheel on tours. They used to roll their eyes at him. Mom had done more than that. She'd pestered, cajoled, and sometimes yelled at Dad to get a license, but he'd insisted that he preferred pedal power. 'Well, then you better get to work on building a bike that can hold a family of three and keep us dry when it rains,' she'd demanded. To which Dad always had laughed and said that he'd get on that.

But when Mom had gotten pregnant with Teddy, she'd put her foot down. Enough, she said. Dad seemed to understand that something had changed. He'd stopped arguing and had gotten a driver's license. He'd also gone back to school to get his teaching certificate. I guess it was OK to be in arrested development with one kid. But with two, time to grow up. Time to start wearing a bow tie.

He has one on this morning, along with a flecked sport coat and vintage wingtips. 'Dressed for the snow, I see,' I say.

'I'm like the post office,' Dad replies, scraping the snow off the car with one of Teddy's plastic dinosaurs that are scattered on the lawn. 'Neither sleet nor rain nor a half inch of snow will compel me to dress like a lumberjack.'

'Hey, my relatives were lumberjacks,' Mom warns. 'No making fun of the white-trash woodsmen.'

'Wouldn't dream of it,' Dad replies. 'Just making stylistic contrasts.'

Dad has to turn the ignition over a few times before the car chokes to life. As usual, there is a battle for stereo dominance. Mom wants the news. Dad wants Frank Sinatra. Teddy wants SpongeBob SquarePants. I want the classical-music station, but recognizing that I'm the only classical fan in the family, I am willing to compromise with Shooting Star.

Dad brokers the deal. 'Seeing as we're missing school today, we ought to listen to the news for a while so we don't become ignoramuses—'

'I believe that's ignoramusi,' Mom says.

Dad rolls his eyes and clasps his hand over Mom's and clears his throat in that schoolteachery way of his. 'As I was saying, the news first, and then when the news is over, the classical station. Teddy, we will not torture you with that. You can use the Discman,' Dad says, starting to disconnect the portable player he's rigged to the car radio. 'But you are not allowed to play to Alice Cooper in my car. I forbid it.' Dad reaches into the glove box to examine what's inside. 'How about Jonathan Richman?'

'I want SpongeBob. It's in the machine,' Teddy shouts, bouncing up and down and pointing to the Discman. The chocolate-chip pancakes dowsed in syrup have clearly only enhanced his hyper excitement.

'Son, you break my heart,' Dad jokes. Both Teddy and I were raised on the goofy tunes of Jonathan Richman, who is Mom and Dad's musical patron saint.

Once the musical selections have been made, we are off. The road has some patches of snow, but mostly it's just wet. But this is Oregon. The roads are always wet. Mom used to joke that it was when the road was dry that people ran into trouble. 'They get cocky, throw caution to the wind, drive like assholes. The cops have a field day doling out speeding tickets.'

I lean my head against the car window, watching the scenery zip by, a tableau of dark-green fir trees dotted with snow, wispy strands of white fog, and heavy gray storm clouds up above. It's so warm in the car that the windows keep fogging up, and I draw little squiggles in the condensation.

When the news is over, we turn to the classical station. I hear the first few bars of Beethoven's Cello Sonata no. 3, which was the very piece I was supposed to be working on this afternoon. It feels like some kind of cosmic coincidence. I concentrate on the notes, imagining myself playing, feeling grateful for this chance to practice, happy to be in a warm car with my sonata and my family. I close my eyes.

You wouldn't expect the radio to work afterward. But it does.

The car is eviscerated. The impact of a four-ton pickup truck going sixty miles an hour plowing straight into the passenger side had the force of an atom bomb. It tore off the doors, sent the front-side passenger seat through the driver's-side window. It flipped the chassis, bouncing it across the road and ripped the engine apart as if it were no stronger than a spider web. It tossed wheels and hubcaps deep into the forest. It ignited bits of the gas tank, so that now tiny flames lap at the wet road.

And there was so much noise. A symphony of grinding, a chorus of popping, an aria of exploding, and finally, the sad clapping of hard metal cutting into soft trees. Then it went quiet, except for this: Beethoven's Cello Sonata no. 3, still playing. The car radio somehow still is attached to a battery and so Beethoven is broadcasting into the once-again tranquil February morning.

At first I figure everything is fine. For one, I can still hear the Beethoven. Then there's the fact that I am standing here in a ditch on the side of the road. When I look down, the jean skirt, cardigan sweater, and the black boots I put on this morning all look the same as they did when we left the house.

I climb up the embankment to get a better look at the car. It isn't even a car anymore. It's a metal skeleton, without seats, without passengers. Which means the rest of my family must have been thrown from the car like me. I brush off my hands onto my skirt and walk into the road to find them.

I see Dad first. Even from several feet away, I can make out the protrusion of the pipe in his jacket pocket. 'Dad,' I call, but as I walk toward him, the pavement grows slick and there are gray chunks of what looks like cauliflower. I know what I'm seeing right away but it somehow does not immediately connect back to my father. What springs into my mind are those news reports about tornadoes or fires, how they'll ravage one house but leave the one next door intact. Pieces of my father's brain are on the asphalt. But his pipe is in his left breast pocket.

I find Mom next. There's almost no blood on her, but her lips are already blue and the whites of her eyes are completely red, like a ghoul from a low-budget monster movie. She seems totally unreal. And it is the sight of her looking like some preposterous zombie that sends a hummingbird of panic ricocheting through me.

I need to find Teddy! Where is he? I spin around, suddenly frantic, like the time I lost him for ten minutes at the grocery store. I'd been convinced he'd been kidnapped. Of course, it had turned out that he'd wandered over to inspect the candy aisle. When I found him, I hadn't been sure whether to hug him or yell at him.

I run back toward the ditch where I came from and

I see a hand sticking out. 'Teddy! I'm right here!' I call. 'Reach up. I'll pull you out.' But when I get closer, I see the metal glint of a silver bracelet with tiny cello and guitar charms. Adam gave it to me for my seventeenth birthday. It's my bracelet. I was wearing it this morning. I look down at my wrist. I'm still wearing it now.

I edge closer and now I know that it's not Teddy lying there. It's me. The blood from my chest has seeped through my shirt, skirt and sweater, and is now pooling like paint drops on the virgin snow. One of my legs is askew, the skin and muscle peeled away so that I can see white streaks of bone. My eyes are closed, and my dark-brown hair is wet and rusty with blood.

I spin away. This isn't right. This cannot be happening. We are a family, going on a drive. This isn't real. I must have fallen asleep in the car. *No! Stop. Please stop. Please wake up!* I scream into the chilly air. It's cold. My breath should smoke. It doesn't. I stare down at my wrist, the one that looks fine, untouched by blood and gore, and I pinch as hard as I can.

I don't feel a thing.

I have had nightmares before – falling nightmares, playing-a-cello-recital-without-knowing-the-music nightmares, break-up-with-Adam nightmares – but I have always been able to command myself to open my eyes, to lift my head from the pillow, to halt the horror movie playing behind my closed lids. I try again. *Wake up!* I scream. *Wake up! Wakeupwakeupwakeup!* But I can't. I don't.

Then I hear something. It's the music. I can still hear the music. So I concentrate on that. I finger the notes of Beethoven's Cello Sonata no. 3 with my hands, as I often do when I listen to pieces I am working on. Adam calls it 'air cello.' He's always asking me if one day we can play a duet, him on air guitar, me on air cello. 'When we're done, we can thrash our air instruments,' he jokes. 'You know you want to.'

I play, just focusing on that, until the last bit of life in the car dies, and the music goes with it.

It isn't long after that the sirens come.

9:23 a.m.

Am I dead?

I actually have to ask myself this.

Am I dead?

At first it seemed obvious that I am. That the standing-here-watching part was temporary, an intermission before the bright light and the life-flashing-before-me business that would transport me to wherever I'm going next.

Except the paramedics are here now, along with the police and the fire department. Someone has put a sheet over my father. And a fireman is zipping Mom up into a plastic bag. I hear him discuss her with another firefighter, who looks like he can't be more than eighteen. The older one explains to the rookie that Mom was probably hit first and killed instantly, explaining the lack of blood. 'Immediate cardiac arrest,' he says. 'When your heart can't pump blood, you don't really bleed. You seep.'

I can't think about that, about Mom seeping. So instead I think how fitting it is that she was hit first, that she was the one to buffer us from the blow. It wasn't her choice, obviously, but it was her way.

But am I dead? The me who is lying on the edge of the road, my leg hanging down into the gulley, is surrounded by a team of men and women who are performing frantic ablutions over me and plugging my veins with I do not know what. I'm half naked, the paramedics having ripped open the top of my shirt. One of my breasts is exposed. Embarrassed, I look away.

The police have lit flares along the perimeter of the scene and are instructing cars in either direction to turn back, the road is closed. The police politely offer alternate routes, back roads that will take people where they need to be.

They must have places to go, the people in these cars, but a lot of them don't turn back. They climb out of their cars, hugging themselves against the cold. They appraise the scene. And then they look away, some of them crying, one woman throwing up into the ferns on the side of the road. And even though they don't know who we are or what has happened, they pray for us. I can feel them praying.

Which also makes me think I'm dead. That and the fact my body seems to be completely numb, though to look at me, at the leg that the sixty m.p.h. asphalt exfoliant has pared down to the bone, I should be in agony. And I'm not crying, either, even though I *know* that something unthinkable has just happened to my family. We are like Humpty Dumpty and all these king's horses and all these king's men cannot put us back together again.

I am pondering these things when the medic with the freckles and red hair who has been working on me answers my question. 'Her Glasgow Coma is an eight. Let's bag her now!' she screams.

She and the lantern-jawed medic snake a tube down my throat, attach a bag with a bulb to it, and start pumping. 'What's the ETA for Life Flight?'

'Ten minutes,' answers the medic. 'It takes twenty to get back to town.'

'We're going to get her there in fifteen if you have to speed like a fucking demon.'

I can tell what the guy is thinking. That it won't do me any good if they get into a crash, and I have to agree. But he doesn't say anything. Just clenches his jaw. They load me into the ambulance; the redhead climbs into the back with me. She pumps my bag with one hand, adjusts my IV and my monitors with the other. Then she smoothes a lock of hair from my forehead.

'You hang in there,' she tells me.

*

I played my first recital when I was ten. I'd been playing cello for two years at that point. At first, just at
school, as part of the music program. It was a fluke
that they even had a cello; they're very expensive and
fragile. But some old literature professor from the
university had died and bequeathed his Hamburg to
our school. It mostly sat in the corner. Most kids
wanted to learn to play guitar or saxophone.

When I announced to Mom and Dad that I was
going to become a cellist, they both burst out laughing. They apologized about it later, claiming that the
image of pint-size me with such a hulking instrument
between my spindly legs had made them crack up.
Once they'd realized I was serious, they immediately
swallowed their giggles and put on supportive faces.

But their reaction still stung – in ways that I never
told them about, and in ways that I'm not sure they
would've understood even if I had. Dad sometimes
joked that the hospital where I was born must have
accidentally swapped babies because I look nothing
like the rest of my family. They are all blond and fair
and I'm like their negative image, brown hair and
dark eyes. But as I got older, Dad's hospital joke took
on more meaning than I think he intended.

Sometimes I did feel like I came from a different tribe. I was not like my outgoing, ironic dad or my tough-chick mom. And as if to seal the deal, instead of learning to play electric guitar, I'd gone and chosen the cello.

But in my family, playing music was still more important than the type of music you played, so when after a few months it became clear that my love for the cello was no passing crush, my parents rented me one so I could practice at home. Rusty scales and triads led to first attempts at 'Twinkle, Twinkle, Little Star' that eventually gave way to basic *études* until I was playing Bach suites. My middle school didn't have much of a music program, so Mom found me a private teacher, a college student who came over once a week. Over the years there was a revolving batch of students who taught me, and then, as my skills surpassed theirs, my student teachers played with me.

This continued until ninth grade, when Dad, who'd known Professor Christie from when he'd worked at the music store, asked if she might be willing to offer me private lessons. She agreed to listen to me play, not expecting much, but as a favor to Dad, she later told me. She and Dad listened downstairs while I was up in my room practicing a Vivaldi sonata. When I came down for dinner, she offered to take over my training.

My first recital, though, was years before I met her. It was at a hall in town, a place that usually showcased local bands, so the acoustics were terrible for unamplified classical. I was playing a cello solo from Tchaikovsky's 'Dance of the Sugar Plum Fairy'.

Standing backstage, listening to other kids play scratchy violin and clunky piano compositions, I'd almost chickened out. I'd run to the stage door and huddled on the stoop outside, hyperventilating into my hands. My student teacher had flown into a minor panic and had sent out a search party.

Dad found me. He was just starting his hipster-to-square transformation, so he was wearing a vintage suit, with a studded leather belt and black ankle boots.

'You OK, Mia Oh-My-Uh?' he asked, sitting down next to me on the steps.

I shook my head, too ashamed to talk.

'What's up?'

'I can't do it,' I cried.

Dad cocked one of his bushy eyebrows and stared

at me with his gray-blue eyes. I felt like some mysterious foreign species he was observing and trying to figure out. He'd been playing in bands for ever. Obviously, he *never* got something as lame as stage fright.

'Well, that would be a shame,' Dad said. 'I've got a dandy of a recital present for you. Better than flowers.'

'Give it to someone else. I can't go out there. I'm not like you or Mom or even Teddy.' Teddy was just six months old at that point, but it was already clear that he had more personality, more verve, than I ever would. And of course, he was blond and blue-eyed. Even if he weren't, he'd been born in a birthing center, not a hospital, so there was no chance of an accidental baby swapping.

'It's true,' Dad mused. 'When Teddy gave his first harp concert, he was cool as cucumber. Such a prodigy.'

I laughed through my tears. Dad put a gentle arm around my shoulder. 'You know that I used to get the most ferocious jitters before a show.'

I looked at Dad, who always seemed absolutely sure of everything in the world. 'You're just saying that.'

He shook his head. 'No, I'm not. It was god-awful. And I was the drummer, way in the back. No one even paid any attention to me.'

'So what did you do?' I asked.

'He got wasted,' Mom interjected, poking her head out the stage door. She was wearing a black vinyl miniskirt, a red tank top, and Teddy, droolingly happy from his BabyBjörn. 'A pair of forty-ouncers before the show. I don't recommend that for you.'

'Your mother is probably right,' Dad said. 'Social services frowns on drunk ten-year-olds. Besides, when I dropped my drumsticks and puked onstage, it was punk. If you drop your bow and smell like a brewery, it will look gauche. You classical-music people are so snobby that way.'

Now I was laughing. I was still scared, but it was somehow comforting to think that maybe stage fright was a trait I'd inherited from Dad; I wasn't just some foundling, after all.

'What if I mess it up? What if I'm terrible?'

'I've got news for you, Mia. There's going to be all kinds of terrible in there, so you won't really stand out,' Mom said. Teddy gave a squeal of agreement.

'But seriously, how do you get over the jitters?'

Dad was still smiling but I could tell he had turned serious because he slowed down his speech. 'You don't. You just work through it. You just hang in there.'

So I went on. I didn't blaze through the piece. I didn't achieve glory or get a standing ovation, but I didn't muck it up entirely, either. And after the recital, I got my present. It was sitting in the passenger seat of the car, looking as human as that cello I'd been drawn to two years earlier. It wasn't a rental. It was mine.

10:12 a.m.

When my ambulance gets to the nearest hospital – not the one in my hometown but a small local place that looks more like an old-age home than a medical center – the medics rush me inside. 'I think we've got a collapsed lung. Get a chest tube in her and move her out!' the nice red-haired medic screams as she passes me off to a team of nurses and doctors.

'Where's the rest?' asks a bearded guy in scrubs.

'Other driver suffering mild concussions, being treated at the scene. Parents DOA Boy, approximately seven years old, just behind us.'

I let out a huge exhale, as though I've been holding my breath for the last twenty minutes. After seeing myself in that ditch, I had not been able to look for Teddy. If he were like Mom and Dad, like me, I . . . I didn't want to even think about it. But he isn't. He is alive.

They take me into a small room with bright lights. A doctor dabs some orange stuff onto the side of my chest and then rams a small plastic tube in me. Another doctor shines a flashlight into my eye. 'Nonresponsive,' he tells the nurse. 'The chopper's here. Get her to Trauma. Now!'

They rush me out of the ER and into the elevator. I have to jog to keep up. Right before the doors close, I notice that Willow is here. Which is odd. We were meant to be visiting her and Henry and the baby at home. Did she get called in because of the snow? Because of us? She rushes around the hospital hall, her face a mask of concentration. I don't think she even knows it is us yet. Maybe she even tried to call, left a message on Mom's cell phone, apologizing that there'd been an emergency and she wouldn't be home for our visit.

The elevator opens right onto the roof. A

helicopter, its blades swooshing the air, sits in the middle of a big red circle.

I've never been in a helicopter before. My best friend, Kim, has. She went on an aerial flight over Mount St Helens once with her uncle, a big-shot photographer for *National Geographic*.

'There he was, talking about the post-volcanic flora and I puked right on him and all over the cameras,' Kim told me in homeroom the next day. She still looked a little green from the experience.

Kim is on yearbook and has hopes of becoming a photographer. Her uncle had taken her on this trip as a favor, to nurture her budding talent. 'I even got some on his cameras,' Kim lamented. 'I'll never be a photographer now.'

'There are all kinds of different photographers,' I told her. 'You don't necessarily need to go flying around in helicopters.'

Kim laughed. 'That's good. Because I'm never going on a helicopter again – and don't you, either!'

I want to tell Kim that sometimes you don't have a choice in the matter.

The hatch in the helicopter is opened, and my stretcher with all its tubes and lines is loaded in. I climb into the helicopter behind it. A medic bounds in next to me, still pumping the little plastic bulb that is apparently breathing for me. Once we lift off, I understand why Kim got so queasy. A helicopter is not like an airplane, a smooth fast bullet. A helicopter is more like a hockey puck bounced through the sky. Up and down, side to side. I have no idea how these people can work on me, can read the small computer print-outs, can drive this thing while they communicate about me through headsets, how they can do any of it with the chopper chopping around.

The helicopter hits an air pocket and by all rights it should make me queasy. But I don't feel anything, at least the me who's a bystander here does not. And the me on the stretcher doesn't seem to feel anything, either. Again I have to wonder if I'm dead but then I tell myself no. They would not have loaded me on this helicopter, would not be flying me across the lush forests if I were dead.

Also, if I were dead, I like to think Mom and Dad would've come for me by now.

I can see the time on the control panel. It's 10:37. I wonder what's happening back down on the ground.

Has Willow figured out who the emergency is? Has anyone phoned my grandparents? They live one town over from us, and I was looking forward to dinner with them. Gramps fishes and he smokes his own salmon and oysters, and we would've probably eaten that with Gran's home-made thick brown beer bread. Then Gran would've taken Teddy over to the giant recycling bins in town and let him swim around for magazines. Lately, he's had a thing for *Reader's Digest*. He likes to cut out the cartoons and make collages.

I wonder about Kim. There's no school today. I probably won't be in school tomorrow. She'll probably think I'm absent because I stayed out late listening to Adam and Shooting Star in Portland.

Portland. I am fairly certain that I'm being taken there. The helicopter pilot keeps talking to Trauma One. Outside the window, I can see the peak of Mount Hood looming. That means Portland is close.

Is Adam already there? He played in Seattle last night but he's always so full of adrenaline after a gig, and driving helps him to come down. The band is normally happy to let him chauffeur while they nap. If he's already in Portland, he's probably still asleep. When he wakes up, will he have coffee on Hawthorne

Boulevard? Maybe take a book over to the Japanese Garden? That's what we did the last time I went to Portland with him, only it was warmer then. Later this afternoon, I know that the band will do a sound check. And then Adam will go outside to await my arrival. At first, he'll think that I'm late. How is he going to know that I'm actually early? That I got to Portland this morning while the snow was still melting?

*

'Have you ever heard of this Yo-Yo Ma dude?' Adam asked me. It was the spring of my sophomore year, which was his junior year. By then, Adam had been watching me practice in the music wing for several months. Our school was one of those progressive ones that always got written up in national magazines because of its emphasis on the arts. We did get a lot of free periods to paint in the studio or practice music. I spent mine in the soundproof booths of the music wing. Adam was there a lot, too, playing guitar. Not the electric guitar he played in his band. Just acoustic melodies.

I rolled my eyes. 'Everyone's heard of Yo-Yo Ma.'

Adam grinned. I noticed for the first time that his smile was lopsided, his mouth sloping up on one side. He hooked his ringed thumb out toward the quad. 'I don't think you'll find five people out there who've heard of Yo-Yo Ma. And by the way, what kind of name is that? Is it ghetto or something? Yo Mama?'

'It's Chinese.'

Adam shook his head and laughed. 'I know plenty of Chinese people. They have names like Wei Chin. Or Lee something. Not Yo-Yo Ma.'

'You cannot be blaspheming the master,' I said. But then I laughed in spite of myself. It had taken me a few months to believe that Adam wasn't taking the piss out of me, and after that we'd started having these little conversations in the corridor.

Still, his attention baffled me. It wasn't that Adam was such a popular guy. He wasn't a jock or a most-likely-to-succeed sort. But he was cool. Cool in that he played in a band with people who went to the college in town. Cool in that he had his own rocker-ish style, procured from thrift stores and garage sales, not from Urban Outfitters knock-offs. Cool in that he seemed totally happy to sit in the lunchroom absorbed in a book, not just pretending to read because he didn't have anywhere to sit or anyone to sit with. That wasn't the case at all. He had a small group of friends and a large group of admirers.

And it wasn't like I was a dork, either. I had friends and a best friend to sit with at lunch. I had other good friends at the music conservatory camp I went to in the summer. People liked me well enough, but they also didn't really know me. I was quiet in class. I didn't raise my hand a lot or sass the teachers. And I was busy, much of my time spent practicing or playing in a string quartet or taking theory classes at the community college. Kids were nice enough to me, but they tended to treat me as if I were a grown-up. Another teacher. And you don't flirt with your teachers.

'What would you say if I said I had tickets to the master?' Adam asked me, a glint in his eyes.

'Shut up. You do not,' I said, shoving him a little harder than I'd meant to.

Adam pretended to fall against the glass wall. Then he dusted himself off. 'I do. At the Schnitzle place in Portland.'

'It's the Arlene Schnitzer Hall. It's part of the Symphony.'

'That's the place. I got tickets. A pair. You interested?'

'Are you serious? Yes! I was dying to go but they're like eighty dollars each. Wait, how did you get tickets?'

'A friend of the family gave them to my parents, but they can't go. It's no big thing,' Adam said quickly. 'Anyhow, it's Friday night. If you want, I'll pick you up at five-thirty and we'll drive to Portland together.'

'OK,' I said, like it was the most natural thing.

By Friday afternoon, though, I was more jittery than when I'd inadvertently drunk a whole pot of Dad's tar-strong coffee while studying for final exams last winter.

It wasn't Adam making me nervous. I'd grown comfortable enough around him by now. It was the uncertainty. What was this, exactly? A date? A friendly favor? An act of charity? I didn't like being on soft ground any more than I liked fumbling my way through a new movement. That's why I practiced so much, so I could rush myself on solid ground and then work out the details from there.

I changed my clothes about six times. Teddy, a kindergartner back then, sat in my bedroom, pulling the Calvin and Hobbes books down from shelves and pretending to read them. He cracked himself up, though I wasn't sure whether it was Calvin's high jinks or my own making him so goofy.

Mom popped her head in to check on my progress. 'He's just a guy, Mia,' she said when she saw me getting worked up.

'Yeah, but he's just the first guy I've ever gone on a maybe-date with,' I said. 'So I don't know whether to wear date clothes or symphony clothes – do people here even dress up for that kind of thing? Or should I just keep it casual, in case it's *not* a date?'

'Just wear something you feel good in,' she suggested. 'That way you're covered.' I'm sure Mom would've pulled out all the stops had she been me. In the pictures of her and Dad from the early days, she looked like a cross between a 1930s siren and a biker chick, with her pixie haircut, her big blue eyes coated in kohl eyeliner, and her rail-thin body always ensconced in some sexy get-up, like a lacy vintage camisole paired with skintight leather pants.

I sighed. I wished I could be so ballsy. In the end, I chose a long black skirt and a maroon short-sleeved sweater. Plain and simple. My trademark, I guess.

When Adam showed up in a sharkskin suit and Creepers (an ensemble that wholly impressed Dad), I realized that this really was a date. Of course, Adam would choose to dress up for the symphony and a 1960s sharkskin suit could've just been his cool take on formal, but I knew there was more to it than that. He seemed nervous as he shook hands with my dad and told him that he had his band's old CDs. 'To use as coasters, I hope,' Dad said. Adam looked surprised, unused to the parent being more sarcastic than the child, I imagine.

'Don't you kids get too crazy. Bad injuries at the last Yo-Yo Ma mosh pit,' Mom called as we walked down the lawn.

'Your parents are so cool,' Adam said, opening the car door for me.

'I know,' I replied.

We drove to Portland, making small talk. Adam played me snippets of bands he liked, a Swedish pop trio that sounded monotonous but then some Icelandic art band that was quite beautiful. We got a little lost downtown and made it to the concert hall with only a few minutes to spare.

Our seats were in the balcony. Nosebleeds. But you don't go to Yo-Yo Ma for the view, and the sound was incredible. That man has a way of making the cello sound like a crying woman one minute, a laughing child the next. Listening to him, I'm always reminded of why I started playing cello in the first place – that there is something so human and expressive about it.

When the concert started, I peered at Adam out of the corner of my eye. He seemed good-natured enough about the whole thing, but he kept looking at his program, probably counting off the movements until intermission. I worried that he was bored, but after a while I got too caught up in the music to care.

Then, when Yo-Yo Ma played 'Le Grand Tango', Adam reached over and grasped my hand. In any other context, this would have been cheesy, the old yawn-and-cop-a-feel move. But Adam wasn't looking at me. His eyes were closed and he was swaying slightly in his seat. He was lost in the music, too. I squeezed his hand back and we sat there like that for the rest of the concert.

Afterward, we bought coffees and doughnuts and walked along the river. It was misting and he took off his suit jacket and draped it over my shoulders.

'You didn't really get those tickets from a family friend, did you?' I asked.

I thought he would laugh or throw up his arm in mock surrender like he did when I beat him in an argument. But he looked straight at me, so I could see the green and browns and grays swimming around in his irises. He shook his head. 'That was two weeks of pizza-delivery tips,' he admitted.

I stopped walking. I could hear the water lapping below. 'Why?' I asked. 'Why me?'

'I've never seen anyone get as into music as you do. It's why I like to watch you practice. You get the cutest crease in your forehead, right there,' Adam said, touching me above the bridge of my nose. 'I'm obsessed with music and even I don't get transported like you do.'

'So, what? I'm like a social experiment to you?' I meant it to be jokey, but it came out sounding bitter.

'No, you're not an experiment,' Adam said. His voice was husky and choked.

I felt the heat flood my neck and I could sense myself blushing. I stared at my shoes. I knew that Adam was looking at me now with as much certainty as I knew that if I looked up he was going to kiss me. And it took me by surprise how much I wanted to be kissed by him, to realize that I'd thought about it so often that I'd memorized the exact shape of his lips, that I'd imagined running my finger down the cleft of his chin.

My eyes flickered upward. Adam was there waiting for me.

That was how it started.

12:19 p.m.

There are a lot of things wrong with me.

Apparently, I have a collapsed lung. A ruptured spleen. Internal bleeding of unknown origin. And most serious, the contusions on my brain. I've also got broken ribs. Abrasions on my legs, which will require skin grafts; and on my face, which will require cosmetic surgery – but, as the doctors note, that is only if I am lucky.

Right now, in surgery, the doctors have to remove my spleen, insert a new tube to drain my collapsed lung, and stanch whatever else might be causing the internal bleeding. There isn't a lot they can do for my brain.

'We'll just wait and see,' one of the surgeons says, looking at the CAT scan of my head. 'In the meantime, call down to the blood bank. I need two units of O neg and keep two units ahead.'

O negative. My blood type. I had no idea. It's not like it's something I've ever had to think about before. I've never been in the hospital unless you count the time I went to the emergency room after I cut my ankle on some broken glass. I didn't even need stitches then, just a tetanus shot.

In the operating room, the doctors are debating what music to play, just like we were in the car this morning. One guy wants jazz. Another wants rock. The anesthesiologist, who stands near my head, requests classical. I root for her, and I feel like that must help because someone pops on a Wagner CD, although I don't know that the rousing 'Ride of the Valkyries' is what I had in mind. I'd hoped for something a little lighter. *Four Seasons*, perhaps.

The operating room is small and crowded, full of blindingly bright lights, which highlight how grubby this place is. It's nothing like on TV, where operating rooms are like pristine theaters that could accom-modate an opera singer, *and* an audience. The floor, though buffed shiny, is dingy with scuff marks and rust streaks, which I take to be old bloodstains.

Blood. It is everywhere. It does not faze the doctors one bit. They slice and sew and suction through a river of it, like they are washing dishes in soapy water. Meanwhile, they pump an ever-replenishing stock into my veins.

The surgeon who wanted to listen to rock sweats a lot. One of the nurses has to periodically dab the perspiration from his face with gauze that she holds in tongs. At one point, he sweats through his mask and has to replace it.

The anesthesiologist has gentle fingers. She sits at my head, keeping an eye on all my vitals, adjusting the amounts of the fluids and gases and drugs they're giving me. She must be doing a good job because I don't appear to feel anything, even though they are yanking at my body. It's rough and messy work, nothing like that game Operation we used to play as kids where you had to be careful not touch the sides as you removed a bone, or the buzzer would go off.

The anesthesiologist absentmindedly strokes my

temples through her latex gloves. This is what Mom used to do when I came down with the flu or got one of those headaches that hurt so bad I used to imagine cutting open a vein in my temple just to relieve the pressure.

The Wagner CD has repeated twice now. The doctors decide it's time for a new genre. Jazz wins. People always assume that because I am into classical music, I'm a jazz aficionado. I'm not. Dad is. He loves it, especially the wild, latter-day Coltrane stuff. He says that jazz is punk for old people. I guess that explains it, because I don't like punk, either.

The operation goes on and on. I'm exhausted by it. I don't know how the doctors have the stamina to keep up. They're standing still, but it seems harder than running a marathon.

I start to zone out. And then I start to wonder about this state I'm in. If I'm not dead – and the heart monitor is bleeping along, so I assume I'm not – but I'm not in my body, either, can I go anywhere? Am I a ghost? Could I transport myself to a beach in Hawaii? Can I pop over to Carnegie Hall in New York City? Can I go to Teddy?

Just for the sake of experiment, I wiggle my nose

like Samantha on *Bewitched*. Nothing happens. I snap my fingers. Click my heels. I'm still here.

I decide to try a simpler maneuver. I walk into the wall, imagining that I'll float through it and come out the other side. Except that what happens when I walk into the wall is that I hit a wall.

A nurse bustles in with a bag of blood, and before the door shuts behind her, I slip through it. Now I'm in the hospital corridor. There are lots of doctors and nurses in blue and green scrubs hustling around. A woman on a gurney, her hair in a gauzy blue shower cap, an IV in her arm, calls out to 'William, William.' I walk a little farther. There are rows of operating rooms, all full of sleeping people. If the patients inside these rooms are like me, why then can't I see the people outside the people? Is everyone else loitering about like I seem to be? I'd really like to meet someone in my condition. I have some questions, like, what is this state I'm in exactly and how do I get out of it? How do I get back to my body? Do I have to wait for the doctors to wake me up? But there's no one else like me around. Maybe the rest of them figured out how to get to Hawaii.

I follow a nurse through a set of automatic double

doors. I'm in a small waiting room now. My grand-parents are here.

Gran is chattering away to Gramps, or maybe just to the air. It's her way of not letting emotion get the best of her. I've seen her do it before, when Gramps had a heart attack. She is wearing her wellies and her gardening smock, which is smudged with mud. She must have been working in her greenhouse when she heard about us. Gran's hair is short and curly and gray; she's been wearing it in a permanent wave, Dad says, since the 1970s. 'It's easy,' Gran says. 'No muss, no fuss.' This is so typical of her. No nonsense. She's so quint-essentially practical that most people would never guess she has a thing for angels. She keeps a collection of ceramic angels, yarn-doll angels, blown-glass angels, you-name-it angels, in a special china hutch in her sewing room. And she doesn't just collect angels; she believes in them. She thinks that they're everywhere. Once, a pair of loons nested in the pond in the woods behind their house. Gran was convinced that it was her long-dead parents, come to watch over her.

Another time, we were sitting outside on her porch and I saw a red bird. 'Is that a red crossbill?' I'd asked Gran.

She'd shaken her head. 'My sister Gloria is a cross-bill,' Gran had said, referring to my recently deceased great-aunt Glo, with whom Gran had never gotten along. 'She wouldn't be coming around here.'

Gramps is staring into the dregs of his Styrofoam cup, peeling away the top of it so that little white balls collect in his lap. I can tell it's the worst kind of swill, the kind that looks like it was brewed in 1997 and has been sitting on a burner ever since. Even so, I wouldn't mind a cup.

You can draw a straight line from Gramps to Dad to Teddy, although Gramps's wavy hair has gone from blond to gray and he is stockier than Teddy, who is a stick, and Dad, who is wiry and muscular from afternoon weight-lifting sessions at the local YMCA gym. But they all have the same watery gray-blue eyes, the color of the ocean on a cloudy day.

Maybe this is why I now find it hard to look at Gramps.

*

Juilliard was Gran's idea. She's from Massachusetts originally, but she moved to Oregon in 1955, on her own. Now that would be no big deal, but I guess fifty-two years ago it was kind of scandalous for a twenty-two-year-old unmarried woman to do that kind of thing. Gran claimed she was drawn to wild open wilderness and it didn't get more wild than the endless forests and craggy beaches of Oregon. She got a job as a secretary working for the Forest Service. Gramps was working there as a biologist.

We go back to Massachusetts sometimes in the summers, to a lodge in the western part of the state that for one week is taken over by Gran's extended family. That's when I see the second cousins and great aunts and uncles whose names I barely recognize. I have lots of family in Oregon, but they're all from Gramps's side.

Last summer at the Massachusetts retreat, I brought my cello so I could keep up my practicing for an upcoming chamber music concert. The flight wasn't full, so the stewardesses let it travel in a seat next to me, just like the pros do it. Teddy thought this was hilarious and kept trying to feed it pretzels.

At the lodge, I gave a little concert one night, in the main room, with my relatives and the dead game animals mounted on the wall as my audience.

It was after that that someone mentioned Juilliard, and Gran became taken with the idea.

At first, it seemed far-fetched. There was a perfectly good music program at the university near us. And, if I wanted to stretch, there was a conservatory in Seattle, which was only a few hours' drive. Juilliard was across the country. And expensive. Mom and Dad were intrigued with the idea of it, but I could tell neither one of them really wanted to relinquish me to New York City or go into hock so that I could maybe become a cellist for some second-rate small-town orchestra. They had no idea whether I was good enough. In fact, neither did I. Professor Christie told me that I was one of the most promising students she'd ever taught, but she'd never mentioned Juilliard to me. Juilliard was for virtuoso musicians, and it seemed arrogant to even think that they'd give me a second glance.

But after the retreat, when someone else, someone impartial and from the East Coast, deemed me Juilliard-worthy, the idea burrowed into Gran's brain. She took it upon herself to speak to Professor Christie about it, and my teacher took hold of the idea like a terrier to a bone.

So, I filled out my application, collected my letters of recommendation, and sent in a recording of my playing. I didn't tell Adam about any of this. I had told myself that it was because there was no point advertising it when even getting an audition was such a long shot. But even then I'd recognized that for the lie that it was. A small part of me felt like even applying was some kind of betrayal. Juilliard was in New York. Adam was here.

But not at high school anymore. He was a year ahead of me, and this past year, my senior year, he'd started at the university in town. He only went to school part-time now because Shooting Star was starting to get popular. There was a record deal with a Seattle-based label, and a lot of traveling to gigs. So only after I got the creamy envelope embossed with THE JUILLIARD SCHOOL and a letter inviting me to audition did I tell Adam that I'd applied and been granted an audition. I explained how many people didn't get that far. At first he looked a little awestruck, like he couldn't quite believe it. Then he gave a sad little smile. 'Yo Mama better watch his back,' he said.

* * *

The auditions were held in San Francisco. Dad had some big conference at the school that week and couldn't get away, and Mom had just started a new job at the travel agency, so Gran volunteered to accompany me. 'We'll make a girls' weekend of it. Take high tea at the Fairmont. Go window-shopping in Union Square. Ride the ferry to Alcatraz. We'll be tourists.'

But a week before we were due to leave, Gran tripped over a tree root and sprained her ankle. She had to wear one of those clunky boots and wasn't supposed to walk. Minor panic ensued. I said I could just go by myself – drive, or take the train, and come right back.

It was Gramps who insisted on taking me. We drove down together in his pickup truck. We didn't talk much, which was fine by me because I was so nervous. I kept fingering the Popsicle-stick good-luck talisman Teddy had presented me with before we left. 'Break an arm,' he'd told me.

Gramps and I listened to classical music and farm reports on the radio when we could pick up a station. Otherwise, we sat in silence. But it was such a calming silence; it made me relax and feel closer to him than any heart-to-heart would have.

Gran had booked us in a really frilly inn, and it was funny to see Gramps in his work boots and plaid flannel amid all the lacy doilies and potpourri. But he took it all in stride.

The audition was grueling. I had to play five pieces: a Shostakovich concerto, two Bach suites, all Tchaikovsky's *Pezzo capriccioso*, which was next to impossible, and a movement from Ennio Morricone's *The Mission*, a fun but risky choice because Yo-Yo Ma had covered this and everyone would compare. I walked out with my legs wobbly and my underarms wet with sweat. But my endorphins were surging and that, combined with the huge sense of relief, left me totally giddy.

'Shall we see the town?' Gramps asked, his lips twitching into a smile.

'Definitely!'

We did all the things Gran had promised we would do. Gramps took me to high tea and shopping, although for dinner, we skipped out on the reservations Gran had made at some fancy place on Fisherman's Wharf and instead wandered into Chinatown, looking for the restaurant with the longest line of people waiting outside, and ate there.

When we got back home, Gramps dropped me off and enveloped me in a hug. Normally, he was a handshaker, maybe a back patter on really special occasions. His hug was strong and tight, and I knew it was his way of telling me that he'd had a wonderful time.

'Me, too, Gramps,' I whispered.

3:47 p.m.

They just moved me out of the recovery room into the trauma intensive-care unit, or ICU. It's a horseshoe-shaped room with about a dozen beds and a cadre of nurses, who constantly bustle around, reading the computer print-outs that churn out from the feet of our beds recording our vital signs. In the middle of the room are more computers and a big desk, where another nurse sits.

I have two nurses who check in on me, along with the endless round of doctors. One is a taciturn doughy man with blond hair and a mustache, who I don't much like. And the other is a woman with skin so black it's blue and a lilt in her voice. She calls me 'sweetheart' and perpetually straightens the blankets around me, even though it's not like I'm kicking them off.

There are so many tubes attached to me that I cannot count them all: one down my throat breathing for me; one down my nose, keeping my stomach empty; one in my vein, hydrating me; one in my bladder, peeing for me; several on my chest, recording my heartbeat; another on my finger, recording my pulse. The ventilator that's doing my breathing has a soothing rhythm like a metronome, in, out, in, out.

No one, aside from the doctors and nurses and a social worker, has been in to see me. It's the social worker who speaks to Gran and Gramps in hushed sympathetic tones. She tells them that I am in 'grave' condition. I'm not entirely sure what that means – grave. On TV, patients are always critical, or stable. Grave sounds bad. Grave is where you go when things don't work out here.

'I wish there was something we could do,' Gran says. 'I feel so useless just waiting.'

'I'll see if I can get you in to see her in a little while,' the social worker says. She has frizzy gray hair and a coffee stain on her blouse; her face is kind. 'She's still sedated from the surgery and she's on a ventilator to help her breathe while her body heals from the trauma. But it can be helpful even for patients in a comatose state to hear from their loved ones.'

Gramps grunts in reply.

'Do you have any people you can call?' the social worker asks. 'Relatives who might like to be here with you. I understand this must be quite a trial for you, but the stronger you can be, the more it will help Mia.'

I startle when I hear the social worker say my name. It's a jarring reminder that it's me they're talking about. Gran tells her about the various people who are en route right now, aunts, uncles. I don't hear any mention of Adam.

Adam is the one I really want to see. I wish I knew where he was so I could try to go there. I have no idea how he's going to find out about me. Gran and Gramps don't have his phone number. They don't carry cell phones, so he can't call them. And I don't know how he'd even know to call them. The people who would normally pass along pertinent information that something has happened to me are in no position to do that.

I stand over the bleeping tubed lifeless form that is me. My skin is gray. My eyes are taped shut. I wish someone would take the tape off. It looks like it itches. The nice nurse bustles over. Her scrubs have lollipops on them, even though this isn't a pediatric unit. 'How's it going, sweetheart?' she asks me, as if we just bumped into each other in the grocery store.

*

It didn't start out so smoothly with Adam and me. I think I had this notion that love conquers all. And by the time he dropped me off from the Yo-Yo Ma concert, I think we were both aware that we were falling in love. I thought that getting to this part was the challenge. In books and movies, the stories always end when the two people finally have their romantic kiss. The happily-ever-after part is just assumed.

It didn't quite work that way for us. It turned out that coming from such far corners of the social universe had its downsides. We continued to see each other in the music wing, but these interactions remained platonic, as if neither one of us wanted to mess with a good thing. But whenever we met at other places in the school – when we sat together in the cafeteria or studied side by side on the quad on a sunny day – something was off. We were uncomfortable. Conversation was stilted. One of us would say something and the other would start to say something else at the same time.

'You go,' I'd say.

'No, you go,' Adam would say.

The politeness was painful. I wanted to push through it, to return to the glow of the night of the concert, but I was unsure of how to get back there.

Adam invited me to see his band play. This was even worse than school. If I felt like a fish out of water in my family, I felt like a fish on Mars in Adam's circle. He was always surrounded by funky, lively people, by cute girls with dyed hair and piercings, by aloof guys who perked up when Adam rock-talked with them. I couldn't do the groupie thing. And I didn't know how to rock talk at all. It was a language I should've understood, being both a musician and Dad's daughter, but I didn't. It was like how Mandarin speakers can sort of understand Cantonese but not really, even though non-Chinese people assume all Chinese can communicate with one another, even though Mandarin and Cantonese are actually different.

I dreaded going to shows with Adam. It wasn't that I was jealous. Or that I wasn't into his kind of music. I loved to watch him play. When he was onstage, it was like the guitar was a fifth limb, a natural extension of his body. And when he came offstage afterward, he would be sweaty but it was such a clean sweat that part of me was tempted to lick the side of his face, like it was a lollipop. I didn't, though.

Once the fans would descend, I'd skitter off to the sidelines. Adam would try to draw me back, to wrap an arm around my waist, but I'd disentangle myself and head back to the shadows.

'Don't you like me anymore?' Adam chided me after one show. He was kidding, but I could hear the hurt behind the offhand question.

'I don't know if I should keep coming to your shows,' I said.

'Why not?' he asked. This time he didn't try to disguise the hurt.

'I feel like I keep you from basking in it all. I don't want you to have to worry about me.'

Adam said that he didn't mind worrying about me, but I could tell that part of him did.

We probably would've broken up in those early weeks were it not for my house. At my house, with my family, we found a common ground. After we'd been together for a month, I took Adam home with me for his first family dinner with us. He sat in the kitchen with Dad, rock-talking. I observed, and I still didn't understand half of it, but unlike at the shows didn't feel left out.

'Do you play basketball?' Dad asked. When it came to observing sports, Dad was a baseball fanatic, but when it came to playing, he loved to shoot hoops.

'Sure,' Adam said. 'I mean, I'm not very good.'

'You don't need to be good; you just need to be committed. Want to play a quick game? You already have your basketball shoes on,' Dad said, looking at Adam's Converse high-tops. Then he turned to me. 'You mind?'

'Not at all,' I said, smiling. 'I can practice while you play.'

They went out to the courts behind the nearby

elementary school. They returned forty-five minutes later. Adam was covered with a sheen of sweat and looking a little dazed.

'What happened?' I asked. 'Did the old man whoop you?'

Adam shook his head and nodded at the same time. 'Well, yes. But it's not that. I got stung by a bee on my palm while we were playing. Your dad grabbed my hand and sucked the venom out.'

I nodded. This was a trick he'd learned from Gran, and unlike with rattlesnakes, it actually worked on bee stings. You got the stinger and the venom out, so you were left with only a little itch.

Adam broke into an embarrassed smile. He leaned in and whispered into my ear: 'I think I'm a little wigged out that I've been more intimate with your dad than I have with you.'

I laughed at that. But it was sort of true. In the few weeks we'd been together, we hadn't done much more than kiss. It wasn't that I was a prude. I *was* a virgin, but I certainly wasn't devoted to staying that way. And Adam certainly wasn't a virgin. It was more that our kissing had suffered from the same painful politeness as our conversations.

'Maybe we should remedy that,' I murmured.

Adam raised his eyebrows as if asking me a question. I blushed in response. All through dinner, we grinned at each other as we listened to Teddy, who was chattering about the dinosaur bones he'd apparently dug up in the back garden that afternoon. Dad had made his famous salt roast, which was my favorite dish, but I had no appetite. I pushed the food around my plate, hoping no one would notice. All the while, this little buzz was building inside me. I thought of the tuning fork I used to adjust my cello. Hitting it sets off vibrations in the note of A – vibrations that keep growing, and growing, until the harmonic pitch fills up the room. That's what Adam's grin was doing to me during dinner.

After the meal, Adam took a quick peek at Teddy's fossil finds, and then we went upstairs to my room and closed the door. Kim is not allowed to be alone in her house with boys – not that the opportunity ever came up. My parents had never mentioned any rules on this issue, but I had a feeling that they knew what was happening with Adam and me, and even though Dad liked to play it all *Father Knows Best*, in reality, he and Mom were suckers when it came to love.

Adam lay down on my bed, stretching his arms above his head. His whole face was grinning – eyes, nose, mouth. 'Play me,' he said.

'What?'

'I want you to play me like a cello.'

I started to protest that this made no sense, but then I realized it made perfect sense. I went to my closet and grabbed one of my spare bows. 'Take off your shirt,' I said, my voice quavering.

Adam did. As thin as he was, he was surprisingly built. I could've spent twenty minutes staring at the contours and valleys of his chest. But he wanted me closer. I wanted me closer.

I sat down next to him on the bed, perpendicular to his hips, so his long body was stretched out in front of me. The bow trembled as I placed it on the bed. I reached with my left hand and caressed Adam's head as if it were the scroll of my cello. He smiled again and closed his eyes. I relaxed a little. I fiddled with his ears as though they were the string pegs and then I playfully tickled him as he laughed softly. I placed two fingers on his Adam's apple. Then, taking a deep breath for courage, I plunged into his chest. I ran my hands up and down the length of his torso, focusing on the sinews in his muscles, assigning each one a string – A, G, C, D. I traced them down, one at a time, with the tip of my fingers. Adam got quiet then, as if he were concentrating on something.

I reached for the bow and brushed it across his hips, where I imagined the bridge of the cello would be. I played lightly at first and then with more force and speed as the song now playing in my head increased in intensity. Adam lay perfectly still, little groans escaping from his lips. I looked at the bow, looked at my hands, looked at Adam's face, and felt this surge of love, lust, and an unfamiliar feeling of power. I had never known that I could make someone feel this way.

When I finished, he stood up and kissed me long and deep. 'My turn,' he said. He pulled me to my feet and started by slipping the sweater over my head and edging down my jeans. Then he sat down on the bed and laid me across his lap. At first Adam did nothing except hold me. I closed my eyes and tried to feel his eyes on my body, seeing me as no one else ever had.

Then he began to play.

He strummed chords across the top of my chest, which tickled and made me laugh. He gently brushed his hands, moving farther down. I stopped giggling. The tuning fork intensified – its vibrations growing every time Adam touched me somewhere new.

After a while he switched to more of a Spanish-style, finger-picking type of playing. He used the top of my body as the fret board, caressing my hair, my face, my neck. He plucked at my chest and my belly, but I could feel him in places his hands were nowhere near. As he played on, the energy magnified; the tuning fork going crazy now, firing off vibrations all over, until my entire body was humming, until I was left breathless. And when I felt like I could not take it one more minute, the swirl of sensations hit a dizzying crescendo, sending every nerve ending in my body on high alert.

I opened my eyes, savoring the warm calm that was sweeping over me. I started to laugh. Adam did, too. We kissed for a while longer until it was time for him to go home.

As I walked him out to his car, I wanted to tell him that I loved him. But it seemed like such a cliché after what we'd just done. So I waited and told him the next day. 'That's a relief. I thought you might just be using me for sex,' he joked, smiling.

After that, we still had our problems, but being overly polite with each other wasn't one of them.

4:39 p.m.

It's almost a crowd now. Gran and Gramps. Uncle Greg. Aunt Diane. Aunt Kate. My cousins Heather and John and David. Dad is one of five kids, so there are still lots more relatives out there. Nobody is talking about Teddy, which leads me to believe that he's not here. He's probably still at the other hospital, being taken care of by Willow.

The relatives gather in the hospital waiting room. Not the little one on the surgical floor where Gran and Gramps were during my operation, but a larger one on the hospital's main floor that is tastefully decorated in shades of mauve and has comfy chairs and sofas and magazines that are almost current. Everyone still talks in hushed tones, as if being respectful of the other people waiting, even though it's only my family in the waiting room. It's all so serious, so ominous. I go back into the hallway to get a break.

I'm so happy when Kim arrives; happy to see the familiar sight of her long black hair in a single braid. She wears the braid every day and always, by lunch time, the curls and ringlets of her thick mane have managed to escape in rebellious little tendrils. But she refuses to surrender to that hair of hers, and every morning, it goes back into the braid.

Kim's mother is with her. She doesn't let Kim drive long distances, and I guess that after what's happened, there's no way she'd make an exception today. Mrs Schein is red-faced and blotchy, like she's been crying or is about to cry. I know this because I have seen her cry many times. She's very emotional. 'Drama queen,' is how Kim puts it. 'It's the Jewish-mother gene. She can't help it. I suppose I'll be like that one day, too,' Kim concedes.

Kim is so the opposite of that, so droll and funny in a low-key way that she's always having to say 'just kidding' to people who don't get her sarcastic sense of humor, that I cannot imagine her ever being like her mother. Then again, I don't have much basis for comparison. There are not a lot of Jewish mothers in our town or that many Jewish kids at our school. And the kids who are Jewish are usually only half, so all it means is that they have a menorah alongside their Christmas trees.

But Kim is really Jewish. Sometimes I have Friday-night dinner with her family when they light candles, eat braided bread, and drink wine (the only time I can imagine neurotic Mrs Schein allowing Kim to drink). Kim's expected to only date Jewish guys, which means she doesn't date. She jokes that this is the reason her family moved here, when in fact it was because her father was hired to run a computer-chip plant. When she was thirteen, she had a bat mitzvah at a temple in Portland, and during the candle-lighting ceremony at the reception, I got called up to light one. Every summer, she goes to Jewish sleep-away camp in New Jersey. It's called Camp Torah Habonim, but Kim calls it *Torah Whore*, because all the kids do all summer is hook up.

'Just like band camp,' she joked, though my summer conservatory program is nothing like *American Pie*.

Right now I can see Kim is annoyed. She's walking

fast, keeping a good ten feet between her and her mother as they march down the halls. Suddenly her shoulders go up like a cat that's just spied a dog. She swerves to face her mother.

'Stop it!' Kim demands. 'If I'm not crying, there's no fucking way you're allowed to.'

Kim never curses. So this shocks me.

'But,' Mrs Schein protests, 'how can you be so . . .' – sob – 'so calm when—'

'Cut it out!' Kim interjects. 'Mia is still here. So I'm not losing it. And if I don't lose it, you don't get to!'

Kim stalks off in the direction of the waiting room, her mother following limply behind. When they reach the waiting room and see my assembled family, Mrs Schein starts sniffling.

Kim doesn't curse this time. But her ears go pink, which is how I know she's still furious. 'Mother. I am going to leave you here. I'm taking a walk. I'll be back later.'

I follow her back out into the corridor. She wanders around the main lobby, loops around the gift shop, visits the cafeteria. She looks at the hospital directory. I think I know where she's headed before she does.

There's a small chapel in the basement. It's hushed in there, a library kind of quiet. There are plush chairs like the kind you find at a movie theater, and a muted soundtrack playing some New-Agey type music.

Kim slumps back in one of the chairs. She takes off her coat, the one that is black and velvet and that I have coveted since she bought it at some mall in New Jersey on a trip to visit her grandparents.

'I love Oregon,' she says with a hiccup attempt at a laugh. I can tell by her sarcastic tone that it's me she's talking to, not God. 'This is the hospital's idea of nondenominational.' She points around the chapel. There is a crucifix mounted on the wall, a flag of a cross draped over the lectern, and a few paintings of the Madonna and Child hanging in the back. 'We have a token Star of David,' she says, gesturing to the six-pointed star on the wall. 'But what about the Muslims? No prayer rugs or symbol to show which way is east toward Mecca? And what about the Buddhists? Couldn't they spring for a gong? I mean there are probably more Buddhists than Jews in Portland anyway.'

I sit down in a chair beside her. It feels so natural the way that Kim is talking to me like she always does. Other than the paramedic who told me to hang in there and the nurse who keeps asking me how I'm doing, no one has talked to me since the accident. They talk about me.

I've never actually seen Kim pray. I mean, she prayed at her bat mitzvah and she does the blessings at Shabbat dinner, but that is because she has to. Mostly, she makes light of her religion. But after she talks to me for a while, she closes her eyes and moves her lips and murmurs things in a language I don't understand.

She opens her eyes and wipes her hands together as if to say *Enough of that.* Then she reconsiders and adds a final appeal. 'Please don't die. I can understand why you'd want to, but think about this: If you die, there's going to be one of those cheesy Princess Diana memorials at school, where everyone puts flowers and candles and notes next to your locker.' She wipes away a renegade tear with the back of her hand. 'I know you'd hate that kind of thing.'

*

Maybe it was because we were too alike. As soon as Kim showed up on the scene, everyone assumed we'd be best friends just because we were both dark, quiet, studious and, at least outwardly, serious. The thing was, neither one of us was a particularly great student (straight B averages all around) or, for that matter, all that serious. We were serious about certain things – music in my case, art and photography in hers – and in the simplified world of junior high school, that was enough to set us apart as separated twins of some sort.

Immediately we got shoved together for everything. On Kim's third day of school, she was the only person to volunteer to be a team captain during a soccer match in PE, which I'd thought was beyond suck-uppy of her. As she put on her red jersey, the coach scanned the class to pick Team B's captain, his eyes settling on me, even though I was one of the least athletic girls. As I shuffled over to put on my jersey, I brushed past Kim, mumbling 'thanks a lot.'

The following week, our English teacher paired us together for a joint oral discussion on *To Kill a Mockingbird*. We sat across from each other in stony silence for about ten minutes. Finally, I said, 'I guess we should talk about racism in the Old South, or something.'

Kim ever so slightly rolled her eyes, which made me want to throw a dictionary at her. I was caught off guard by how intensely I already hated her. 'I read this book at my old school,' she said. 'The racism thing is kind of obvious. I think the bigger thing is people's goodness. Are they naturally good and turned bad by stuff like racism or are we naturally bad and need to work hard not to be?'

'Whatever,' I said. 'It's a stupid book.' I didn't know why I'd said that because I'd actually loved the book and had talked to Dad about it; he was using it for his student teaching. I hated Kim even more for making me betray a book I loved.

'Fine. We'll do your idea, then,' Kim said, and when we got a B minus, she seemed to gloat about our mediocre grade.

After that, we just didn't talk. That didn't stop teachers from pairing us together or everyone in the school from assuming that we were friends. The more that happened, the more we resented it – and each other. The more the world shoved us together, the more we shoved back – and against each other. We tried to pretend the other didn't exist even though the existence of our nemeses kept us both occupied for hours.

I felt compelled to give myself reasons why I hated Kim: She was a Goody Two-shoes. She was annoying. She was a show-off. Later, I found out that she did the same thing about me, though her major complaint was that she thought I was a bitch. And one day, she even wrote it to me. In English class, someone flung a folded-up square of notebook paper onto the floor next to my right foot. I picked it up and opened it. It read, *Bitch!*

Nobody had ever called me that before, and though I was automatically furious, deep down I was also flattered that I had elicited enough emotion to be worthy of the name. People called Mom that a lot, probably because she had a hard time holding her tongue and could be brutally blunt when she disagreed with you. She'd explode like a thunderstorm, and then be fine again. Anyhow, she didn't care that people called her a bitch. 'It's just another word for feminist,' she told me with pride. Even Dad called her that sometimes, but always in a jokey, complimentary way. Never during a fight. He knew better.

I looked up from my grammar book. There was only one person who would've sent this note to me, but I still scarcely believed it. I peered at the class.

Everyone had their faces in their books. Except for Kim. Her ears were so red that it made the little sideburn-like tendrils of dark hair look like they were also blushing. She was glaring at me. I might have been eleven years old and a little socially immature, but I recognized a gauntlet being thrown down when I saw it, and I had no choice but to take it up.

When we got older, we liked to joke that we were so glad we had that fist fight. Not only did it cement our friendship but it also provided us our first and likely *only* opportunity for a good brawl. When else were two girls like us going to come to blows? I wrestled on the ground with Teddy, and sometimes I pinched him, but a fist fight? He was just a baby, and even if he were older, Teddy was like half kid brother and half my own kid. I'd been babysitting him since he was a few weeks old. I could never hurt him like that. And Kim, an only child, didn't have any siblings to sock. Maybe at camp she could've gotten into a scuffle, but the consequences would've been dire: hours-long conflict-resolution seminars with the counselors and the rabbi. 'My people know how to fight with the best of them, but with words, with lots and lots of words,' she told me once.

But that fall day, we fought with fists. After the last bell, without a word, we followed each other out to the playground, dropped our backpacks on the ground, which was wet from the day's steady drizzle. She charged me like a bull, knocking the wind out of me. I punched her on the side of the head, fist closed, like men do. A crowd of kids gathered around to witness the spectacle. Fighting was novelty enough at our school. Girl-fighting was extra special. And good girls going at it was like hitting the jackpot.

By the time teachers separated us, half of the sixth grade was watching us (in fact, it was the ring of students loitering that alerted the playground monitors that something was up). The fight was a tie, I suppose. I had a split lip and a bruised wrist, the latter inflicted upon myself when my swing at Kim's shoulder missed her and landed squarely on the pole of the volleyball net. Kim had a swollen eye and a bad scrape on her thigh as a result of her tripping over her backpack as she attempted to kick me.

There was no heartfelt peacemaking, no official détente. Once the teachers separated us, Kim and I looked at each other and started laughing. After finagling ourselves out of a visit to the principal's office, we limped home. Kim told me that the only reason that she volunteered for team captain was that if you did that at the beginning of a school year, coaches tended to remember and that actually kept them from picking you in the future (a handy trick I co-opted from then on). I explained to her that I actually agreed with her take on *To Kill a Mockingbird*, which was one of my favorite books. And then that was it. We were friends, just as everyone had assumed all along that we would be. We never laid a hand on each other again, and even though we'd get into plenty of verbal clashes, our tiffs tended to end the way our fist fight had, with us cracking up.

After our big brawl, though, Mrs Schein refused to let Kim come over to my house, convinced that her daughter would return on crutches. Mom offered to go over and smooth things out, but I think that Dad and I both realized that given her temper, her diplomatic mission might end up with a restraining order against our family. In the end, Dad invited the Scheins over for a roast-chicken dinner, and though you could see Mrs Schein was still a little weirded out by my family – 'So you work in a record store while you study to become a teacher? And *you* do the cooking? How unusual,' she said to Dad – Mr Schein declared my parents decent and our family non-violent and told Kim's mother that Kim ought to be allowed to come and go freely.

For those few months in sixth grade, Kim and I shed our good-girl personas. Talk about our fight circulated, the details growing more exaggerated – broken ribs, torn-off fingernails, bite marks. But when we came back to school after winter break, it was all forgotten. We were back to being the dark, quiet, good-girl twins.

We didn't mind anymore. In fact, over the years that reputation has served us well. If, for instance, we were both absent on the same day, people automatically assumed we had come down with the same bug, not that we'd ditched school to watch art films being shown in the film-survey class at the university. When, as a prank, someone put our school up for sale, covering it with signs and posting a listing on eBay, suspicious eyes turned to Nelson Baker and Jenna McLaughlin, not to us. Even if we had owned up to the prank – as we'd planned to if anyone else got in trouble – we'd have had a hard time convincing anyone it really was us.

This always made Kim laugh. 'People believe what they want to believe,' she said.

4:47 p.m.

Mom once snuck me into a casino. We were going on vacation to Crater Lake and we stopped at a resort on an Indian reservation for the buffet lunch. Mom decided to do a bit of gambling, and I went with her while Dad stayed with Teddy, who was napping in his stroller. Mom sat down at the dollar blackjack tables. The dealer looked at me, then at Mom, who returned his mildly suspicious glance with a look sharp enough to cut diamonds followed by a smile more brilliant that any gem. The dealer sheepishly smiled back and didn't say a word. I watched Mom play, mesmerized. It seemed like we were in there for fifteen minutes but then Dad and Teddy came in search of us, both of them grumpy. It turned out we'd been there for over an hour.

The ICU is like that. You can't tell what time of day it is or how much time has passed. There's no natural light. And there's a constant soundtrack of noise, only instead of the electronic beeping of slot machines and the satisfying jangle of quarters, it's the hum and whir of all the medical equipment, the endless muffled pages over the PA, and the steady talk of the nurses.

I'm not entirely sure how long I've been in here. A while ago, the nurse I liked with the lilting accent said she was going home. 'I'll be back tomorrow, but I want to see you here, sweetheart,' she said. I thought that was weird at first. Wouldn't she want me to be home, or moved to another part of the hospital? But then I realized that she meant she wanted to see me in this ward, as opposed to dead.

The doctors keep coming around and pulling up my eyelids and waving around a flashlight. They are rough and hurried, like they don't consider eyelids worthy of gentleness. It makes you realize how little in life we touch one another's eyes. Maybe your parents will hold an eyelid up to get out a piece of dirt, or maybe your boyfriend will kiss your eyelids, light as a butterfly, just before you drift off to sleep. But eyelids are not like elbows or knees or shoulders, parts of the body accustomed to being jostled.

The social worker is at my bedside now. She is looking through my chart and talking to one of the nurses who normally sits at the big desk in the middle of the room. It is amazing the ways they watch you here. If they're not waving penlights in your eyes or reading the print-outs that come tumbling out from the bedside printers, then they are watching your vitals from a central computer screen. If anything goes slightly amiss, one of the monitors starts bleeping. There is always an alarm going off somewhere. At first, it scared me, but now I realize that half the time, when the alarms go off, it's the machines that are malfunctioning, not the people.

The social worker looks exhausted, as if she wouldn't mind crawling into one of the open beds. I am not her only sick person. She has been shuttling back and forth between patients and families all afternoon. She's the bridge between the doctors and the people, and you can see the strain of balancing between those two worlds.

After she reads my chart and talks to the nurses, she goes back downstairs to my family, who have stopped talking in hushed tones and are now all engaged in solitary activities. Gran is knitting. Gramps is pretending to nap. Aunt Diane playing sudoku. My cousins are taking turns on a GameBoy, the sound turned to mute.

Kim has left. When she came back to the waiting room after visiting the chapel, she found Mrs Schein a total wreck. She'd seemed so embarrassed and had hustled her mother out. Actually, I think having Mrs Schein there probably helped. Comforting her gave everyone else something to do, a way to feel useful. Now they're back to feeling useless, back to the endless wait.

When the social worker walks into the waiting room, everyone stands up, like they're greeting royalty. She gives a half smile, which I've seen her do several times already today. I think it's her signal that everything is OK, or status quo, and she's just here to deliver an update, not to drop a bomb.

'Mia is still unconscious, but her vital signs are improving,' she tells the assembled relatives, who have abandoned their distractions haphazardly on the chairs. 'She's in with the respiratory therapists right now. They're running tests to see how her lungs are functioning and whether she can be weaned off the ventilator.'

'That's good news, then?' Aunt Diane asks. 'I mean if she can breathe on her own, then she'll wake up soon?'

The social worker gives a practiced sympathetic nod. 'It's a good step if she can breathe on her own. It shows her lungs are healing and her internal injuries are stabilizing. The question mark is still the brain contusions.'

'Why is that?' Cousin Heather interrupts.

'We don't know when she will wake up on her own, or the extent of the damage to her brain. These first twenty-four hours are the most critical and Mia is getting the best possible care.'

'Can we see her?' Gramps asks.

The social worker nods. 'That's why I'm here. I think it would be good for Mia to have a short visit. Just one or two people.'

'We'll go,' Gran says, stepping forward. Gramps is by her side.

'Yes, that's what I thought,' the social worker says. 'We won't be long,' she says to the rest of the family.

The three of them walk down the hall in silence. In the elevator, the social worker attempts to prepare my grandparents for the sight of me, explaining the extent of my external injuries, which look bad, but are treatable. It's the internal injuries that they're worried about, she says.

She's acting like my grandparents are children. But they're tougher than they look. Gramps was a medic in Korea. And Gran, she's always rescuing things: birds with broken wings, a sick beaver, a deer hit by a car. The deer went to a wildlife sanctuary, which is funny because Gran usually hates deer; they eat up her garden. 'Pretty rats,' she calls them. 'Tasty rats' is what Gramps calls them when he grills up venison steaks. But that one deer, Gran couldn't bear to see it suffer, so she rescued it. Part of me suspects she thought it was one of her angels.

Still, when they come through the automatic double doors into the ICU both of them stop, as if repelled by an invisible barrier. Gran takes Gramps's hand, and I try to remember if I've ever seen them hold hands before. Gran scans the beds for me, but just as the social worker starts to point out where I am, Gramps sees me and he strides across the floor to my bed.

'Hello, duck,' he says. He hasn't called me that in ages, not since I was younger than Teddy. Gran walks slowly to where I am, taking little gulps of air as she comes. Maybe those wounded animals weren't such good prep after all.

The social worker pulls over two chairs, setting them up at the foot of my bed. 'Mia, your grandparents are here.' She motions for them to sit down. 'I'll leave you alone now.'

'Can she hear us?' Gran asks. 'If we talk to her, she'll understand?'

'Truly, I don't know,' the social worker responds. 'But your presence can be soothing so long as what you say is soothing.' Then she gives them a stern look, as if to tell them not to say anything bad to upset me. I know it's her job to warn them about things like this and that she is busy with a thousand things and can't always be so sensitive, but for a second, I hate her.

After the social worker leaves, Gran and Gramps sit in silence for a minute. Then Gran starts prattling on about the orchids she's growing in her greenhouse. I notice that she's changed out of her gardening smock into a clean pair of corduroy pants and a sweater. Someone must have stopped by her house to bring her fresh clothes. Gramps is sitting very still, and his hands are shaking. He's not much of a talker, so it must be hard for him being ordered to chat with me now.

Another nurse comes by. She has dark hair and

dark eyes brightened with lots of shimmery eye make-up. Her nails are acrylic and have heart decals on them. She must have to work hard to keep her nails so pretty. I admire that.

She's not my nurse but she comes up to Gran and Gramps just the same. 'Don't you doubt for a second that she can hear you,' she tells them. 'She's aware of everything that's going on.' She stands there with her hands on her hips. I can almost picture her snapping gum. Gran and Gramps stare at her, lapping up what she's telling them. 'You might think that the doctors or nurses or all this is running the show,' she says, gesturing to the wall of medical equipment. 'Nuh-uh. *She's* running the show. Maybe she's just biding her time. So you talk to her. You tell her to take all the time she needs, but to come on back. You're waiting for her.'

*

Mom and Dad would never call Teddy or me mistakes. Or accidents. Or surprises. Or any of those other stupid euphemisms. But neither one of us was planned, and they never tried to hide that.

Mom got pregnant with me when she was young.

Not teenager-young, but young for their set of friends. She was twenty-three and she and Dad had already been married for a year.

In a funny way, Dad was always a bow-tie wearer, always a little more traditional than you might imagine. Because even though he had blue hair and tattoos and wore leather jackets and worked in a record store, he wanted to marry Mom back at a time when the rest of their friends were still having drunken one-night stands. '*Girlfriend* is such a stupid word,' he said. 'I couldn't stand calling her that. So, we had to get married, so I could call her "wife".'

Mom, for her part, had a messed-up family. She didn't go into the gory details with me, but I knew her father was long gone and for a while she had been out of touch with her mother, though now we saw Grandma and Papa Richard, which is what we called Mom's stepfather, a couple of times a year.

So Mom was taken not just with Dad but with the big, mostly intact, relatively normal family he belonged to. She agreed to marry Dad even though they'd been together just a year. Of course, they still did it their way. They were married by a lesbian justice of the peace while their friends played a guitar-feedback-heavy version of 'The Wedding March.' The bride wore a white fringed flapper dress and black spiked boots. The groom wore leather.

*   *   *

They got pregnant with me because of someone else's wedding. One of Dad's music buddies who'd moved to Seattle had gotten his girlfriend pregnant, so they were doing the shotgun thing. Mom and Dad went to the wedding, and at the reception, they got a little drunk and back at the hotel weren't as careful as usual. Three months later there was a thin blue line on the pregnancy test.

The way they tell it, neither felt particularly ready to be parents. Neither one felt like an adult yet. But there was no question that they would have me. Mom was adamantly pro-choice. She had a bumper sticker on the car that read IF YOU CAN'T TRUST ME WITH A CHOICE, HOW CAN YOU TRUST ME WITH A CHILD? But in her case the choice was to keep me.

Dad was more hesitant. More freaked out. Until the minute the doctor pulled me out and then he started to cry.

'That's poppycock,' he would say when Mom recounted the story. 'I did no such thing.'

'You didn't cry then?' Mom asked in sarcastic amusement.

'I *teared*. I did not cry.' Then Dad winked at me and pantomimed weeping like a baby.

Because I was the only kid in Mom and Dad's group of friends, I was a novelty. I was raised by the music community, with dozens of aunties and uncles who took me in as their own little foundling, even after I started showing a strange preference for classical music. I didn't want for real family, either. Gran and Gramps lived nearby, and they were happy to take me for weekends so Mom and Dad could act wild and stay out all night for one of Dad's shows.

Around the time I was four, I think my parents realized that they were actually doing it – raising a kid – even though they didn't have a ton of money or 'real' jobs. We had a nice house with cheap rent. I had clothes (even if they were hand-me-downs from my cousins) and I was growing up happy and healthy. 'You were like an experiment,' Dad said. 'Surprisingly successful. We thought it must be a fluke. We needed another kid as a kind of control group.'

They tried for four years. Mom got pregnant twice and had two miscarriages. They were sad about it, but they didn't have the money to do all the fertility stuff that people do. By the time I was nine, they'd decided that maybe it was for the best. I was becoming independent. They stopped trying.

As if to convince themselves how great it was not to be tied down by a baby, Mom and Dad bought us tickets to go visit New York for a week. It was supposed to be a musical pilgrimage. We would go to the infamous punk club CBGB's and Carnegie Hall. But when to her surprise, Mom discovered she was pregnant, and then to her greater surprise, stayed pregnant past the first trimester, we had to cancel the trip. She was tired and sick to her stomach and so grumpy Dad joked that she'd probably scare the New Yorkers. Besides, babies were expensive and we needed to save.

I didn't mind. I was excited about a baby. And I knew that Carnegie Hall wasn't going anywhere. I'd get there someday.

* * *

5:40 p.m.

I am a little freaked out right now. Gran and Gramps left a while ago, but I stayed behind here in the ICU. I am sitting in one the chairs, going over their conversation, which was very nice and normal and non-disturbing. Until they left. As Gran and Gramps walked out of the ICU, with me following, Gramps turned to Gran and asked: 'Do you think she decides?'

'Decides what?'

Gramps looked uncomfortable. He shuffled his feet. 'You know? Decides,' he whispered.

'What are you talking about?' Gran sounded exasperated and tender at the same time.

'I don't know what I'm talking about. You're the one who believes in all the angels.'

'What does that have to do with Mia?' Gran asked.

'If they're gone now, but still here, like you believe, what if they want her to join them? What if she wants to join them?'

'It doesn't work like that,' Gran snapped.

'Oh,' was all Gramps said. The inquiry was over.

After they left, I was thinking that one day maybe

I'll tell Gran that I never much bought into her theory that birds and such could be people's guardian angels. And now I'm more sure than ever that there's no such thing.

My parents aren't here. They are not holding my hand, or cheering me on. I know them well enough to know that if they could, they would. Maybe not both of them. Maybe Mom would stay with Teddy while Dad watched over me. But neither of them is here.

And it's while contemplating this that I think about what the nurse said. *She's running the show.* And suddenly I understand what Gramps was really asking Gran. He had listened to that nurse, too. He got it before I did.

If I stay. If I live. It's up to me.

All this business about medically induced comas is just doctor talk. It's not up to the doctors. It's not up to the absentee angels. It's not even up to God who, if He exists, is nowhere around right now. It's up to me.

How am I supposed to decide this? How can I possibly stay without Mom and Dad? How can I leave without Teddy? Or Adam? This is too much. I don't even understand how it all works, why I'm here in the state that I'm in or how to get out of it if I wanted to. If I were to say, *I want to wake up*, would I wake up right now? I already tried snapping my heels to find Teddy and trying to beam myself to Hawaii, and that didn't work. This seems a whole lot more complicated.

But in spite of that, I believe it's true. I hear the nurse's words again. I am running the show. Everyone is waiting on me.

I decide. I know this now.

And this terrifies me more than anything else that has happened today.

Where the hell is Adam?

*

A week before Halloween of my junior year, Adam showed up at my door triumphant. He was holding a dress bag and wearing a shit-eating grin.

'Prepare to writhe in jealousy. I just got the best costume,' he said. He unzipped the bag. Inside was a frilly white shirt, a pair of breeches, and a long wool coat with epaulets.

'You're going to be Seinfeld with the puffy shirt?' I asked.

'Pff. *Seinfeld*. And you call yourself a classical musician. I'm going to be Mozart. Wait, you haven't seen the shoes.' He reached into the bag and pulled out clunky black leather numbers with metal bars across the tops.

'Nice,' I said. 'I think my mom has a pair like them.'

'You're just jealous because you don't have such a rockin' costume. And I'll be wearing tights, too. I'm just that secure in my manhood. Also, I have a wig.'

'Where'd you get all this?' I asked, fingering the wig. It felt like it was made of burlap.

'Online. Only a hundred bucks.'

'You spent a hundred dollars on a Halloween costume?'

And the mention of the world *Halloween* Teddy zoomed down the stairs, ignoring me and yanking on Adam's wallet chain. 'Wait here!' he demanded and then ran back upstairs and returned a few seconds later holding a bag. 'Is this a good costume? Or will it make me look babyish?' Teddy asked, pulling out a pitchfork, a set of devil ears, a red tail and a pair of red feetie pajamas.

'Ohh.' Adam stepped backward, his eyes wide. 'That

outfit scares the hell out of me and you aren't even wearing it.'

'Really? You don't think the pajamas make it look dumb. I don't want anyone to laugh at me,' Teddy declared, his eyebrows furrowed in seriousness.

I grinned at Adam, who was trying to swallow his own smile. 'Red pajamas plus pitchfork plus devil ears and pointy tail is so fully satanic no one would dare challenge you, lest they risk eternal damnation,' Adam assured him.

Teddy's face broke into a wide grin, showing off the gap of his missing front tooth. 'That's kind of what Mom said, but I just wanted to make sure she wasn't just telling me that so I wouldn't bug her about the costume. You're taking me trick-or-treating, right?' He looked at me now.

'Just like every year,' I answered. 'How else am I gonna get candy?'

'You're coming, too?' he asked Adam.

'I wouldn't miss it.'

Teddy turned on his heel and whizzed back up the stairs. Adam turned to me. 'That's Teddy settled. What are you wearing?'

'Ahh, I'm not much of a costume girl.'

Adam rolled his eyes. 'Well, become one. It's Halloween, our first one together. Shooting Star has a big show that night. It's a costume concert, and you promised to go.'

Inwardly, I groaned. After six months with Adam, I had just gotten used to us being the odd couple at school – people called us Groovy and the Geek. And I was starting to become more comfortable with Adam's bandmates, and had even learned a few words of rock talk. I could hold my own now when Adam took me to the House of Rock, the rambling house near the college where the rest of the band all lived. I could even participate in the band's punk-rock pot-luck parties when everyone invited had to bring something from their fridge that was on the verge of spoiling. We took all the ingredients and made something out of it. I was actually pretty good at finding ways to turn the vegetarian ground beef, beets, feta cheese and apricots into something edible.

But I still hated the shows and hated myself for hating them. The clubs were smoky, which hurt my eyes and made my clothes stink. The speakers were always turned up so high that the music blared, causing my ears ring so loudly afterward that the high-pitched drone would actually keep me up. I'd lie in bed, replaying the awkward night and feeling shittier about it with each playback.

'Don't tell me you're gonna back out,' Adam said, looking equal parts hurt and irritated.

'What about Teddy? We promised we'd take him trick-or-treating—'

'Yeah, at five o'clock. We don't have to be at the show until ten. I doubt even Master Ted could trick-or-treat for five solid hours. So you have no excuse. And you'd better get a good outfit together because I'm going to look hot, in an eighteenth-century kind of way.'

After Adam left to go to work delivering pizzas, I had a pit in my stomach. I went upstairs to practice the Dvořák piece Professor Christie had assigned me, and to work out what was bothering me. Why didn't I like his shows? Was it because Shooting Star was getting popular and I was jealous? Did the ever-growing masses of girl groupies put me off? This seemed like a logical enough explanation, but it wasn't it.

After I'd played for about ten minutes, it came to me: My aversion to Adam's shows had nothing to do with music or groupies or envy. It had to with the doubts. The same niggling doubts I always had about not belonging. I didn't feel like I belonged with my family, and now I didn't feel like I belonged with Adam, except unlike my family, who was stuck with me, Adam had chosen me, and this I didn't understand. Why had he fallen for *me*? It didn't make sense. I knew it was music that brought us together in the first place, put us in the same space so we could even get to know each other. And I knew that Adam liked how into music I was. And that he dug my sense of humor, 'so dark you almost miss it,' he said. And, speaking of dark, I knew he had a thing for dark-haired girls because all of his girlfriends had been brunettes. And I knew that when it was the two of us alone together, we could talk for hours, or sit reading side by side for hours, each one plugged into our own iPod, and still feel completely together. I understood all that in my head, but I still didn't believe it in my heart. When I was with Adam, I felt picked, chosen, special, and that just made me wonder *Why me?* even more.

And maybe this was why even though Adam willingly submitted to Schubert symphonies and attended any recital I gave, bringing me stargazer lilies, my favorite flower, I'd still rather have gone to the dentist than to one of his shows. Which was so churlish of me. I thought of what Mom sometimes said to me when I was feeling insecure: 'Fake it till you make it.' By the time I finished playing the piece three times over, I decided that not only would I go to his show, but for once I'd make as much of an effort to understand his world as he did mine.

'I need your help,' I told Mom that night after dinner as we stood side by side doing dishes.

'I think we've established that I'm not very good at trigonometry. Maybe you can try the online tutor thing,' Mom said.

'Not math help. Something else.'

'I'll do my best. What do you need?'

'Advice. Who's the coolest, toughest, hottest rocker girl you can think of?'

'Debbie Harry,' Mom said.

'Tha—'

'Not finished,' Mom interrupted. 'You can't ask me to pick only one. That's so *Sophie's Choice*. Kathleen

Hannah. Patti Smith. Joan Jett. Courtney Love, in her demented destructionist way. Lucinda Williams, even though she's country she's tough as nails. Kim Gordon from Sonic Youth, pushing fifty and still at it. That woman from Cat Power. Joan Armatrading. Why, is this some kind of social-studies project?'

'Kind of,' I answered, toweling off a chipped plate. 'It's for Halloween.'

Mom clapped her soapy hands together in delight. 'You planning on impersonating one of us?'

'Yeah,' I replied. 'Can you help me?'

Mom left work early so we could trawl through vintage-clothing stores. She decided we should go for a pastiche of rocker looks, rather than trying to copy any one artist. We bought a pair of tight, lizard-skin pants. A blond bobbed wig with severe bangs, à la early-eighties Debbie Harry, which Mom streaked with purple Manic Panic. For accessories, we got a black leather armband for one wrist and about two dozen silver bangles for the other. Mom fished out her own vintage Sonic Youth T-shirt – warning me not to take it off lest someone grab it and sell it on eBay for a couple hundred bucks – and the pair of black, pointy-toed leather spiked boots that she'd worn to her wedding.

On Halloween, she did my make-up, thick streaks of black liquid eyeliner that made my eyes look dangerous. White powder that made my skin pale. Blood-red gashes on my lips. A stick-on nose ring. When I looked in the mirror, I saw Mom's face peering back at me. Maybe it was the blond wig, but this was the first time I ever thought I actually looked like any of my immediate family.

My parents and Teddy waited downstairs for Adam while I stayed in my room. It felt like this was prom or something. Dad held the camera. Mom was practically dancing with excitement. When Adam came through door, showering Teddy with Skittles, Mom and Dad called me down.

I did a slinky walk as best as I could in the heels. I'd expected Adam to go crazy when he saw me, his jeans-and-sweaters girlfriend all glammed out. But he smiled his usual greeting, chuckling a bit. 'Nice costume,' was all he said.

'Quid pro quo. Only fair,' I said, pointing to his Mozart ensemble.

'I think you look scary, but pretty,' Teddy said. 'I'd say sexy, too, but I'm your brother, so that's gross.'

'How do you even know what *sexy* means?' I asked. 'You're six.'

'Everyone knows what *sexy* means,' he said.

Everyone but me, I guess. But that night, I kind of learned. When we trick-or-treated with Teddy, my own neighbors who'd known me for years didn't recognize me. Guys who'd never given me a second glance did a double take. And every time that happened, I felt a little bit more like the risky sexy chick I was pretending to be. Fake it till you make it actually worked.

The club where Shooting Star was playing was packed. Everyone was in costume, most of the girls in the kinds of racy get-ups – cleavage-bearing French maids, whip-wielding dominatrixes, slutty *Wizard of Oz* Dorothys with skirts hiked up to show their ruby garters – that normally made me feel like a big oaf. I didn't feel oafish at all that night, even if nobody seemed to recognize that I was wearing a costume.

'You were supposed to dress up,' a skeleton guy chastised me before offering me a beer.

'I fucking LOVE those pants,' a flapper girl screamed into my ear. 'Did you get them in Seattle?'

'Aren't you in the Crack House Quartet?' a guy in a Hillary Clinton mask asked me, referring to some hard-core band that Adam loved and I hated.

When Shooting Star went on, I didn't stay backstage, which is what I normally did. Backstage I can sit on a chair and have an uninterrupted view and not have to talk to anybody. This time, I lingered out by the bar, and then, when the flapper girl grabbed me, I joined her dancing in the mosh pit.

I'd never gone into the mosh pit before. I had little interest in running around in circles while drunk, brawny boys in leather trod on my toes. But tonight, I totally got into it. I understood what it was like to merge your energy with the mob's and to absorb theirs as well. How in the pit, when things got going, you weren't so much walking or dancing as being sucked into a whirlpool.

When Adam finished his set, I was as panting and sweaty as he was. I didn't go backstage to greet him before everyone else got to him. I waited for him to go to the floor of the club, to meet his public like he did at the end of every show. And when he came out, a towel around his neck, sucking on a bottle of water, I flung myself into his arms and kissed him open mouthed and sloppy in front of everyone. I could feel him smiling as he kissed me back.

'Well, well, looks like someone has been infused with spirit of Debbie Harry,' he said, wiping some of the lipstick off his chin.

'I guess so. What about you? Are you feeling very Mozarty?'

'All I know about him is from what I saw in that movie. But I remember he was kind of a horndog, so after that kiss, I guess I am. You ready to go? I can load up and we can get out of here.'

'No, let's stay for the last set.'

'*Really?*' Adam asked, his eyebrows rising in surprise.

'Yeah. I might even go into the pit with you.'

'Have you been drinking?' he teased.

'Just the Kool-Aid,' I replied.

We danced, stopping every now and again to make out, until the club closed.

On the way home, every so often Adam would turn to look at me and smile while shaking his head.

'So you like me like this?' I asked.

'Hmm,' he responded.

'Is that a yes or a no?'

'Of course I like you.'

'No, like this. Did you like me tonight?'

Adam straightened up. 'I liked that you got into the show and weren't chomping to leave ASAP. And I loved dancing with you. And I loved how comfortable you seemed to be with all us riffraff.'

'But did you like me like this? Like me better?'

'Than what?' he asked. He looked genuinely perplexed.

'Than normal.' I was getting irritated now. I'd felt so brazen tonight, like the Halloween costume had imbued me with a new personality, one more worthy of Adam, of my family. I tried to explain that to him, and to my dismay, found myself near tears.

Adam seemed to sense that I was upset. He pulled the car off onto a logging road and turned to me. 'Mia, Mia, Mia,' he said, stroking the tendrils of my hair that had escaped from the wig. 'This *is* the you I like. You definitely dressed sexier and are, you know, blond and that's different. But the you who you are tonight is the same you I was in love with yesterday, the same you I'll be in love with tomorrow. I love that you're fragile and tough, quiet and kick-ass. Hell, you're one of the punkest girls I know, no matter who you listen to or what you wear.'

After that, whenever I started to doubt Adam's feelings, I'd think about my wig, gathering dust in my closet, and it would bring back the memory of that night. And then I wouldn't feel insecure. I'd just feel lucky.

7:13 p.m.

He's here.

I have been hanging out in an empty hospital room in the maternity ward, wanting to be far away from my relatives and even farther away from the ICU and that nurse, or more specifically what that nurse said and what I now understand. I needed to be somewhere where people wouldn't be sad, where the thoughts concerned life, not death. So I came here, the land of screaming babies. Actually, the wail of the newborns is comforting. They have so much fight in them already.

But it's quiet in this room now. So I'm sitting on the windowsill, staring out at the night. A car screeches into the parking garage, shaking me out of my reverie. I peer down in time to catch a glimpse of the taillights of a pink car disappear into the darkness. Sarah, who is the girlfriend of Liz, Shooting Star's drummer, has a pink Dodge Dart. I hold my breath, waiting for Adam to appear out of the tunnel. And then he's here, walking up the ramp, hugging his leather jacket against the winter night. I can see the chain of his wallet glinting in the floodlights. He stops, turns around to talk to someone behind him. I see the soft figure of a woman emerge from the shadows. At first, I think it must be Liz. But then I see the braid.

I wish I could hug her. To thank her for always being one step ahead of what I need.

Of course Kim would go to Adam, to tell him in person as opposed to breaking the news over the phone, and then to bring him here, to me. It was Kim who knew that Adam was playing a show in town. Kim who must have somehow managed to cajole her mother into driving downtown. Kim, who judging by. Mrs Schein's absence, must have convinced her mother to go home, to let her stay with Adam and me. I remember how it took Kim two months to get permission to take that helicopter flight with her uncle, so I'm impressed that she managed this amount of emancipation within the space of a few hours. It was Kim who must have braved any number of intimidating bouncers and hipsters to find Adam. And Kim who must have braved telling Adam.

I know this sounds ridiculous, but I'm glad it wasn't me. I don't think I could have borne it. Kim had to bear it.

And now, because of her, he is finally here.

All day long, I've been imagining Adam's arrival, and in my fantasy, I rush to greet him, even though he can't see me and even though, from what I can tell so far, it's nothing like that movie *Ghost*, where you can walk through your loved ones so that *they* feel your presence.

But now that Adam is here, I'm paralyzed. I'm scared to see him. To see his face. I've seen Adam cry twice. Once when we watched *It's a Wonderful Life*. And another time when we were in the train station in Seattle and we saw a mother yelling and swatting her son who had Downs syndrome. He just got quiet and it was only when we were walking away that I saw the tears rolling down his cheeks. And it damn near tore my heart out. If he is crying, it *will* kill me. Forget this *my choice* business. That alone will do me in.

I'm such a chicken-shit.

I look at the clock on the wall. It's past seven now. Shooting Star will not be opening for Bikini after all. Which is a shame. It was a huge break for them. For a second, I wonder if the rest of the band will go on without Adam. I very much doubt it, though. It's not just that he is the lead singer and the lead guitar player. The band has this kind of code. Loyalty to feelings is important. Last summer, when Liz and Sarah broke up (for what turned out to be all of a month) and Liz was too distraught to play, they canceled their five-night tour, even though this guy Gordon who plays drums in another band offered to sub for her.

I watch Adam make his way to the hospital's main entrance, Kim trailing behind him. Just before he comes to the covered awning and the automatic doors, he looks up into the sky. He is waiting for Kim but I also like to think he's looking for me. His face, illuminated by the lights, is blank, like someone vacuumed away all his personality, leaving only a mask. He doesn't look like him. But at least he's not crying.

That gives me the guts to go to him now. Or rather to me, to the ICU, which is where I know he will want to go. Adam knows Gran and Gramps and the cousins, and I imagine he'll join the waiting-room vigil later. But right now he's here for me.

Back in the ICU time stands still as always. One of the surgeons who worked on me earlier – the one who sweated a lot and, when it was his turn to pick the music, blasted Weezer – is checking in on me.

The light is dim and artificial and kept to the same level all the time, but even so, the circadian rhythms win out and a nighttime hush has fallen over the place. It is less frenetic than it was during the day, like the nurses and machines are all a little tired and have reverted to power-save mode.

So when Adam's voice reverberates from the hall-way outside the ICU, it really wakes everyone up.

'What do you mean I can't go in?' he booms.

I make my way across the ICU, standing just on the

other side of the automatic doors. I hear the orderly outside explain to Adam that he is not allowed in this part of the hospital.

'This is bullshit!' Adam yells.

Inside the ward, all the nurses look toward the door, their heavy eyes wary. I am pretty sure they're thinking: *Don't we have enough to deal with inside without having to calm down crazy people outside?* I want explain to them that Adam isn't crazy. That he never yells, except for very special occasions.

The graying middle-aged nurse who doesn't attend to the patients but sits by and monitors the computers and phones, gives a little nod and stands up as if accepting a nomination. She straightens her creased white pants and makes her way toward the door. She's really not the best one to talk to him. I wish I could warn them that they ought to send Nurse Ramirez, the one who reassured my grandparents (and freaked me out). She'd be able to calm him down. But this one is only going to make it worse. I follow her through the double doors where Adam and Kim are arguing with an orderly. The orderly looks at the nurse. 'I told them they're not authorized to be up here,' he explains. The nurse dismisses him with the wave of a hand.

'Can I help you, young man?' she asks Adam. Her voice sounds irritated and impatient, like some of Dad's tenured colleagues at school who Dad says are just counting the days till retirement.

Adam clears his throat, attempting to pull himself together. 'I'd like to visit a patient,' he says, gesturing toward the doors blocking him from the ICU.

'I'm afraid that's not possible,' she replies.

'But my girlfriend, Mia, she's—'

'She's being well cared for,' the nurse interrupts. She sounds tired, too tired for sympathy, too tired to be moved by young love.

'I understand that. And I'm grateful for it,' Adam says. He's trying his best to play by her rules, to sound mature, but I hear the catch in his voice when he says: 'I really need to see her.'

'I'm sorry, young man, but visits are restricted to immediate family.'

I hear Adam gasp. *Immediate family.* The nurse doesn't mean to be cruel. She's just clueless, but Adam won't know that. I feel the need to protect him and to protect the nurse from what he might do to her. I reach for him, on instinct, even though I cannot really touch him. But his back is to me now. His shoulders are hunched over, his legs starting to buckle.

Kim, who was hovering near the wall, is suddenly at his side, her arms encircling his falling form. With both arms locked around his waist, she turns to the nurse, her eyes blazing with fury. 'You don't understand!' she cries.

'Do I need to call security?' the nurse asks.

Adam waves his hand, surrendering to the nurse, to Kim. '*Don't,*' he whispers to Kim.

So Kim doesn't. Without saying another word, she hoists his arm around her shoulder and shifts his weight onto her. Adam has about a foot and fifty pounds on Kim, but after stumbling for a second, she adjusts to the added burden. She bears it.

*

Kim and I have this theory that almost everything in the world can be divided into two groups.

There are people who like classical music. People who like pop. There are city people. And country people. Coke drinkers. Pepsi drinkers. There are conformists and freethinkers. Virgins and non-virgins. And there are the kind of girls who have boyfriends in high school, and the kind of girls who don't.

Kim and I had always assumed that we both belonged to the latter category. 'Not that we'll be forty-year-old virgins or anything,' she reassured. 'We'll just be the kinds of girls who have boyfriends in college.'

That always made sense to me, seemed preferable even. Mom was the sort of girl who had had boyfriends in high school and often remarked that she wished she hadn't wasted her time. 'There's only so many times a girl wants to get drunk on cheap beer, go cow-tipping, and make out in back of a pickup truck. As far as the boys I dated were concerned, that amounted to a romantic evening.'

Dad on the other hand, didn't really date till college. He was shy in high school, but then he started playing drums and freshman year of college joined a punk band, and boom, girlfriends. Or at least a few of them until he met Mom, and boom, a wife. I kind of figured it would go that way for me.

So, it was a surprise to both Kim and me when I wound up in Group A, with the boyfriended girls. At first, I tried hide it. After I came home from the Yo-Yo Ma concert, I told Kim the vaguest of details. I didn't mention the kissing. I rationalized the omission: There was no point getting all worked up about a kiss. One kiss does not a relationship make. I'd kissed boys before, and usually by the next day the kiss had evaporated like a dewdrop in the sun.

Except I knew that with Adam it *was* a big deal. I knew from the way the warmth flooded my whole body that night after he dropped me off at home, kissing me once more at my doorstep. By the way I stayed up until dawn hugging my pillow. By the way that I could not eat the next day, could not wipe the smile off my face. I recognized that the kiss was a door I had walked through. And I knew that I'd left Kim on the other side.

After a week, and a few more stolen kisses, I knew I had to tell Kim. We went for coffee after school. It was May but it was pouring rain as though it were November. I felt slightly suffocated by what I had to do.

'I'll buy. You want one of your froufrou drinks?' I asked. That was another one of the categories we'd determined: people who drank plain coffee and people who drank gussied-up caffeine drinks like the mint-chip lattes Kim was so fond of.

'I think I'll try the cinnamon-spice chai latte,' she

said, giving me a stern look that said, *I will not be ashamed of my beverage selection.*

I bought us our drinks and a piece of marionberry pie with two forks. I sat down across from Kim, running the fork along the scalloped edge of the flaky crust.

'I have something to tell you,' I said.

'Something about having a boyfriend?' Kim's voice was amused, but even though I was looking down, I could tell that she'd rolled her eyes.

'How'd you know?' I asked, meeting her gaze.

She rolled her eyes again. 'Please. Everyone knows. It's the hottest gossip this side of Melanie Farrow dropping out to have a baby. It's like a Democratic presidential candidate marrying a Republican presidential candidate.'

'Who said anything about marrying?'

'I'm just being metaphoric,' Kim said. 'Anyhow, I know. I knew even before you knew.'

'Bullshit.'

'Come on. A guy like Adam going to a Yo-Yo Ma concert. He was buttering you up.'

'It's not like that,' I said, though of course, it was totally like that.

'I just don't see why you couldn't tell me sooner,' she said in a quiet voice.

I was about to give her my whole one-kiss-not-equaling-a-relationship spiel and to explain that I didn't want to blow it out of proportion, but I stopped myself. 'I was afraid you'd be mad at me,' I admitted.

'I'm not,' Kim said. 'But I will be if you ever lie to me again.'

'OK,' I said.

'Or if you turn into one of those girlfriends, always ponying around after her boyfriend, and speaking in the first-person plural. "*We* love the winter. *We* think Velvet Underground is seminal."'

'You know I wouldn't rock-talk to you. First person singular or plural. I promise.'

'Good,' Kim replied. 'Because if you turn into one of those girls, I'll shoot you.'

'If I turn into one of those girls, I'll hand you the gun.'

Kim laughed for real at that, and the tension was broken. She popped a hunk of pie into her mouth. 'How did your parents take it?'

'Dad went through the five phases of grieving –

denial, anger, acceptance, whatever – in like one day. I think he's more freaked out that he is old enough to have a daughter who has a boyfriend.' I paused, took a sip of my coffee, letting the word *boyfriend* rest out in the air. 'And he claims he can't believe that I'm dating a musician.'

'You're a musician,' Kim reminded me.

'You know, a punk, pop musician.'

'Shooting Star is emo-core,' Kim corrected. Unlike me, she cared about the myriad pop musical distinctions: punk, indie, alternative, hard-core, emo-core.

'It's mostly hot air, you know, part of his whole bow-tie-Dad thing. I think Dad likes Adam. He met him when he picked me up for the concert. Now he wants me to bring him over for dinner, but it's only been a week. I'm not quite ready for a meet-the-folks moment yet.'

'I don't think I'll ever be ready for that.' Kim shuddered at the thought of it. 'What about your mom?'

'She offered to take me to Planned Parenthood to get the Pill and told me to make Adam get tested for various diseases. In the meantime, she ordered me to buy condoms now. She even gave me ten bucks to start my supply.'

'Have you?' Kim gasped.

'No, it's only been a week,' I said. 'We're still in the same group on that one.'

'For now,' Kim said.

* * *

One other category that Kim and I devised was people who tried to be cool and people who did not. On this one, I thought that Adam, Kim, and I were in the same column, because even though Adam was cool, he didn't try. It was effortless for him. So, I expected the three of us to become the best of friends. I expected Adam to love everyone I loved as much as I did.

And it did work out like that with my family. He practically became the third kid. But it never clicked with Kim. Adam treated her the way that I'd always imagined he would treat a girl like me. He was nice enough – polite, friendly, but distant. He didn't attempt to enter her world or gain her confidence. I suspected he thought she wasn't cool enough and it made me mad. After we'd been together about three months, we had a huge fight about it.

'I'm not dating Kim. I'm dating you,' he said, after I accused him of not being nice enough to her.

'So what? You have lots of female friends. Why not add her to the stable?'

Adam shrugged. 'I don't know. It's just not there.'

'You're such a snob!' I said, suddenly furious.

Adam eyed me with furrowed brows, like I was a math problem on the blackboard that he was trying to figure out. 'How does that make me a snob? You can't force friendship. We just don't have a lot in common.'

'*That's* what makes you a snob! You only like people like you,' I cried. I stormed out, expecting him to follow after me, begging forgiveness, and when he didn't, my fury doubled. I rode my bike over to Kim's house to vent. She listened to my diatribe, her expression purposefully blasé.

'That's just ridiculous that he only likes people like him,' she scolded when I'd finished spewing. 'He likes you, and you're not like him.'

'That's the problem,' I mumbled.

'Well, then deal with that. Don't drag me into your drama,' she said. 'Besides, I don't really click with him, either.'

'You don't?'

'No, Mia. Not everyone swoons for Adam.'

'I didn't mean it like that. It's just that I want you guys to be friends.'

'Yeah, well, I want to live in New York City and have normal parents. As the man said, "You can't always get what you want."'

'But you're two of the most important people in my life.'

Kim looked at my red and teary face and her expression softened into a gentle smile. 'We know that, Mia. But we're from different parts of your life, just like music and me are from different parts of your life. And that's fine. You don't have to choose one or the other, at least not as far as I'm concerned.'

'But I want those parts of my life to come together.'

Kim shook her head. 'It doesn't work that way. Look, I accept Adam because you love him. And I assume he accepts me because you love me. If it makes you feel any better, your love binds us. And that's enough. Me and him don't have to love each other.'

'But I want you to,' I wailed.

'Mia,' Kim said, an edge of warning in her voice

signaling the end of her patience. 'You're starting to act like one of those girls. Do you need to get me a gun?'

Later that night, I stopped by Adam's house to say I was sorry. He accepted my apology with a bemused kiss on the nose. And then nothing changed. He and Kim remained cordial but distant, no matter how much I tried to sell them on each another. The funny thing was, I never really bought into Kim's notion that they were somehow bound together through me – until just now when I saw her half carrying him down the hospital corridor.

8:12 p.m.

I watch Kim and Adam disappear down the hall. I mean to follow them but I'm glued to the linoleum, unable to move my phantom legs. It's only after they disappear around a corner that I rouse myself and trail after them, but they've already gone inside the elevator.

By now I've figured out that I don't have any super-natural abilities. I can't float through walls or dive down stairwells. I can only do the things I'd be able do in real life, except that apparently what I do in my world is invisible to everyone else. At least that seems to be the case because no one looks twice when I open doors or hit the elevator button. I can touch things, even manipulate door handles and the like, but I can't really *feel* anything or anybody. It's like I'm experiencing everything through a fishbowl. It doesn't really make sense to me, but then again, nothing that's happening today makes much sense.

I assume that Kim and Adam are headed to the waiting room to join the vigil, but when I get there, my family is not there. There's a stack of coats and sweaters on the chairs and I recognize my cousin Heather's bright-orange down jacket. She lives in the country and likes to hike in the woods, so she says that the neon colors are necessary to keep drunk hunters from mistaking her for a bear.

I look at the clock on the wall. It could be dinner time. I wander back down the halls to the cafeteria, which has the same fried-food, boiled-vegetable stench as cafeterias everywhere. Unappetizing smell aside, it's full of people. The tables are crammed with doctors and nurses and nervous-looking medical students in short white jackets and stethoscopes so shiny that they look like toys. They are all chowing down on cardboard pizza and freeze-dried mashed potatoes. It takes me a while to locate my family, huddled around a table. Gran is chatting to Heather. Gramps is paying careful attention to his turkey sandwich.

Aunt Kate and Aunt Diane are in the corner, whispering about something. 'Some cuts and bruises. He was already released from the hospital,' Aunt Kate is saying, and for a second I think she's talking about Teddy and am so excited I could cry. But then I hear her say something about there being no alcohol in his system, how our car just swerved into his lane and some guy named Mr Dunlap says he didn't have time to stop, and then I realize it's not Teddy they're talking about; it's the other driver.

'The police said it was probably the snow, or a deer that caused them to swerve,' Aunt Kate continues. 'And apparently, this lopsided outcome is fairly common. One party is just fine and the other suffers catastrophic injuries . . .' She trails off.

I don't know that I'd call Mr Dunlap 'just fine', no matter how superficial his injuries. I think about what it must be like to be him, to wake up one Tuesday morning and get into your truck to head off to work at the mill or maybe to the feed-supply store or maybe to Loretta's Diner to have eggs over easy. Mr Dunlap, who was maybe perfectly happy or perfectly miserable, married with kids or a bachelor. But whatever and whoever he was early this morning, he isn't that person any longer. His life has changed irrevocably, too. If what my aunt says is true, and the crash wasn't his fault, then he was what Kim would call 'a poor schmuck,' in the wrong place at the wrong time. And because of his bad luck and because he was in his truck, driving eastbound on Route 27 this morning, two kids are now parentless and at least one of them is in grave condition.

How do you live with that? For a second, I have a fantasy of getting better and getting out of here and going to Mr Dunlap's house, to relieve him of his burden, to reassure him that it's not his fault. Maybe we'd become friends.

Of course, it probably wouldn't work like that. It would be awkward and sad. Besides, I still have no idea what I will decide, still have no clue how I would determine to stay or not stay in the first place. Until I figure that out, I have to leave things up to the fates, or to the doctors, or whoever decides these matters when the decider is too confused to choose between the elevator and the stairs.

I *need* Adam. I take a final look for him and Kim but they're not here, so I head back upstairs to the ICU.

I find them hiding out on the trauma floor, several halls away from the ICU. They're trying to look casual as they test out the doors to various supply closets. When they finally find an unlocked one, they sneak inside. They fumble around in the dark for a light switch. I hate to break it to them, but it's actually back out in the hall.

'I'm not sure this kind of thing works outside of the movies,' Kim tells Adam as she feels along the wall.

'Every fiction has its base in fact,' he tells her.

'You don't really look like the doctor type,' she says.

'I was hoping for orderly. Or maybe janitor.'

'Why would a janitor be in the ICU?' Kim asks. She's a stickler for these kinds of details.

'Broken lightbulb. I don't know. It's all in how you pull it off.'

'I still don't understand why you don't just go to her family?' asks Kim, pragmatic as ever. 'I'm sure her grandparents could explain, could get you in to see Mia.'

Adam shakes his head. 'You know, when the nurse threatened to call security, my first thought was *I'll just call Mia's parents to fix this.*' Adam stops, takes a few breaths. 'It just keeps walloping me over and over, and it's like it's the first time every time,' he says in a husky voice.

'I know,' Kim replies in a whisper.

'Anyhow,' Adam says, resuming his search for the light switch, 'I can't go to her grandparents. I can't add anything more to their burden. This is something I have to do for myself.'

I'm sure my grandparents would actually be happy to help Adam. They've met him a bunch of times, and they like him a lot. On Christmas, Gran is always sure to make maple fudge for him because he once mentioned how much he liked it.

But I also know that sometimes Adam needs to do things the dramatic way. He is fond of the Grand

Gesture. Like saving up two weeks of pizza-delivery tips to take me to Yo-Yo Ma instead of just asking me out on a regular date. Like decorating my windowsill with flowers every day for a week when I was contagious with the chicken pox.

Now I can see that Adam is concentrating on the new task at hand. I'm not sure what exactly he has in mind, but whatever the plan, I'm grateful for it, if only because it's pulled him out of his emotional stupor I saw in the hallway outside the ICU. I've seen him get like this before, when he's writing a new song or is trying to convince me to do something I won't want to do – like go camping with him – and nothing, not a meteorite crashing into the planet, not even a girlfriend in the ICU, can dissuade him.

Besides, it's the girlfriend in the ICU that's necessitating Adam's ruse to begin with. And from what I can guess, it's the oldest hospital trick in the book, taken straight from that movie *The Fugitive*, which Mom and I recently watched on TNT. I have my doubts about it. So does Kim.

'Don't think that nurse might recognize you?' Kim asks. 'You did yell at her.'

'She won't have to recognize me if she doesn't see

me. Now I get why you and Mia are such peas in a pod. A pair of Cassandras.'

Adam has never met Mrs Schein, so he doesn't get that implying that Kim is a worrywart is fighting words. Kim scowls, but then I can see her give in. 'Maybe this retarded plan of yours would work better if we could actually see what we're doing.' She fumbles around in her bag and pulls out the cell phone her mother made her start carrying when she was ten – child-GPS, Kim called it – and turned it on. A square of light softens the darkness.

'Now, that's more like the brilliant girl Mia brags about,' Adam says. He turns on his own cell phone and now the room is illuminated by a dull glow.

Unfortunately, the glow shows that the tiny broom closet is full of brooms, a bucket, and a pair of mops, but is lacking any of the disguises that Adam was hoping for. If I could, I would inform them that the hospital has locker rooms, where the doctors and nurses can stow their street clothes and where they change into their scrubs or their lab coats. The only generic hospital garb sitting around are those embarrassing gowns that they put the patients in. Adam probably could throw on a gown and cruise the hallways in a wheelchair with no one the wiser, but such an outfit would still not get him into the ICU.

'Shit,' Adam says.

'We can keep trying,' Kim says, suddenly the cheerleader. 'There are like ten floors in this place. I'm sure there are other unlocked closets.'

Adam sinks to the floor. 'Nah. You're right. This is stupid. We need to come up with a better plan.'

'You could fake a drug overdose or something so you wind up in the ICU,' Kim says.

'This is Portland. You're lucky if a drug overdose gets you into the ER,' Adam replies. 'No, I was thinking more like a distraction. You know, like making the fire alarm go off so the nurses all come running out.'

'Do you really think sprinklers and panicked nurses are good for Mia?' Kim asks.

'Well, not that exactly, but something so that they all look away for half a second and I stealthily sneak in.'

'They'll find you out right away. They'll throw you out on your backside.'

'I don't care,' Adam responds. 'I only need a second.'

'Why? I mean what can you do in a second?'

Adam pauses for a second. His eyes, which are normally a kind of mutt's mixture of gray and brown and green, have gone dark. 'So I can show her that I'm here. That someone's still here.'

Kim doesn't ask any more questions after that. They sit there in silence, each lost in their own thoughts, and it reminds me of how Adam and I can be together but quiet and separate and I realize that they're friends now, friends for real. No matter what happens, at least I have achieved that.

After about five minutes, Adam knocks on his forehead. 'Of course,' he says.

'What?'

'Time to activate the Bat Signal.'

'Huh?'

'Come on. I'll show you.'

*

When I first started playing the cello, Dad was still playing drums in his band, though that all started to taper off a couple years later when Teddy arrived. But right from the get-go, I could see that there was something different about playing my kind of music, something more than my parents' obvious bewilderment with my classical tastes. My music was solitary. I mean Dad might hammer on his drums for a few hours by himself or write songs alone at the kitchen table, plinking out the notes on his beat-up acoustic guitar, but he always said that songs really got written as you played them. That was what made it so interesting.

When I played, it was most often by myself, in my room. Even when I practiced with the rotating college students, other than during lessons, I still usually played solo. And when I gave a concert or recital, it was alone, on a stage, my cello, myself, and an audience. And unlike Dad's shows, where enthusiastic fans jumped the stage and then dive-bombed into the crowd, there was always a wall between the audience and me. After a while playing like this got lonely. It also got kind of boring.

So in the spring of eighth grade I decided to quit. I planned to trail off quietly, by cutting back my obsessive practices, not giving recitals. I figured that if I laid off gradually, by the time I entered high school in the fall, I could start fresh, no longer be known as 'the cellist.' Maybe then I'd pick up a new instrument, guitar or bass, or even drums. Plus, with Mom too busy with Teddy to notice the length of my cello practice, and Dad swamped with lesson plans and grading papers at his new teaching job, I figured nobody would even realize that I'd stopped playing until it was already a done deal. At least that's what I told myself. The truth was, I could no sooner quit cello cold turkey than I could stop breathing.

I might have quit for real, were it not for Kim. One afternoon, I invited her to go downtown with me after school.

'It's a weekday. Don't you have practice?' she asked as she twisted the combination on her locker.

'I can skip it today,' I said, pretending to search for my earth-science book.

'Have the pod people stolen Mia? First no recitals. And now you're skipping out on practice. What's going on?'

'I don't know,' I said, tapping my fingers against the locker. 'I'm thinking of trying a new instrument. Like drums. Dad's kit is down in the basement gathering dust.'

'Yeah, right. You on drums. That's rich,' Kim said with a chuckle.

'I'm serious.'

Kim had looked at me, her mouth agape, like I'd just told her I planned on sautéing up a platter of slugs for dinner. 'You can't quit cello,' she said after a moment of stunned silence.

'Why not?'

She looked pained as the tried to explain. 'I don't know but it just seems like your cello is part of who you are. I can't imagine you without that thing between your legs.'

'It's stupid. I can't even play in the school marching band. I mean, who plays the cello anyhow? A bunch of old people. It's a dumb instrument for a girl to play. It's so dorky. And I want to have more free time, to do fun stuff.'

'What kind of "fun stuff"?" Kim challenged.

'Um, you know? Shopping. Hanging out with you . . .'

'Please,' Kim said. 'You hate to shop. And you hang out with me plenty. But fine, skip practice today. I want to show you something.' She took me home with her and dragged out a CD of *Nirvana MTV Unplugged* and played me 'Something in the Way'.

'Listen to that,' she said. 'Two guitar players, a

drummer, and a *cello player*. Her name is Lori Goldston and I bet when she was younger, she practiced two hours a day like some other girl I know because if you want to play with the philharmonic, or with Nirvana, that's what you have to do. And I don't think anyone would dare call *her* a dork.'

I took the CD home and listened to it over and over for the next week, pondering what Kim said. I pulled my cello out a few times, played along. It was a different kind of music than I'd played before, challenging, and strangely invigorating. I planned to play 'Something in the Way' for Kim the following week when she came over for dinner.

But before I had a chance, at the dinner table Kim casually announced to my parents that she thinks I ought to go to summer camp.

'What, you trying to convert me so I'll go to your Torah camp?' I asked.

'Nope. It's music camp.' She pulled out a glossy brochure for the Franklin Valley Conservatory, a summer program in British Columbia. 'It's for *serious* musicians,' Mia said. 'You have to send a recording of your playing to get in. I called. The deadline for applications is May first, so there's still time.' She turned to face me head-on, as if she were daring me to get mad at her for interfering.

I wasn't mad. My heart was pounding, as if Kim had announced that my family won a lottery and she was about to reveal how much. I looked at her, the nervous look in her eyes betraying the 'you wanna piece of me?' smirk on her face, and I was overwhelmed with gratitude to be friends with someone who often seemed to understand me better than I understood myself. Dad asked me if I wanted to go, and when I protested about the money, he said never mind about that. Did I want to go? And I did. More than anything.

Three months later, when Dad dropped me off in a lonely corner of Vancouver Island, I wasn't so sure. The place looked like a typical summer camp, log cabins in the woods, kayaks strewn on the beach. There were about fifty kids who, judging by the way they were hugging and squealing, had all known one another for years. Meanwhile, I didn't know anybody. For the first six hours, no one talked to me except for the camp's assistant director, who assigned me to a cabin, showed me my bunk bed, and pointed the way to the cafeteria, where that night, I was given a plate of something that appeared to be meat loaf.

I stared miserably at my plate, looking out at the gloomy gray evening. I already missed my parents, Kim, and especially Teddy. He was at that fun stage, wanting to try new things and constantly asking 'What's that?' and saying the most hilarious things. The day before I left, he informed me that he was 'nine-tenths thirsty' and I almost peed myself laughing. Homesick, I sighed and moved the mass of meatloaf around my plate.

'Don't worry, it doesn't rain every day. Just every other day.'

I looked up. There was an impish kid who couldn't have been more than ten years old. He had a blond buzz cut and a constellation of freckles falling down his nose.

'I know,' I said. 'I'm from the Northwest, though it was sunny where I lived this morning. It's the meatloaf I'm worried about.'

He laughed. 'That doesn't get better. But the peanut-butter-and-jelly is always good,' he said, gesturing to a table where a half-dozen kids were fixing themselves sandwiches. 'Peter. Trombone. Ontario,' he said. This, I would learn, was standard Franklin greeting.

'Oh, hey. I'm Mia. Cello. Oregon, I guess.'

Peter told me that he was thirteen, and this was his second summer here; almost everyone started when they were twelve, which is why they all knew one another. Of the fifty students, about half did jazz, the other half classical, so it was a small crew. There were only two other cello players, one of them a tall lanky red-haired guy named Simon who Peter waved over.

'Will you be trying for the concerto competition?' Simon asked me as soon as Peter introduced me as Mia. Cello. Oregon. Simon was Simon. Cello. Leicester, which turned out to be a city in England. It was quite the international group.

'I don't think so. I don't even know what that is,' I answered.

'Well, you know how we all perform in an orchestra for the final symphony?' Peter asked me.

I nodded my head, though really I had only a vague idea. Dad had spent the spring reading out loud from the camp's literature, but the only thing I'd cared about was that I was going to camp with other classical musicians. I hadn't paid too much attention to the details.

'It's the summer's end symphony. People from all over come to it. It's a quite a big deal. We, the youngster musicians, play as a sort of cute sideshow,' Simon explained. 'However, one musician from the camp is chosen to play with the professional orchestra and to perform a solo movement. I came close last year but it went to a flutist. This is my second-to-last chance before I graduate. It hasn't gone to strings in a while, and Tracy, the third of our little trio here, isn't trying out. She's more of a hobby player. Good but not terribly serious. I heard you were serious.'

Was I? Not so serious that I hadn't been on the verge of quitting. 'How'd you hear that?' I asked.

'The teachers hear all the application reels and word gets around. Your audition tape was apparently quite good. It's unusual to admit someone in year two. So I was hoping for some bloody good competition, to up my game, as it were.'

'Whoa, give the girl a chance,' Peter said. 'She's only just tasted the meat loaf.'

Simon shriveled his nose. 'Beg pardon. But if you want to put heads together about audition choices, let's have a little chat about that,' he said, and disappeared off in the direction of the sundae bar.

'Forgive Simon. We haven't had high-quality cellists for a couple years, so he's excited about new blood. In a purely aesthetic way. He's gay, though it may be hard to tell.'

'Oh. I see. But what did he say? I mean it sounds like he *wants* me to compete against him.'

'Of course he does. That's the fun. That's why we're all at camp in the middle of a flipping rainforest,' he said, gesturing outside. 'That and the amazing cuisine.' Peter looked at me. 'Isn't that why you're here?'

I shrugged. 'I don't know. I haven't played with that many people, at least that many serious people.'

Peter scratched his ears. 'Really? You said you're from Oregon. Ever done anything with the Portland Cello Project?'

'The what?'

'Avant-garde cello collective, eh. Very interesting work.'

'I don't live in Portland,' I mumbled, embarrassed that I'd never even *heard* of any Cello Project.

145

'Well then, who do you play with?'

'Other people. College students mostly.'

'No orchestra? No chamber-music ensemble? String quartet?'

I shook my head, remembering a time when one of my student teachers invited me to play in a quartet. I'd turned her down because playing one-on-one with her was one thing; playing with complete strangers was another. I'd always believed that the cello was a solitary instrument, but now I was starting to wonder if maybe *I* was the solitary one.

'Hmm. How are you any good?' Peter asked. 'I don't mean to sound like an asshole, but isn't that how you get good? It's like tennis. If you play someone crappy, you end up missing shots or serving all sloppy, but if you play with an ace player, suddenly you're all at the net, lobbing good volleys.'

'I wouldn't know,' I told Peter, feeling like the most boring, sheltered person ever. 'I don't play tennis, either.'

The next few days went by in a blur. I had no idea why they put out the kayaks. There was no time for playing. Not that kind, anyway. The days were totally grueling. Up at six-thirty, breakfast by seven, private study time for three hours in the morning and in the afternoon, and orchestra rehearsal before dinner.

I'd never played with more than a handful of musicians before, so the first few days in orchestra were chaotic. The camp's musical director, who was also the conductor, scrambled to get us situated and then it was everything he could do to get us playing the most basic of movements in any semblance of time. On the third day, he trotted out some Brahms lullabies. The first time we played, it was painful. The instruments didn't blend so much as collide, like rocks caught in a lawn mower. 'Terrible!' he screamed. 'How can any of you ever expect to play in a professional orchestra if you cannot keep time on a lullaby? Now again!'

After about a week, it started to gel and I got my first taste of being a cog in the machine. It made me hear the cello in an entirely new way, how its low tones worked in concert with the viola's higher notes, how it provided a foundation for the woodwinds on the other side of the orchestra pit. And even though you might think that being part of a group would make you relax a little, not care so much how you sounded blended among everyone else, if anything, the opposite was true.

I sat behind a seventeen-year-old viola player named Elizabeth. She was one of the most accomplished musicians in the camp – she'd been accepted into the Royal Conservatory of Music in Toronto – and she was also model-gorgeous: tall, regal, with skin the color of coffee, and cheekbones that could carve ice. I would've been tempted to hate her were it not for her playing. If you're not careful, the viola can make the most awful screech, even in the hands of practiced musicians. But with Elizabeth the sound rang out clean and pure and light. Hearing her play, and watching how deeply she lost herself in the music, I wanted to play like that. Better even. It wasn't just that I wanted to beat her, but also that I felt like I owed it to her, to the group, to myself, to play at her level.

'That's sounding quite beautiful,' Simon said toward the end of camp as he listened to me practice a movement from Haydn's Cello Concerto No. 2, a piece that had given me no end of trouble when I'd first attempted it last spring. 'Are you using that for the concerto competition?'

I nodded. Then I couldn't help myself, I grinned. After dinner and before lights-out every night, Simon and I had been bringing our cellos outside to hold impromptu concerts in the long twilight. We took turns challenging each other to cello duels, each trying to out-crazy-play the other. We were *always* competing, always trying to see who could play something better, faster, from memory. It had been so much fun, and was probably one reason why I was feeling so good about the Haydn.

'Ahh, someone's awfully confident. Think you can beat me?' Simon asked.

'At soccer. Definitely,' I joked. Simon often told us that he was the black sheep in his family not because he was gay, or a musician, but because he was such a 'shitey footballer'.

Simon pretended that I'd shot him in the heart. Then he laughed. 'Amazing things happen when you stop hiding behind that hulking beast?' he said, gesturing to my cello. I nodded. Simon smiled at me. 'Well, don't go getting quite so cocky. You should hear my Mozart. It sounds like the bloody angels singing.'

Neither one of us won the solo spot that year. Elizabeth did. And though it would take me four more years, eventually I'd nab the solo.

9:06 p.m.

'I've got exactly twenty minutes before our manager has a total shit fit.' Brooke Vega's raspy voice booms in the hospital's now-quiet lobby. So this is Adam's idea: Brooke Vega, the indie-music goddess and lead singer of Bikini. In a trademark punky glam outfit – tonight it's a short bubble skirt, fishnets, high black leather boots, an artfully ripped-up 'Shooting Star' T-shirt, topped off with a vintage fur shrug and a pair of black Jackie O glasses – she stands out in the hospital lobby like an ostrich in a chicken coop. She's surrounded by people: Liz and Sarah; Mike and Fitzy, Shooting Star's rhythm guitarist and bass player, respectively, plus a handful of Portland hipsters who I vaguely recognize. With her magenta hair, she's like the sun, around which her admiring planets revolve. Adam is like a moon, standing off to the side, stroking his chin. Meanwhile, Kim looks shell-shocked, like a bunch of Martians just entered the building. Or maybe it's because Kim worships Brooke Vega. In fact, so does Adam. Aside from me, this was one of the few things they had in common.

'I'll have you out of here in fifteen,' Adam promises, stepping into her galaxy.

She strides toward him. 'Adam, baby,' she croons. 'How you holding up?' Brooke encircles him in a hug as if they are old friends, though I know that they only met for the first time today; just yesterday Adam was saying how nervous he was about it. But now she's here acting like his best friend. That's the power of the scene, I guess. As she embraces Adam, I see every guy and girl in that lobby watching enviously, wishing that they were the ones getting the consolatory cuddle from Brooke.

I can't help but wonder if I were here, if I were watching this as regular old Mia, would I feel jealous, too? Then again, if I were regular old Mia, Brooke Vega would not be in this hospital lobby as part of some great ruse to get Adam in to see me.

'OK, kids. Time to rock-and-roll. Adam, what's the plan?' Brooke asks.

'*You* are the plan. I hadn't really thought beyond you going up to the ICU and making a ruckus.'

Brooke licks her bee-stung lips. 'Making a ruckus is one of my favorite things to do. What do you think we should do? Let out a primal scream? Strip? Smash a guitar? Wait, I didn't bring my guitar. Damn.'

'You could sing something?' someone suggests.

'How about that old Smiths song "Girlfriend in a Coma"?' someone calls.

Adam blanches at this sudden reality check and Brooke raises her eyebrows in a stern rebuke. Everyone goes serious.

Kim clears her throat. 'Um, it doesn't do us any good if Brooke is a diversion in the lobby. We need to go upstairs to the ICU and then maybe someone could shout that Brooke Vega is here. That might do it. If it doesn't, then sing. All we really want is to lure a couple of curious nurses out, and that grouchy head nurse after them. Once she comes out of the ICU and sees all of us in the hall, she'll be too busy dealing with us to notice that Adam has slipped inside.'

Brooke appraises Kim. Kim in her rumpled black pants and unflattering sweater. Then Brooke smiles and links arms with my best friend. 'Sounds like a plan. Let's motor, kids.'

I lag behind, watching this procession of hipsters barrel through the lobby. The sheer noisiness of them, of their heavy boots, and loud voices, buzzed on by their sense of urgency, ricochets through the quiet hush of the hospital and breathes some life into the place. I remember watching a TV program once about old-age homes that brought in cats and dogs to cheer the elderly and dying patients. Maybe all hospitals should import groups of rabble-rousing punk rockers to kick-start the languishing patients' hearts.

They stop in front of the elevator, waiting endlessly for one empty enough to ferry them up as a group. I decide that I want to be next to my body when Adam makes it to the ICU. I wonder if I will be able to *feel* his touch on me. While they wait at the elevator banks, I scramble up the stairs.

I've been gone from the ICU for more than two hours, and a lot has changed. There is a new patient in one of the empty beds, a middle-aged man whose face looks like one of those surrealist paintings: half of it looks normal, handsome even, the other half is a mess of blood, gauze, and stitching, like someone just blew it off. Maybe a gunshot wound. We get a lot of hunting accidents around here. One of the other patients, one who was so swaddled in gauze and bandages that I couldn't see if he/she was a man or woman, is gone. In his/her place is a woman whose neck is immobilized in one of those collar things.

As for me, I'm off my ventilator now. I remember the social worker telling my grandparents and Aunt Diane that this was a positive step. I stop to check if I feel any different, but I don't feel anything, not physically anyhow. I haven't since I was in the car this morning, listening to Beethoven's Cello Sonata No. 3. Now that I'm breathing on my own, my wall of machines bleeps far less, so I get fewer visits from the nurses. Nurse Ramirez, the one with the nails, looks over at me every now and again, but she's busy with the new guy with the half face.

'Holy crud. Is that Brooke Vega?' I hear someone ask in a totally fakey dramatic voice from outside the ICU's automatic doors. I've never heard any of Adam's friends talk so PG-13 before. It's their sanitized hospital version of 'holy fucking shit'.

'You mean Brooke Vega of Bikini? Brooke Vega

who was on the cover of *Spin* magazine last month? Here in this very hospital?' This time it's Kim talking. She sounds like a six-year-old reciting lines from a school play about the food groups: *You mean you're supposed to eat five servings of fruit and vegetables a day?*

'Yeah, that's right,' says Brooke's raspy voice. 'I'm here to offer some rock-and-roll succor to all the people of Portland.'

A couple of the younger nurses, the ones who probably listen to pop radio or watch MTV and have heard of Bikini, look up, their faces excited question marks. I hear them whispering, eager to see if it's really Brooke, or maybe just happy for the break in the routine.

'Yeah. That's right. So I thought I might sing a little song. One of my favorites. It's called "Eraser",' Brooke says. 'One of you guys want to count me in?'

'I need something to tap with,' Liz answers. 'Anyone got some pens or something?'

Now the nurses and orderlies in the ICU are very curious and heading toward the doors. I'm watching it all play out, like a movie on the screen. I stand next to my bed, my eyes trained on the double doors, waiting for them to open. I'm itching with suspense.

I think of Adam, of how calming it feels when he touches me, how when he absent-mindedly strokes the nape of my neck or blows warm air on my cold hands, I could melt into a puddle.

'What's going on?' the older nurse demands. Suddenly every nurse on the floor is looking at her, not out toward Brooke anymore. No one is going to try to explain to her that a famous pop star is outside. The moment has broken. I feel the tension ease into disappointment. The door isn't going to open.

Outside, I hear Brooke start belting out the lyrics to 'Eraser'. Even *a cappella*, even through the automatic double doors, she sounds good.

'Somebody call security now,' the nurse growls.

'Adam, you better just go for it,' Liz yells. 'Now or never. Full-court press.'

'Go!' screams Kim, suddenly an army general. 'We'll cover you.'

The door opens. In tumble more than a half-dozen punkers, Adam, Liz, Fitzy, some people I don't know, and then Kim. Outside, Brooke is still singing, as though this were the concert she'd come to Portland to give.

As Adam and Kim charge through the door, they

both look determined, happy even. I'm amazed by their resilience, by their hidden pockets of strength. I want to jump up and down and root for them like I used to do at Teddy's T-ball games when he'd be rounding third and heading for home. It's hard to believe, but watching Kim and Adam in action, I almost feel happy, too.

'Where is she?' Adam yells. 'Where's Mia?'

'In the corner, next to the supply closet!' someone shouts. It takes me a minute to realize it's Nurse Ramirez.

'Security! Get him! Get him!' the grumpy nurse shouts. She has spotted Adam through all the other invaders and her face has gone pink with anger. Two hospital security guards and two orderlies run inside. 'Dude, was that Brooke Vega?' one asks as he snags Fitzy and flings him toward the exit.

'Think so,' the other answers, grabbing Sarah and steering her out.

Kim has spotted me. 'Adam, she's here!' she screams, and then turns to look at me, the scream dying her throat. '*She's here*,' she says again, only this time it's a whimper.

Adam hears her and he is dodging nurses and

making his way to me. And then he's there at the foot of my bed, his hand reaching out to touch me. His hand about to be on me. Suddenly I think of our first kiss after the Yo-Yo Ma concert, how I didn't know how badly I'd wanted his lips on mine until the kiss was imminent. I didn't realize just how much I was craving his touch, until now that I can almost feel it on me.

Almost. But suddenly he's moving away from me. Two guards have him by the shoulders and have yanked him back. One of the same guards grabs Kim's elbow and leads her out. She's limp now, offering no resistance.

Brooke's still singing in the hallway. When she sees Adam, she stops. 'Sorry, honey,' she says. 'I gotta jet before I miss my show. Or get arrested.' And then she's off down the hall, trailed by a couple of orderlies begging for her autograph.

'Call the police,' the old nurse yells. 'Have him arrested.'

'We're taking him down to security. That's protocol,' one guard says.

'Not up to us to arrest,' the other adds.

'Just get him off my ward.' She harrumphs and

turns around. 'Miss Ramirez, that had better not have been you abetting these hoodlums.'

'Of course not. I was in the supply closet. I missed all the hubbub,' she replies. She's such a good liar that her face gives nothing away.

The old nurse claps her hands. 'OK. Show's over. Back to work.'

I bolt back out the ICU door, chasing after Adam and Kim, who are being led into the elevators. I jump in with them. Kim looks dazed, like someone flipped her reset button and she's still booting up. Adam's lips are set in a grim line. I can't tell if he's about to cry or about to punch the guard. For his sake, I hope it's the former. For my own, I hope the latter.

Downstairs, the guards hustle Adam and Kim toward a hallway filled with darkened offices. They're about to go inside one of the few offices with lights on when I hear someone scream Adam's name.

'Adam! Stop. Is that you?'

'Willow?' Adam yells.

'Willow?' Kim mumbles.

'Excuse me, where are you taking them?' Willow yells at the guards as she runs toward them.

'I'm sorry but these two were caught trying to break into the ICU,' one guard explains.

'Only because they wouldn't let us in,' Kim explains weakly.

Willow catches up to them. She's still wearing her nursing clothes, which is strange, because she normally changes out of what she calls 'orthopedic couture' as soon as she can. Her long, curly auburn hair looks lank and greasy, like she's forgotten to wash it these past few weeks. And her cheeks, normally rosy like apples, have been repainted beige. 'Excuse me. I'm an RN over at Cedar Creek. I did my training here, so if you like we can go straighten this out with Richard Caruthers.'

'Who's he?' one guard asks.

'Director of community affairs,' the other replies. Then he turns to Willow. 'He's not here. It's not business hours.'

'Well, I have his home number,' Willow says, brandishing her cell phone like a weapon. 'I doubt he'd be pleased if I were to call him now and tell him how his hospital was treating someone trying to visit his critically wounded girlfriend. You know that the director values compassion as much as efficiency, and this is not the way to treat a concerned loved one.'

'We're just doing our job, ma'am. Following orders.'

'How about I save you two the trouble and take it from here. The patient's family is all assembled upstairs. They're waiting for these two to join them. Here, if you have any problems, you tell Mr Caruthers to get in touch with me.' She reaches into her bag and pulls out a card and hands it over. One of the guards looks at it, hands it to the other, who stares at it and shrugs.

'Might as well save ourselves the paperwork,' he says. He lets go of Adam, whose body slumps like a scarecrow taken off his pole. 'Sorry, kid,' he says to Adam, brushing off his shoulders.

'I hope your girlfriend's OK,' the other mumbles. And then they disappear toward the glow of some vending machines.

Kim, who has met Willow all of twice, flings herself into her arms. 'Thank you!' she murmurs into her neck.

Willow hugs her back, pats her on the shoulders before letting go. She rubs her eyes and winces out a brittle laugh. 'What in the hell were you two thinking?' she asks.

'I want to see Mia,' Adam says.

Willow turns to look at Adam and it's like someone has unscrewed her valve, letting all her air escape. She deflates. She reaches out and touches Adam's cheek. 'Of course you do.' She wipes her eyes with the heel of her hand.

'Are you OK?' Kim asks.

Willow ignores the question. 'Let's see about getting you in to Mia.'

Adam perks up when he hears this. 'You think you can? That old nurse has it in for me.'

'If that old nurse is who I think she is, it doesn't matter if she has it in for you. It's not up to her. Let's check in with Mia's grandparents and then I'll find out who's in charge of breaking the rules around here and get you in to see your girl. She needs you now. More than ever.'

Adam swivels around and hugs Willow with such force that her feet lift up off the ground.

Willow to the rescue. Just the way she rescued Henry, Dad's best friend and bandmate, who, once upon a time, was a total drunk playboy. When he and Willow had been dating a few weeks, she told him to straighten out and dry out or say goodbye. Dad said that lots of girls had given Henry ultimatums, tried to force him to settle down, and lots of girls had been left crying on the sidewalk. But when Willow packed her toothbrush and told Henry to grow up, Henry was the one who cried. Then he dried his tears, grew up, got sober and monogamous. Eight years later, here they are, with a baby, no less. Willow is formidable that way. Probably why after she and Henry got together she became Mom's best friend; she was another tough-as-nails, tender-as-kittens, feminist bitch. And probably why she was one of Dad's favorite people, even though she hated the Ramones and thought baseball was boring, while Dad lived for the Ramones and thought baseball was a religious institution.

Now Willow is here. Willow the nurse. Willow who doesn't take no for an answer is here. She'll get Adam in to see me. She'll take care of everything. *Hooray!* I want to shout. *Willow is here!*

I'm so busy celebrating Willow's arrival that the implication of her being here takes a few moments to sink in, but when it does, it hits me like a jolt of electricity.

Willow is here. And if she's here, if she's in my

hospital, it means that there isn't any reason for her to be in her hospital. I know her well enough to know that she never would have left him there. Even with me here, she would've stayed with him. He was broken, and brought to her for fixing. He was her patient. Her priority.

I think about the fact that Gran and Gramps are in Portland with me. And that all anyone in that waiting room is talking about is me, how they are avoiding mentioning Mom or Dad or Teddy. I think about Willow's face, which looks like it has been scrubbed clean of all joy. And I think about what she told Adam, that I need him now. More than ever.

And that's how I know. Teddy. He's gone, too.

*

Mom went into labor three days before Christmas, and she insisted we go holiday shopping together.

'Shouldn't you like lie down or go to the birthing center or something?' I asked.

Mom grimaced through a cramp. 'Nah. The contractions aren't that bad and are still like twenty minutes apart. I cleaned our entire house, from top to bottom, while I was in early labor with you.'

'Putting the labor in labor,' I joked.

'You're a smart-ass, you know that?' Mom said. She took a few breaths. 'I've got a ways to go. Now come on. Let's take the bus to the mall. I'm not up to driving.'

'Shouldn't we call Dad?' I asked.

Mom laughed at that. 'Please, it's enough for me to have to birth *this* baby. I don't need to deal with him, too. We'll call him when I'm ready to pop. I'd much rather have you around.'

So Mom and I wandered around the mall, stopping every couple minutes so she could sit down and take deep breaths and squeeze my wrist so hard it left angry red marks. Still, it was a weirdly fun and productive morning. We bought presents for Gran and Gramps (a sweater with an angel on it and a new book about Abraham Lincoln) and toys for the baby and a new pair of rain boots for me. Usually we waited for the holiday sales to buy stuff like that, but Mom said that this year we'd be too busy changing diapers. 'Now's not the time to be cheap. Ow, fuck. Sorry, Mia. Come on. Let's go get pie.'

We went to Marie Callender's for pie. Mom had a slice of pumpkin and of banana cream. I had blue-berry. When she was done, she pushed her plate away and announced she was ready to go to the midwife.

We'd never really talked about my being there or not being there. I went everywhere with Mom and Dad at that point, so it was just kind of assumed. We met a nerve-racked Dad at the birthing center, which was nothing like a doctor's office. It was the ground floor of a house, the inside decked out with beds and Jacuzzi tubs, the medical equipment discreetly tucked away. The hippie midwife led Mom inside and Dad asked me if I wanted to come, too. By now, I could hear Mom screaming profanities.

'I can call Gran and she'll pick you up,' Dad said, wincing at Mom's barrage. 'This might take a while.'

I shook my head. Mom needed me. She'd said so. I sat down on one of the floral couches and picked up a magazine with a goofy-looking bald baby on the cover. Dad disappeared into the room with the bed.

'Music! Goddammit! Music!' Mom screamed.

'We have some lovely Enya. Very soothing,' the midwife said.

'Fuck Enya!' Mom screamed. 'Melvins. Earth. Now!'

'I've got it covered,' Dad said. Then he popped a CD of the loudest, churningest, guitar-heaviest music I'd ever heard. It made all the fast-paced punk songs Dad normally listened to sound like harp music. This music was primal and that seemed to make Mom feel better. She started making these low guttural noises. I just sat there quietly. Every so often she'd scream my name and I'd scamper inside. Mom would look up at me, her face plastered with sweat. *Don't be scared*, she'd whisper. *Women can handle the worst kind of pain. You'll find out one day.* Then she'd scream *fuck* again.

I'd seen a couple of births on that cable-TV show, and people usually yelled for a while; sometimes they swore and it had to be bleeped, but it never took longer than half an hour. After three hours, Mom and the Melvins were still screaming along. The whole birthing center felt tropically humid, even though it was forty degrees outside.

Henry dropped by. When he came inside and heard the noise, he froze in his tracks. I knew that the whole kid-thing freaked him out. I'd overheard Mom and Dad talking about that, and Henry's refusal to grow up. He'd apparently been shocked when Mom and Dad had me, and now was completely bewildered that they chose to have a second. They'd both been relieved when he and Willow had gotten back together. 'Finally, a grown-up in Henry's life,' Mom had said.

Henry looked at me; his face was pale and sweaty. 'Holy shit, Mee. Should you be hearing this? Should I be hearing this?'

I shrugged. Henry sat down next to me. 'I've got the flu or something, but your dad just called asking me to bring some food. So here I am,' he said, proffering a Taco Bell bag reeking of onions. Mom let out another moan. 'I should go. Don't want me spreading germs or anything.' Mom screamed even louder and Henry practically jumped in his seat. 'You sure you wanna hang around for this? You can come back to my place. Willow's there, taking care of me.' He grinned when he mentioned her name. 'She can take care of you, too.' He stood up to leave.

'No. I'm fine. Mom needs me. Dad's kind of freaking out, though.'

'Did he puke yet?' Henry asked, sitting back down on the couch. I laughed, but then saw from his face that he was serious.

'He threw up when you were coming. Almost fainted on the floor. Not that I can blame him. But the dude was a mess, the doctors wanted to kick him out . . . said they were going to if you didn't come out within a half hour. That got your mom so pissed off she pushed you out five minutes later.' Henry smiled, leaning back into the sofa. 'So the story goes. But I'll tell you this: He cried like a mother-fucking baby when you were born.'

'I've heard that part.'

'Heard what part?' Dad asked breathlessly. He grabbed the bag from Henry. 'Taco Bell, Henry?'

'Dinner of champions,' Henry said.

'It'll do. I'm starving. It's intense in there. Got to keep up my strength.'

Henry winked at me. Dad pulled out a burrito and offered one to me. I shook my head. Dad had started unwrapping his meal when Mom let out a growl and then started screaming at the midwife that she was ready to push.

The midwife poked her head out the door. 'I think we're getting close, so maybe you should save dinner for later,' she said. 'Come on back.'

Henry practically bolted out the front door. I followed Dad into the bedroom where Mom was sitting now, panting like a sick dog. 'Would you like to watch?' the midwife asked Dad, but he just swayed and turned a pale shade of green.

'I'm probably better up here,' he said, grasping Mom's hand, which she violently shook off.

No one asked me if I wanted to watch. I just automatically went to stand next to the midwife. It was pretty gross, I'll admit. Lots of blood. And I'd certainly never seen my mom so full-on frontal before. But it felt strangely normal for me to be there. The midwife was telling Mom to push, then hold, then push. 'Go baby, go baby, go baby go,' she chanted. 'You're almost there!' she cheered. Mom looked like she wanted to smack her.

When Teddy slid out, he was head up, facing the ceiling, so that the first thing he saw was me. He didn't come out squalling like you see on TV. He was just quiet. His eyes were open, staring straight at me. He held my gaze as the midwife suctioned out his nose. 'It's a boy,' she shouted.

The midwife put Teddy on Mom's belly. 'Do you want to cut the cord?' she asked Dad. Dad waved his hands no, too overcome or nauseous to speak.

'I'll do it,' I offered.

The midwife held the cord taut and told me where

to cut. Teddy lay still, his gray eyes wide open, still staring at me.

Mom always said that it was because Teddy saw me first, and because I cut his cord, that somewhere deep down he thought I was his mother. 'It's like those goslings,' Mom joked. 'Imprinting on a zoologist, not the mama goose, because he was the first one they saw when they hatched.'

She exaggerated. Teddy didn't really think I was his mother, but there were certain things that only I could do for him. When he was a baby and going through his nightly fussy period, he'd only calm down after I played him a lullaby on my cello. When he started getting into *Harry Potter*, only I was allowed to read a chapter to him every night. And when he'd skin a knee or bump his head, if I was around he would not stop crying until I bestowed a magic kiss on the injury, after which he'd miraculously recover.

I know that all the magic kisses in the world probably couldn't have helped him today. But I would do anything to have been able to give him one.

* * *

10:40 p.m.

I run away.

I leave Adam, Kim, and Willow in the lobby and I just start careening through the hospital. I don't realize I'm looking for the pediatric ward until I get there. I tear through the halls, past rooms with nervous four-year-olds sleeping restlessly before tomorrow's tonsillectomies, past the neonatal ICU with babies the size of fists, hooked up to more tubes than I am, past the pediatric oncology unit where bald cancer patients sleep under cheerful murals of rainbows and balloons. I'm looking for him, even though I know I won't find him. Still, I have to keep looking.

I picture his head, his tight blond curls. I love to nuzzle my face in those curls, have done since he was a baby. I keep waiting for the day when he'll swat me away, say 'You're embarrassing me,' the way he does to Dad when Dad cheers too loudly at T-ball games. But so far, that hadn't happened. So far, I've been allowed constant access to that head of his. So far. Now there is no more so far. It's over.

I picture myself nuzzling his head one last time,

and I can't even imagine it without seeing myself crying, my tears turning his blond curlicues straight.

Teddy is never going to graduate from T-ball to baseball. He's never going to grow a mustache. Never going to get into a fist fight or shoot a deer or kiss a girl or have sex or fall in love or get married or father his own curly-haired child. I'm only ten years older than him, but it's like I've already had so much more life. It is unfair. If one of us should have been left behind, if one of us should be given the opportunity for more life, it should be him.

I race through the hospital like a trapped wild animal. *Teddy?* I call. *Where are you? Come back to me!*

But he won't. I know it's fruitless. I give up and drag myself back to my ICU. I want to break the double doors. I want to smash the nurses' station. I want it all to go away. I want to go away. I don't want to be here. I don't want to be in this hospital. I don't want to be in this suspended state where I can see what's happening, where I'm aware of what I'm feeling without being able to actually feel it. I cannot scream until my throat hurts or break a window with my fist until my hand bleeds, or pull my hair out in clumps until the pain in my scalp overcomes the one in my heart.

I'm staring at myself, at the 'live' Mia now, lying in her hospital bed. I feel a burst of fury. If I could slap my own lifeless face, I would.

Instead, I sit down in the chair and close my eyes, wishing it all away. Except I can't. I can't concentrate because there's suddenly so much noise. My monitors are blipping and chirping and two nurses are racing toward me.

'Her BP and pulse ox are dropping,' one yells.

'She's tachycardic,' the other yells. 'What happened?'

'Code blue, code blue in Trauma,' blares the PA.

Soon the nurses are joined by a bleary-eyed doctor, rubbing the sleep out of his eyes, which are ringed by deep circles. He yanks down the covers and lifts my hospital gown. I'm naked from the waist down, but no one notices these things here. He puts his hands on my belly, which is swollen and hard. His eyes widen and then narrow into slits. 'Abdomen's rigid,' he says angrily. 'We need to do an ultrasound.'

Nurse Ramirez runs to a back room and then wheels out what looks like a portable laptop with a long white attachment. She squirts some jelly on my stomach, and the doctor runs the attachment over my stomach.

'Damn. Full of fluid,' he says. 'Patient had surgery this afternoon?'

'A splenectomy,' Nurse Ramirez replies.

'Could be a missed blood vessel that wasn't cauterized,' the doctor says. 'Or a slow leak from a perforated bowel. Car accident, right?'

'Yes. Patient was medevacced in this morning.'

The doctor flips through my chart. 'Doctor Sorensen was her surgeon. He's still on call. Page him, get her to the OR. We need to get inside and find out what's leaking, and why, before she drops any further. Jesus, brain contusions, collapsed lung. This kid's a train wreck.'

Nurse Ramirez shoots the doctor a dirty look, as if he had just insulted me.

'Miss Ramirez,' the grumpy nurse at the desk scolds. 'You have patients of your own to deal with. Let's get this young woman intubated and transferred to the OR. That will do her more good than all this dilly-dallying around!'

The nurses work rapidly to detach the monitors and catheters and run another tube down my throat. A pair of orderlies rush in with a gurney and heave me onto it. I'm still naked from the waist down as they hustle me out, but right before I reach the back door, Nurse Ramirez calls, 'Wait!' and then gently closes the hospital gown around my legs. She taps me three times on the forehead with her fingers, like it's some kind of Morse-code message. And then I'm gone into the maze of hallways leading toward the OR for another round of cutting, but this time I don't follow myself. This time I stay behind in the ICU.

I am starting to get it now. I mean, I don't totally fully understand. It's not like I somehow commanded a blood vessel to pop open and start leaking into my stomach. It's not like I wished for another surgery. But Teddy is gone. Mom and Dad are gone. This morning I went for a drive with my family. And now I am here, as alone as I've ever been. I am seventeen years old. This is not how it's supposed to be. This is not how my life is supposed to turn out.

In the quiet corner of the ICU I start to really think about the bitter things I've managed to ignore so far today. What would it be like if I stay? What would it feel like to wake up an orphan? To never smell Dad smoke a pipe? To never stand next to Mom quietly talking as we do the dishes? To never read Teddy another chapter of *Harry Potter*? To stay without them?

I'm not sure this is a world I belong in anymore. I'm not sure that I want to wake up.

*

I've only ever been to one funeral in my life and it was for someone I hardly knew.

I might have gone to Great Aunt Glo's funeral after she died of acute pancreatitis. Except her will was very specific about her final wishes. No traditional service, no burial in the family plot. Instead, she wanted to be cremated and have her ashes scattered in a sacred Native American ceremony somewhere in the Sierra Nevada Mountains. Gran was pretty annoyed by that, by Aunt Glo in general, who Gran said was always trying to call attention to how different she was, even after she was dead. Gran ended up boycotting the ash scattering, and if she wasn't going, there was no reason for the rest of us to.

Peter Hellman, my trombonist friend from conservatory camp, he died two years ago, but I didn't find out until I returned to camp and he wasn't there. Few of us had known that he'd had lymphoma. That was the funny thing about conservatory camp; you got so close with the people over the summer, but it was some unwritten rule that you didn't keep in touch during the rest of the year. We were summer friends. Anyhow, we had a memorial concert at camp in Peter's honor, but it wasn't really a funeral.

Kerry Gifford was a musician in town, one of Mom and Dad's people. Unlike Dad and Henry, who as they got older and had families became less music performers than music connoisseurs, Kerry stayed single and stayed faithful to his first love: playing music. He was in three bands and he earned his living doing the sound at a local club, an ideal setup because at least one of his bands seemed to play there every week, so he just had to hop up on the stage and let someone take the controls for his set, though sometimes you'd see him jumping down in the middle of a set to adjust the monitors himself. I had known Kerry when I was little and would go to shows with Mom and Dad and then I sort of re-met him when Adam and I got together and I started going to shows again.

He was at work one night, doing the sound for a Portland band called Clod, when he just keeled over on the soundboard. He was dead by the time the ambulance got there. A freak brain aneurysm.

Kerry's death caused an uproar in our town. He was kind of fixture around here, an outspoken guy with a big personality and this mass of wild white-boy dreadlocks. And he was young, only thirty-two. Everyone we knew was planning on going to his funeral, which was being held in the town where he grew up, in the mountains a couple of hours' drive away. Mom and Dad were going, of course, and so was Adam. So even though I felt a little bit like an impostor crashing someone's death day, I decided to go along. Teddy stayed with Gran and Gramps.

We caravanned to Kerry's hometown with a bunch of people, squeezing into a car with Henry and Willow, who was so pregnant the seat belt wouldn't fit over her bump. Everyone took turns telling funny stories about Kerry. Kerry the avowed left-winger who decided to protest the Iraq war by getting a bunch of guys to dress up in drag and go down to the local army recruiting office to enlist. Kerry the atheist curmudgeon, who hated how commercialized Christmas had become and so threw an annual Merry Anti-Christmas Celebration at the club, where he held a contest for which band could play the most distorted versions of Christmas carols. Then he invited everyone to throw all their crappy presents into a big pile in the middle of the club. And contrary to local lore, Kerry did not burn the stuff in a bonfire; Dad told me that he donated it to St Vincent de Paul.

As everyone talked about Kerry, the mood in the car was fizzy and fun, like we were going to the circus, not a funeral. But it seemed right, it seemed true to Kerry, who was always overflowing with frenetic energy.

The funeral, though, was the opposite. It was horribly depressing – and not just because it was for someone who'd died tragically young and for no particular reason aside from some bad arterial luck. It was held in a huge church, which seemed strange considering Kerry was an outspoken atheist, but that part I could understand. I mean where else do you have a funeral? The problem was the service itself. It was obvious that the pastor had never even met Kerry because when he talked about him, it was generic, about what a kind heart Kerry had and how even though it was sad that he was gone, he was getting his 'heavenly reward'.

And instead of having eulogies from his band-mates or the people in town who he'd spent the last fifteen years with, some uncle from Boise got up and talked about teaching Kerry how to ride a bike when he was six, like learning to ride a bike was the defining moment in Kerry's life. He concluded by reassuring us that Kerry was walking with Jesus now. I could see my mom getting red when he said that, and I started to get a little worried that she might say something. We went to church sometimes, so it's not like Mom had anything against religion, but Kerry totally did and Mom was ferociously protective of the people she loved, so much that she took insults upon them personally. Her friends sometimes called her Mama Bear for this reason. Steam was practically blowing out of Mom's ears by the time the service ended with a rousing rendition of Bette Midler's 'Wind Beneath My Wings'.

'It's a good thing Kerry's dead, because that funeral would've sent him over the edge,' Henry said. After the church service, we'd decided to skip the formal luncheon and had gone to a diner.

' "Wind Beneath My Wings"?' Adam asked, absent-mindedly taking my hand into his and blowing on it, which is what he did to warm my perpetually cold fingers. 'What's wrong with "Amazing Grace"? It's still traditional—'

'But doesn't make you want to puke,' Henry interjected. 'Or better yet, "Three Little Birds" by Bob Marley. That would have been a more Kerry-worthy song. Something to toast the guy he was.'

'That funeral wasn't about celebrating Kerry's life,' Mom growled, yanking at her scarf. 'It was about repudiating it. It was like they killed him all over again.'

Dad put a calming hand over Mom's clenched fist. 'Now come on. It was just a song.'

'It wasn't just a song,' Mom said, snatching her hand away. 'It was what it represented. That whole charade back there. You of all people should understand.'

Dad shrugged and smiled sadly. 'Maybe I should. But I can't be angry with his family. I imagine this funeral was their way of reclaiming their son.'

'Please,' Mom said, shaking her head. 'If they wanted to claim their son, why didn't they respect the life he chose to live? How come they never came to visit? Or supported his music?'

'We don't know what they thought about all that,' Dad replied. 'Let's not judge too harshly. It has to be heartbreaking to bury your child.'

'I can't believe you're making excuses for them,' Mom exclaimed.

'I'm not. I just think you might be reading too much into a musical selection.'

'And I think you're confusing being empathetic with being a pushover!'

Dad's wince was barely visible, but it was enough to make Adam squeeze my hand and Henry and Willow exchange a look. Henry jumped in, to Dad's rescue, I think. 'It's different for you, with your parents,' he told Dad. 'I mean they're old-fashioned but they always were into what you did, and even in your wildest days, you were always a good son, a good father. Always home for Sunday dinner.'

Mom guffawed, as if Henry's statement had proven her point. We all turned to her, and our shocked expressions seemed to snap her out of her rant. 'Clearly I'm just emotional right now,' she said. Dad seemed to understand that was as much an apology as he was going to get right now. He covered her hand with his and this time she didn't snatch it away.

Dad paused, hesitating before speaking. 'I just think that funerals are a lot like death itself. You can have your wishes, your plans, but at the end of the day, it's out of your control.'

'No way,' Henry said. 'Not if you make your wishes known to the right people.' He turned to Willow and spoke to the bump in her belly. 'So listen up, family. At my funeral no one is allowed to wear black. And for music, I want something poppy and old-school, like Mr T Experience.' He looked up at Willow. 'Got that?'

'Mr T Experience. I'll make sure of it.'

'Thanks, and what about you, honey?' he asked her.

Without missing a beat, Willow said: 'Play "P.S. You Rock My World" by the Eels. And I want one of those green funerals where they bury you in the ground under a tree. So the funeral itself would be in nature. And no flowers. I mean, give me all the peonies you want when I'm alive, but once I'm dead, better to give donations on my behalf to a good charity like Doctors Without Borders.'

'You've got all the details figured out,' Adam said. 'Is that a nurse thing?'

Willow shrugged.

'According to Kim, that means you're deep,' I said. 'She says that the world is divided into the people who imagine their own funerals and the people who don't, and that smart and artistic people naturally fall into the former category.'

'So which are you?' Adam asked me.

'I'd want Mozart's Requiem,' I said. I turned to Mom and Dad. 'Don't worry, I'm not suicidal or anything.'

'Please,' Mom said, her mood lightening as she stirred her coffee. 'When I was growing up I'd have elaborate fantasies about my funeral. My deadbeat father and all the friends who'd wronged me would weep over my casket, which would be red, naturally, and they'd play James Taylor.'

'Let me guess,' Willow said. ' "Fire and Rain"?'

Mom nodded and she and Willow started laughing and soon everyone at the table was cracking up so hard that tears ran down our faces. And then we were crying, even me, who didn't know Kerry all that well. Crying and laughing, laughing and crying.

'So what now?' Adam asked Mom when we'd calmed down. 'Still harbor a soft spot for Mr Taylor?'

Mom stopped and blinked hard, which is what she does when she's thinking about something. Then she reached over to stroke Dad's cheek, a rare demonstration of PDA. 'In my ideal scenario, my big-hearted pushover husband and I die quickly and simultaneously when we're ninety-two years old. I'm not sure how. Maybe we're on a safari in Africa – 'cause in the future, we're rich; hey, it's my fantasy – and we come down with some exotic sickness and go to sleep one night feeling fine and then never wake up. And no James Taylor. Mia plays at our funeral. If, that is, we can tear her away from the New York Philharmonic.'

Dad was wrong. It's true you might not get to control your funeral, but sometimes you do get to choose your death. And I can't help thinking that part of Mom's wish *did* come true. She went with Dad. But I won't be playing at her funeral. It's possible that her funeral will also be mine. There's something comforting in that. To go down as a family. No one left behind. That said, I can't help thinking Mom would not be happy about this. In fact, Mama Bear would be absolutely furious with the way events are unfolding today.

2:48 a.m.

I'm back where I started. Back in the ICU. My body, that is. *I've* been sitting here all along, too tired to move. I wish I could go to sleep. I wish there was some kind of anesthesia for *me*, or at least something to make the world shut up. I want to be like my body, quiet and lifeless, putty in someone else's hands. I don't have the energy for this decision. I don't want this anymore. I say it out loud. *I don't want this*. I look around the ICU, feeling kind of ridiculous. I doubt all the other messed-up people in the ward are exactly thrilled to be here, either.

My body wasn't gone from the ICU for too long. A few hours for surgery. Some time in the recovery room. I don't know exactly what's happened to me, and for the first time today, I don't really care. I shouldn't have to care. I shouldn't have to work this hard. I realize now that dying is easy. Living is hard.

I'm back on the ventilator, and once again there's tape over my eyes. I still don't understand the tape. Are the doctors afraid that I'll wake up mid-surgery and be horrified by the scalpels or blood? As if those things could faze me now. Two nurses, the one assigned to me and Nurse Ramirez, come over to my bed and check all my monitors. They call out a chorus of numbers that are as familiar to me now as my own name: BP, pulse ox, respiratory rate. Nurse Ramirez looks like an entirely different person from the one who arrived here yesterday afternoon. The make-up has all rubbed off and her hair is flat. She looks like she could sleep standing up. Her shift must be over soon. I'll miss her but I'm glad she'll be able to get away from me, from this place. I'd like to get away, too. I think I will. I think it's just a matter of time – of figuring out how to let go.

I haven't been back in my bed fifteen minutes when Willow shows up. She marches through the double doors and goes to speak to the one nurse behind the desk. I don't hear what she says, but I hear her tone: it's polite, soft-spoken, but leaving no room for questions. When she leaves the room a few minutes later, there's a change in the air. Willow's in charge now. The grumpy nurse at first looks pissed off, like *Who is this woman to tell me what to do?* But then she seems to resign, to throw her hands up in surrender. It's been a crazy night. The shift is almost over. Why bother? Soon, me and all of my noisy, pushy visitors will be somebody else's problem.

Five minutes later, Willow is back, bringing Gran and Gramps with her. Willow has worked all day and now she is here all night. I know she doesn't get enough sleep on a good day. I used to hear Mom give her tips for getting the baby to sleep through the night.

I'm not sure who looks worse, me or Gramps. His cheeks are sallow, his skin looks gray and papery, and his eyes are bloodshot. Gran, on the other hand, looks just like Gran. No sign of wear and tear on her. It's like exhaustion wouldn't dare mess with her. She bustles right over to my bed.

'You've sure got us on a roller-coaster ride today,' Gran says lightly. 'Your mom always said she couldn't believe what an easy girl you were and I remember telling her, "Just wait until she hits puberty." But you proved me wrong. Even then you were such a breeze. Never gave us any trouble. Never the kind of girl to make my heart race in fear. You made up for a life-time of that today.'

'Now, now,' Gramps says, putting a hand on her shoulder.

'Oh, I'm only kidding. Mia would appreciate it.

She's got a sense of humor, no matter how serious she sometimes seems. A wicked sense of humor, this one.'

Gran pulls the chair up next to my bed and starts combing through my hair with her fingers. Someone has rinsed it out, so, while it's not exactly clean, it's not caked with blood, either. Gran starts untangling my bangs, which are about chin length. I'm forever cutting bangs, then growing them. It's about as radical a makeover as I can give myself. She works her way down, pulling the hair out from under the pillow so it streams down my chest, hiding some of the lines and tubes connected to me. 'There, much better,' she says. 'You know, I went outside for a walk today and you'll never guess what I saw? A crossbill. In Portland in February. Now, that's unusual. I think it's Glo. She always had a soft spot for you. Said you reminded her of your father, and she adored him. When he cut his first crazy Mohawk hairdo, she practically threw him a party. She loved that he was rebellious, so different. Little did she know your father couldn't stand her. She came to visit us once when your dad was around five or six, and she had this ratty mink coat with her. This was before she got all into the animal rights and crystals and the like. The coat smelled terrible, like mothballs, like the old linens we kept in a trunk in the attic, and your father took to calling her "Auntie Trunk Smell". She never knew that. But she loved that he'd rebelled against us, or so she thought, and she thought it was something that you rebelled all over again by becoming a classical musician. Though much as I tried to tell her that it wasn't the way it was, she didn't care. She had her own ideas about things; I suppose we all do.'

Gran twitters on for another five minutes, filling me in on mundane news: Heather has decided she wants to become a librarian. My cousin Matthew bought a motorcycle and my aunt Patricia is not pleased about that. I've heard her keep up a running stream of commentary like this for hours while she's cooking dinner or potting orchids. And listening to her now, I can almost picture us in her greenhouse, where even in winter, the air is always warm and humid and smells musty and earthy like soil with the slightest tinge of manure. Gran hand-collects cow-shit, 'cow-patties', she calls them, and mixes them in with mulch to make her own fertilizer. Gramps thinks she should patent the recipe and sell it because she uses it on her orchids, which are always winning awards.

I try to meditate on the sound of Gran's voice, to be carried away by her happy babble. Sometimes I can almost fall asleep while sitting on the bar stool at her kitchen counter and listening to her, and I wonder if I could do that here today. Sleep would be so welcome. A warm blanket of black to erase everything else. Sleep without dreams. I've heard people talk about the sleep of the dead. Is that what death would feel like? The nicest, warmest, heaviest never-ending nap? If that's what it's like, I wouldn't mind. If that's what dying is like, I wouldn't mind that at all.

I jerk myself up, a panic destroying whatever calm listening to Gran had offered. I am still not entirely clear on the particulars here, but I do know that once I fully commit to going, I'll go. But I'm not ready. Not yet. I don't know why, but I'm not. And I'm a little scared that if I accidentally think, I wouldn't mind an endless nap, it will happen and be irreversible, like the way my grandparents used to warn me that if I made a funny face as the clock struck noon, it would remain like that for ever.

I wonder if every dying person gets to decide

whether they stay or go. It seems unlikely. After all, this hospital is full of people having poisonous chemicals pumped into their veins or submitting to horrible operations all so they can stay, but some of them will die anyway.

Did Mom and Dad decide? It hardly seems like there would have been time for them to make such a momentous decision, and I can't imagine them choosing to leave me behind. And what about Teddy? Did he want to go with Mom and Dad? Did he know that I was still here? Even if he did, I wouldn't blame him for choosing to go without me. He's little. He was probably scared. I suddenly picture him alone and frightened, and for the first time in my life, I hope that Gran is right about the angels. I pray they were all too busy comforting Teddy to worry about me.

This is all too much for a seventeen-year-old girl to have to decide. Why can't someone else decide this for me? Why can't I get a death proxy?

Gran is gone. Willow is gone. The ICU is tranquil. I close my eyes. When I open them again, Gramps is there. He's crying. He's not making any noise, but tears are cascading down his cheeks, wetting his entire face. I've never seen anyone cry like this. Quiet but gushing, a faucet behind his eyes mysteriously turned on. The tears fall onto my blanket, onto my freshly combed hair. *Plink. Plink. Plink.*

Gramps doesn't wipe his face or blow his nose. He just lets the tears fall where they may. And when the well of grief is momentarily dry, he steps forward and kisses me on the forehead. He looks like he's about to leave, but then he doubles back to my bedside, bends so his face is level with my ear, and whispers into it.

'It's OK,' he tells me. 'If you want to go. Everyone wants you to stay. *I* want you to stay more than I've ever wanted anything in my life.' His voice cracks with emotion. He stops, clears his throat, takes a breath, and continues. 'But that's what I want and I could see why it might not be what you want. So I just wanted to tell you that I understand if you go. It's OK if you have to leave us. It's OK if you want to stop fighting.'

For the first time since I realized that Teddy was gone, too, I feel something unclench. I feel myself breathe. I know that Gramps can't be that death proxy I'd hoped for. He won't unplug my breathing tube or overdose me with morphine or anything like that. But this is the first time today that anyone has acknowledged what I have lost. I know that the social worker warned Gran and Gramps not to upset me, but Gramps's recognition, and the permission he just offered me – it feels like a gift.

Gramps doesn't leave me. He slumps back into the chair. It's quiet now. So quiet that you can almost hear other people's dreams. So quiet that you can almost hear me tell Gramps, 'Thank you.'

*

When Mom had Teddy, Dad was still playing drums in the same band he'd been in since college. They'd released a couple of CDs; they'd gone on a tour every summer. The band was by no means big, but they had a following in the Northwest and in various college towns between here and Chicago. And, weirdly, they had a bunch of fans in Japan. The band was always getting letters from Japanese teenagers begging them to come play, and offering up their homes as crash pads. Dad was always saying that if they went, he'd take me and Mom. Mom and I even learned a few words of Japanese just in case.

Konnichiwa. *Arigatou*. It never panned out, though.

After Mom announced she was pregnant with Teddy, the first sign that changes were afoot was when Dad went and got himself a learner's permit. At age thirty-three. He tried letting Mom teach him to drive, but she was too impatient, he said. Dad was too sensitive to criticism, Mom said. So Gramps took Dad out along the empty country lanes in his pickup truck, just like he'd done with the rest of Dad's siblings – except they'd all learned to drive when they were sixteen.

Next up was the wardrobe change, but it wasn't something any of us noticed right away. It wasn't like one day he stripped off the tight black jeans and band tees in exchange for suits. It was more subtle. First the band tees went out in the window in favor of button-up 1950s rayon numbers, which he dug up at the Goodwill until they started getting trendy and he had to buy them from the fancy vintage-clothing shop. Then the jeans went in the bin, except for one pair of impeccable, dark blue Levi's, which Dad ironed and wore on weekends. Most days he wore neat, flat-front cuffed trousers. But when, a few weeks after Teddy was born, Dad gave away his leather jacket – his prized beat-up motorcycle jacket with the fuzzy leopard belt – we finally realized that a major transformation was under way.

'Dude, you cannot be serious,' Henry said when Dad handed him the jacket. 'You've been wearing this thing since you were a kid. It even smells like you.'

Dad shrugged, ending the conversation. Then he went to pick up Teddy, who was squalling from his bassinet.

A few months later, Dad announced he was leaving the band. Mom told him not to do it for her sake. She said it was OK to keep playing as long as he didn't take off on month-long tours, leaving her alone with two kids. Dad said not to worry, he wasn't quitting for her.

Dad's other bandmates took his decision in stride, but Henry was devastated. He tried to talk him out of it. Promised they'd only play in town. Wouldn't have to tour. Ever be gone overnight. 'We can even start playing shows in suits. We'll look like the Rat Pack. Do Sinatra covers. Come on, man,' Henry reasoned.

When Dad refused to reconsider, he and Henry had

a huge blowout. Henry was furious with Dad for unilaterally quitting the band, especially since Mom had said he could still play shows. Dad told Henry that he was sorry, but he'd made his decision. By this time, he'd already filled out his applications for grad school. He was going to be a teacher now. No more dicking around. 'One day you'll understand,' Dad told Henry.

'The fuck I will,' Henry shot back.

Henry didn't speak to Dad for a few months after that. Willow would drop by from time to time, to play peacemaker. She'd explain to Dad that Henry was just sorting some stuff out. 'Give him time,' she said, and Dad would pretend to not be hurt. Then she and Mom would drink coffee in the kitchen and exchange knowing smiles that seemed to say: *Men are such boys.*

Henry eventually resurfaced, but he didn't apologize to Dad, not right away, anyhow. Years later, shortly after his daughter was born, Henry called our house one night in tears. 'I get it now,' he told Dad.

* * *

Strangely enough, in some ways Gramps seemed as upset with Dad's metamorphosis as Henry had been. You would have thought he would love the new Dad. On the surface, he and Gran seem so old-school, it's like a time warp. They don't use computers or watch cable TV, and they never curse and have this thing about them that makes you want to be polite. Mom, who swore like a prison guard, never cursed around Gran and Gramps. It was like no one wanted to disappoint them.

Gran got a kick out of Dad's stylistic transformation. 'Had I known that all that stuff was going to come back in style, I would've saved Gramps's old suits,' Gran said one Sunday afternoon when we'd stopped by for lunch and Dad pulled off a trench coat to reveal a pair of wool gabardine trousers and a 1950s cardigan.

'It hasn't come back into style. *Punk* has come into style, so I think this is your son's way of rebelling all over again,' Mom said with a smirk. 'Whose daddy's a rebel? Is your daddy a rebel?' Mom baby-talked as Teddy gurgled in delight.

'Well, he sure does look dapper,' Gran said. 'Don't you think?' she said, turning to Gramps.

Gramps shrugged. 'He always looks good to me. All my children and grandchildren do.' But he looked pained as he said it.

* * *

Later that afternoon, I went outside with Gramps to help him collect firewood. He needed to split some more logs, so I watched him take an ax to a bunch of dried alder.

'Gramps, don't you like Dad's new clothes?' I asked.

Gramps halted the ax in midair. Then he set it down gently next to the bench I was sitting on. 'I like his clothes just fine, Mia,' he said.

'But you looked so sad in there when Gran was talking about it.'

Gramps shook his head. 'Don't miss a thing, do you? Even at ten years old.'

'It's not easy to miss. When you feel sad, you look sad.'

'I'm not sad. Your father seems happy and I think he'll make a good teacher. Those are some lucky kids who get to read *The Great Gatsby* with your dad. I'll just miss the music.'

'Music? You never go to Dad's shows.'

'I've got bad ears. From the war. The noise hurts.'

'You should wear headphones. Mom makes me do that. Earplugs just fall out.'

'Maybe I'll try that. But I've always listened to your dad's music. At low volume. I'll admit, I don't much care for all that electric guitar. Not my cup of tea. But I still admired the music. The words, especially. When he was about your age, your father used to come up with these great stories. He'd sit down at his little table and write them down, then give them to Gran to type up, then he'd draw pictures. Funny stories about animals, but real and smart. Always reminded me of that book about the spider and the pig – what's it called?'

'*Charlotte's Web*?'

'That's the one. I always thought your dad would grow up to be a writer. And in a way, I always felt like he did. The words he writes to his music, they're poetry. You ever listen carefully to the things he says?'

I shook my head, suddenly ashamed. I hadn't even realized that Dad wrote lyrics. He didn't sing so I just assumed that the people in front of the microphones wrote the words. But I *had* seen him sit at the kitchen table with a guitar and a notepad a hundred times. I'd just never put it together.

That night when we got home, I went up to my room with Dad's CDs and a Discman. I checked the liner notes to see which songs Dad had written and then I painstakingly copied down all the lyrics. It was only after I saw them scrawled in my science lab book that I saw what Gramps meant. Dad's lyrics were not just rhymes. They were something else. There was one song in particular called 'Waiting for Vengeance' that I listened to and read over and over until I had it memorized. It was on the second album, and it was the only slow song they ever did; it sounded almost country, probably from Henry's brief infatuation with hillbilly punk. I listened to it to so much that I started singing it to myself without even realizing it.

'Well, what is this?
What am I coming to?
And beyond that, what am I gonna do?
Now there's blankness

Where once your eyes held the light
But that was so long ago
That was last night

'Well, what was that?
What's that sound that I hear?
It's just my lifetime
It's whistling past my ear
And when I look back
Everything seems smaller than life
The way it's been for so long
Since last night

'Now I'm leaving
Any moment I'll be gone
I think you'll notice
I think you'll wonder what went wrong
I'm not choosing
But I'm running out of fight
And this was decided so long ago
It was last night . . .'

'What are you singing, Mia?' Dad asked me, catching me serenading Teddy as I pushed him around the kitchen in his stroller in a vain attempt to get him to nap.

'Your song,' I said sheepishly, suddenly feeling like I'd maybe illegally trespassed into Dad's private territory. Was it wrong to go around singing other people's music without their permission?

But Dad looked delighted. 'My Mia's singing "Waiting for Vengeance" to my Teddy. What do you think about that?' He leaned over to muss my hair and to tickle Teddy on his chubby cheek. 'Well, don't let me stop you. Keep going. I'll take over this part,' he said, taking the stroller.

I felt embarrassed to sing in front of him now, so I just sort of mumbled along, but then Dad joined in and we sang softly together until Teddy fell asleep. Then he put a finger over his lips and gestured for me to follow him into the living room.

'Want to play some chess?' he asked. He was always trying to teach me to play, but I thought it was too much work for a supposed game.

'How about checkers?' I asked.

'Sure.'

We played in silence. When it was Dad's move, I'd steal looks at him in his button-down shirt, trying to remember the fast-fading picture of the guy with peroxided hair and a leather jacket.

'Dad?'

'Hmm.'

'Can I ask you a question?'

'Always.'

'Are you sad that you aren't in a band anymore?'

'Nope,' he said.

'Not even a little bit?'

Dad's gray eyes met mine. 'What brought this all on?'

'I was talking to Gramps.'

'Oh, I see.'

'You do?'

Dad nodded. 'Gramps thinks that he somehow exerted pressure on me to change my life.'

'Well, did he?'

'I suppose in an indirect way he did. By being who he is, by showing me what a father is.'

'But you were a good dad when you played in a band. The *best* dad. I wouldn't want you to give that up for me,' I said, feeling suddenly choked up. 'And I don't think Teddy would, either.'

Dad smiled and patted my hand. 'Mia Oh-My-Uh.

I'm not giving anything up. It's not an either-or proposition. Teaching or music. Jeans or suits. Music will always be a part of my life.'

'But you quit the band! Gave up dressing punk!'

Dad sighed. 'It wasn't hard to do. I'd played that part of my life out. It was time. I didn't even think twice about it, in spite of what Gramps or Henry might think. Sometimes you make choices in life and sometimes choices make you. Does that make any sense?'

I thought about the cello. How sometimes I didn't understand why I'd been drawn to it, how some days it seemed as if the instrument had chosen me. I nodded, smiled, and returned my attention to the game. 'King me,' I said.

4:57 a.m.

I can't stop thinking about 'Waiting for Vengeance.' It's been years since I've listened to or thought of that song, but after Gramps left my bedside, I've been singing it to myself over and over. Dad wrote the song ages ago, but now it feels like he wrote it yesterday.

Like he wrote it from wherever he is. Like there's a secret message in it for me. How else to explain those lyrics? *I'm not choosing. But I'm running out of fight.*

What does it mean? Is it supposed to be some kind of instruction? Some clue about what my parents would choose for me if they could? I try to think about it from their perspectives. I know they'd want to be with me, for us all to be together again eventually. But I have no idea if that even happens after you die, and if it does, it'll happen whether I go this morning or in seventy years. What would they want for me *now*? As soon as I pose the question, I can see Mom's pissed-off expression. She'd be livid with me for even contemplating anything *but* staying. But Dad, he understood what it meant to run out of fight. Maybe, like Gramps, he'd understand why I don't think I *can* stay.

I'm singing the song, as if buried within its lyrics are instructions, a musical road map to where I'm supposed to go and how to get there.

I'm singing and concentrating and singing and thinking so hard that I barely register Willow's return to the ICU, barely notice that she's talking to the grumpy nurse, barely recognize the steely determination in her tone.

Had I been paying attention, I might have realized that Willow was lobbying for Adam to be able to visit me. Had I been paying attention, I might have somehow got away before Willow was – as always – successful.

I don't want to see him now. I mean, of course I do. I ache to. But I know that if I see him, I'm going to lose the last wisp of peacefulness that Gramps gave me when he told me that it was OK to go. I'm trying to summon the courage to do what I have to do. And Adam will complicate things. I try to stand up to get away, but something has happened to me since I went back into surgery. I no longer have the strength to move. It takes all my effort to sit upright in my chair. I can't run away; all I can do is hide. I curl my knees into my chest and close my eyes.

I hear Nurse Ramirez talking to Willow. 'I'll take him over,' she says. And for once, the grumpy nurse doesn't order her back to her own patients.

'That was a pretty boneheaded move you pulled earlier,' I hear her tell Adam.

'I know,' Adam answers. His voice is a throaty

whisper, the way it gets after a particularly screamy concert. 'I was desperate.'

'No, you were romantic,' she tells him.

'I was idiotic. They said she was doing better before. That she'd come off the ventilator. That she was getting stronger. But after I came in here that she got worse. They said her heart stopped on the operating table . . .' Adam trails off.

'And they got it started. She had a perforated bowel that was slowly leaking bile into her abdomen and it threw her organs out of whack. This kind of thing happens all the time, and it had nothing to do with you. We caught it and fixed it and that's what matters.'

'But she was doing better,' Adam whispers. He sounds so young and vulnerable, like Teddy used to sound when he got the stomach flu. 'And then I came in and she almost died.' His voice chokes into a sob. The sound of it wakes me up like a bucket of ice water dropped down my shirt. Adam thinks that *he* did this to me? No! That's beyond absurd. He's so wrong.

'And I *almost* stayed in Puerto Rico to marry a fat SOB,' the nurse snaps. 'But I didn't. And I have a different life now. *Almost* don't matter. You got to deal with the situation at hand. And she's still here.' She whips the privacy curtain around my bed. 'In you go,' she tells Adam.

I force my head up and my eyes open. Adam. God, even in this state, he is beautiful. His eyes are dipping with fatigue. He's sprouting stubble, enough of it that if we were to make out, it would make my chin raw. He is wearing his typical band uniform of a T-shirt, skinny pegged pants, and Converse, with Gramps's plaid scarf draped over his shoulders.

When he first sees me, he blanches, like I'm some hideous Creature from the Black Lagoon. I do look pretty bad, hooked back up to the ventilator and a dozen other tubes, the dressing from my latest surgery seeping blood. But after a moment, Adam exhales loudly and then he's just Adam again. He searches around, like he's dropped something and then finds what he's looking for: my hand.

'Jesus, Mia, your hands are freezing.' He squats down, takes my right hand into his, and careful to not bump into my tubes and wires, draws his mouth to them, blowing warm air into the shelter he's created. 'You and your crazy hands.' Adam is always amazed at how even in middle of summer, even after the sweatiest of encounters, my hands stay cold. I tell him it's bad circulation but he doesn't buy it because my feet are usually warm. He says I have bionic hands, that this is why I'm such a good cello player.

I watch him warm my hands as he has done a thousand times before. I think of the first time he did it, at school, sitting on the lawn, as if it were the most natural thing in the world. I also remember the first time he did it in front of my parents. We were all sitting on the porch on Christmas Eve, drinking cider. It was freezing outside. Adam grabbed my hands and blew on them. Teddy giggled. Mom and Dad didn't say anything, just exchanged a quick look, something private that passed between them and then Mom smiled ruefully at us.

I wonder if I tried, if I could feel him touching me. If I were to lie down on top of myself in the bed, would I become one with my body again? Would I feel him then? If I reached out my ghostly hand to his, would he feel me? Would he warm the hands he cannot see?

Adam drops my hand and steps forward to look at me. He is standing so close that I can almost smell him and I'm overpowered by the need to touch him. It's basic, primal, and all-consuming the way a baby needs its mother's breast. Even though I know, if we touch, a new tug-of-war – one that will be even more painful than the quiet one Adam and I have been waging these past few months – will begin.

Adam is mumbling something now. In a low voice. Over and over he is saying: please. *Please. Please. Please. Please. Please. Please. Please. Please. Please.* Finally, he stops and looks at my face. 'Please, Mia,' he implores. 'Don't make me write a song.'

*

I'd never expected to fall in love. I was never the kind of girl who had crushes on rock stars or fantasies about marrying Brad Pitt. I sort of vaguely knew that one day I'd probably have boyfriends (in college, if Kim's prediction was anything to go by) and get married. I wasn't totally immune to the charms of the opposite sex, but I wasn't one of those romantic, swoony girls who had pink fluffy daydreams about falling in love.

Even as I was falling in love – full throttle, intense, can't-erase-that-goofy-smile love – I didn't really register what was happening. When I was with Adam, at least after those first few awkward weeks, I felt so good that I didn't bother thinking about what was going on with me, with us. It just felt normal and right, like slipping into a hot bubble bath. Which isn't to say we didn't fight. We argued over lots of stuff: him not being nice enough to Kim, me being antisocial at shows, how fast he drove, how I stole the covers. I got upset because he never wrote any songs about me. He claimed he wasn't good with sappy love songs: 'If you want a song, you'll have to cheat on me or something,' he said, knowing full well that wasn't going to happen.

This past fall, though, Adam and I started to have a different kind of fight. It wasn't even a fight, really. We didn't shout. We barely even argued, but a snake of tension quietly slithered into our lives. And it seemed like it all started with my Juilliard audition.

'So did you knock them dead?' Adam asked me when I got back. 'They gonna let you in with a full scholarship?'

I had a feeling that they were going to let me in, at least – even before I told Professor Christie about the one judge's 'long time since we've had an Oregon country girl' comment, even before she hyper-ventilated because she was so convinced this was a tacit promise of admission. Something had happened to my playing in that audition; I had broken through some invisible barrier and could finally play the pieces like I heard them being played in my head, and the result had been something transcendent: the mental and physical, the technical and emotional sides of my abilities all finally blend-ing. Then, on the drive home, as Gramps and I were approaching the California-Oregon border, I just had this sudden flash – a vision of me lugging a cello through New York City. And it was like I *knew*, and that certainty planted itself in my belly like a warm secret. I'm not the kind of person who's prone to pre-monitions or overconfidence, so I suspected that there was more to my flash than magical thinking.

'I did OK,' I told Adam, and as I said it, I realized that I'd just straight-out lied to him for the first time, and that this was different from all the lying by omission I'd been doing before.

I had neglected to tell Adam that I was applying to Juilliard in the first place, which was actually harder than it sounded. Before I sent in my application, I had to practice every spare moment with Professor Christie to fine-tune the Shostakovich concerto and the two Bach suites. When Adam asked me why I was so busy, I gave purposely vague excuses about learning tough new pieces. I justified this to myself because it was technically true. And then Professor Christie arranged for me to have a recording session at the university so I could submit a high-quality CD to Juilliard. I had to be at the studio at seven in the morning on a Sunday and the night before I'd pretended to be feeling out of sorts and told Adam he probably shouldn't stay over. I'd justified that fib, too. I was feeling out of sorts because I was so nervous. So, it wasn't a real lie. And besides, I thought, there was no point in making a big fuss about it. I hadn't told Kim, either, so it wasn't like Adam was getting special deception treatment.

But after I told him I'd only done OK at the audition, I had the feeling that I was wading into quicksand, and that if I took one more step, there'd be no extricating myself and I'd sink until I suffocated. So I took a deep breath and heaved myself back onto solid ground. 'Actually, that's not true,' I told Adam. 'I did really well. I played better than I ever have in my life. It was like I was possessed.'

Adam's first reaction was to smile with pride. 'I wish I could've seen that.' But then his eyes clouded over and his lips fell into a frown. 'Why'd you down-play it?' he asked. 'Why didn't you call me after the audition to brag?'

'I don't know,' I said.

'Well, this is great news,' Adam said, trying to mask his hurt. 'We should be celebrating.'

'OK, let's celebrate,' I said, with a forced gaiety. 'We can go to Portland Saturday. Go to the Japanese Gardens and go out for dinner at Beau Thai.'

Adam grimaced. 'I can't. We're playing in Olympia and Seattle this weekend. Mini-tour. Remember? I'd love for you to come, but I don't know if that's really a celebration for you. But I'll be back Sunday late afternoon. I can meet you in Portland Sunday night if you want.'

'I can't. I'm playing in a string quartet at some professor's house. What about next weekend?'

Adam looked pained. 'We're in the studio the next couple weekends, but we can go out during the week somewhere. Around here. To the Mexican place?'

'Sure. The Mexican place,' I said.

Two minutes before, I hadn't even wanted to celebrate, but now I was feeling dejected and insulted at being relegated to a midweek dinner at the same place we always went to.

When Adam graduated from high school last spring and moved out of his parents' place and into the House of Rock, I hadn't expected much to change. He'd still live nearby. We'd still see each other all the time. I'd miss our little powwows in the music wing, but I would also be relieved to have our relationship out from under the microscope of high school.

But things had changed when Adam moved into the House of Rock and started college, though not for the reasons I'd thought they would. At the beginning of the fall, just as Adam was getting used to college life, things suddenly started heating up with Shooting Star. The band was offered a record deal with a medium-size label based in Seattle and now were busy in the studio recording. They were also playing more shows, to larger and larger crowds, almost every weekend. Things were so hectic that Adam had dropped half his course load and was going to college part-time, and if things kept up at this rate, he was thinking of dropping out altogether. 'There are no second chances,' he told me.

I was genuinely excited for him. I knew that Shooting Star was something special, more than just a college-town band. I hadn't minded Adam's increasing absences, especially since he made it so clear how much he minded them. But somehow, the prospect of Juilliard made things different – somehow it made me mind. Which didn't make any sense at all because if anything, it should have leveled the field. Now I had something exciting happening, too.

'We can go to Portland in a few weeks,' Adam promised. 'When all the holiday lights are up.'

'OK,' I said sullenly.

Adam sighed. 'Things are getting complicated, aren't they?'

'Yeah. Our schedules are too busy,' I said.

'That's not what I meant,' Adam said, turning my face toward his so I was looking at him in the eye.

'I know that's not what you meant,' I replied, but then a lump lodged itself in my throat and I couldn't talk anymore.

* * *

218

We tried to defuse the tension, to talk about it without really talking about it, to joke-ify it. 'You know I read in *US News and World Report* that Willamette University has a good music program,' Adam told me. 'It's in Salem, which is apparently getting hipper by the moment.'

'According to who? The governor?' I replied.

'Liz found some good stuff at a vintage-clothing store there. And you know, once the vintage places come in, the hipsters aren't far behind.'

'You forget, I'm not a hipster,' I reminded him. 'But speaking of, maybe Shooting Star should move to New York. I mean, it's the heart of the punk scene. The Ramones. Blondie.' My tone was frothy and flirtatious, an Oscar-worthy performance.

'That was thirty years ago,' Adam said. 'And even if I wanted to move to New York, there's no way the rest of the band would.' He stared mournfully at his shoes and I recognized the joking part of the conversation had ended. My stomach lurched, an appetizer before the full portion of heartache I had a feeling was going to be served at some point soon.

Adam and I had never been the kind of couple to talk about the future, about where our relationship was going, but with things suddenly so unclear, we avoided talking about *anything* that was happening more than a few weeks away, and this made our conversations as stilted and awkward as they'd been in those early weeks together before we'd found our groove. One afternoon in the fall, I spotted a beautiful 1930s silk gown in the vintage store where Dad bought his suits and I almost pointed it out to Adam and asked if he thought I should wear that to the prom, but prom was in June and maybe Adam would be on tour in June or maybe I'd be too busy getting ready for Juilliard, so I didn't say anything. Not long after that, Adam was complaining about his decrepit guitar, saying he wanted to get a vintage Gibson SG, and I offered to get it for him for his birthday. But then he said that those guitars cost thousands of dollars, and besides his birthday wasn't until September, and the way he said *September*, it was like a judge issuing a prison sentence.

A few weeks ago, we went to a New Year's Eve party together. Adam got drunk, and when midnight came, he kissed me hard. 'Promise me. Promise me you'll spend New Year's with me next year,' he whispered into my ear.

I was about to explain that even if I did go to Juilliard, I'd be home for Christmas and New Year's, but then I realized that wasn't the point. So I promised him because I wanted it to be true as much as he did. And I kissed him back so hard, like I was trying to merge our bodies through our lips.

On New Year's Day, I came home to find the rest of my family gathered in the kitchen with Henry, Willow and the baby. Dad was making breakfast: smoked-salmon hash, his specialty.

Henry shook his head when he saw me. 'Look at the kids. Seems like just yesterday that stumbling home at eight o'clock felt early. Now I'd kill just to be able to sleep until eight.'

'We didn't even make it till midnight,' Willow admitted, bouncing the baby on her lap. 'Good thing, because this little lady decided to start her new year at five-thirty.'

'I stayed up till midnight!' Teddy yelled. 'I saw the ball drop on TV at twelve. It's in New York, you know? If you move there, will you take me to see it drop in real life?' he asked.

'Sure, Teddy,' I said feigning enthusiasm. The idea of me going to New York was seeming more and more real, and though this generally filled me with a nervous, if conflicted, excitement, the image of me and Teddy hanging out together on New Year's Eve left me feeling unbearably lonely.

Mom looked at me, eyebrows arched. 'It's New Year's Day, so I won't give you shit for coming in at this hour. But if you're hungover, you're grounded.'

'I'm not. I had one beer. I'm just tired.'

'Just tired, is it? You sure?' Mom grabbed a hold of my wrist and turned me toward her. When she saw my stricken expression, she tilted her head to the side as if to say, *You OK?* I shrugged and bit my lip to keep from losing it. Mom nodded. She handed me a cup of coffee and led me to the table. She put down a plate of hash and a thick slice of sourdough bread, and even though I couldn't imagine being hungry, my mouth watered and my stomach rumbled and I was suddenly ravenous. I ate silently, Mom watching me all the while. After everyone was done, Mom sent the rest of them into the living room to watch the Rose Parade on TV.

'Everyone out,' she ordered. 'Mia and I will do the washing up.'

As soon as everyone was gone, Mom turned to me and I just fell against her, crying and releasing all of the tension and uncertainty of the last few weeks. She stood there silently, letting me blubber all over her sweater. When I stopped, she held out the sponge. 'You wash. I'll dry. We'll talk. I always find it calming. The warm water, the soap.'

Mom picked up the dish towel and we went to work. And I told her about Adam and me. 'It was like we had this perfect year and a half,' I said. 'So perfect that I never even thought about the future. About it taking us in different directions.'

Mom's smile was both sad and knowing. 'I thought about it.'

I turned to her. She was staring straight out the window, watching a couple of sparrows bathe in a puddle. 'I remember last year when Adam came over for Christmas Eve. I told your father that you'd fallen in love too soon.'

'I know, I know. What does a dumb kid know about love?'

Mom stopped drying a skillet. 'That's not what I meant. The opposite, really. You and Adam never struck me as a "high-school" relationship,' Mom said making quote marks with her hands. 'It was nothing like the drunken roll in the back of some guy's Chevy that passed for a relationship when I was in high school. You guys seemed, still seem, in love, truly, deeply.' She sighed. 'But seventeen is an inconvenient time to be in love.'

That made me smile and made the pit in my stomach soften a little. 'Tell me about it,' I said. 'Though if we weren't both musicians, we could go to college together and be fine.'

'That's a cop-out, Mia,' Mom countered. 'All relationships are tough. Just like with music, sometimes you have harmony and other times you have cacophony. I don't have to tell you that.'

'I guess you're right.'

'And come on, music brought you two together. That's what your father and I always thought. You were both in love with music and then you fell in love with each other. It was a little like that for your dad and me. I didn't play but I listened. Luckily, I was a little older when we met.'

I'd never told Mom about what Adam had said that night after the Yo-Yo Ma concert, when I'd asked him *Why me?* How the music was totally a part of it. 'Yeah, but now I feel like it's music that's going to pull us apart.'

Mom shook her head. 'That's bullshit. Music can't do that. Life might take you down different roads. But each of you gets to decide which one to take.' She turned to face me. 'Adam's not trying to stop you going to Juilliard, is he?'

'No more than I'm trying to get him to move to New York. And it's all ridiculous anyway. I might not even go.'

'No, you might not. But you're going somewhere. I think we all get that. And the same is true for Adam.'

'At least he can go somewhere while still living here.'

Mom shrugged. 'Maybe. For now anyhow.'

I put my face in my hands and shook my head. 'What am I going to do?' I lamented. 'I feel like I'm caught in a tug-of-war.'

Mom shot me a sympathetic grimace. 'I don't know. But I do know that if you want to stay and be with him, I'd support that, though maybe I'm only saying that because I don't think you'd be able to turn down Juilliard. But I'd understand if you chose love, Adam-love, over music-love. Either way you win. And either way you lose. What can I tell you? Love's a bitch.'

Adam and I talked about it once more after that. We were at House of Rock, sitting on his futon. He was riffing about on his acoustic guitar.

'I might not get in,' I told him. 'I might wind up at school here, with you. In a way, I hope I don't get accepted so I don't have to choose.'

'If you get in, the choice is already made, isn't it?' Adam asked.

It was. I would go. It didn't mean I'd stop loving Adam or that we'd break up, but Mom and Adam were both right. I wouldn't turn down Juilliard.

Adam was silent for a minute, plinking away at his guitar so loud that I almost missed it when he said, 'I don't want to be the guy who doesn't want you to go. If the tables were turned, you'd let me go.'

'I kind of already have. In a way, you're already gone. To your own Juilliard,' I said.

'I know,' Adam said quietly. 'But I'm still here. And I'm still crazy in love with you.'

'Me, too,' I said. And then we stopped talking for a

while as Adam strummed an unfamiliar melody. I asked him what he was playing.

'I'm calling it "The Girlfriend's-Going-to-Juilliard-Leaving-My-Punk-Heart-in-Shreds Blues",' he said, singing the title in an exaggeratedly twangy voice. Then he smiled that goofy shy smile that I felt like came from the truest part of him. 'I'm kidding.'

'Good,' I said.

'Sort of,' he added.

5:42 a.m.

Adam is gone. He suddenly rushed out, calling to Nurse Ramirez that he'd forgotten something important and would be back as soon as he could. He was already out the door when she told him that she was about to get off work. In fact, she just left, but not before making sure to inform the nurse who'd relieved Old Grumpy that 'the young man with the skinny pants and messy hair' is allowed to see me when he returns.

Not that it matters. Willow rules the school now. She has been marching the troops through here all morning. After Gran and Gramps and Adam, Aunt Patricia stopped by. Then it was Aunt Diane and Uncle Greg. Then my cousins shuffled in. Willow's running to and fro, a gleam in her eye. She's up to something, but whether it's trotting out loved ones to lobby on behalf of my continuing my earthly existence or whether she's simply bringing them in to say goodbye, I can't say.

Now it's Kim's turn. Poor Kim. She looks like she slept in a Dumpster. Her hair has staged a full-scale rebellion and more of it has escaped her mangled braid than remains tucked inside. She's wearing one of what she calls her 'turd sweaters', the greenish, grayish, brownish lumpy masses her mom is always buying her. At first, Kim squints at me, as if I'm a bright, glaring light. But then it's like she adjusts to the light and decides that even though I may look like a zombie, even though there are tubes sticking out of every which orifice, even though there's blood on my thin blanket from where it's seeped through the bandages, I'm still Mia and she's still Kim. And what do Mia and Kim like to do more than anything? Talk.

Kim settles into the chair next to my bed. 'How are you doing?' she asks.

I'm not sure. I'm exhausted, but at the same time Adam's visit has left me ... I don't know what. Agitated. Anxious. Awake, definitely awake. Though I couldn't feel it when he touched me, his presence stirred me up anyhow. I was just starting to feel grateful that he was here when he booked out of here like the devil was chasing him. Adam has spent the last ten hours trying to get in to see me, and now that he finally succeeded, he left ten minutes after arriving. Maybe I scared him. Maybe he doesn't want to deal. Maybe I'm not the only chicken-shit around here. After all, I spent the last day dreaming of him coming to me, and when he finally staggered into the ICU, if I had the strength, I would've run away.

'Well, you would not believe the crazy night it's been,' Kim says. Then she starts telling me about it. About her mom's hysterics, about how she lost it in front of my relatives, who were very gracious about the whole thing. The fight they had outside the Roseland Theater in front of a bunch of punks and hipsters. When Kim shouted at her crying mother to 'pull it together and start acting like the adult around here' and then stalked off into the club leaving a shocked Mrs Schein at the curb, a group of guys in spiked leather and fluorescent hair cheered and high-fived her. She tells me about Adam, his determination to get in to see me, how after he got kicked out of the ICU, he enlisted the help of his music friends, who were not at all the snobby scenesters she'd imagined them to be. Then she told me that a bona fide rock star had come to the hospital on my behalf.

Of course, I know almost everything that Kim is telling me, but there is no way that she'd know that. Besides, I like having her recount the day to me. I like how Kim is talking to me normally, like Gran did earlier, just jabbering on, spinning a good yarn, as if we were together on my porch, drinking coffee (or an iced caramel Frappuccino in Kim's case) and catching up.

I don't know if once you die you remember things that happened to you when you were alive. It makes a certain logical sense that you wouldn't. That being dead will feel like before you were born, which is to say, a whole lot of nothingness. Except that for me, at least, my prebirth years aren't entirely blank. Every now and again, Mom or Dad will be telling a story about something, about Dad catching his first salmon with Gramps, or Mom remembering the amazing Dead Moon concert she saw with Dad on their first date, and I'll have an overpowering déjà vu. Not just a sense that I've heard the story before, but that I've lived it. I can picture myself sitting on the riverbank as Dad pulls a hot-pink coho out of the water, even though Dad was all of twelve at the time. Or I can hear the feedback when Dead Moon played 'DOA' at the X-Ray, even though I've never heard Dead Moon play live, even though the X-Ray Café shut down before I was born. But sometimes the memories feel so real, so visceral, so personal, that I confuse them with my own.

I never told anyone about these 'memories'. Mom probably would've said that I was there – as one of the eggs in her ovaries. Dad would've joked that he and Mom had tortured me with their stories one too many times and had inadvertently brainwashed me. And Gran would've told me that maybe I *was* there as an angel before I chose to become Mom and Dad's kid.

But now I wonder. And now I hope. Because when I go, I want to remember Kim. And I want to remember her like this: telling a funny story, fighting with her crazy mom, being cheered on by punkers, rising to the occasion, finding little pockets of strength in herself that she had no idea she possessed.

Adam is a different story. Remembering Adam would be like losing him all over again, and I'm not sure if I can bear that on top of everything else.

Kim's up to the part of Operation Distraction, when Brooke Vega and a dozen assorted punks descended upon the hospital. She tells me that before they got to the ICU, she was so scared of getting into trouble, but how when she burst inside the ward, she'd felt exhilarated. When the guard had grabbed her, she hadn't been scared at all. 'I kept thinking, what's the worst that could happen? I go to jail. Mom has a conniption. I get grounded for a year.' She stops for a minute. 'But after what's happened today, that would be nothing. Even going to jail would be easy compared to losing you.'

I know that Kim's telling me this to try to keep me alive. She probably doesn't realize that in a weird way, her remark frees me, just like Gramps's permission did. I know it will be awful for Kim when I die, but I also think about what she said, about not being scared, about jail being easy compared to losing me. And that's how I know that Kim will be

OK. Losing me will hurt; it will be the kind of pain that won't feel real at first, and when it does, it will take her breath away. And the rest of her senior year will probably suck, what with her getting all that cloying your-best-friend's-dead sympathy that will drive her so crazy, and also because really, we are each other's only close friend at school. But she'll deal. She'll move on. She'll leave Oregon. She'll go to college. She'll make new friends. She'll fall in love. She'll become a photographer, the kind who never has to go on a helicopter. And I bet she'll be a stronger person because of what she's lost today. I have a feeling that once you live through something like this, you become a little bit invincible.

I know that makes me a bit of a hypocrite. If that's the case, shouldn't *I* stay? Soldier through it? Maybe if I'd had some practice, maybe if I'd had more devastation in my life, I would be more prepared to go on. It's not that my life has been perfect. I've had disappointments and I've been lonely and frustrated and angry and all the crappy stuff everyone feels. But in terms of heartbreak, I've been spared. I've never toughened up enough to handle what I'd have to handle if I were to stay.

Kim is now telling me about being rescued from certain incarceration by Willow. As she describes how Willow took charge of the whole hospital, there is such admiration in her voice. I picture Kim and Willow becoming friends, even though there are twenty years between them. It makes me happy to imagine them drinking tea or going to the movies together, still connected to each other by the invisible chain of a family that no longer exists.

Now Kim is listing all the people who are at the hospital or who have been, during the course of the day, ticking them off with her fingers: 'Your grandparents and aunts, uncles, and cousins. Adam and Brooke Vega and the various rabble-rousers who came with her. Adam's bandmates Mike and Fitzy and Liz and her girlfriend, Sarah, all of whom have been downstairs in the waiting room since they got heaved out of the ICU Professor Christie, who drove down and stayed half the night before driving back so she could sleep a few hours and shower and make some morning appointment she had. Henry and the baby, who are on their way over right now because the baby woke up at five in the morning and Henry called us and said that he could not stay at home any longer. And me and Mom,' Kim concludes. 'Shoot. I lost count of how many people that was. But it was a lot. And more have called and asked to come, but your aunt Diane told them to wait. She says that we're making enough nuisance of ourselves. And I think by "us", she means me and Adam.' Kim stops and smiles for a split second. Then she makes this funny noise, a cross between a cough and a throat-clearing. I've heard her make this sound before; it's what she does when she's summoning her courage, getting ready to jump off the rocks and into the bracing river water.

'I do have a point to all this,' she continues. 'There are like twenty people in that waiting room right now. Some of them are related to you. Some of them are not. But we're all your family.'

She stops now. Leans over me so that the wisps of her hair tickle my face. She kisses me on the forehead. *'You still have a family,'* she whispers.

*

Last summer, we hosted an accidental Labor Day party at our house. It had been a busy season. Camp for me. Then we'd gone to Gran's family's

Massachusetts retreat. I felt like I had barely seen Adam and Kim all summer. My parents were lamenting that they hadn't seen Willow and Henry and the baby in months. 'Henry says she's starting to walk,' Dad noted that morning. We were all sitting in the living room in front of the fan, trying not to melt. Oregon was having a record heat wave. It was ten in the morning and pushing ninety degrees.

Mom looked up at the calendar. 'She's ten months old already. Where has the time gone?' Then she looked at Teddy and me. 'How is it humanly possible that I have a daughter who's starting her senior year in high school? How in the hell can my baby boy be starting second grade?'

'I'm not a baby,' Teddy shot back, clearly insulted.

'Sorry, kid, unless we have another one, you'll always be my baby.'

'Another one?' Dad asked with mock alarm.

'Relax. I'm kidding – for the most part,' Mom said. 'Let's see how I feel when Mia leaves for college.'

'I'm gonna be eight in December. Then I'm a man and you'll have to call me "Ted",' Teddy reported.

'Is that so?' I laughed, spraying orange juice through my nose.

'That's what Casey Carson told me,' Teddy said, his mouth set into a determined line.

My parents and I groaned. Casey Carson was Teddy's best friend, and we all liked him a lot and thought his parents seemed like such nice people, so we didn't get how they could give their child such a ridiculous name.

'Well, if Casey Carson says so,' I said, giggling, and soon Mom and Dad were laughing, too.

'What's so funny?' Teddy demanded.

'Nothing, Little Man,' Dad said. 'It's just the heat.'

'Can we still do sprinklers today?' Teddy asked. Dad had promised him he could run through the sprinklers that afternoon even though the governor had asked everyone in the state to conserve water this summer. That request had peeved Dad, who claimed that we Oregonians suffer eight months of rain a year and should be exempt from ever worrying about water conservation.

'Damn straight you can,' Dad said. 'Flood the place if you want.'

Teddy seemed placated. 'If the baby can walk, then she can walk through the sprinklers. Can she come into the sprinklers with me?'

Mom looked at Dad. 'That's not a bad idea,' she said. 'I think Willow's off today.'

'We could have a barbecue,' Dad said. 'It is Labor Day and grilling in this heat would certainly qualify as labor.'

'Plus, we've got a freezer full of steaks from when your father decided to order that side of beef,' Mom said. 'Why not?'

'Can Adam come?' I asked.

'Of course,' Mom said. 'We haven't seen much of your young man lately.'

'I know,' I said. 'Things are starting to happen for the band,' I said. At the time I was excited about it. Genuinely and completely. Gran had only recently planted the seed of Juilliard in my head, but it hadn't taken root. I hadn't decided to apply yet. Things with Adam had not gotten weird yet.

'If the rock star can handle a humble picnic with squares like us,' Dad joked.

'If he can handle a square like me, he can handle squares like you,' I joked back. 'I think I'll invite Kim, too.'

'The more the merrier,' Mom said. 'We'll make it a blowout like in the olden days.'

'When dinosaurs roamed the earth?' Teddy asked.

'Exactly,' Dad said. 'When dinosaurs roamed the earth and your mom and I were young.'

About twenty people showed up. Henry, Willow, the baby, Adam, who brought Fitzy, Kim, who brought a cousin visiting from New Jersey, plus a whole bunch of friends of my parents whom they had not seen in ages. Dad hauled our ancient barbecue out of the basement and spent the afternoon scrubbing it. We grilled up steaks and, this being Oregon, tofu pups and veggie burgers. There was watermelon, which we kept cool in a bucket of ice, and a salad made with vegetables from the organic farm that some of Mom and Dad's friends had started. Mom and I made three pies with wild blackberries that Teddy and I had picked. We drank Pepsi out of these old-fashioned bottles that Dad had found at some ancient country store, and I swear they tasted better than the regular kind. Maybe it was because it was so hot, or that the party was so last minute, or maybe because everything tastes better on the grill, but it was one of those meals that you know you'll remember.

When Dad turned on the sprinkler for Teddy and the baby, everyone else decided to run through it. We left it on so long that the brown grass turned into a big slippery puddle and I wondered if the governor himself might come and tell us off. Adam tackled me and we laughed and squirmed around on the lawn. It was so hot, I didn't bother changing into dry clothes, just kept dousing myself whenever I got too sweaty. By the end of the day, my sundress was stiff. Teddy had taken his shirt off and had streaked himself with mud. Dad said he looked like one of the boys from *Lord of the Flies*.

When it started to get dark, most people left to catch the fireworks display at the university or to see a band called Oswald Five-0 play in town. A handful of people, including Adam, Kim, Willow, and Henry, stayed. When it cooled off, Dad lit a campfire on the lawn, and we roasted marshmallows. Then the musical instruments appeared. Dad's snare drum from the house, Henry's guitar from his car, Adam's spare guitar from my room. Everyone was jamming together, singing songs: Dad's songs, Adam's songs, old Clash songs, old Wipers songs. Teddy was dancing around, the blond of his hair reflecting the golden flames. I remember watching it all and getting that tickling in my chest and thinking to myself: *This is what happiness feels like.*

At one point, Dad and Adam stopped playing and I caught them whispering about something. Then they went inside, to get more beer, they claimed. But when they returned they were carrying my cello.

'Oh, no, I'm not giving a concert,' I said.

'We don't want you to,' Dad said. 'We want you to play with us.'

'No way,' I said. Adam had occasionally tried to get me to 'jam' with him and I always refused. Lately he'd started joking about us playing air-guitar–air-cello duets, which was about as far as I was willing to go.

'Why not, Mia?' Kim said. 'Are you such a classical-music snob?'

'It's not that,' I said, suddenly feeling panicked. 'It's just that the two styles don't fit together.'

'Says who?' Mom asked, her eyebrows raised.

'Yeah, who knew you were such a musical segregationist?' Henry joked.

Willow rolled her eyes at Henry and turned to me. 'Pretty please,' she said as she rocked the baby to sleep in her lap. 'I never get to hear you play anymore.'

'C'mon, Mee,' Henry said. 'You're among family.'

'Totally,' Kim said.

Adam took my hand and caressed the inside of my wrist with his fingers. 'Do it for me. I really want to play with you. Just once.'

I was about to shake my head, to reaffirm that my cello had no place among the jamming guitars, no place in the punk-rock world. But then I looked out at Mom, who was smirking at me, as if issuing a challenge, and Dad, who was tapping on his pipe, pretending to be nonchalant so as not to apply any pressure, and Teddy, who was jumping up and down – though I think it was because he was hopped up on marshmallows, not because he had any desire to hear me play – and Kim and Willow and Henry all peering at me like this really mattered, and Adam, looking as awed and proud as he always did when he listened to me play. And I was a little scared of falling on my face, of not blending, of making bad music. But everyone was looking at me so intently, wanting me to join in so much, and I realized that sounding bad wasn't the worst thing in the world that could happen.

So I played. And even though you wouldn't think

it, the cello didn't sound half bad with all those guitars. In fact, it sounded pretty amazing.

7:16 a.m.

It's morning. And inside the hospital, there's a different kind of dawn, a rustling of covers, a clearing of the eyes. In some ways, the hospital never goes to sleep. The lights stay on and the nurses stay awake, but even though it's still dark outside, you can tell that things are waking up. The doctors are back, yanking on my eyelids, shining their lights at me, frowning as they scribble notes in my chart as though I've let them down.

I don't care anymore. I'm tired of this all, and it will be over soon. The social worker is back on duty again, too. It looks like the night's sleep had little impact on her. Her eyes are still heavy, her hair a kinky mess. She reads my chart and listens to updates from the nurses on my bumpy night, which seems to make her even more tired. The nurse with the blue-black skin is also back. She greeted me by telling me how glad she was to see me this morning, how she'd been thinking about me last night, hoping I'd be here. Then she noticed the bloodstain on my blanket and *tsked tsked* before hustling off to get me a new one.

After Kim left, there haven't been any more visitors. I guess Willow has run out of people to lobby me with. I wonder if this deciding business is something that all the nurses are aware of. Nurse Ramirez sure knew about it. And I think the nurse with me now knows it, too, judging by how congratulatory she's acting that I made it through the night. And Willow seems like she knows it, too, with the way she's been marching everyone through here. I like these nurses so much. I hope they will not take my decision personally.

I am so tired now that I can barely blink my eyes. It's all just a matter of time, and part of me wonders why I'm delaying the inevitable. But I know why. I'm waiting for Adam to come back. Though it seems like he has been gone for an eternity, it's probably only been an hour. And he asked me to wait, so I will. That's the least I can do for him.

My eyes are closed so I hear him before I see him. I hear the raspy, quick rushes of his lungs. He is panting like he just ran a marathon. Then I smell the sweat on him, a clean musky scent that I'd bottle and wear as perfume if I could. I open my eyes. Adam has closed his. But the lids are puffy and pink, so I know what he's been doing. Is that why he went away? To cry without my seeing?

He doesn't so much sit in the chair as fall into it, like clothes heaped onto the floor at the end of a long day. He covers his face with his hands and takes deep breaths to steady himself. After a minute, he drops his hands into his lap. 'Just listen,' he says with a voice that sounds like shrapnel.

I open my eyes wide now. I sit up as much as I can. And I listen.

'Stay.' With that one word, Adam's voice catches, but he swallows the emotion and pushes forward. 'There's no word for what happened to you. There's no good side of it. But there is something to live for. And I'm not talking about me. It's just . . . I don't know. Maybe I'm talking shit. I know I'm in shock. I know I haven't digested what happened to your parents, to Teddy . . .' When he says *Teddy*, his voice cracks and an avalanche of tears tumbles down his face. And I think: *I love you*.

I hear him take gulpfuls of air to steady himself. And then he continues: 'All I can think about is how fucked up it would be for your life to end here, now. I mean, I know that your life is fucked up no matter what now, for ever. And I'm not dumb enough to think that I can undo that, that anyone can. But I can't wrap my mind around the notion of you not getting old, having kids, going to Juilliard, getting to play that cello in front of a huge audience, so that they can get the chills the way I do every time I see you pick up your bow, every time I see you smile at me.

'If you stay, I'll do whatever you want. I'll quit the band, go with you to New York. But if you need me to go away, I'll do that, too. I was talking to Liz and she said maybe coming back to your old life would just be too painful, that maybe it'd be easier for you to erase us. And that would suck, but I'd do it. I can lose you like that if I don't lose you today. I'll let you go. If you stay.'

Then it is Adam who lets go. His sobs burst like fists pounding against tender flesh.

I close my eyes. I cover my ears. I cannot watch this. I cannot hear this.

But then, it is no longer Adam that I hear. It's that sound, the low moan that in an instant takes flight and turns into something sweet. It's the cello. Adam has placed headphones over my lifeless ears and is laying an iPod down on my chest. He's apologizing, saying that he knows this isn't my favorite but it was the best he could do. He turns up the volume so I can hear the music floating across the morning air. Then he takes my hand.

It is Yo-Yo Ma. *Andante con moto e poco rubato*. The low piano plays almost as if in warning. In comes the cello, like a heart bleeding. And it's like something inside of me implodes.

I am sitting around the breakfast table with my family, drinking hot coffee, laughing at Teddy's chocolate-chip mustache. The snow is blowing outside.

I am visiting a cemetery. Three graves under a tree on a hill overlooking the river.

I am lying with Adam, my head on his chest, on a sandy bank next to the river.

I am hearing people say the word *orphan* and realize that they're talking about me.

I am walking through New York City with Kim,

the skyscrapers casting shadows on our faces.

I am holding Teddy on my lap, tickling him as he giggles so hard he keels over.

I am sitting with my cello, the one Mom and Dad gave me after my first recital. My fingers caress the wood and the pegs, which time and touch have worn smooth. My bow is poised over the strings now. I am looking at my hand, waiting to start playing.

I am looking at my hand, being held by Adam's hand.

Yo-Yo Ma continues to play, and it's like the piano and cello are being poured into my body, the same way that the IV and blood transfusions are. And the memories of my life as it was, and the flashes of it as it might be, are coming so fast and furious. I feel like I can no longer keep up with them but they keep coming and everything is colliding, until I cannot take it anymore. Until I cannot be like this one second longer.

There is a blinding flash, a pain that rips through me for one searing instant, a silent scream from my broken body. For the first time, I can sense how fully agonizing staying will be.

But then I feel Adam's hand. Not sense it, but feel

it. I'm not sitting huddled in the chair anymore. I'm lying on my back in the hospital bed, one again with my body.

Adam is crying and somewhere inside of me I am crying, too, because I'm feeling things at last. I'm feeling not just the physical pain, but all that I have lost, and it is profound and catastrophic and will leave a crater in me that nothing will ever fill. But I'm also feeling all that I have in my life, which includes what I have lost, as well as the great unknown of what life might still bring me. And it's all too much. The feelings pile up, threatening to crack my chest wide open. The only way to survive them is to concentrate on Adam's hand. Grasping mine.

And suddenly I just *need* to hold his hand more than I've ever needed anything in this world. Not just be held by it, but hold it back. I aim every remaining ounce of energy into my right hand. I'm weak, and this is so hard. It's the hardest thing I will ever have to do. I summon all the love I have ever felt, I summon all the strength that Gran and Gramps and Kim and the nurses and Willow have given me. I summon all the breath that Mom, Dad, and Teddy would fill me with if they could. I summon all my own strength, focus it like a laser beam into the fingers and palm of my right hand. I picture my hand stroking Teddy's hair, grasping a bow poised above my cello, interlaced with Adam's.

And then I squeeze.

I slump back, spent, unsure of whether I just did what I did. Of what it means. If it registered. If it matters.

But then I feel Adam's grip tighten, so that the grasp of his hand feels like it is holding my entire body. Like it could lift me up right out of this bed. And then I hear the sharp intake of his breath followed by the sound of his voice. It's the first time today I can truly hear him.

'Mia?' he asks.

Acknowledgments

Several people came together in a short amount of time to make *If I Stay* possible. It starts with Gillian Aldrich, who started crying (in a good way) when I told her about my idea. This proved to be quite a good motivator to get started.

Tamara Glenny, Eliza Griswold, Kim Sevcik and Sean Smith took time out of their hectic schedules to read early drafts of my work and to offer much-needed encouragement. For that and for their enduring generosity and friendship, I love and thank them. Some people help you keep your head straight; Marjorie Ingall helps me keep my heart straight, and for that I love and thank her. Thank you also to Jana and Moshe Banin.

Sarah Burnes is my agent in the truest sense of the

word, harnessing her formidable intelligence, insight, passion and warmth to shepherd the words that I write to the people who should read them. She, along with the superb Courtney Hammer and Stephanie Cabot, has made miracles happen where this book is concerned. Across the pond, Caspian Dennis and Abner Stein worked miracles of their own.

Selina Walker at Transworld was the first publisher to believe in this book and for that I am indebted to her as well as to the wonderful Clare Argar and Annie Eaton at Random House Children's Books. Back in the US at Penguin, my thanks go to my extraordinary editor, Julie Strauss-Gabel, as well as Don Weisberg and the indefatigable sales, marketing, publicity and design teams who worked so hard for this book.

Music is a huge part of this story, and I drew a lot of inspiration from Yo-Yo Ma – whose own work informs much of Mia's story – and from Glen Hansard and Marketa Irglova, whose song 'Falling Slowly' I probably listened to more than 200 times while working on the book.

Thanks to my Oregon contingent: Greg and Diane Rios, who have been our compatriots through all this. John and Peg Christie, whose grace, dignity, and generosity continue to move me. Jennifer Larson, MD, an old friend and, as luck would have it, an emergency-room doctor, who enlightened me about Glasgow Coma Scales, among other medical details.

Thanks to my parents – Lee and Ruth Forman – and my siblings – Tamar Schamhart and Greg Forman – all of whom are my cheerleaders and most steadfast fans, who ignore my failings (professional ones, anyhow) and celebrate my successes as if they were their own (which they are).

I didn't immediately recognize how much of this book is about the way parents transform their lives for their children. Willa Tucker teaches me this lesson every day and is occasionally forgiving when I am too absorbed playing make believe in my head to play make believe with her.

Without my husband, Nick Tucker, none of this would be. I owe him everything.

Finally, my deepest thanks go to R.D.T.J., who inspire me in so many ways and who show me every single day that there is such a thing as immortality.

The Story Behind the Story

Once upon a time, there was a family: a mother, a father, a boy like Teddy and a baby. And once upon a time, there was a snowy day. And a drive in a car. And a devastating car accident. And an unfathomable tragedy.

Once upon a time, one of those family members held on a little longer, though by the time the news reached me, all the way across the country in New York City, the tragedy was complete. But the child's act of tenacity, followed by his surrender, haunted me. Did he know what had happened to the rest of his family? Did he choose to go with them?

Once upon a time there was a vibrant family of four. And then there wasn't. And what was left was heart-break. Mine, and other people's.

But what was left was also important, in that it became something with which I simply could not come to terms from outside my own grief. As friends from around the country spontaneously gathered in the Oregon town where our friends had once lived, as we rushed headlong into the hell of our loss, I found a clarity, a guidance, a moral compass.

How would the tragedy change us? How would *we* change us? How would we rise to the occasion – not just of their deaths but of our lives? And, as I experienced a depth of grief unknown to me previously, I found something that felt divine. Was this our newly departed friends watching out for us? Was this God?

Of course, this transcendent grieving doesn't last. Gloom descends, the awfulness of your loss hits you, again and again. Real life gets on with itself. And eventually your loss normalizes, it integrates into part of your everyday life, and you find yourself three or five years later doing OK, changed but . . . but still able to hear your friends' voices, still telling stories about them, still thinking of them every day. And still pondering questions about them – like did one of them choose to die knowing the rest of his family had been obliterated?

It was out of the fog of this persistent question that one day, almost seven years later, a stranger popped into my consciousness.

Her name was Mia. She was seventeen-years-old. And a cello player (news to me; I knew nothing about the cello and not so much about classical music). And she had no relation whatsoever to the people I knew. But the minute I met her I knew she was going to take me on a journey, to answer that question that had been living in me for years: *What would I do if I had to choose?* I didn't know what Mia's answer would be when I started the book, though I knew it would be her own decision based upon the life that she and I were creating together.

People often ask me if the book was emotional or difficult to write. Emotional, yes. I typed through a lot of tears. But it was the opposite of difficult. Some of that grace from the days after the tragedy returned. Maybe that was because I was creating characters somewhat based on friends I loved and so I was deeply ensconced in their world again. It was as if they were right there in the room with me as I wrote.

And in a way they were. In a way, they have never left me. And that's just it, isn't it? That's how we manage to survive loss. Because love never dies; it never goes away; and it never fades. As long as you hang onto it.

Gayle Forman

January 2010

Behind the Music

Music is a major part of *If I Stay*, with both rock and classical references and allusions woven throughout the story. If you want to hear more of the songs mentioned in the book, head to www.gayleforman.com. But if you want to learn *why* I chose to include certain songs or mentioned specific artists or just get some music recommendations, here's a behind-the-scenes listening tour.

Page 17: 'School's Out' by Alice Cooper: When he hears that school's closed for the day, Teddy sings the requisite song for ditching school. I still can't imagine him joyfully bellowing this out without getting a pit in my stomach.

Page 20: Jonathan Richman: In the car, Dad suggests – and Teddy rejects – playing Jonathan Richman, who Mia describes as her parents' 'musical patron saint.' OK, he's actually mine! Rockin', sweet, tender, edgy, goofy, Jonathan is considered by many to be the Godfather of

Punk. Go listen to his debut, *Jonathan Richman and The Modern Lovers*; released in 1976, it *still* sounds fresh. Tunes like 'I'm A Little Dinosaur,' also make him a fave among children.

Page 20: Teddy begs to listen to SpongeBob, by which I was actually referring to the very cool Flaming Lips song 'SpongeBob and Patrick Confront The Psychic Wall of Energy' from the SpongeBob Soundtrack. Teddy has impeccable taste in music, too.

Page 21: Beethoven's Cello Sonata no. 3: This is the piece that comes on right before the accident, the one that Mia was meant to be practicing that day. I chose it because it announces that Mia is a serious and accomplished cellist.

Page 31: Tchaikovsky's 'Dance of the Sugar Plum Fairy.' This is what Mia plays at her first recital when she's eight. It seemed like one of those popular pieces kids would choose to play – and mangle. Not Mia, though.

Page 44: The Icelandic art band Adam plays for Mia is Sigur Rós.

Page 45: Yo-Yo-Ma. 'Le Grand Tango.' Recently, the master of all things cello has been doing all kinds of cool experimental crossover stuff, so I decided that he'd be playing some of his more contemporary work – which seemed like something that would move Adam at the concert he and Mia go to on their first date. But the tango recordings were done in 1997, so strictly speaking Yo-Yo-Ma would not have been playing them in 2005. I'm afraid I cheated a little here.

Page 48: To me (and the doctors), Mia's surgery seemed like a battle, hence Wagner's 'Ride of the Valkyries'.

Page 58: Mia's Juilliard audition pieces are all taken straight from the school's website, which lists a menu of what applicants can play for their auditions. I choose Ennio Morricone's piece from *The Mission* because when I saw that movie when I was sixteen, I loved the score so much, I immediately ran out and bought a cassette of the soundtrack.

Pages 104–5: Although Mia namedrops classical musicians like Dvořák and Schubert, I have to admit that personally I'm much more comfortable firing off a bunch of rock divas like Mia's mother does when Mia asks her who the hottest rocker girl she can think of is – and she replies with a list that includes Kathleen Hanna (of Bikini Kill and Le Tigre) Joan Jett (Kristen Stewart is playing her in a new movie) and Lucinda Williams.

Page 139: 'Something in the Way' by Nirvana. When Kim wanted to play Mia a modern band that used a cellist, there was no question who to pick. Nirvana from the *MTV Unplugged in New York* album.

Page 152: 'Girlfriend in a Coma' by the Smiths. Because a little gallows humour never hurts.

Page 155: 'Eraser' by Bikini. This is a fake song by a fake band. There is no Bikini. And there is no Shooting Star, either. I took the name Shooting Star from a short-lived band my husband played in called The Redmond Shooting Stars. When I checked to see if there was an actual band called Shooting Star, I was surprised to see there was only some defunct Euro hair band from the eighties.

Page 166: Melvins. Earth. I must come clean now. I *really* dislike the heavy, heavy sound of these two bands. But it seemed like Mia's mother would totally want to labour to them.

Pages 181–2: 'Wind Beneath My Wings' by Bette Midler. Just hearing that synthesizer at the beginning of this song activates my gag reflex. Just hearing the opening notes of 'Amazing Grace', though, never fails to raise the hairs on the back of my neck – in a good way.

Page 182: 'Three Little Birds' by Bob Marley. I never really thought of this as a funeral song until I thought of Kerry and then it just fit. Characters, even minor ones, speak to you.

Page 184: Henry requests the Mr T Experience at his funeral. Specifically I was thinking of the song 'Love American Style.' Someone I was in love with made me a mixed tape with that track on it and to this day some of the lyrics are like the pinnacle of romance to me. I can see Henry making a mixed tape like this for Willow so that's why I had him request this band.

Page 184: 'P.S. You Rock My World' by the Eels. Willow's personal funeral selection is off one of my favorite albums, Electro-Shock Blues, a record about grieving that helped me through a hard time in my own life.

Page 185: Mozart's Requiem. Mia's funeral choice. Haunting. Intense. Beautiful. Just like my girl.

Page 185: 'Fire and Rain' by James Taylor. Classic folky tear-jerker song. Would be cheesy if it weren't so good.

Pages 202–4: 'Waiting for Vengeance.' Even though Dad's band is nameless, and fictional, this particular lyric is adapted from an actual song by Oswald-Five-O. I suck at writing lyrics and this particular song worked eerily well for the story.

Page 231: 'DOA' by Dead Moon. This is the song that Mia swears she can 'remember' her parents listening to on their first date (before she was born). Dead Moon is this great, semi-obscure garage band from Portland, and while I recognize that including a track titled DOA might be metaphoric overkill, it's my favorite Dead Moon song so I did it anyway.

Page 240: Clash. Many of you will know the Clash, and if you don't, go listen to *London Calling* now. The Wipers are a less known punk band from Portland, who rockers like Mia's Dad and Adam would worship. Pick up a copy of *Is This Real?* if you want to rock it old-school Northwest style.

Page 247: *Andante con moto e poco rubato* by George Gershwin, performed by Yo-Yo Ma. Finding the piece that would bring Mia back was a challenge. First, I had to figure which Yo-Yo Ma album Adam would be able to readily download in the middle of the night. I decided that Adam would choose compilations. So I downloaded a couple of likely comps and then lay down on my couch, closed my eyes, and listened. The song that gave me the strongest emotional reaction – goose bumps, palpitations – won.

An Interview with Gayle Forman

You've already spoken about what inspired you to write *If I Stay*. And yet it was envisaged first of all as a book for children. Why was that?

Because of the personal nature of *If I Stay*, I wasn't quite sure when I started it whether it was meant to be a book, or if it was just some therapeutic exercise. So I wasn't really thinking about whether it was for children or adults. I was really thinking: *is this even a book?* In fact, when I saved the first few chapters on my computer, the name of the file was Why Not? – as in, not quite sure this is viable, but hey, why not go with it and see where it takes me?

As I kept going and it became clear that this was a book – and it got a proper title and file name – I thought it was teen fiction. It was about a seventeen-year-old girl, after all. And my first novel, *Sisters in Sanity*, had been a teen book. For whatever reason, I'm drawn to writing about this age group, perhaps because I feel in some ways as though I am still sixteen. But at the same time, Mia had a voice that seemed more mature than my own voice, an outlook that was so wise, and she was grappling with issues that even in the murky world of teen fiction, seemed rather intense. So I began to wonder if I wasn't writing myself out of the teen market? In the end, I decided not to worry about any of this, not to put the cart before the horse (after all, I didn't have a publishing contract at this point), and just write the book as I needed to write it and let the experts sort it out. And indeed, the consensus among the publishing experts was, for the most part, that it was a children's book that adults should read.

As for the readers themselves, they don't seem to care about such parameters. I hear from everyone from thirteen-year-old girls to sixty-five-year-old grandmothers to fifty-year-old bachelors who have read and been moved by this book. Maybe it's because I wrote a book about a teenager, but I also wrote a book about her parents, and grandparents and about music. It's multigenerational in the telling, and, I hope, in the reading.

And yet it's a serious novel with big themes. Which theme is the most important for you?

Is it too cheesy to say that, for me, the most important theme is love? I mean I know that this is a book about choices. And although most of us – thank goodness – will never have to make the kind of decision that Mia has to, we all know what it's like to grapple with a tough decision. But at the core of Mia's choice are the various forces of love: familial love, friendship love, romantic love, musical love – I think the book is really a series of love stories, and the theme – or takeaway, really – is that love endures. All those memories Mia is reliving from the hospital are moments of love from her life, moments that will never leave her so long as she draws breath.

And there's one love story that matters above all in *If I Stay*.

Yes, I'm a sucker for a love story in books and movies so there's no way I'd write a book without some kind of romantic interest. But it wasn't until I wrote that first scene when Adam and Mia are at the Yo-Yo Ma concert that I realized that this was going to be a Love Story, that these two were going to have a love that doesn't often happen at such a young age, and when it does, it causes complications. As I kept writing, I realized that the whole notion of staying worked on multiple levels because even before the accident, Mia was already grappling with whether or not to stay – with Adam or go to Juilliard. Of course, after the accident, the notion of staying takes on a much greater significance.

Yet *If I Stay* is also about death. Why do you think it's not more depressing?

I guess a book about death can also be equally about life. In *If I Stay* Mia's reliving the highlights of her life – her first kiss with her boyfriend, her silly antics with her little brother, the moment that she transcended some block and played music with all of her being – and readers are right in the room with her. Many readers have spoken about the odd sensation of being in tears one moment and bursting with joy the next. I can't say that I set out to create an emotional rollercoaster but I'm gratified to hear it is. It means that readers are engaging with Mia, feeling the love that infused her life, the anguish of her loss and the agony of her decision. I think too that the highs of Mia's life would not feel as true and intense if you didn't feel the loss on her behalf. I realize that *If I Stay* is an emotionally difficult book in places, but because Mia's life is filled with such love and joy, and readers get to experience that with her – and maybe to connect it to happy parts of their own life – there's a payoff for the pain?

Mia is a wonderfully warm, quirky heroine. Is she drawn from personal experience?

It's a funny question. Usually I can see elements of myself in my characters but Mia just seems so much wiser and braver and more driven and mature that I didn't see much commonality. Moreover, unlike Mia, I'm not a musician. But my sister, who knows me about as well as anyone, thought that Mia and I were a lot alike and initially she had a difficult time reading the novel because of it. I suppose that, like Mia, I always felt a little fish-out-of water in life (though not in my family; I don't have uber-cool parents like Mia did). And I suppose that I was working out some of my own grief through Mia. Of all the characters in the book, I think I'm the most like Willow in that I'm very bossy and I'm the kind of person who marches into a situation and takes charge. My husband calls me the 'charismatic leader's right hand man' for this habit, a designation that I used to resent; I wanted to be the charismatic leader! But I see what he means. I'm an organizer. A rallier of the troops.

One of the things that most attracted me to *If I Stay* was that I wasn't sure what Mia would choose to do at its end. Did you know as you were writing it which she would choose?

Not in the beginning, no, because in the real-life story that inspired the novel, there were no survivors. But I wanted Mia's story to take on a life (or death) of its own, so I didn't know what her choice would be until about halfway through the book when I realized I'd created this character who was so deeply in love with music, who had this incredibly bright future, and who had found a romantic love at seventeen that many of us search our whole lives for. Which isn't to say that any of that would be enough to make it all OK, but simply that it would be enough for her to take that leap of faith, to see that life might still have something to offer her.

You have two time-schemes operating in the novel, both of which meld seamlessly together. Was it difficult to put them in place?

I had no idea when I sat down to write that I'd use this flashback format – nor did I know, though I have since learned, that in literary circles, the use of extended flashbacks is normally considered the kiss of death for a book. I just sat down and starting writing this family. I wrote them having breakfast. And then I wrote the accident scene. And that scene was so gruesome and difficult for me that I needed a break. So when the paramedic says to Mia, 'You hang in there,' it clicked this idea of a young Mia having stage fright at a cello recital and her father telling her to hang in there. That was how the flashback structure was born. Other flashbacks weren't quite so linear or logical. I can't quite explain the rhyme or reason behind what went where – they are not chronological and not necessarily thematic to what's happening during the present tense narrative. And they weren't mapped out, either. Sometimes I didn't know what flashback I would write until the morning before I got to work (I often get insomnia while I'm working on a novel so I'll be up at 4 a.m., lying in bed and pondering the next day's writings). Sometimes, I wouldn't figure out the flashback until a few pages before I got to it. Such is the wondrous magic of writing. There's a wall. And then suddenly, there's a door.

When I finished the book, one of the things it made me think about most was the responsibility of living, and what I would do if I was in Mia's situation. Is this something that other readers have said to you?

Yes, and I have to say, it's been something of a surprise. When you write a book you don't lace it with messages or themes. Or at least I don't. You just tell a story. And then you hear people telling you how the book reverberated in their life, how it made them realize how quickly things could change, how they need to treat every day as precious, treasure every relationship. I've heard from lots of teen readers that they put the book down and went to their parents and told them that they loved them. One reader told me that after reading this she gave up touching her cell phone while driving – even though the cause of the crash is never explained. The idea that life is fleeting and can be gone in an instant – it's an easy thing to forget in the hectic pace of daily life. I'm certainly guilty of that. But for me, it's so important to stop, even if just for a moment, to do that little gratitude check – to look at my family and remind myself that *this* is life, this is what matters. As for what I'd do in Mia's situation, I can't even go there. I'm a wuss!

I believe there's some serious film interest. Could you tell us about this?

Summit, the studio that produces the *Twilight* films, among others, has optioned the rights to *If I Stay*, and they seem very enthusiastic about the book. But Hollywood being Hollywood, everything is in flux until filming actually begins. If you're interested in the nitty-gritty of it all, I keep readers pretty up-to-date on my website at www.gayleforman.com.

How exciting – I can't wait to see the film! Many thanks, Gayle Forman, for talking to us.

Gayle Forman is an award-winning author and journalist whose articles have appeared in numerous publications, including *Seventeen*, *Cosmopolitan*, *The Nation* and *The New York Times Magazine* in the US. She lives in Brooklyn with her family.

Visit her at www.gayleforman.com

By the same author

The Sunne In Splendour
Lionheart
A King's Ransom

THE WELSH TRILOGY SERIES

Here Be Dragons
Falls the Shadow
The Reckoning

THE HENRY II TRILOGY SERIES

When Christ and His Saints Slept
Time and Chance
Devil's Brood

THE QUEEN'S MAN SERIES

The Queen's Man
Cruel as the Grave
Dragon's Lair
Prince of Darkness

PRINCE OF DARKNESS

SHARON PENMAN is the author of eight critically acclaimed historical novels: *The Sunne in Splendour*, *Here Be Dragons*, *Falls the Shadow*, *The Reckoning*, *When Christ and His Saints Slept*, *Time and Chance*, *Devil's Brood* and *Lionheart*. She has also written four medieval mysteries. Her first, *The Queen's Man*, was a finalist for an Edgar Award for Best First Mystery from the Mystery Writers of America. Her other mysteries are *Cruel as the Grave*, *Dragon's Lair*, and *Prince of Darkness*. She lives in New Jersey.

PRINCE OF DARKNESS

The Queen's Man IV

SHARON PENMAN

HEAD of ZEUS

First published in 2005 by Marian Wood Books, an imprint of G. P. Putnam's Sons, New York

This paperback edition first published in the UK in 2014 by Head of Zeus Ltd

9 7 5 3 1 2 4 6 8

A catalogue record for this book is available from the British Library.

ISBN (PB): 9781781857090
ISBN (E): 9781781857076

Printed and bound by Clays Ltd, St Ives PLC

Head of Zeus Ltd
Clerkenwell House
45-47 Clerkenwell Green
London EC1R 0HT

WWW.HEADOFZEUS.COM

For Mic Cheetham

PROLOGUE

December 1193
St-Malo, Brittany

They came together on a damp December evening in a pirate's den. That was how she would one day describe this night to her son, Constance decided. The men of St-Malo were legendary as sea wolves, prideful and bold, and so were the men gathered in this drafty, unheated chapter house. Torches flared from wall sconces, casting smoky shadows upon the cold stone walls, upon their intent, expectant faces. Several of them already knew what she would say; the "unholy trinity," as she liked to call them, three of the duchy's most powerful lords, knew. So did their host, an affable gambler with a corsair's nerve and a bishop's miter. As for the others, they'd embraced the aim, needed only to be apprised of the means.

Turning toward the man hovering by the door, Constance beckoned him forward. He came slowly, as if reluctant to leave the shadows, and it occurred to her that she'd rarely seen him in the full light of day. Although a man of God, he had the polished manners of a courtier, and he bent over her hand, murmuring "My lady duchess," as if offering a benediction.

Constance did not like him very much, this unctuous instrument of her enemy's doom, and she withdrew her fingers as soon as his lips grazed her skin. She felt no gratitude; he'd been very well paid, after all. In truth, she found herself scorning him for the very betrayal that would serve her son so well. Loyalty was the currency of kingship, and he'd already proven that he dealt in counterfeit.

"This is Robert, a canon from St Étienne's Cathedral in Toulouse." She did not introduce the lords or Bishop Pierre. When she nodded, Robert produced a parchment sheet. All eyes were upon him as he unrolled it and carefully removed the silk seal-bags, revealing plaited cords and tags impressed with green wax, coated with varnish. Savoring the suspense, Constance held the letter out to the closest of her barons, André de Vitré.

André was already familiar with the letter, but he made a show of reading it as if for the first time. Rising from his seat in a gesture of respect for Raoul de Fougères's years and stature, he passed the letter to the older man. Raoul read without comment, offered it to Alain de Dinan. One by one, they read the letter, studying those dangling wax seals with the exaggerated care due a holy relic. Only after the letter had made a circuit of the chapter-house and was once more in Constance's hands did the questions begin to flow. Did Her Grace believe the seals were genuine? Who else knew of this letter? And how had it come into the possession of Canon Robert?

"Does it truly matter?" she challenged. "This letter is evidence of a foul crime, a mortal sin. Once its contents become known, it will give the Holy Church a potent weapon to use against the ungodly heresies that have taken root in Toulouse.

And it will be of great interest to the king of the French and to the Lionheart."

Richard Coeur de Lion. England's charismatic crusader-king, celebrated throughout Christendom for his courage, his bravura deeds on the bloody battlefields of the Holy Land, his mastery of the arts of war. But in Constance's mouth, the admiring sobriquet became a sardonic epithet, for her loathing of her Angevin in-laws burned to the very bone.

"This letter will draw as much blood as any dagger thrust," she said, "and I will not pretend that does not give me pleasure. But there is far more at stake than past wrongs and unhealed grievances." She paused, and for the first time that night, they saw her smile. "With this, we shall make my son England's king."

CHAPTER I

December 1193
Genêts, Normandy

A pallid winter sun had broken through the clouds shrouding the harbor, although the sea remained the color of slate. Brother Andrev's mantle billowed behind him like a sail as he strode toward the water's edge, but he was as indifferent to the wind's bite as he was to the damp, invasive cold. No true Breton was daunted by foul weather; Brother Andrev liked to joke that storms were their birthright and squalls their meat and drink.

As always, his gaze was drawn to the shimmering silhouette of Mont St Michel. Crowned by clouds and besieged by foam-crested waves, the abbey isle seemed to be floating above the choppy surface of the bay, more illusion than reality, Eden before the Fall. During low tide, pilgrims would trudge out onto those wet sands, intent upon saying prayers and making offerings to Blessed St Michael. The prudent ones hired local men to guide them through the quicksand bogs, men who would be able to get them safely to the rocky citadel before the tides came roaring back into the bay. When warned of the fearsome speed of those surging waters, people sometimes scoffed, refusing to believe that even a horse at full gallop could not outrun that incoming tide. The bodies that washed up on the beaches of the bay would be given decent Christian burial by the monks of Mont St Michel; for those swept out to sea and not recovered, only prayers could be said.

In the three years since Brother Andrev had been assigned to the abbey's cell at Genêts, not a day passed when he'd not blessed his good fortune at being able to serve both God and St Michael. This December noon was no different, and as he filled his eyes with the majesty of the motherhouse, his soul rejoiced in a deep and profound sense of peace.

"Father Andrev!" A towheaded youngster was running toward him, skimming over the beach as nimbly as a sandpiper. Recognizing the son of Eustace the shipwright, Brother Andrev waved back. He no longer corrected them when they called him "Father" instead of "Brother," for he understood their confusion. Brother Andrev was that rarity, both ordained priest and Benedictine monk, and thus more intimately involved with the daily lives of the villagers than his monastic brethren, saying Mass, hearing their confessions, baptizing their babies, and burying their dead.

"Where are you off to in such a hurry, Eudo? I've rarely seen you move so fast... unless you were on your way to dinner, of course."

The boy grinned. "I was fleeing from Brother Bernard," he said cheekily. "He caught Giles and me throwing dice in the churchyard and I bolted, not wanting to hear another of his sermons about our slothful, sinful ways."

Brother Andrev knew he ought to pick up the gauntlet flung down by Brother Bernard and lecture Eudo about the evils of gambling, especially on the Lord's Day. But he liked to play hasard and raffle himself, and he did not count hypocrisy among his sins. Too often he'd wanted to flee, too, when Brother Bernard launched into one of his interminable homilies.

Before he could respond, Eudo's head came up sharply. "Oh, crud! I cannot believe he's tracked me this far—" With that, he spun around and began to sprint up the beach, leaving Brother Andrev to gape after him in puzzlement—until he turned and saw the stout figure in Benedictine black bearing down upon him.

"Was that Eudo?" Brother Bernard was panting, his normally florid complexion now beet-red with annoyance and exertion. But when Brother Andrev would have offered up a defense of the errant youngster, the other monk waved it aside impatiently; whatever had brought him onto the windswept beach, it was not Eudo's tomfoolery. "I have been looking for you everywhere, Brother André. I should have known you'd be here," he said, churlishly enough to give his words an accusatory edge.

At first Brother Andrev had done his best to master his dislike of Brother Bernard. He was no saint, though, and his good intentions had frayed under constant exposure to the other monk's surly disposition and sour outlook upon life. "Ahn-DRAY-oh," he said coolly, "not André. It is a Breton name, not a French one. You'd like it not if I called you Bernez instead of Bernard."

Brother Bernard ignored the rebuke, for he shared the common belief of his French countrymen that Bretons were uncivilized, ignorant rustics. "I came to tell you that you are wanted back at the church. That woman has come again."

He invested the words "that woman" with such scorn that Brother Andrev knew at once the identity of their guest: Lady

Arzhela de Dinan. His friendship with Lady Arzhela was one of the joys of his life, but he knew that in Brother Bernard's eyes, her sins were manifold. She was Breton, proudly so. She was known to be bastard-born, yet she was also highborn. She was thrice wed, thrice widowed, and barren, for she'd never been with child. She was no stranger to controversy; her free and easy ways had often given rise to rumors and gossip. And although she was the kindest woman Brother Andrev had ever met, she was one for speaking her mind. On her last visit to Genêts, she had scolded Brother Bernard for chasing beggars away from the church and then earned his undying enmity by laughing at his attempt at offended dignity.

"Lady Arzhela? That is indeed welcome news and it was good of you to let me know straightaway," he said blandly, and started off across the sand. To his vexation, Brother Bernard fell into step beside him. It seemed the sermon was not yet over.

"She said that she wanted you to hear her confession." Brother Bernard sounded out of breath, for he was laboring to keep pace with Brother Andrev's longer strides. "Do you not think it odd that she keeps coming to you for the sacrament of penance?"

"No, I do not."

"Well, I do. Genêts is not her parish and you are not her priest."

Brother Andrev understood the insinuation, that Lady Arzhela was parish-shopping, seeking a priest who'd be more indulgent of her sins, impose a lighter penance. He stopped abruptly and swung around to confront the older man angrily. "If you must know, Lady Arzhela has a fondness for our church. Abbot Robert consecrated it in God's Year 1157, the year of her birth. She was baptized there, had one of her

8

weddings there, and has always avowed that she wants to be buried in the choir, near to the high altar."

Brother Bernard gasped. "That is outrageous," he said indignantly. "A woman like that does not deserve to be buried inside the church! I do not care if she is the widow of a Breton lord, she is also a wanton and—"

"She is the widow of three Breton barons, but were she not, she'd still have the right to be buried here in our church of Notre Dame and Saint-Sebastien, in the abbey of Blessed St Michael, or even in Bishop Herbert's great cathedral at Rennes. Do you not know—"

"What—that she is a count's bastard?"

It had been years since Brother Andrev had lost his temper like this; his fists clenched at his sides as he fought back an alarming urge to take aim at the other monk's sneer. "Yes, she is the Count of Nantes's natural daughter," he said tautly, "which makes her the aunt of our late lord, Duke Conan, and the cousin of our duchess, the Lady Constance. She is of the Royal House of Brittany, and not to be judged by the likes of you!"

Brother Bernard was not as impressed by Lady Arzhela's illustrious pedigree as Brother Andrev had hoped. His was an easy face to read, and his disdain for the royal Breton bloodlines was all too evident. But if he did not respect Lady Arzhela's heritage, he did understand the significance of her kinship to the duchess. She might well be the Whore of Babylon, but only a fool would make an enemy of a woman with such proximity to power. Swallowing his bile as best he could, he turned on his heel and marched off.

Brother Andrev watched him go, more bemused now than angry. Embarrassed by his own fervor, he could only marvel at Lady Arzhela's ability to befuddle male minds and heat their blood. She was no longer young, was not even present, and yet she'd managed to bring two men of God almost to blows.

WOMEN WERE CONFESSED IN OPEN CHURCH, and a shriving stool had been set up for Lady Arzhela at the front of the chancel. The three parts of confession had been satisfied. Arzhela had expressed contrition, confessed her sins, and accepted the fasting penance imposed by Brother Andrev. Now it was for him to offer absolution, but he found himself hesitating. What if Brother Bernard were right? If Arzhela deliberately chose him, knowing he'd give out light penances? Was she truly contrite?

"Brother Andrev?" Arzhela was looking up at him, a quizzical smile parting her lips. She had captivating eyes, wide-set and long-lashed, a vivid shade of turquoise, like sunlight on seawater. At first glance, a man might not find her beautiful—the fairness of her skin was marred by a sprinkling of freckles and her hair was the color of fire, thought to be unlucky since the time of Judas—but then he'd look into those amazing eyes, and he'd be lost.

Brother Andrev blinked, came back to himself, and hastily said, "I absolve you from your sins in the name of the Father and of the Son and of the Holy Spirit."

Arzhela lowered her lashes, murmured a demure "Amen," and then her grin broke free. "You had me worried that you were not going to give me absolution."

"And if I did not?" Brother Andrev asked, and she wrinkled her nose and then grinned again.

"Well, if I eat a portion of cabbage and onions without complaint, I want my honey wafers and hippocras afterward!" When he did not join in her laughter, her eyebrows shot upward. "Surely that deserves a smile, even a small one? You cannot expect me to believe that my petty sins are too terrible to be forgiven. Why, I've done much worse and even told you so in shameful but provocative detail—"

She stopped suddenly, frowning. "Oh, no! Do not tell me that nasty little man talked to you, too, about my confessions?"

"What 'nasty little man,' my lady?"

"Brother Bertrand or Barnabus or whatever his name is. When I told him I wanted you to hear my confession, he mumbled something about that being 'such a surprise.' His sarcasm was thick enough to choke on, and when I challenged him, he said it was not fitting for me to do penance to a priest who was besotted with me. Well, I gave him a right sharp talking-to for that bit of impertinence, but obviously not sharp enough. I am right, am I not? He did mention this to you?"

Brother Andrev nodded reluctantly. "He did plant one of his poison seeds, and I was foolish enough to let it take root."

"Indeed you were." She held out her hand, let him help her to her feet. "Of course, he was not entirely wrong. We both know you are besotted with me, for what man is not?"

She had a low laugh, an infectious chuckle that had always been music to his ears... until now. He could feel the heat rising in his face and he lowered his head, hoping she'd not notice.

She did, and her attitude changed dramatically. "Oh, Andrev, I am so sorry! I ought not to have been teasing you. But you know me; I'll be flirting with the Devil on my deathbed. You are very dear to me and there is nothing sinful or shameful about our friendship. I come to you for confession because you can see into my heart, because you know that my contrition is genuine, that I truly mean it when I vow not to sin again... even knowing that I will."

11

She kept up an easy flow of conversation as they walked down the nave, and he blessed her social skills, for by the time they'd reached the cloisters, his discomfort had faded and when she called Brother Bernard a profane name that cast aspersions on his manhood, he grinned appreciatively.

Arzhela was pleased that she'd got him into a better mood. But she was not done with Brother Bernard, not yet, for she was as protective as a mother lion when it came to those she cared about. That nasty little man would not be harassing Andrev again if she had anything to say about it, and she damned well did. "Tell me," she said, favoring him with her most innocent smile, "does Mont St Michel have any alien priories or cells in other lands... say, Ireland? Mayhap Wales?"

Brother Andrev was accustomed to Arzhela's non sequiturs; part of her charm was her unpredictability. "No," he said thoughtfully, "not that I know of. The abbey does have lands in England, though. Several in Devon and a grange up in Yorkshire."

"Yorkshire," Arzhela said happily. Perfect. Making a mental note to have a little talk with Abbot Jourdain the next time she visited the abbey, she gestured toward a bench in one of the carrels. "May we sit for a while? I have a private matter to discuss with you."

"More private than the confessional?" Brother Andrev joked, gallantly using the corner of his mantle to wipe the bench clean for her. "What may I do for you, my lady?"

"I have a dilemma," she confided. "I have learned something I'd rather not have known, for now I must make a choice. If I do nothing, great harm will come to one who... well, let us just say I have fond memories of him. But if I warn him, someone else I care for will be adversely affected. What would you do, Brother Andrev, if you were faced with such a predicament?"

"Well, I think I would probably just toss a coin in the air. Lady Arzhela, I cannot possibly answer your question based upon the meager information you have given me."

Arzhela did not know whether to scowl or smile. In the end, she did both, and then sighed. "No, I do not suppose you can," she agreed. "But I cannot tell you what you'd need to know to give me an honest answer. This friend of mine will be in grave danger if this accusation is made against him. I cannot be more specific, though."

"Is the accusation true?"

"No, I do not think it is."

"But you cannot be sure of that?"

She considered the question. "He is not a man overly burdened with scruples. I do not believe, though, that he is guilty of this charge." With a wry smile, she said, "He is too clever to make a mistake of this magnitude."

"Can you tell me anything about the other person involved, the one you said you 'care for'?" He was not surprised when she shook her head, for he felt reasonably certain that Duchess Constance was the other player in this mysterious drama. "What, then, of the consequences, my lady? What happens if you warn your 'friend' of the danger? And what happens if you do not?"

Arzhela was quiet for several moments. "You are right," she said at last. "That does clarify matters for me, for the scales do not balance. On the one hand, disappointment, and on the other, destruction." Rising, she leaned over and kissed him on the cheek. "Thank you, dear friend. You've helped more than you know. Now I've taken up enough of your time. The provost has invited me to dine with him this evening. I hope to see you there, too. But for the love of God Everlasting, please do not let him include your favorite monk and mine!"

She did not wait for his response, blew him a playful kiss, and started up the walkway. She'd only taken a few steps before Brother Andrev jumped to his feet. "My lady, wait! There is something I must ask you, something I should have asked at the first. If you involve yourself in this, would you be putting yourself at risk?"

She looked at him for a moment, her expression grave, but amusement was shimmering in the depths of those beautiful blue-green eyes, and it was not long in spilling over into laughter. "I do hope so," she said, "for life without risk would be like meat without salt!"

CHAPTER II

December 1193
St Albans, England

The two men were loitering by the roadside with such
suspicious intent that they at once drew Sarra's attention.
Turning in the saddle, she was relieved to see that Justin de
Quincy had noticed them, too, and was already taking
protective measures. Nudging his stallion toward the Lady
Claudine's mare, he carefully transferred the blanket-wrapped
bundle in his arms to her embrace, and then opened his mantle
to give himself quick access to the sword at his hip. As Sarra
had hoped and Justin had expected, the mere sight of the
weapon was enough to discourage any villainy the men had in
mind. Tipping their caps with sardonic deference, they backed
away from the road, prudently preferring to await easier prey.

Justin did not let down his guard, though, not until they'd
reached the outskirts of St Albans. Only then did he dare to
reclaim that precious cargo. The infant settled back into the
crook of his arm with a soft sigh, and her contentment caught
at his heart.

"We are almost there," Sarra said quietly, giving him a sympathetic sideways glance as she tightened her hold upon her own baby.

Justin nodded, never taking his eyes from his daughter's flower-petal little face. He said nothing, for what was there to say?

As soon as he heard the footsteps outside, Baldwin leaped to his feet. He flung the door open wide, his welcoming smile faltering at the sight of his sister. "Rohese!" Attempting to disguise his disappointment, he made a great fuss out of ushering her inside, seating her close to the hearth, and fetching her a cup of his best ale. "This is indeed a pleasant surprise," he said heartily. "But where is Brian? Surely he did not let you make this trip on your own?"

"Of course not." Her eyes no longer met his, though, as she explained that Brian had stopped by the local alehouse upon their arrival in town. "He had a great thirst after so many hours on the road..."

It was a weak excuse, feebly offered. But Baldwin bit back any comments, knowing from experience that an attack upon her husband would only spur her to his defense. A pity it was, but there was naught to be done about it. Baldwin liked his brother-by-marriage, in truth he did. Brian was a charmer, quick with a joke, always willing to offer a helping hand. He was never a nasty drunk, but a drunk he was, and Rohese alone refused to admit it.

"Where is Sarra?" she asked abruptly, eager to turn the conversation away from her missing husband. "And the bairns—never have I heard your house so quiet!"

"The children are with Sarra's mother. Sarra... Sarra has been away for the past fortnight. She said she'd be back by the last week of Advent, so I hope she'll get home today or tomorrow."

He was not keen to explain his wife's absence, but he knew he'd have to satisfy Rohese's curiosity; no respectable wife and mother left her home and hearth unless her need was a strong one. And indeed, his sister blinked in surprise, at once wanting to know where Sarra had gone. He supposed he could lie and claim she was visiting an ailing aunt, but for what purpose? Sooner or later, the rest of the family would have to know.

"Sarra has agreed to be the wet nurse for a lady's newborn."

Rohese's eyes widened. "Truly, Baldwin?" She knew that Sarra's mother had been the wet nurse to King Richard in his infancy and her entire family had benefited greatly from it. Sarra's brother Alexander not only enjoyed bragging rights as the king's milk-brother, he had received an excellent education at St Albans and Paris. So she understood why Baldwin and Sarra might be tempted by such an opportunity. Yet there were drawbacks, too, in accepting so serious a trust.

"Are you sure you want to do this, Baldwin? I know Sarra would never agree to live in as her mother was required to do. But you'll be taking a stranger's child into your home, into your lives, for at least a year, mayhap two, until the babe is weaned."

She did not mention the greatest deterrent to breast-nursing— that sexual intercourse was forbidden as long as the baby suckled. Since it was widely believed that breast-feeding prevented pregnancy and a highborn woman's first duty was to provide her husband with heirs, women of the nobility hired wet nurses for their children. For those of lesser status or affluence, this was not possible, and their choices were unpalatable. A woman could sleep chastely in the marriage bed while she nursed her baby. Or her husband could refrain

17

from spilling his seed within her body; "thresh within and winnow without," as Rohese's Brian cheerfully put it. But this practice was a mortal sin in the eyes of the Holy Church. Most couples chose the lesser sin and yielded to the temptations of the flesh. If a nursing mother then became pregnant, it was just God's Will.

A wet nurse did not dare take such a risk, though. All knew that mother's milk was purified blood. This made conception during nursing dangerous to the nursing baby, for a pregnant woman's good blood would be needed to nurture the child within her womb, leaving only her impure blood to feed the child at her breast. Moreover, pregnancy would soon dry up her milk, impure or not, and she would no longer be of use to her highborn employer.

Rohese did not think she had the right to lecture, though, for Baldwin was her elder brother. She contented herself with repeating, "You are sure?"

"Yes," he said, not sounding all that convinced. He was quiet for some moments, watching as flames licked the hearth log. "We could hardly say no, not when the queen was the one doing the asking. She sent for Sarra's mother, told Hodierna that she needed a wet nurse she could trust, a woman who was healthy, between twenty-five and thirty-five, willing to forswear spicy and sour foods whilst nursing, and above all, discreet."

Rohese had straightened on her stool at the first mention of the queen. It all made sense now. Understandably eager to please Eleanor, Hodierna must have mentioned that her youngest daughter was nursing her own babe. "No," she agreed, "you could hardly turn down the Queen of England." Her eyes shining, she leaned forward, patting Baldwin's knee. "This is so exciting, Baldwin! For the queen to take a hand, surely the babe must be of high birth. You think... could it be her son John's?"

Sarra would never have answered Rohese's question, but Sarra was not there. Baldwin already had misgivings and the baby had not even arrived yet. "I wondered that, too," he admitted. "But I met the father, or the lad claiming to be the father. He came a fortnight ago to escort Sarra to Godstow Priory. That is where the mother had her lying-in, and I gathered that Justin—the only name he gave me—has been staying nearby since the babe's birth. The baby was not due till December, but she was born early. They had to find a local girl to nurse the child until arrangements could be made to get her to St Albans."

Rohese had not yet abandoned her theory that the baby could be Lord John's, and she felt a small dart of disappointment, for she imagined a father would be more involved in a son's life than a daughter's. "The child is a girl, then?"

Baldwin nodded. "She is called Aline. Justin said it was his mother's name." Anticipating her curious questions, he raised a hand in playful protest. "I can tell you very little about him, Rohese, other than the fact that he has excellent manners and wears a sword with the comfort of a man who knows how to use it."

"What is his connection to the queen? Could he... could he be a natural son of the old king?"

Baldwin shook his head, chuckling. "He has grey eyes like the old king, but he is dark as a Saracen. Moreover, I do not think the queen would have warm, fond feelings for one of King Henry's bastards. This Justin cannot be much more than twenty or twenty-one, and by then the queen was being held prisoner by her husband."

"Oh," Rohese said, deflated. At least two of King Henry's

19

bastards had been raised at his court, with the queen's consent. But if Justin were born after the queen had rebelled against King Henry, he'd not have known her during his childhood and it was unlikely that she'd be bestirring herself on his behalf. "Well, then, it must be the baby's mother who has the queen's favor. What do you know about her?"

"Even less than I know about Justin. We've been told her name is Clarice, but it is most likely false—" This time Baldwin was certain of the step outside the door. With a grin, he hurried over to open it for his wife.

BALDWIN WAS STRUCK BY THE BEAUTY of the woman introduced to him as "the Lady Clarice." He was struck, too, by her unease. Her smile was perfunctory, her demeanor distracted, and her eyes darted around the room as if measuring the confines of a cage. Conversation was stilted, sporadic, for Justin was no more talkative than "Clarice." Unlike her, though, he did not seem nervous, just sad. He was holding baby Aline as if she were as delicate as a snowflake and would melt if breathed upon. Baldwin remembered how he'd felt when he'd cradled his firstborn—awed and thankful and so protective of that fragile little life that it was actually painful—and he thawed toward the younger man. But his newfound empathy for Justin did nothing to ease the awkwardness, and he was relieved when Sarra reached again for her mantle, declaring that she could not wait another moment to see her children.

Once out in the street, Rohese was obviously eager to interrogate Sarra about Aline's parents, but she won Baldwin's gratitude by curbing her curiosity and declaring she was off to fetch Brian from the alehouse. Sarra and Baldwin stood for several moments in a wordless embrace, cuddling their young daughter between them until she started to squirm. Giving her to Baldwin, Sarra linked her arm in his and they started walking up the street toward her mother's residence.

"Well, Ella," he joked, "how do you feel about having a new milk-sister?" The little girl gurgled and cooed, and his anxiety began to ebb away in his joy at having his family together again. "So, what do you think, Sarra?"

"It will be well," she said, and he was comforted by her certainty, for she'd never been one for sweetening the truth. "Our greatest fear was that they'd be haughty and demanding. We need not worry about that. The girl is highborn, as we suspected, but I saw no malice in her, no spite, and I did not see her at her best, for she is still recovering from the birthing. She had a hard time of it, Baldwin, bled enough to scare the midwife half to death."

Ella let out a sudden squeal, and Aline and her mysterious parents were forgotten. Sarra wanted reassurance that their other children had behaved themselves during her absence, and Baldwin was happy to spin some tall tales about their mischief-making. It was not until they'd almost reached her mother's house that he thought to thank her for bringing that awkward cottage encounter to a merciful end.

"Actually," she said, "I wanted to give them some time alone with their little one."

"Ah... so it will be a painful parting?"

"I think so," she said, and then amended that to "Certainly for him."

CLAUDINE HAD FOLLOWED JUSTIN TO THE door and was watching as he untied the cradle from their packhorse. But after a moment, she realized that the chill was not good for the baby, and she hurriedly retreated toward the hearth. Aline hiccupped, and she patted the infant gingerly on the back as she'd seen Sarra do. To her surprise, it worked and Aline burped.

Justin came in, then, with the cradle. Once it was set up, Claudine relinquished the baby and went to pour a cup of ale. Justin was leaning over the cradle, murmuring to Aline. Returning with the ale, Claudine smiled when she was close enough to catch his words.

"What did you call her? Butterfly?"

"The swaddling looks like a cocoon to me." When Claudine studied the linen bands binding the baby's body, she saw what he meant; only Aline's head and hands were visible. "Sarra assured me that it is necessary to keep her warm and make sure her limbs develop properly. She says an infant's body is so soft and pliable that it needs special support, and I daresay she is right, but it does not look comfortable, does it?"

"This is the way it is always done, Justin." Reaching over to straighten the pannus, the cloth covering Aline's loins, Claudine wrinkled her nose. "Not again!"

"She does leak a lot," Justin agreed, grinning, and went rooting for a dry cloth in Aline's coffer. Neither one had fully mastered the skill of diapering a baby yet, but between the two of them, they managed to get Aline into a clean one. Claudine retrieved her ale cup while he continued to play with their daughter. She watched him for a few moments before saying,

"Justin... I have a favor to ask of you."

He glanced up, and although he smiled, she thought he looked faintly wary, too. "It may be months before the queen and King Richard return from Germany. Since I need not be in attendance upon the queen, I have decided to pay a visit to my family, first to my cousin Petronillla in Paris and then home to Poitou. Will you escort me to Southampton?"

"Of course I will," Justin said, doing his best to conceal his relief that she had not asked him to accompany her to France. If she had, he'd have felt honor-bound to accept. His own mother had died giving him birth, and the midwife had told him that Claudine had come fearfully close to trading her life for Aline's. Had he ever loved Claudine? He remembered how much it had hurt to discover that she was John's spy, and how troubling it had been to discover, too, that he could still desire a woman he could not trust. When she'd told him that she was pregnant, a very ugly suspicion had surfaced; had she been John's concubine as well as his spy?

Claudine was a distant kinswoman of Queen Eleanor, and ostensibly this was why the queen had been so willing to help with Claudine's pregnancy. Or was it that she'd wondered if Claudine could be carrying her grandchild? Justin had never discussed this with the queen. He'd had difficulty even admitting the suspicion to himself. He had no proof, after all, that Claudine had ever lain with John, much less that she'd been sharing his bed when Aline was conceived. The doubts had remained, though—until the first time he'd held Aline in his arms. But if he'd given his heart utterly and willingly to his baby daughter, it was far more complicated with Claudine.

"Justin... ?" She was watching him intently. "What is it? Your words do not match your face. Surely it is not too much to ask?"

"Not at all! I'll gladly take you to Southampton, Claudine."

"I'd ask you to come with me to France, but I dare not—you understand."

He did. She could hardly invite him to meet her family. How would she introduce him? As her lower-class lover? She was the daughter of one highborn baron, widow of another, and he was the bastard son of a bishop. Her father was not likely to be impressed that he was also the queen's man. They were the queen's kindred.

Claudine had wandered to the door. Opening it a crack, she turned to face Justin with a radiant, relieved smile. "Sarra and her husband are coming back, with a flock of children trailing after them. We ought to leave whilst there is still daylight, Justin."

"I suppose." As he reached over to make sure Aline's blankets were securely tucked around her, she opened her eyes. They'd been blue at birth, but they'd been darkening daily, and Sarra had told him that they might eventually become as brown as Claudine's. When he touched her hand, her tiny fingers clamped on to his thumb. "I have to go, Butterfly," he said softly. "But I'll be back."

WINCHESTER WAS ON THE SOUTHAMPTON ROAD, AND JUSTIN suggested that they stop there for the night in order to visit with his friend, Luke de Marston, the shire's under-sheriff. Claudine had met Luke during one of his London trips and they'd got along very well, so she was amenable to the idea. Reaching the city at dusk, they were made welcome by Luke and the woman he loved, Aldith. But within an hour of their arrival, Claudine sensed that they were sharing their cottage with trouble. It lurked in the corners, flitted about in the shadows, hovered in the air, and she was worldly enough to recognize that this was the age-old war that men and women had been fighting since God breathed life into Adam's rib.

Justin was not oblivious to the tension, either. He caught the oblique glances that Aldith cast in Luke's direction when he wasn't looking. He felt the heaviness of the silences between them. He noticed how often Luke reached for the wine flagon. He noticed, too, how uncomfortable Aldith seemed in

Claudine's presence; Aldith usually made other women feel uncomfortable. But she knew Claudine was a lady-in-waiting to the Queen of England while she was a poor potter's daughter of dubious reputation. Her unease told Justin that she'd learned Luke was under pressure to end their liaison, and he was sorry, for Aldith was his friend, the most seductive, shapely of friends, but a friend, nonetheless.

The only one who was enjoying the stay in Winchester was Justin's dog, Shadow, for he was utterly and enthusiastically smitten with Jezebel, Aldith's mastiff. Rescued by Justin from drowning in the River Fleet, Shadow had finally grown into his long, rangy frame, but he was still dwarfed by the enormous mastiff, who was not receptive to his wooing. He continued his high-risk courtship, though, until a snarl and yelp told them that Jezebel's latest rebuff had drawn blood.

"Poor sap," Luke said unsympathetically. "I have to make one last sweep of the town tonight. Come with me, de Quincy, and we'd best bring your besotted hound with us ere Jezebel bites him where it will hurt the most."

Claudine and Aldith shared a common expression for a moment, one of dismay at the prospect of being left alone together. Justin snatched up his mantle, hoping he did not appear too eager to escape the stifling atmosphere of the cottage, and he and Shadow followed the under-sheriff out into the night.

THEY ENDED UP IN A TAVERN ON CALPE STREET. AS USUAL, Luke insisted upon being the one to order a flagon of heavily spiced red wine. An under-sheriff could run up charges indefinitely, for no alehouse or tavern owner would be foolish enough to push for payment. Justin coaxed Shadow under the table where he'd be in no danger of being stepped on and then apologized for showing up at Luke's door with no warning.

"What you really mean," Luke said, "is that you're sorry you did not want to pay for a night's stay at a Winchester inn. The worst of our flea-ridden hovels is looking better and better when compared to the harmony and joy at Castle de Marston."

"You know me, anything to save a few pence. So... Aldith knows?"

Luke nodded morosely and they drank in silence for several moments. They'd met when Justin had been investigating the death of a Winchester goldsmith the previous year. Aldith had been the man's longtime mistress, but Luke had been willing to offer her what the goldsmith could not—marriage. When word of his intentions got out, though, he'd encountered opposition from the sheriff and the Bishop of Winchester. Marriage would elevate Aldith into the gentry, and Winchester society had far more stringent standards for an under-sheriff's wife than for his bedmate. Unwilling to lose his office, and equally unwilling to lose Aldith, Luke had been concocting excuses for delaying the wedding while he tried to find a way out of the trap. Justin had advised him to tell Aldith the truth. Apparently that had not worked too well.

"She blames you for not defying them?" he asked in surprise, for that did not mesh with what he knew of Aldith.

"No, she says not. She said she understood and she chided me for not telling her sooner. But nothing has been right between us since then. We fight more and we watch what we say and..." Luke doused the rest of his words in his wine cup. When he set it down again, he signaled that he was done discussing his family woes by saying hastily, "Well, enough of that. What is the latest news about the queen and King Richard?"

The English king had been seized by his enemies on his way home from the Crusade, and after much negotiation and scheming, he was to be freed upon payment of a vast ransom to his royal captor, Heinrich, the Holy Roman Emperor. Queen Eleanor had sailed for Germany that past November to deliver the ransom. But Richard's release was not a foregone conclusion. The French king, Philippe, and Richard's younger brother, John, Count of Mortain, had been doing all in their power to prolong Richard's confinement, and they were not known for being gracious losers. Rumor had it that they'd offered Heinrich an even larger sum to keep Richard prisoner, and Luke hoped that Justin, one of the queen's men, might be a better source than local alehouse gossip.

He was to be disappointed, though. All Justin could tell him was that the queen had safely arrived in Germany and that John was still in France, reported to be at the French king's court. Peering into the wine flagon, Luke motioned to the serving maid for another. He was about to recount a story about a local vintner who'd evaded the tax imposed to pay King Richard's ransom, but remembered in time that Justin would probably not see the humor in it. The Crown had demanded that all of Richard's subjects contribute fully a fourth of their annual income to the Exchequer, a huge burden that had eroded some of the king's popularity, at least in Winchester. But Justin's loyalty to his queen was absolute and Luke thought it was unlikely he'd question the exorbitant price the English were paying for the return of their king.

"I had to make a trip to London," he said, "the week of Michaelmas. I stopped by to see you, de Quincy, but your friends at the alehouse said you'd been gone since the summer. I assume you were off skulking and lurking on the queen's behalf?"

"I was in Wales," Justin said, reaching over to pour them more wine. "Some of King Richard's ransom had gone missing, and the queen sent me to recover it."

"Just another ordinary summer, then," Luke said with a grin. "Did you get it back?"

"Eventually," Justin said, and he grinned, too, then, imagining Luke's reaction if he'd been able to give the deputy a candid account of his time in Wales.

The Welsh prince, Davydd ab Owain, was fighting a civil war with his nephew, Llewelyn ab Iorwerth. He staged a false robbery of the ransom to put the blame on Llewelyn, but he was outwitted by his not-so-loving wife, Emma, the bastard sister of the old king. Emma arranged to have the ransom really stolen, with the help of a partner in crime and a dangerous spy called "the Breton." I followed Emma to an abbey grange and discovered that her confederate was none other than the queen's son John, who decided that the best way to protect his aunt Emma was to shut my mouth by filling it with grave-soil. Since a prince never dirties his own hands, he left it for Durand to do.

You remember Durand, Luke? John's henchman from Hell, who secretly serves the queen when he is not doing the Devil's work. Durand had the grace to apologize to me first, wanting me to know there was nothing personal in his actions as he was about to spill my guts all over the chapel floor. Obviously it did not go as he expected, thanks to Llewelyn. Did I mention that Llewelyn and I had become allies of a sort? Anyway, I got the ransom back for the queen, too many men died, and John decided that Paris was healthier than Wales.

Of course Justin could never say that. Of all he owed the queen, not the least was his silence. She wanted John's misdeeds covered up, not exposed to the light of day. Nor was he being completely honest, not even in his own mental musings. His mocking tone softened the harsh edges of memory—trapped in that torch-lit chapel, disarmed and defenseless, hearing John say dispassionately, "*Kill him.*"

"I was somewhat surprised to have you turn up with the Lady Claudine," Luke admitted, "for I thought you ended it once you found out that she was spying for John in her spare time."

"I did, but..." Justin shrugged, for he could hardly explain about Aline. It got confusing at times, remembering who knew which secrets. Claudine knew that the Bishop of Chester was his father. But she did not know that her spying had been discovered by Justin and the queen. Luke knew about Justin's connection to Claudine, but not about his blood ties to the bishop. Molly, a childhood friend and recent bedmate, had guessed the truth about his father. She did not know, though, that he served the queen. The irony was not lost upon Justin that he, who'd never cared much for secrets, should now have so many.

Misreading his shrug, Luke laughed. "I know; when it comes to a choice between common sense and a beautiful woman, guess which one wins every time? Just be sure you sleep with one eye open, de Quincy, especially once you reach Paris. That is where John is amusing himself these days, is it not?"

"I am not accompanying Claudine to Paris. I go no farther than the docks at Southampton."

Luke blinked. "You do remember that the queen is away? Why pass up a chance to see Paris? Take advantage of this free time, de Quincy. Trust me on this—of all the cities in Christendom, none offers a man as many opportunities to sin as Paris does!"

"I daresay you're right. But there is a town that I find even more tempting than Paris," Justin confided, and laughed outright at the baffled expression on Luke's face when he said, "St Albans."

CHAPTER III

January 1194
London, England

A brisk wind had chased most Londoners indoors. The man shambling along Gracechurch Street encountered no other passersby, only two cats snarling and spitting at each other on the roof of an apothecary's shop. The shop was closed, for customers were scarce once the winter dark had descended. Farther down the street, though, he saw light leaking from the cracked shutters of the local alehouse, and he quickened his pace. But the door did not budge when he shoved it, and as he pounded for entry, a voice from within shouted, "We are closed, so be off with you!"

He was not easily discouraged and continued to beat upon the door for several moments, to no avail. He was finally stumbling away, cursing under his breath, when he almost collided with a younger man just turning the corner. He reeled backward, would have fallen if the other man had not caught his arm and hauled him upright, saying, "Have a care, Ned."

The face smiling down at him looked blearily familiar, but his brain had been marinating in wine since mid-afternoon

31

and his memory refused to summon up a name. His new friend had a grip on his elbow and was steering him back toward the alehouse. He submitted willingly to the change of direction, although he thought it only fair to warn mournfully, "They'll not let us in."

"I think they will," Justin assured him, turning his head to avoid the wine fumes gusting from Ned's mouth. "Nell closed the alehouse tonight for Cicily's churching. You know Cicily—the chandler's wife? Remember she had a baby last month?" Ned was looking up at him with such little comprehension that Justin abandoned any further explanations. Rapping sharply upon the alehouse door, he said, "It's Justin," and when it opened, he pulled Ned in with him.

Nell was a tiny little thing, barely five feet tall, but when she frowned grown men cringed, for her tempers were feared the length and breadth of Gracechurch Street. She was scowling now at Ned, who instinctively shrank back behind Justin. "Passing strange, but I do not remember inviting this swill-pot to the churching!"

"Have a heart, Nell. All they'll find is a frozen lump in the morning if he does not get somewhere to sober up."

Nell grumbled, as he expected. But she also waved Ned on in, as he'd expected, too. Justin snatched an ale from Odo the barber and guided Ned over to an empty seat, where he settled down happily with the ale, utterly oblivious of the celebration going on all around him. Justin shed his mantle, exchanged greetings with those closest to the door, and went to get Odo another ale. Coming back, he acknowledged his dog's enthusiastic if belated welcome, and wandered over to eavesdrop as Odo's wife, Agnes, tried to explain to Nell's young daughter, Lucy, what a churching was.

"... and after giving birth, she is welcomed back into the

Church, lass, where she is purified with holy water and blessed by the priest. Afterward, there is a gathering of her friends and family, and Cicily has so many of them that your mama insisted it be held at the alehouse."

"Mama said she was the baby's..." Lucy frowned, trying to remember, her expression a mirror in miniature of her mother's. "... the baby's godmother!"

Agnes, a wise woman, detected the unspoken admission of jealousy and did her best to reassure Lucy that her mother's new goddaughter was not a rival for her affections. "It is not like having a child of your own blood, not like you, Lucy. Nonetheless, it is a great honor to be a godparent. You ought to be pleased that your mama was chosen."

Lucy did not seem overly impressed with the honor, but Justin felt a sudden stab of guilt. Agnes's words reminded him that a godmother was only one of the benefits other children enjoyed and Aline would be denied. How could he and Claudine seek out godparents for a child whose very existence must be kept secret?

At that moment, he happened to see Aldred leaning against the far wall. The young Kentishman worked for Jonas, the one-eyed sergeant who was Justin's sometime partner and the fulltime scourge of the London underworld. Justin began to weave his way across the common room. Aldred was hoarding a pile of Nell's savory wafers and they staged a mock struggle over possession, which ended with several wafers sliding off the platter into the floor rushes. Justin and Aldred reacted as one, hastily looking around to make sure Nell hadn't noticed the mishap.

Justin whistled for Shadow, who eagerly volunteered for wafer cleanup, and then followed Aldred toward a vacant space on the closest bench. Watching the revelries, Justin felt a quiet contentment, a sense of belonging that he'd rarely experienced. He knew that he did not truly belong on Gracechurch Street, but thanks to his friendship with Nell and Aldred and Gunter the blacksmith, he'd been accepted as if he did, and that was an unusual occurrence in his life. Even before he'd learned the truth about his paternity, he'd always felt like an outsider, the foundling without family in a world in which family was paramount.

But on Gracechurch Street, he knew these people, knew their secrets and their hopes. He knew that the cartwright's brother was smitten with the weaver's daughter, knew that Avice, the tanner's widow, fed her children by taking in laundry and an occasional male customer when her pantry ran bare, knew that Aldred was besotted with Nell and Gunter still mourned his dead wife, and that his neighbors no longer looked upon him with suspicion, that they'd learned to trust him enough to take pride in knowing that one of the queen's men was living in their midst.

The new mother, Cicily, was basking in the attention, and she'd just dramatically declared that her next child would be a boy since the first sight to fill her eyes upon leaving the church was a little lad. At that moment, there was a sudden, loud pounding at the door. Nell hastened over and slid back the latch. It was soon apparent to the others that she was arguing with the Watch, for snatches of conversation came wafting in with each blast of cold air.

"... curfew rung at St Mary-Le-Bow!"

"But we are closed to the public!" Nell protested. "My friends and I are celebrating Cicily's churching."

"... heard that one before... hauled into the wardmoot... huge fine..."

"Oh, Splendor of God!" Nell threw up her hands in frustration. "Justin, will you please come tell these ⟨...⟩ not open for business?" Ignoring his obvious re⟨...⟩ swung back toward the Watch, arms akimbo, eyes ⟨...⟩ "Hear it from the queen's man if you doubt my word!"

Knowing Nell was not to be denied, Justin got to his fee⟨...⟩ and crossed to the door. With a reproachful glance toward Nell that was utterly wasted, he stepped outside to talk to the Watch. Returning soon thereafter, he muttered that the Watch was satisfied and grabbed Nell in time to stop her from opening the door and shouting a triumphant "I told you so!"

Conversation resumed and once it had reached a festive level again, Aldred elbowed Justin in the ribs and murmured, "So how did you 'satisfy' the Watch?" for he knew Justin well enough to feel confident that he'd not clubbed them over the heads with the queen's name.

"How do you think? I bribed them," Justin confessed quietly, and they exchanged grins, for they'd both learned by now that the less authority men had, the more likely they were to defend it jealously. But it was then that the banging began again, even louder this time.

"I'll get it," Aldred offered quickly, for Nell's outraged expression did not bode well for a peaceful resolution. Before she could object, he darted to the door. "It is not the Watch come back," he announced with palpable relief, and opened the door wide. "Someone is asking after you, Justin."

The man was a stranger. He was clad in a costly wool mantle that told Justin he was no ordinary courier; so did his self-assurance, which bordered on arrogance. "I'd been told that if you were not to be found at the cottage by the smithy, I should seek you at the alehouse," he said, drawing out a tightly rolled parchment. "This was to be delivered into your hands and yours alone."

gent communications in the past. But
be sending him messages from Germany.
it, he wondered if it could be from his father.
Justi, he dismissed that idea; the bishop had never
th learn how to reach him in London. A wax seal
from the scroll, its imprint unfamiliar to him.
ning the letter, he headed into the kitchen in search of
light and privacy.

He broke the seal and unrolled the letter as soon as he reached the hearth. The handwriting was not known to him, and his eyes flicked to the last line, seeking the identity of the sender. He caught his breath at the sight of Claudine's name, elegantly inscribed across the bottom of the page. He read rapidly by the flickering light of the kitchen fireplace, then went back and read it a second time.

"Justin?"

His head coming up sharply, he saw Nell standing in the doorway. "I do not mean to pry," she said. Not even Nell could carry that off with a straight face, and her lips were twitching. "All right, I do. But it is my experience that mysterious messages arriving in the middle of the night rarely bear good news. Does this one?"

"No, most likely not, Nell. I shall have to leave at first light. I'd be grateful if you could care for Shadow whilst I am gone."

Nell grimaced and sighed and looked put-upon, but eventually agreed, as they both knew she'd do. "At least tell me where you'll be going."

Justin glanced down at the letter again. "Dover," he said, "where I'll be taking ship for France."

IN HIS TWENTY-ONE YEARS, JUSTIN HAD NEVER SET FOOT ON shipboard, and he'd have been content to go to his grave without ever having that experience. He'd done his best to make the trip tolerable, seeking out a priest to be shriven even before booking passage, and then searching for the dockside alehouse frequented by the crew of his ship, the *Holy Ghost*. It was easy enough to befriend the sailors, taking no more than an offer to buy them an ale, and by the time he was ferried out to their ship, he had earned an exemption from the casual contempt that sailors worldwide bestowed upon their land-loving passengers.

His alehouse companions found him a sheltered spot on deck, pointed out the steering oar that acted as a rudder, and showed him how the compass worked—a needle magnetized by a lodestone, then placed on a pivot in a shallow pan of water. One even shared a pinch of ground ginger, swearing it would settle his stomach and keep him from feeding the fish. Justin was grateful for their goodwill. It did not make the voyage any less unpleasant for him, though. He shuddered every time the ship sank into a slough, holding his breath until it battled its way back. The ship was so low in the water that he was doused with sea spray, chilled to the very marrow of his bones, but the sailors insisted that his queasiness would worsen within the crowded, rank confines of the canvas tent set up to shelter the passengers, where men were "puking their guts up" and there was not room enough to "swing a dead cat." So Justin stayed out on the deck, bracing himself against the gunwale of the *Holy Ghost* and clinging to the Infinite Mercy of Almighty God.

JUSTIN HAD CHOSEN THE PORT OF DOVER OVER SOUTHAMPTON because of its closer proximity to London. Claudine's letter had been sparing with details, but her urgency had been unmistakable. Trouble was brewing, she'd written, and she entreated him to make haste to Paris if ever he'd loved her. Had her family learned about Aline? Had she confided in her cousin Petronilla, only to be betrayed? If she had indeed been disowned by her father and brothers, he did not know what he could do to heal so grievous a wound. He had to try, though. To ease her fears of childbirth and disgrace, he'd promised her that he would always be there when she and Aline had need of him. If that meant Paris and a hellish sea voyage, so be it.

The *Holy Ghost* took more than twelve hours to cross the Channel, entering Boulogne harbor that night with the incoming tide. Justin had seen few sights as beautiful to him as the beacon fire lit in the old Roman lighthouse on the hill overlooking the estuary. The customs fee demanded of disembarking passengers was outrageously high, but Justin paid it without complaint, so eager was he to get back upon ground that did not tremble and quake like one of Nell's egg custards. The next morning he purchased a horse, too impatient to bargain the price down by much, and took the road south toward Paris.

Four days later, Justin saw the walls of Saint-Denis in the distance, and his spirits rose, for he'd been told the abbey was only seven miles from Paris. Regretting that he could not spare the time to visit the magnificent abbey church, he resolutely pushed on. The road wound its way through open fields and vineyards, deserted and barren under an overcast sky. He had chosen a well-traveled road, though, one paved by long-dead Roman engineers, and he did not lack for company. Heavily laden carts, messengers on lathered horses, pilgrims with sturdy ash-wood staffs, beggars, merchants, soldiers, an occasional barefoot penitent, dogs, several elderly monks on mules, peddlers, a raucous band of students, and a well-mounted lord and his retinue—all converging upon Paris, paying scant heed to the body dangling from a roadside gallows, for the end of their journey was at hand.

Several years earlier, the French king had begun replacing the wooden stockade that sheltered the Right Bank of the Seine with a wall of stone. It was soon within view, and the weary travelers surged forward, eager to reach the city before darkness descended. After paying the toll, Justin was allowed to pass through the gate of Saint-Merri. Although Claudine's letter had been vexingly terse, she had at least provided directions to her cousin Petronilla's town house, located there on the Right Bank.

He had no difficulty finding it for it overlooked a large, open area called the Grève, the city's wine market. All he'd known about Petronilla was that she was wed to a much older French lord, and divided her time between their estates in Vermandois and their residence in Paris. Now he knew, too, that her husband was wealthy. Most urban dwellings were constructed at right angles to the street, for it was cheaper to build that way. This house was different. Its great hall was parallel to the street, set back in its own courtyard, flanked by stables and a kitchen and other wooden buildings. Dismounting, Justin found himself hesitating to enter, for Claudine's lavish lodgings were yet further proof of the great gulf between her world and his.

HE WAS ADMITTED AT ONCE, AND within moments, Claudine was hastening into the great hall to bid him welcome. "How it gladdens my eyes to see you, Justin!" Her time in Paris seemed to have suited Claudine, for she looked rested and relaxed, not at all like a woman in peril. But his questions would have to wait, for her cousin had followed her into the hall.

Petronilla had none of Claudine's dark, sultry beauty, but she was elegant and graceful and vivacious, obviously an old man's pampered darling who had the wit to recognize her good fortune. She greeted Justin with surprising warmth. He'd not expected her to approve of Claudine's liaison with a man who was not even a knight. Claudine must have taken her cousin into her confidence, though, for she was making no attempt to hide their intimacy, linking her arm in his as she led him toward the stairwell, insisting that he must be hungry and bone-weary and in need of tender care.

He was ushered into a comfortable bedchamber abovestairs, lit by thick wax candles and heated by a charcoal-filled iron brazier. A servant was pouring warm water into a washing laver, and a platter had already been set out on a table, piled with bread and thick slices of beef. When he tried to speak, Claudine gently placed her finger to his lips.

"We'll talk later. Rest for a while first. You've had a long journey." She beckoned to the servant and slipped away before Justin could respond. As the door closed quietly behind her, he removed his mantle, slowly unbuckled his scabbard. There was a wine cup on the table. Picking it up, he took a swallow; as he expected, it was an expensive vintage. A pair of soft leather shoes lay neatly aligned by the side of the bed. They were very stylish, fastened at the ankle with a decorative brooch, and familiar to him. It was only then that he realized Claudine had taken him to her own bedchamber.

JUSTIN HADN'T MEANT TO SLEEP, BUT the bed was invitingly close at hand, and he'd been in the saddle since dawn. When he awoke, one glance at the marked candle told him that he'd been asleep for several hours. He swung off the bed, hastily groping for his boots. He was still groggy, but splashing his face with water from the laver helped. After cleaning away the dust and road grime of the past few days, he collected his scabbard and mantle and stepped out into the stairwell.

Claudine was awaiting him in the great hall. "I was beginning to fear you'd sleep till the week's end," she teased. "No matter, though. You're awake now, so we can talk. Let's go up to Petronilla's solar where we can have privacy."

Justin was more than willing, for none of this made sense so far. If she were in some sort of danger, why did she seem so nonchalant? And if she were not, why had she summoned him with such urgency? He was done with waiting, and as soon as they entered the solar, he said, with poorly concealed impatience, "Claudine, what is going on? Why did you send for me?"

His answer did not come from Claudine. As the door closed behind them, a figure stepped from the shadows, into the flickering circle of light cast by a smoking oil lamp. "Well, actually, de Quincy," John said affably, "I was the one who sent for you."

CHAPTER IV

January 1194
Paris, France

"I hope you are not angry with me for my little deception, Justin." Claudine was giving him her most irresistible smile, the one that set her dimples to flashing like shooting stars. "Lord John said that he had an urgent matter to discuss with you and he doubted that you would have agreed to come if he had asked you. I'll not blame you for being irked, but he convinced me that this was the best way to do it..."

His utter silence was beginning to erode some of her self-confidence. "Justin?" She reached out to stroke his arm and gasped when he jerked away from her touch. By then John was at her side, gently cupping her elbow and turning her toward the door as he expressed his gratitude. Before she could protest, she found herself out in the stairwell, listening to the latch slide into place.

"She'll probably hover by the door," John predicted cheerfully. "There's not a woman born who could resist the chance to eavesdrop. There is wine over there, and ale, too, as Claudine says you've a liking for it."

He started toward the table, stopping when Justin recoiled, dropping his hand to the hilt of his sword. "What—you think I got you here to do you harm? Good God, man, use your common sense. If I wanted you dead—"

"You did want me dead!"

John paused. "Well, yes, I suppose so," he conceded. "I'll not deny that I did tell Durand to kill you. But that was not personal, de Quincy. I was simply trying to protect my aunt."

"Very gallant of you, my lord," Justin snarled, and John's eyebrows rose.

"I like to think so." Moving toward the table, he observed, "I am not about to lunge at you, am merely pouring myself a drink. I'd offer you one, too, but I fear you might fling it in my face." Taking a swallow of wine, he regarded Justin thoughtfully over the rim of his cup. "Time for some blunt speaking, I see. Yes, I did give Durand that command. You know it, I know it, and by now, I expect my lady mother knows it, too."

She didn't, but Justin was not about to tell him that. He was still badly shaken, not only by John's ambush and Claudine's betrayal, but by the surge of hot, raw rage that had flooded his brain and submerged his self-control. He'd learned at an early age to keep his emotions under a tight rein, for a runaway temper was an indulgence few orphans could afford. Life could be cruel to the weak and the innocent. Nor was it kind to the unwary or the careless. In the world he'd grown up in, men paid dearly for their mistakes—unless they were fortunate enough to have the royal blood of England coursing through their veins.

"Put yourself in my place, de Quincy. What was I to do—let you go free to tell my mother that my aunt Emma had been plotting with me against her beloved Richard? If you'd been a more reasonable sort, I could have bought your silence. An argument might even be made that you brought some of your troubles upon yourself by being so incorruptible, so damnably honest."

It was one of John's saving graces that he found humor in the un-likeliest places, pools of water in the driest deserts, and Justin had long suspected that this was one reason he'd so often been able to beguile his way back into Eleanor's favor. Even Claudine's playful nickname for him, "the Prince of Darkness," hinted at the seductive nature of his sins. But his sardonic charm was wasted upon Justin. "Out of morbid curiosity," he said coldly, "how did Durand explain his failure to murder me?"

"As Durand told it, he was overpowered by a score of Welshmen masquerading as monks. Why? Is there more to the tale than that?"

"No," Justin said grudgingly. Leave it to Durand to tell just enough of the truth to save his worthless skin. Justin's loathing for Queen Eleanor's spy made his distrust of John seem positively benign in comparison, yet he could deny neither the other man's ice-blooded courage nor his unholy quickness of wit. Strangely enough, he did believe John's claim that he'd been seeking to shield Emma from exposure. But he could find no excuses at all for Durand's willingness to obey that lethal order.

John made another casual offer of wine, shrugging at Justin's terse refusal. "So... where was I? Ah, yes, complaining about your unwillingness to take bribes. It is not as if I bore you some bitter, vengeful grudge, de Quincy. Since the risk of death is a natural hazard of your precarious profession, I do not see why you are taking this so much to heart. Hellfire, man, you won, did you not? You thwarted Durand, outwitted Davydd and Emma, recovered the ransom, and probably even earned a few words of my lady mother's sparing praise. Now that I think about it, I am more the injured party than you are!"

Justin was not amused. "Why did you lure me here, my lord John?"

"Must you make it sound so underhanded and sly?" John protested, the corner of his mouth twitching. "I need your help, de Quincy. It is urgent that I speak with Emma as soon as possible. I want you to deliver a letter from me, convince her if she has qualms, and escort her safely to Paris."

Justin shook his head in disbelief. "You cannot be serious. I am the last man in Christendom whom the Lady Emma would heed."

"I agree that she has no fondness for you. But you are the also the queen's man, as she well knows. She'll not dare refuse you."

In spite of himself, Justin felt a flicker of interest stirring. So John wanted the cover of the Crown. What was he up to and what part did Emma play in his scheme? "Why would I ever agree?"

"I can make it well worth your while." John did not elaborate, nor did he need to. They both knew he was offering more than a pouch full of coins. He was offering, too, the favor of a future king. Richard had no heirs of his body. If he died before he sired a son, a distinct possibility for a man who flirted with Death on a daily basis, there were two claimants for his crown—his brother John and his nephew Arthur, the six-year-old son of his dead brother Geoffrey and Geoffrey's highborn widow, Constance, Duchess of Brittany. The smart money was on John.

"I serve the Queen's Grace, and I somehow doubt that her interests and yours are likely to coincide."

"Actually," John said, "in this case, they do."

Justin did not reply; his incredulous expression spoke for him. John frowned, for he'd hoped to avoid trusting Justin with the specifics of his plight. "I have learned that I am about to be accused of a crime I did not commit, compliments of that Breton bitch, my sister-in-law Constance."

"A crime you did not commit?" Justin echoed, with enough skepticism to deepen John's scowl.

"Is that so hard to believe? Constance would accuse me of murdering babies and drinking their blood if she thought she could discredit me in Richard's eyes."

"Or she could let you do that all by yourself."

"Damnation, de Quincy, will you listen to me? I am in trouble, and for once, none of it is my doing!"

"And that would grieve me because... ?"

"Because it would grieve my mother, you fool!"

"Would it?" Justin did not know if that was true or not, and at the moment, he did not care. He'd had enough. "That is not for me to say," he said, and started toward the door.

John moved swiftly to intercept him. "We are not done yet! At the least, you can hear me out!"

Justin discovered now that their difference in height gave him the advantage, for the queen's son had to look up to him. "No, my lord, we *are* done," he said, and pushed past John to the door.

As John had predicted, Claudine was waiting out in the stairwell. "Justin, we have to talk!"

"No, we do not," he said, and continued on down the stairs.

She followed hastily behind him. "Justin, wait! I know you are wroth with me, but you do not understand. If you'd let me explain—"

"There is nothing you can say!" As Justin shoved the door open, she caught at his arm, crying out his name. Emerging from the stairwell, they came to an abrupt halt, for all in the hall were staring at them.

"Justin, please," Claudine entreated softly. She was still clutching his arm, and when she would not release her grip, he pried her fingers loose, one by one, until he was free. He turned, then, and stalked away, ignoring her plea that he wait, that he listen. He'd almost reached the door when his gaze fell on Durand de Curzon, lounging against the wall, arms folded across his chest. As their eyes met, Durand raised his hand in a sarcastic salute.

TEMPERATURES HAD DROPPED SHARPLY WITH THE setting sun, and Justin shivered as he strode across the courtyard toward the stables. Within moments, he heard the door slam and quick footsteps sounded behind him. He spun around to see Claudine hurrying toward him.

"Go back to the hall!"

"Not until we talk!"

He continued on into the stables, with Claudine almost running in order to keep pace. "Go back inside," he snapped. Noticing for the first time that she'd neglected to take her mantle, he added impatiently, "You'll freeze out here."

"I do not care if I do!" Her defiance might have sounded more convincing if her teeth hadn't been chattering. She half expected him to offer her his own mantle, was taken aback when he did not. "Justin, why are you being so stubborn? Why will you not listen to me?"

Justin ignored her and went to look for his saddle. She trailed after him, wrapping her arms around herself in a futile attempt at warmth. "You are going to hear me out if I have to follow you across half of Paris. I met Lord John at the French court, and he asked for my help. I could hardly refuse him, Justin. You may have forgotten that he is the queen's son, but I do not have that luxury. Moreover, I saw no harm in doing what he asked. He said he needed to talk to you. Why is that so dreadful? Why are you acting as if I'd lured you into a viper's den?"

Justin whirled, angry words of accusation hovering on his lips, only to be silenced by the look of honest bewilderment on her face. Remembering just in time that she did not know what had happened in Wales. She did not know that John had passed a sentence of death upon him. Nor was she aware that her spying for John had been discovered. And the queen did not want her to know.

"Justin, talk to me, please. Tell me what I've done that is so unforgivable," she pleaded, and he stared at her mutely, overwhelmed by the burden of so many secrets. Not knowing what else to do, not trusting himself to hold his tongue, he turned away from her and fled out into the night.

THE GRÈVE WAS DESERTED AND STILL, swallowed up in shadows. The only signs of life came from the river, where several boats were moored. Justin headed in that direction, tightening his hold upon his mantle as he faced into the wind. As he'd hoped, he soon caught a glimmer of light, and followed it to a small dockside tavern. It was half empty, the only customers a sleeping sailor and several men lingering over their drinks to delay going out into the cold. Justin found a table out of range of the door's drafts and ordered a flagon.

The wine was wretched, so impure that he had to spit out sediment into the floor rushes. Shoving it aside, he made a resolute attempt to banish John and Claudine from his thoughts and focus upon where he was to spend the night. It made sense to leave his horse in Petronilla's stable; he could claim it in the morning. Curfew must be nigh, so he had no time to roam the streets in search of an inn. After some thought, he beckoned to the tavern owner, and negotiated a bed for the night. The man agreed to provide a pallet in his kitchen, but he looked as shifty as any London cutpurse, and Justin decided he'd best sleep with one eye open.

Overhearing this negotiation, one of the other customers suggested he look for lodgings at St-Gervais, by the Baudoyer Gate, and Justin was getting directions when the door was thrust open and Durand de Curzon entered. He was wearing an elegant wool mantle trimmed with fox fur, a garment that looked utterly out of place in the seedy little tavern, and he attracted a few covetous, conjectural glances. When he swaggered toward Justin, though, men moved out of his way, theirs the instinctive unease of a flock sensing a predator in their midst.

"This day keeps getting better and better," Justin said as Durand claimed a stool and a place at his table.

"You were too easy to track down," the knight announced, reaching over for the wine flagon. "Had I been a hired killer, you'd have been a lamb to the slaughter." Lacking a cup, he drank directly from the flagon, gagged, and spat into the floor rushes. "Christ on the Cross, de Quincy, I'd sooner drink horse piss!"

"What do you want, Durand?"

"I want you to fetch the Lady Emma for John and bring her back to Paris."

"And I want you to repent your multitude of mortal sins and take the Cross, pledging to walk barefoot to Jerusalem. What are the chances of that happening?"

"If you are expecting me to offer an apology for what I did in Wales, you'll still be waiting on the Day of Judgment. As I told you then, I had to choose which mattered more to the queen, that I continued to protect her son or that you continued to breathe. The hard truth, de Quincy, is that the queen needs me more than she needs you."

"So does the Devil," Justin said, pushing his stool away from the table. Once he was on his feet, though, with a clear path to the door, he paused. He did not doubt that Durand's first loyalty was to Durand, not the queen. But he also knew that the queen would have expected him to hear the other man out.

Durand correctly interpreted his hesitation. "Sit down ere you attract attention and I'll tell you what I know and why I think you ought to do as John bids you." As soon as Justin reclaimed his seat, the knight leaned forward, saying quietly, "John got a letter from Brittany that rattled him good and proper. He balked at showing it to me, saying only that Constance was contriving his destruction. But I knew his favorite hiding places, so I just bided my time until I got a chance to read it for myself. It was a message from a woman named Arzhela de Dinan, warning him that Constance had written proof that he and the Count of Toulouse's son were plotting to lure Richard to Toulouse once he is ransomed and there have him slain."

Justin caught his breath, for John was right. Such a charge could indeed be his ruin. Richard had never seemed threatened by John's attempts to steal his crown. Even in German confinement, he'd dismissed John's intrigues with laughter and a mocking comment that John was not the man to conquer a kingdom if there was anyone to offer the feeblest resistance. Justin had often marveled at how often John eluded the consequences of his treachery, concluding that fortune had thrice favored him. He benefited from his brother's amiable contempt and his mother's protection, but above all from his position as heir-apparent. Most people were willing to turn a blind eye to the misdeeds of a man who might one day be England's king.

But what if proof existed that he had connived at Richard's murder? To kill a crowned king, God's anointed, was regicide. Richard would not overlook that. Nor would Eleanor forgive. Justin suspected that John would have more to fear from the mother than from the queen, for Richard claimed her heart and John could only claim her blood.

"Two questions," he said, his eyes searching Durand's impassive, unreadable face. "Is there any chance this is true? And what have you been able to find out about this Arzhela de Dinan? How reliable is she?"

"Those are three questions," Durand pointed out. "But no, I do not see how it can be true. It is a charge that could eventually be disproved—assuming John was given the chance to disprove it. On the surface, though, it has enough plausibility to hearten his enemies and fire Richard's Angevin temper, for he has long been at odds with the lords of Toulouse. It is easy to believe that Raymond would concoct a murder plot, given the oceans of bad blood there. He is already suspect because of the heresies he and his father tolerate in their lands."

Justin knew that the Church was increasingly alarmed by the spread of a heretical doctrine that denied some of the basic tenets of the True Faith, but his knowledge went no further than that. He had more pressing concerns now than outlaw sects, and he interrupted before Durand could continue. "Tell me about the woman."

"Arzhela de Dinan's warning has to be taken seriously, for

she is well placed to know the secrets of the Breton court. She is a first cousin to Duchess Constance, and to judge by the tone of her letter, she was once John's bedmate. She told John that she has not yet seen the letter for herself, but she is sure it exists. She believes it to be a forgery, or at least pretends to believe that. I'd say John has good reason for concern. He has enough penance due for past sins without adding regicide to the list."

"But what does Emma have to do with a Breton plot?"

"I do not know," Durand admitted reluctantly. "All I've been able to get out of John is that he has sent an urgent message to his favorite spy, the Breton. But Emma's part in this remains murky. With luck, I'll have been able to find out more by the time you get back to Paris with Emma."

Opening his mouth to protest, Justin realized that there was nothing he could say. As little as he liked the idea of being drawn into John's web, he had no choice. He knew what his queen would want, what she always wanted—to save John from himself.

DURAND HAD TOLD JUSTIN THAT LADY Petronilla had invited John to spend the night, for his lodgings with the Templars were outside the city gate, now shut until daybreak. Returning to the house, he felt like Daniel going into the lions' den and wondered grimly if he'd emerge alive like Daniel or if the lions would have the mastery of him.

Claudine was not in the great hall, to his relief. But John was still there, with the Lady Petronilla fluttering about him flirtatiously. His attention was distracted, though, his thoughts obviously elsewhere, and when he noticed Justin, he jumped to his feet with betraying alacrity. Extricating himself from Petronilla's orbit, he strode toward Justin, saying, "Follow me."

He led Justin across the hall into the small oratory, the most private place he could find. As soon as he closed the door, he demanded, "Why did you come back?" eagerly enough to reveal how dismayed he'd been by Justin's abrupt departure.

Justin shrugged. "After traveling all this way, I decided I wanted to hear the end of the story."

"Then you agree to escort Emma to Paris?"

"Only if I know why you have such an urgent need to see her, my lord."

"That is not your concern," John said curtly, and Justin shrugged again.

"As you will, my lord," he said, and turned toward the door.

John impatiently waved him back. "If you must know, I need to contact the Breton. I daresay you remember him from your foray into Wales. He has never been an easy man to find, and the messages I've left for him have gone unanswered. Emma has more of a history with him than I do and she is likely to know other ways to reach him."

Justin suspected there was more to it than that. For now, though, it would do. "I will leave on the morrow. But if the lady is not willing to come, I can hardly stuff her into my saddlebag."

"She may not come for me," John admitted, surprising Justin with his candor. "But she'll come for the queen's man. Emma is a clever woman, and she well knows how urgently she needs to regain my mother's favor. Now, what will your cooperation cost me, de Quincy?"

"The queen pays me two shillings a day. For you, my lord, I would charge three, plus my expenses."

"No more than that?" John tilted his head to the side,

regarding Justin quizzically. "Why am I getting off so cheaply?"

"Because," Justin said, "I am not doing this for money. After this, you will owe me a debt, my lord, a debt I may collect at my pleasure."

"I see..." John's eyes caught the torchlight above his head, giving off a golden glitter. After a moment, he laughed abruptly. "Since when did you become so crafty, de Quincy? I think you've been passing too much time with me!"

JUSTIN WAS GIVEN BLANKETS AND HE joined the other men bedding down for the night in the great hall. He was folding his mantle to use as a pillow when he heard a light step behind him, a step he well knew.

"Justin." Claudine was standing only a few feet away. Acutely aware of the men within earshot, she said, very low, "I have too much on my mind to sleep, and will be awake very late tonight."

"I expect to be asleep very soon myself. Good night, Lady Claudine." Stretching out under the blankets, he turned his back on her, lying very still until he finally heard the soft rustle in the floor rushes as she withdrew. Her perfume lingered after she'd gone, a fragrant, ghostly reminder of all he'd rather forget. His body was treacherously tempted to accept her invitation, but he would not yield to the weakness of the flesh, not tonight. The bedchamber was her battlefield; he had no intention of giving her such a tactical advantage. He believed her avowal that she'd never meant him harm. But she was too susceptible to John's inducements. Nor had she asked the question that would have been foremost in his mind if their positions had been reversed and she had been the one coming from England to join him in Paris. Not once had she asked him about Aline.

CHAPTER V

January 1194
St Albans, England

JUSTIN WAS SPRAWLED IN BALDWIN AND Sarra's best chair, long legs stretched toward the hearth, his the boneless, easy abandon of youth, and Baldwin felt a twinge of envy, remembering when he, too, had been able to spend hours in the saddle without suffering cramps and blisters and spasms of the spine. The baby cradled in the crook of Justin's arm was sleeping peacefully, and Justin's own lashes were flickering drowsily. With an indulgent smile, Baldwin watched him fight his sleepiness. When he'd first realized how often Justin would be visiting Aline, Baldwin had been dubious, not eager to have a stranger so often under his roof, but Justin did his best to make his calls as unobtrusive as possible, and it could always have been worse. It could have been "the Lady Clarice" hovering underfoot.

"What happened to that handsome chestnut stallion of yours? Did you sell him?"

"Jesu forfend," Justin said with a smile. "I'd sooner give up a body part than I would Copper. The horse I'm riding is one

I bought in Dover. I'll sell him in Southampton ere I take ship for France."

"You do get about," Baldwin marveled. "Just back from Paris and now off to Wales and then France again. I feel bone-weary merely listening to your plans, lad."

"Me, too," Justin admitted. He was dreading this trip into Wales, so much so that he found himself tempted to confide his fears to Baldwin. He didn't, of course, for reticence was a lifetime's habit, bred into his bones even before he'd become the queen's man and the bearer of too many secrets. "I almost forgot," he said. "I bought a rattle for Aline in Boulogne. It is over there in my saddlebag..."

"Sit still," Baldwin instructed, "lest you awake the little lass. I'll fetch it." Rising with a creaking of what he ruefully called his "old bones," he soon found the rattle. Straightening up, he smiled at the sight that met his eyes, for Justin had dozed off, joining his infant daughter in sleep. Sarra had also noticed, and gently freed the baby from Justin's grasp, returning Aline to her cradle. Picking up a blanket, Baldwin tucked it around the young man's shoulders, and smiled again, this time at his wife. "I think," he said, "this might work out."

DUSK WAS BLURRING THE LAST LIGHT of day as Justin rode across the Dee Bridge and into the city of Chester. He stopped first at the castle, for he was hoping that the earl would provide him with an armed escort for his foray into Wales. He'd given Prince Davydd good reason to wish him ill, and Davydd was not a man to listen to his better instincts—assuming he had any. The earl's steward remembered Justin from past visits and he was made welcome. But when Justin asked to see the earl, the steward had disquieting, disappointing news for him. The Earl of Chester was gone from the city, gone from the country, having crossed over to his estates in Normandy and Brittany more than a month ago.

Thinking this was not an auspicious beginning to his mission, Justin sought solace at Molly's cottage. The shutters were drawn, no smoke smudged the sky over the roof, and his knocking went unanswered. Hoping that Molly was not off with Piers Fitz Turold, the wealthy vintner who was her protector and the suspected source for much of Chester's criminal activity, Justin headed for the dockside tavern owned by Fitz Turold and run by Molly's brother, Bennet.

Bennet was not there, nor was Berta, the sullen, buxom serving maid. The man pouring drinks was a stranger to Justin, a burly, scarred redhead with unfriendly eyes and a mouth like a padlock. Justin's questions about Bennet's whereabouts were met with shrugs, suspicion, and silence. Justin was not surprised by the lack of cooperation; Fitz Turold was not known for hiring Good Samaritans. He was brooding over a flagon of wine, keeping an eye peeled for Bennet when a voice bellowed in his ear, "By God, it's Ben's friend!"

The youth beaming at him was vaguely familiar, but it was the salutation Justin remembered more than the face. Algar was one of the tavern regulars, a good-natured lad with a crush on Berta and an annoying habit of addressing Justin as "Ben's friend." For once, though, Justin was glad to see him and he gestured for Algar to pull up a stool. "You always know what is going on around here, Algar. Where is Bennet? And for that matter, where is Berta?"

"Berta is home, drunker than a peddler's bitch," Algar said, grinning. "She has been ailing for days with a bad tooth. We finally coaxed her into letting the barber pull it, but she refused to do it sober and damned near drained one of Ben's kegs dry all by herself!"

"And Bennet? Is that where he is, with Berta?"

"No, Ben has been away all week. Molly went off to Dunham-on-the-Hill to tend to a friend whose time was nigh, and Ben went along to keep her safe."

"Do you know when they'll be back?"

"I suppose," Algar said, "it depends upon how fast her friend has the baby!"

JUSTIN TOOK ADVANTAGE OF HIS CONNECTION to the earl to get a bed for the night at the castle. Sleep wouldn't come, though. He'd faced danger before, greater danger than he was likely to encounter at Davydd's court. But if he died in Wales, what would happen to Aline? She would continue to be cared for; the queen and Claudine would see to that. But who would tell her about her blood-kin, her true identity? He'd lived twenty years before finding out that the Bishop of Chester was his father. All he knew about his mother was her name, and he'd only learned that a few months ago. He did not want Aline to travel down that same lonely road.

The next morning, he asked the castle steward for parchment, pen, and ink. He did not have much to bequeath. He'd drawn up a will that spring, leaving his stallion to Gunter, the blacksmith who'd once saved his life, and his dog to Nell's Lucy. His legacy to Aline must be the truth. She had the right to know her own history, her own heritage, and for several hours, he labored over a testament, trying to anticipate any questions she might have about the father she'd never known. He then wrote a brief letter to the queen, and carefully sealed both documents with borrowed wax, for the first time within memory sorry that he did not have a seal of his own.

No seal, no land, not even a name that truly belonged to him. It had not mattered that much until he had a baby daughter and nothing to leave her but regrets.

AFTER DEPARTING THE CASTLE, JUSTIN RODE straight for the Bishop of Chester's palace on the outskirts of the city. He was nervous, for encounters with his father were invariably tense. Waiting for the bishop in the entrance hall, he could not help stealing sidelong glances at the chapel, for it was there that he'd confronted Aubrey de Quincy, and there that his father had denied his paternity until challenged to swear upon his own crucifix.

He turned at the sound of footsteps, saw his father emerging from the stairwell. "Well, Justin, this is a surprise." The bishop's smile was tentative, wary. "Come with me. I've given orders to have wine fetched."

As he followed his father into the great hall, it occurred to Justin that this was the first time that the bishop had not whisked him out of sight and hearing of any witnesses. He must be feeling confident that there'd be no scenes. Justin supposed that, in an ironic sort of way, this was Aubrey's declaration of faith, as close as he was ever likely to come to acceptance.

After taking seats near the central hearth, they drank their wine in an awkward silence that was broken at last by Aubrey. "The Earl of Chester told me that you'd recovered the ransom. I imagine the queen was very pleased with your performance. Are you... are you here on her behalf?"

"Yes," Justin said, watching closely enough to catch the subtle signs of Aubrey's relief that this was an official visit. "I have to go back into Wales." Drawing the sealed letters from his mantle, he held them out to his father. "If you would make sure that these are dispatched to the Queen's Grace, I would be very grateful. I need you to wait, though, until you hear that she has returned to England. I am sorry I cannot explain why—"

Aubrey waved aside his apologies as he accepted the letters. "There is no need. You have information meant for the queen's eyes alone. I understand the confidential nature of your work," he said, and there was an approving tone to his voice that Justin had rarely heard before. Apparently the queen's favor carried weight even with a bishop.

"Thank you, my lord." Justin hesitated, taken aback by a sudden, mad urge to tell his father the truth, to tell him about Aline, the granddaughter he'd likely never see. He raised his cup hastily, drowning the impulse in a swallow of Aubrey's spiced hippocras.

The bishop had reached for his own wine cup, but he was not drinking. "There is something you need to know," he said, speaking so softly that Justin had to lean forward to hear his words. "I was sorely troubled when you told me Lord Fitz Alan had learned that you were now using the de Quincy name."

"Yes," Justin said quietly, "I remember."

Aubrey was staring down into his wine cup, fair brows furrowed. "I told him that you were a bastard son of my younger brother, Reynald. That would explain not only why you'd dared to lay claim to the name, but also why I'd gone to the trouble of placing you in his service. I thought it best that you know this since it is likely you'll be encountering him at court."

"I see." Justin did not know what else to say. He'd not thought much about his father's kindred, for what was the point? His father would never acknowledge him, never admit him into the de Quincy family circle. But those ghostly, faceless strangers had suddenly become real, made flesh and blood by the most simple of spells—the unexpected use of a given name. He had an uncle, Reynald, cousins he'd never get to know. He started to rise, then, for their business was done.

Aubrey rose, too, but he lingered for a moment longer. "God keep you safe in Wales, Justin."

"Thank you," Justin said, surprised. "Let's hope that Davydd agrees with the Almighty."

The bishop frowned. "The queen is sending you back to Davydd's court? Is that wise?"

So his father knew of Davydd's animosity. The Earl of Chester must have been more forthcoming than he'd thought. "I am not eager myself to see Davydd again," Justin conceded, "but I have no choice, as I have an urgent message for the Lady Emma."

Aubrey blinked and then his face cleared. "If it is Emma you seek, then you need not venture into Wales at all," he said with a smile. "You can find her in Shropshire, at her Ellesmere manor."

JUSTIN COULD SCARCELY CREDIT HIS GREAT good luck. Being spared a trip into Davydd's domains was like getting a reprieve on the very steps of the gallows. And Ellesmere lay less than twenty miles to the south. He'd broken his night's fast with only a cup of ale and a piece of bread, and he decided that he could treat himself to a full meal before heading into Shropshire. He re-entered the city and had just turned onto Fleshmonger's Lane in search of a cook-shop when he heard his name being shouted. Swinging about in the saddle, he saw two familiar figures hurrying toward him—the fishmonger's brats who'd banded together with a bishop's foundling to

61

navigate the shoals of a precarious Chester childhood.

Bennet was as tall and thin and supple as a mountain ash; he had the gaunt, lean look of a man who'd often gone to bed hungry. That had indeed been true in his hardscrabble youth, for he and his older sister, Molly, had been accursed with a downtrodden drudge of a mother who'd sadly vanished from their lives, and a mean drunkard of a father who'd sadly stayed. Molly was a flower grown amongst weeds, as graceful and natural and self-willed as the grey cat she so doted upon, as quick to purr or show her claws. She'd easily captured Justin's fourteen-year-old heart, and five months ago, their unexpected reunion had ended up in her bed. Now, as soon as Justin dismounted, she flung herself into his arms and kissed him with enough enthusiasm to earn a round of cheers from male passersby.

"We got back last night," she explained as soon as she had breath for speech, "and found out this morning that you'd been at the tavern!"

"Well, Drogo did not remember your name," Bennet chimed in, "but he described you as tall and dark and shifty-looking, and I said to Moll, 'Damn me if that does not sound like Justin's evil twin!' "

"Pay him no mind," Molly directed, linking her arm in Justin's and drawing him away from the noisome stench coming from the street's center gutter. "Algar was at my cottage ere cockcrow, bursting to tell his news, and we've been scouring the city for you ever since. You gave us such a scare, Justin, for I was sure you'd be long gone!"

"You almost did miss me, Molly. I ought to have been on the road into Shropshire by now, but I decided to find a cook-shop first—"

Molly wrapped her arms around his neck and rose on

tiptoe until her mouth was tantalizingly close to his own. "Are you hungry, lover?" she murmured, laughing up at him with such overdone innocence that Justin rapidly revised his travel plans. What difference could one more day make to John? Like as not, the Devil had been holding a space for him in Hell since he drew his first breath.

CHAPTER VI

January 1194
Ellesmere, England

Justin's first view of Ellesmere was an impressive one—a castle perched on a high ridge overlooking a placid lake. The scene was peaceful and pastoral, deceptively so, for this had been a Marcher lord's stronghold, often caught up in the border wars with the Welsh and the skirmishes of that unhappy time known as The Anarchy, when the country had been convulsed by a power struggle so bloody that people had whispered that Christ and his saints must surely sleep. It was a Crown property by the reign of Henry II, who had given Ellesmere to Davydd ab Owain as part of Emma's marriage portion, pleasing Davydd. Nothing would have pleased Emma, who'd been a most unwilling wife to the prince of Gwynedd.

Justin prudently chose to scout out the lay of the land before riding into the castle bailey and putting himself in Emma's power, and he halted in the village. Even the smallest hamlets usually had an alewife and Ellesmere's was a stout, fair-haired widow with a booming laugh and shrewd blue eyes. Upon spying the telltale ale-stake, Justin had drawn rein in front of her cottage and purchased a tankard of well-brewed ale, a chunk of newly baked bread, and some casual gossip about the lady of the manor.

Lady Emma was indeed in residence at the castle, the alewife affirmed, not surprising Justin with the slight emphasis she placed on Emma's title; it had been his experience that other women did not like Emma much. If he wanted to see her ladyship, though, she continued, he'd best push on toward Shrewsbury, for that was where she was to be found, enriching the town merchants at her lord husband's expense.

EVEN THOUGH IT MEANT ANOTHER FIFTEEN-MILE ride, Justin was pleased to learn that Emma was in Shrewsbury. He'd spent the first eight years of his life in that river town and knew it almost as well as he did Chester. He did not really think Emma posed the same danger as her impulsive, vengeful husband—she was much more clever than Davydd—but it would not hurt to approach her on more neutral ground than her Ellesmere manor.

Reaching Shrewsbury at dusk, he entered through the north gate. This was the only access by land, for Shrewsbury was situated in a horseshoe bend of the muddy River Severn, and it was securely guarded by a more formidable castle than Ellesmere, manned by Justin's former lord and Shropshire's sheriff, William Fitz Alan. Justin was not surprised to learn that Emma was not staying at the castle, for its accommodations were old-fashioned and Emma was particular about her comforts. Justin guessed that she'd be accepting the hospitality of Hugh de Lacy, the abbot of the prosperous Benedictine Abbey of St Peter and St Paul located on the outskirts of the town. Before he continued on to the abbey, he used his all-purpose letter from the queen—declaring him to be in her service—to secure lodgings at Shrewsbury Castle for himself and his gelding. Since he had no objection to spending John's money, he bought a sturdy horn lantern and then headed out onto the Alms Vicus, Shrewsbury's high street and major thoroughfare.

By the time he'd reached the bottom of Gombestole Street, the savory aromas wafting from cook-shops reminded him that the supper hour was nigh. He resisted the temptation to stop, though, wanting to get his interview with Emma done as soon as possible. As he hastened down the steep hill of the street called The Wyle, he found his path blocked by people milling about in the road. Weaving among them, he soon saw the cause of the delay. A cart was stuck in the middle of the thoroughfare, its wheels mired in mud. The carter was in a fury, cursing and lashing at his horse, a scrawny animal not much larger than a pony. This was such a common occurrence that few of the spectators had pity to spare for the beast. But Justin had always had a fondness for horses and underdogs, and the sight of that heaving, wheezing animal, lathered and bloodied, stirred his anger. He was shoving his way toward the cart when another man darted from the crowd and grabbed the carter's whip as he lifted it to strike again.

"Do that and by God, I'll make you eat it!" he threatened, wrenching the whip from the carter's grasp and flinging it aside. The carter was sputtering in outrage and the spectators elbowed closer, anticipating a fight. The newcomer was of only average height, several inches shorter than the carter, but he was broad-chested and well-muscled, and the coiled tension in his stance communicated a willingness to see this through to the bloody end. The carter hesitated, glancing around for allies. Not finding any, he began fumbling with the knife at his belt. It was obvious that he did not really want to unsheathe it, but Justin knew that pride and the jostling bystanders could prod him into it if the confrontation were allowed to ferment.

Swaggering forward, he said loudly, in his best Luke de Marston manner, "Who is the fool blocking the road? Carts are stacking up like firewood! What are you all waiting for—Easter? You, you, and you—"

Pointing at random to the closest men, he directed them to help him free the mired cart, and so convincing was his assumption of authority that no one thought to question it. The carthorse's champion had taken hold of the animal's reins, coaxing it on as men put their shoulders to the wheels. The cart was soon free, and he reluctantly turned the reins over to the carter. But his grey eyes blazed when the carter started to clamber up into the cart, and Justin swiftly intervened again, pointing out that the hill was a high one and the horse would do better if it did not have to lug the carter's weight, too. The carter scowled and swore under his breath. He dared not challenge Justin's under-sheriff imitation, though, and walked alongside the laboring horse as they started up The Wyle.

"You did what you could," Justin said to the carthorse's defender as they stood in the street watching the cart lumber up the hill.

"I suppose..." The other man shook his head, keeping his gaze fixed upon the slow-moving carthorse. "But you know damned well that lout will waste no time finding another switch."

"True, but the last I heard, they still hang horse thieves," Justin said, and got a stare in return, followed by a quick smile.

"Aye, so they do," the man said, conceding that the carthorse's fate was beyond his control, and then, "I am Morgan Bloet."

"Justin de Quincy."

Falling in step, they began walking down The Wyle. Justin judged Morgan to be in his early twenties. He interested Justin because he seemed such a mix of contradictions. His given name was Welsh, but his French was colloquial, with no hint of a Welsh accent. His hair was dark, but his skin was fair enough to sport a few freckles. His garb was plain but finely woven, not homespun. He had no sword, but when the carter had been groping for his knife, Justin had seen Morgan's hand drop instinctively to his left hip, where a scabbard would have been worn. He looked like a man who'd be handy in a brawl, but the carthorse's plight had moved him almost to tears. And most intriguing of all, he seemed vaguely familiar to Justin, even though he felt sure they'd never met before.

They talked amiably as they passed through the town gate and onto the bridge that linked Shrewsbury with the abbey community of St Peter and St Paul. After paying the toll, they continued on toward the abbey's gatehouse. "If you are in need of lodgings," Morgan cautioned once they'd been waved into the monastery precincts, "you're out of luck. The guest hall is full to bursting, mostly with my lady's men. Mayhap if you tell the monks that you're queasy, they'll let you have a bed in the infirmary. No, not a stomach ailment," he corrected himself, with a grin, "for then you'd get naught but broth for supper. Tell them you're feverish."

Morgan's jesting was wasted on Justin, for he'd stopped listening at the words "my lady's men." "I heard the Lady Emma was staying here. Are you in her service, Morgan?"

"Aye, I am. Not for long, just since Christmas. But she says I am the best of her grooms, and of course she is quite right!"

That explained Morgan's empathy for the abused carthorse. "I am seeking an audience with the Lady Emma," Justin said, and Morgan gave him another quick smile.

"Well, mayhap you're in luck, after all. Come, I'll try to get you in," he offered, so obviously proud of his standing in Emma's household that Justin was touched in spite of all he knew about the Lady Emma. He followed Morgan into the guest hall, and watched as the groom approached one of Emma's handmaidens on his behalf. He was back so soon that Justin knew his news could not be good.

"Lady Mabella says Lady Emma is dining with Abbot Hugh, so you'll have to wait till the morrow. Let's see if we can talk the hosteller into squeezing you in with the other grooms—"

"You!" There was so much fury in that one word that Justin and Morgan both spun around in alarm. At the sight of the wrathful figure limping toward them, Justin suppressed a sigh, for Oliver was no stranger to him. The aging Norman knight was Emma's faithful retainer, bodyguard, and co-conspirator, perhaps the one man whom she truly trusted.

"I cannot believe my own eyes! That you would dare to show your face after all the grief you caused my lady!"

I know; it was very unchivalrous of me to thwart her plans to steal the king's ransom. The sarcastic retort hovered on Justin's lips and he had to bite the words back, for Emma and John's scheme had not been publicized; John's crimes rarely were. "At the risk of being rude, I do not answer to you, Sir Oliver."

Oliver's mouth thinned. "Ah, yes, I know. You answer only to the queen. But you also answer to the Almighty, and that day of reckoning may be sooner than you think!"

By now they'd become the center of attention. Several monks were rapidly approaching, and Justin decided that a strategic retreat was in order. Morgan was staring at him, but he did not acknowledge their acquaintanceship in front of the furious Oliver, and Justin gave him credit for good sense.

While avoiding the appearance of haste, he exited the hall before the monks could descend upon him.

Outside, he paused to consider his options, concluding that he had no choice but to return the next day. Before leaving the monastery, he slipped into the great abbey church and offered a prayer at the altar of St Winifred, or Gwenfrewi, for he'd become fond of the little Welsh saint who'd died in defense of her honor and then been reborn so long, long ago. Afterward, he decided to go back to Shrewsbury Castle, for it was now fully dark and he did not want to be shut out of the town when the gates closed.

There were still people about, all hurrying home before the curfew horn sounded, and Justin joined the flowing tide of humanity. By the time he'd retraced his steps to Gombestole Street, the crowd had thinned considerably. Making his way past a cook-shop, he remembered he hadn't yet eaten, but it was tightly shuttered.

His steps slowed as he approached the entrance to Grope Lane, for the narrow footpath was a favorite shortcut into the Fleshambles, Chepyn Street, and the town marketplace. He was tempted to take it, for the wind was picking up, but it was more than a popular haunt for street harlots. So many cutthroats lurked there after dark that locals called it Ambush Alley. Wisely bypassing this dangerous detour, Justin continued on.

Wet snowflakes were falling and the street was empty as Justin turned onto Altus Vicus. He quickened his pace, grateful that he had a meal and bed awaiting him at the castle. He knew several of the castle garrison from his years in Lord Fitz Alan's service, and if memory served, there were likely to be a few dice games going after supper.

A high-pitched scream suddenly ripped through the night's quiet. Justin whirled toward the sound, for it seemed to have come from the Fleshambles. The cry came again, and then a woman's slight figure stumbled from the darkness. She took only a few steps, though, before collapsing onto the ground.

Justin broke into a run. Even before he reached the prostrate woman, he'd flipped back his mantle to give himself swift access to his sword. Setting his lantern down on the ground, he knelt by her side. Her face was hidden by the hood of her mantle, but she moaned as he touched her shoulder.

"You're safe now," he assured her. "Are you hurt? Were you attacked?"

She gasped and clutched at his arm fearfully, then began to sob. Justin was never to know precisely what activated his sixth sense, his survival sense. Had he heard a muffled step, an indrawn breath? The sudden rush of air as the club swung downward? His body reacting before his brain realized his danger, he was already moving as his attacker rushed him.

He flung himself sideways and the blow aimed at his head glanced off his upraised arm. There was a sharp spurt of pain, but he kept rolling. A hulking form loomed over him; his lantern light caught a glimpse of bared teeth, an unkempt beard, and a thick wooden club. He kicked out, his boot connecting with flesh and bone, and the club missed him by inches. "Run!" he yelled to the woman, lurching to his feet and reaching for his sword. But his injured arm made him clumsy and his assailant was upon him before the blade could clear its scabbard.

The man's lips were drawn back in a fierce grin; he actually seemed to be enjoying himself. Justin's weapons training came to his rescue, though, for he'd been taught to counter a cut from above with a half-sword thrust. As the club was raised to strike, he dove under it and rammed his head into his foe's belly. They both went down, the club flying from the man's grip. Justin managed to get to it first, kicking it into the shadows as he succeeded in freeing his sword.

But he had no time to enjoy his triumph, for he was about to get a rude shock. The woman had shed her mantle and gown, revealing herself to be a man, albeit one as thin and puny as a beardless boy. He was gripping a full-sized dagger, though, and Justin did not fancy the odds he now faced, two to one. "End this ere someone dies," he panted, pivoting to keep both men in view. "You made a bad choice, for I have no money."

"We've already been paid!" the youth jeered, and looked offended when his companion cursed his "babbling big mouth."

By now they were deeper in the Fleshambles. Justin could see a black slit off to his right, knew it gave entry to Grope Lane. He was close enough to reach it before his adversaries, but it was so narrow that he'd have no room to use his sword. The first knave had reclaimed his club, and they were circling, wary of his blade but persisting in their attack. It was then that a man emerged from the shadows of the alley, glanced their way, and then ambled over, for all the world as if he were taking a mid-afternoon market stroll.

The felons gaped at his approach. The one with the club recovered first. "Get out of here whilst you still can, you stupid son of a whore!"

"Comments like that are uncalled for," the new arrival objected mildly, reaching down to pick up Justin's lantern, "especially when your own mother rutted with half the swine in Shropshire."

The words were not yet out of his mouth before the lantern was flying through the air, pitched with utter accuracy toward his antagonist's face. The knave threw up his arm to deflect it, losing the club as the lantern struck his shoulder, and Justin lunged forward, bringing him down with a slashing cut to the back of his leg. The boy abandoned his partner without a qualm, spinning around and taking off at a dead run. Justin's new ally had already reached the dropped club and, as the outlaw struggled to rise, the newcomer struck him with his own weapon. The outlaw crumpled, twitched, and then lay still.

"Merciful God," Justin said softly, and got a heartfelt "Amen" in return. The lantern's light had been extinguished when it took flight, but they were close enough now for recognition. Stepping back, Justin regarded Morgan Bloet in openmouthed amazement. "I never thought I had a guardian angel of my own, but how else can I explain your turning up like this?"

"I do not suppose you'd believe that I was just passing by? No, I thought not. You are entitled to an explanation, and I am willing to offer one. But first we ought to decide what we want to do with Cain here," Morgan said, nudging the body at his feet with the tip of his boot.

"Cain? You are not going to tell me that this is a friend of yours?"

"Not exactly. We do work together, if that interests you. Aye, I thought it might."

"Are you telling me this snake slithered out of Emma's den?"

Morgan grinned. "Well, I doubt I would have put it quite that way. But yes, you had the dubious pleasure tonight of meeting Oliver's favorite henchman. Two of them, in fact, for Cain's little helper works as a stable lad at Ellesmere. It must sound as if we have half the felons in the shire under our roof, but I am reasonably certain that these are the only two. Well,

I do have my suspicions about one of the cooks, for the man cannot even boil water—"

Morgan sensed rather than saw Justin's impatience, for the street was too dark for much scrutiny. "Sorry! My mama always said I'd be joking as they put the noose around my neck. As I told you, I'll answer any questions you want, provided that you answer one of mine. But I do think we ought to get out of here ere the Watch blunders by."

Justin knelt and felt for the pulse in Cain's neck. "He is still alive. More's the pity, for I cannot turn him over to the law, and I hate to turn him loose on the good people of Shrewsbury. The hellspawn came very close to killing me."

"Actually, I do not think that was his intent. At least it was not his orders. I saw Cain trailing after you when you left the abbey, and knowing the nasty work he does, knowing the nasty piece of goods he is, I decided to tag along, too."

"Thank God you did! But why do you think he did not have murder in mind?"

"First things first," Morgan said, looking down thoughtfully at Cain. "You are right. It does not seem fair to let him off with just a bump on the head and a gashed leg." Before Justin could anticipate what he was about to do, he brought his boot down hard upon Cain's open hand, grinding until they heard the crunch of bones breaking. "There," Morgan said in satisfaction. "That ought to slow him up for a while. Even Cain won't be able to wreak his usual havoc one-handed."

Justin was startled by the other man's action, but on reflection, he could find no fault with it. "Let's go," he said, and they set off across the empty market square, leaving Cain for the Watch to find. Justin was intent upon confronting Emma as soon as possible, and he was moving so rapidly that the shorter-legged Morgan was hard-pressed to keep up.

When he complained, Justin slowed his pace, but not by much. "I want to get to the abbey bridge ere they shut it for the night," he explained. "We can talk as we go. What question did you want to ask of me?"

"Are you really one of the queen's men?"

Justin confirmed he was, wishing he still had his lantern, for he'd like to have seen Morgan's reaction to that. "Go on with your story," he prompted. "You followed Cain from the abbey. What then?"

"Tiny—that is what we call the lad, for obvious reasons— Tiny ran to catch up with him, carrying a bundle under his arm. I ducked into one of the shuts in time to avoid him seeing me. Shuts are what they call byways between buildings in Shrewsbury—"

"I know," Justin cut in, marveling at how Morgan seemed able to talk without ever pausing for breath. "Go on."

"They were easy to follow, never once looked back. When they disappeared into Grope Lane, I waited and then went in after them. They were lurking at the mouth of the alley whilst Tiny was pulling something over his head. I dared not get close enough to see, thought he might be putting on a monk's habit—"

"A woman's gown."

Morgan laughed softly. "Clever! I'll have to remember that if I ever take to crime. Anyway, as they left the alley, I heard Cain say, 'Remember now. We're not to kill him, just to make him wish we had.' Of course that does not mean they could not have got carried away with zeal for their work. You see, Cain enjoys pain—other people's pain."

Remembering Cain's wolfish grin, Justin found that easy to believe. "What if he finds out you were the one who came to my aid?"

"He never got a good look at my face, and it was so dark out there, he probably could not have recognized his own father, assuming he knew who he was. Needless to say, I'd rather that Sir Oliver never hears about my part in tonight's adventures."

"He'll not hear it from me," Justin promised. The sound he'd been dreading now reached his ears—the blaring of the horns that signaled the coming of curfew to Shrewsbury. He came to a halt then, for it was too late. The town gates were closing; his reckoning with Emma would have to wait till the morrow. "You'd best come back with me to the castle, Morgan. I'll see that you get a bed there for the night. But I do have one more question." Cursing the darkness that cloaked them both so utterly, he said, "Why did you go to so much trouble for me? Mind you, I am right glad you did. But I do wonder, for not many men are so willing to risk their lives for strangers."

"Heroes always do!" Morgan protested playfully. After they'd walked a few moments in silence he said, more seriously, "It is true I do not know much about you, but what I do know, I like. You did not just look away like the others when you saw that poor nag being beaten on The Wyle. You laughed at most of my jokes. And for certes, you are a damned better man than that whoreson Cain and his little weasel!"

"Thank you," Justin said, matching the other man's light tone. But one question still lingered in the back of his mind. Had Morgan helped him because he'd heard Oliver call him the queen's man, and if so, why?

JUSTIN KNEW HE SHOULD BE GRATEFUL that he'd escaped the night's attack with so few injuries. It was difficult to remember that the next morning, though, when he awakened stiff, sore, and scraped. He told himself he was lucky that his arm was only badly bruised from wrist to elbow. But his rage still smoldered. He was bone-weary of being a target for godless men and women.

He was one of the first out of the town gate, and bypassed the abbey gatehouse, preferring to slip unobtrusively onto the monastery grounds via a wicket that opened into the monks' cemetery. As he expected, Oliver was pacing up and down before the main entrance, obviously keeping vigil for his missing henchmen and just as obviously alarmed by their continued absence. Staying out of Oliver's view, Justin found a vantage point that overlooked the guest hall, and settled down to wait.

Soon after the abbey church bells began to peal for Morrow Mass, Emma emerged from the guest hall. Justin intercepted her as she neared the chapter-house. She stopped abruptly, looking genuinely startled, but he knew how finely honed her acting skills were. "We need to talk," he said, adding "my lady" with such lethal courtesy that her eyes narrowed. Dismissing her ladies-in-waiting and other attendants, she followed silently as Justin led the way onto the small bridge over the mill-race and on into the abbey gardens.

It was a blustery morning, the sky clotted with clouds, and the gardens looked bleak and forbidding. Emma tucked her hands inside her mantle to warm them. She voiced no complaints, and the profile she turned to Justin was as delicate and translucent as the finest alabaster, and as cold. She was in her forties now, well past her youth, but she was stubbornly fighting a rearguard action against the advancing years and, so far, she seemed to be holding her own. Despite the two decades between them, Justin was not blind to her beauty, though he gave her no credit for it, thinking uncharitably that any woman blessed with good bones, fair skin, and enough servants to indulge her every whim could resist the ravages of aging as successfully as Emma.

Emma was the first to speak. Halting before the ice-glazed abbey fishponds, she said coolly, "Do you know what 'nemesis' means, Master de Quincy?"

"As a matter of fact, I do, Lady Emma. I am also familiar with the term '*Dies Irae.*' "

Her lashes lifted, unsheathing eyes bluer than sapphires, sharper than daggers. " 'Day of Judgment'? If that is meant as a threat, it is rather heavy-handed. You seem to have lost your sense of subtlety since we last met, Master de Quincy."

"Most likely I mislaid it in the Fleshambles when you set your dogs loose on me, my lady."

Her fashionably plucked eyebrows rose in perfect arches. "What in Heaven's Name are you talking about?"

"A savage mastiff named Cain and his boastful whelp, Tiny." When Emma continued to look politely puzzled, he said impatiently, "They are your hirelings, eating your bread and taking your orders, and it would be easy enough to prove it!"

"I am not denying it!" she protested. "You may well be right. You can hardly expect me to remember the names of all my servants, after all. But even if these men are mine, what of it? What are you accusing me of now?"

Justin caught a blurred movement and turned to see Oliver hovering by the bridge. "Do not be shy, Sir Oliver," Justin called out loudly. "Come and join us. We're discussing how dangerous the streets of Shrewsbury are becoming, and I daresay you have some thoughts on the matter."

The expression on Oliver's face would have been amusing under other circumstances, for he looked as if he'd swallowed his own tongue. One glance at the horrified knight was enough for Emma. "Stay right there," she commanded, as he began to back away. When Justin would have accompanied her, she flung up a hand in the imperious manner of one who was a sister and an aunt to kings. "I do not need your assistance, Master de Quincy."

Justin could have made an issue of it, but he didn't. Emma and Oliver conferred together for several moments, their heads almost touching, and even from a distance he could see the blood rushing up into Oliver's face and throat. Emma soon strode back to him, and he was struck at once by the difference in her demeanor, for her antagonism had been replaced by wariness.

"Well," she said briskly, "at least now I understand your lapse in manners. I did not tell Sir Oliver to set those men on you. I did not even know you were in Shrewsbury. Sir Oliver has been with me for many years, since my first marriage in Normandy, and he is very loyal, very protective. He ought not to have acted so rashly, but fortunately there was no great harm done."

"Fortunately," Justin echoed, with as much sarcasm as he could muster, and Emma gestured toward a bench by the water's edge. When she indicated that he could sit beside her, he knew that she was more disturbed than she'd have him believe. Queen Eleanor often allowed him to sit in her presence, but in her veins flowed the princely blood of Aquitaine and she felt no need to remind others of her lofty heritage. Emma, the out-of-wedlock issue of an Angevin count and one of his many light o' loves, clung to her royal prerogatives like a barnacle to a ship's hull. With a flicker of black humor, he wondered how she'd respond if he told her he understood her self-doubts, one bastard to another.

"I trust... I hope you do not intend to pursue this matter further with Oliver," she said, betraying her discomfort by the rising color in her cheeks, for she'd had little practice in requesting favors from inferiors. "He made a mistake, but it was done from the best of motives."

Taking Justin's incredulous silence for assent, she allowed a small sigh of relief to escape her lips. "Why are you here? I would have thought your royal mistress would be too busy securing Richard's release to have any time to spare for me. What does she want now?"

Once, Justin would have marveled that a she-wolf could see herself as the one wronged by the sheep. His dealings with John had cured him of that particular naïveté. "I have a letter for you," he said, and reached for the leather pouch clipped to his belt.

Emma's eyes widened at the sight of the wax seal, obviously recognizing it as John's. She read in silence, her head bent over the parchment. When she looked up at Justin, he thought he could detect curiosity and possibly even relief in her eyes. "I assume that the queen has an interest in this outcome, since you are the bearer of Lord John's letter."

Justin regarded her impassively. "You could assume that."

Emma looked down at the message again. "You truly do stand high in the queen's favor, Master de Quincy, if she trusts you with matters of this... nature," she said, and when she glanced up at him, it was with a grudging respect, the acknowledgment that he was a more significant piece on the chessboard than she'd first thought.

"What is your answer, my lady? Will you be returning with me to Paris?"

"Yes," she said, "I will," and Justin did not know whether to be glad of that.

Rising in a swirl of skirts, Emma began to pace. "There is so much to do. I suppose if I send to Ellesmere straightaway, I might be able to leave on the morrow. I may be able to buy some of what I need in Shrewsbury... If I take Oliver and Lionel and several men-at-arms..."

She was obviously thinking aloud, Justin's presence forgotten. But the mention of Oliver's name pricked him in a place still sore from the night's attack. "Oliver? I do not fancy going on the road with the man responsible for ambushing me!"

She turned in surprise. "Do not be silly. It is not as if Oliver wielded the club himself!" she pointed out, giving Justin an unexpected and unsettling insight into the thought processes of those with power enough to insulate themselves from the consequences of their actions.

EMMA HAD PROMISED SHE'D BE READY to leave on the morrow, and taking her at her word, Justin showed up as soon as the abbey gate was unbarred. The first person he saw was Morgan, who came hurrying toward him.

"Guess what?" he said, barely containing himself until Justin had swung from the saddle. "I am to go with you and my lady to Paris! She said she'd need a man who is good with horses."

His grin was contagious, impossible to resist, and Justin grinned back. "Ah, but are you good with ships?"

Morgan dismissed that drawback with an airy wave of his hand. "If I can drink the swill that passes for wine at the Doggepol Street tavern, I can survive a sea voyage. Speaking of queasy stomachs, Sir Oliver will not be accompanying us, after all. It seems he ate something putrid, and the poor soul has been sick as a dog all night, groaning and moaning and clutching his belly in a truly pitiful manner."

Justin studied Morgan thoughtfully. "Did he, indeed?"

The groom met his eyes innocently, the ghost of his grin still tugging at the corners of his mouth. "Is that all you have to say? You are not going to tell me that you'll miss old Oliver's company, are you?"

"No... I am thinking that you'd make a bad enemy, Morgan."

The other nodded as if he'd been given a great compliment. "Aye, that I would. But I also make a good friend."

Justin nodded, too. "Yes, you do," he agreed readily, wishing he could be sure which one Morgan was.

CHAPTER VII

January 1194
Paris, France

Justin's third Channel crossing was no less unpleasant than his first two had been. By the time their cog had entered Barfleur harbor, he'd decided that sailors were either the bravest men in Christendom or the most demented. But twelve queasy shipboard hours was only one toll on the costly, dangerous, and discomforting road to Paris. Never before had he traveled with someone who was the wife of a prince and the aunt of a king, and he earnestly hoped that he'd never have to do so again.

Emma had insisted upon an entourage: her handmaiden Mabella, her tiny, feathery lapdog, the young knight Lionel, who was substituting for the ailing Oliver, her groom Morgan, and three men-at-arms, Rufus, Jaspaer, and Crispin. She'd insisted, too, upon transporting their horses across the Channel, for she was accustomed to riding the well-bred Belle, her favorite palfrey, and was disdainful of the caliber of mounts offered for sale in French ports. Horses were even less enthusiastic about sea travel than Justin was, and had to be blindfolded before they could be coaxed onto the gangway; once on board they would have to be separated by hurdles and fitted with canvas belly slings to keep them on their feet. Consequently, not all ships' masters were willing to accept live cargo, and it had taken additional time to find a suitable vessel.

Justin had once been told an amazing story about Hannibal, an enemy of ancient Rome who'd somehow got elephants over the Alps. He'd never understood what had possessed Hannibal to attempt such a mad undertaking until now. Hannibal and the Lady Emma were kindred spirits, so single-minded in the pursuit of their own interests that nothing else mattered to them. And like Hannibal's unfortunate elephants and Emma's hapless horses, he was being dragged along against his will, feeling as powerless as those poor beasts of burden.

DARKNESS HAD DESCENDED BY THE TIME they reached Paris, and the city gates were closed for the night. Fortunately for them, John was staying at the Temple, the sprawling compound of the Templars in the Barres, just east of the Baudoyer Gate, and they had no need to enter the city itself. Justin was glad, for he had no desire to pass the house on the Grève where Claudine was living with her cousin. It was with a vast sense of relief that he escorted Emma into the guest hall to be warmly welcomed by John. As they disappeared into the stairwell in search of privacy, Justin sprawled in the closest window seat and, too tired even to eat, promptly fell asleep.

He was awakened when John sent a servant down into the hall in search of Durand. The knight smirked at Justin as he headed for the stairs, obviously seeing the summons as some sort of victory, and as Justin slid back into sleep, he decided that Durand was as deranged as any sailor. The next thing he knew, Durand was looming over him, scowling. "Get up, de Quincy," the knight said curtly. "He wants to see you now."

JOHN WAS PERCHED ON THE EDGE of a table, wine cup in hand. Emma was seated in a high-backed chair, as close as she could get to a charcoal brazier. Durand was in his favorite position, leaning against a wall in a deceptively languid pose, utterly motionless except for his eyes. Justin sat stiffly upon a wooden bench, making no attempt to disguise either his wariness or his reluctance to be there.

John had been more forthcoming than in their earlier meeting, telling Justin much of what he'd already learned from Durand. He freely acknowledged that Arzhela de Dinan was his source, admitted that Constance and the Breton court planned to accuse him of plotting Richard's murder, insisted that he was innocent, and ignored Justin's involuntary muttered "For once." He had yet to hear from the Breton, he revealed, although Emma had kindly shared several other ways to contact the celebrated spy.

Justin had never met the Breton face-to-face—few men had—but he'd learned more about the man since discovering his role as the go-between in John and Emma's scheme to steal Richard's ransom. The Breton was a legend at royal courts throughout Christendom, known for his expertise at surveillance and espionage, although it was rumored he had other, darker skills for hire. The mystery swirling about him— not even his name was known for sure—was part of his mystique. Justin understood why John would seek the Breton's aid. But he did not understand why he'd been summoned to John's presence or why the queen's son was suddenly being so candid. Why did he have to know all this?

"Lady Arzhela has sent me a second letter," John continued,

"in which she confides she means to find out more about this plot. I advised her against this, warning her that it might be dangerous, but she is not likely to listen to me. Lord knows, she never did," John allowed, with a faint, nostalgic smile that made Justin wonder about the nature of his past involvement with Arzhela. Expressing concern for her safety, John actually sounded sincere.

"Lady Arzhela is a remarkable woman," John said, still in that mellow, reminiscing tone. "She has many admirable qualities, but caution is not one of them. She makes a habit of jumping from the fry pan into the fire and never even notices the heat. She needs looking after, in other words. Fortunately," he added, with a mocking glance at Durand, "I have someone in mind. Sir Durand is going to escort Lady Emma to Laval and then continue on into Brittany to confer with Lady Arzhela to find out what she has been able to discover and keep her out of harm's way."

"I wish him well," Justin said, starting to rise. "If that is all, my lord... ?" He did not really expect to make his escape so easily, and was not surprised when John waved him back onto the bench. He still did not know what was coming, only that he'd not like it.

"Do you not want to know why Lady Emma is going to Laval? My real reason for needing to talk to her?"

Justin had rarely heard a question so fraught with peril and he slowly shook his head.

John grinned. "You need not feign indifference with me, de Quincy. I know you're afire with curiosity. Lady Arzhela gave me the names of the men involved in Constance's scheme. One of them happens to be Emma's son Guy. It occurred to me that the lad could use some maternal counsel, and Lady Emma is in agreement with me about that."

Emma narrowed her eyes, murmuring something under her breath too softly for Justin to hear. Her expression did not bode well for Guy, though. Justin knew that Emma had been wed to a Norman lord, Guy de Laval, and that after she was widowed, her brother, King Henry, had compelled her to marry the Welsh prince, Davydd ab Owain. Twenty years later, that was still a festering grievance with her, and since Henry was beyond earthly retribution, she'd passed on her rancor to the next generation, to his son Richard. Justin cast her a speculative glance, wondering about the source of her discontent. Was she angry with Guy for involving himself in such high-stakes intrigue? Or for doing it without consulting her beforehand?

"So," John said, "now you know it all. Get a good night's sleep, de Quincy, for you'll be leaving on the morrow." He saw Justin's sharp look, and said smoothly, "I forgot to mention that, did I? Lady Emma wants you to accompany her."

Justin suffered a sudden crick in his neck, so hastily did he swing around to stare at Emma. "Good God, why? I ought to be the last man whose company you crave!"

"Very amusing, Master de Quincy," Emma said, not sounding amused at all. "I may not like you, but you've proven yourself to be quick-witted, intrepid, and in your own infuriating way, honorable. I prefer to put my trust in a man I know, the queen's man," she concluded coolly, with a dismissive glance toward the man she did not know, her nephew's man.

Durand said nothing, but even his vaunted self-control could not prevent the surge of angry color that rose in his face and throat. Justin took a moment to enjoy the other man's discomfiture, and then did something he'd never expected to do—offer up praise for Durand de Curzon.

"I know Sir Durand does not always make a favorable first impression. I can vouch for him, though, my lady. He wields a sword with deadly skill and few men are as comfortable dealing with the lawless and the ungodly."

John chuckled into his wine cup, and Durand glowered at Justin, but Emma merely shrugged. "I did not mean to disparage Sir Durand," she said, with an indifference more wounding than simple contempt. "But I will feel more comfortable if Master de Quincy escorts us."

The tone of her voice made it obvious that she considered the matter closed. Rising to her feet, she said, "I assume quarters have been prepared for us, John? I will leave you, then, and retire for the night." Waiting until John summoned a candle-bearing servant, she swept from the chamber in a departure as queenly as any Eleanor herself could have made.

There was a long and heavy silence after Emma had gone. Well aware that Justin's eyes were boring into his back, John turned reluctantly to face him. "I know," he said before Justin could speak, "I know. I owe you, de Quincy."

So, too, Justin thought unhappily, did the Queen's Grace.

JUSTIN AWOKE THE NEXT MORNING IN a grim mood. He was not sure which he minded more, being sucked deeper into John's quagmire or facing another fortnight of catering to the Lady Emma's aristocratic whims. The only consolation he could take from his plight was the realization that Durand was in an equally dark frame of mind. Even the cheerful, irrepressible Morgan was downhearted, disappointed that they'd be leaving Paris so soon. But the atmosphere in the guest hall changed, although not for the better, with Emma's entrance.

The Lady Mabella was ailing, she announced, burning with fever and as feeble as any newborn. Her handmaiden had been feeling poorly since they landed at Barfleur. Justin had got the impression from Morgan and the men-at-arms that Mabella was always complaining about one malady or another. That her illness was genuine now, none could doubt; Emma was not one for coddling those in her service. Their journey would have to be delayed until Mabella was well enough to travel, Emma declared, for she could not do without a handmaiden. Nor could she leave Mabella to languish in the Templars' care, for they were knights, not nursemaids. No, she insisted, overriding John's objections with an impatient wave of her hand, they would just have to wait.

That pleased no one except Morgan, who brightened at the prospect of getting to explore Paris, after all. Durand was in favor of setting out anyway, arguing that Mabella could recuperate at the Hôtel-Dieu, which was said to be the finest hospital in Paris, and adding snidely that he had every confidence that the Lady Emma would be able to brush and braid her own hair and buckle her own shoes. Emma retorted scornfully that she would never consider leaving a gently born lady in a public hospital, nor did she care to debate the matter with one of Lord John's hirelings. Listening morosely from a window seat, Justin fantasized about slipping away while they were squabbling and riding for the coast as if the Devil were on his tail.

It was John who put an end to the quarreling and came up with a feasible solution to their dilemma. He would send to the Lady Petronilla, he stated in a voice that brooked no further arguments, and ask her if she could spare one of her maids to attend Lady Emma, at the same time requesting her hospitality for the stricken Mabella. As he was shrewd enough to mention both Emma's rank as a princess and her blood-ties to the English Royal House in his message, none doubted that Petronilla would be more than happy to comply. And indeed, she responded with alacrity, arriving at the Temple in less than an hour's time, creating quite a stir with an escort that the French king would not have spurned, a richly accoutred horse litter for Mabella, a pretty, dark-eyed young girl named Ivetta for Emma, and her beautiful cousin, Claudine.

PETRONILLA WAS FLIRTING WITH JOHN. DURAND was sulking. Mabella had been taken away in the horse litter to convalesce as Petronilla's houseguest. Claudine and Emma were making polite, desultory conversation. And Justin was doing his best to keep the length of the hall between Claudine and himself. But then John joined Emma and Claudine, and beckoned both Durand and Justin to his side.

Compelled by courtesy to acknowledge Claudine's presence, Justin greeted her with the averted eyes and rigid demeanor of a monk finding himself in close proximity to Eve. Durand, however, played the courtier's role with his usual panache, snatching up Claudine's hand and kissing it with a lover's intimacy. She murmured "Sir Durand" with what passed for a smile, but as soon as she'd freed her hand from his grasp, she wiped it against the skirt of her gown. Her insult could only have been more overt had she spat in his face, and Durand drew a breath as sharp as any sword. Justin looked away to hide a smile, remembering that Claudine's loathing of Durand was one of her more endearing attributes.

Emma had noticed this byplay, but ignored it since neither Claudine nor Durand were of any interest to her. "I am beholden to you and your cousin, Lady Claudine. Your kindness will not be forgotten." Her expression of gratitude was gracefully rendered, if somewhat formulaic in tone, and she inclined her head graciously, obviously expecting equally polished banalities in return.

But Claudine had grown tired of trading polite platitudes and she chose that moment to reveal her real reason for accompanying Petronilla to the Temple. "It was our pleasure, Lady Emma. I think you will be pleased with Ivetta; my cousin says she is very skillful at styling hair. I regret to say that she is not as well-born as your Lady Mabella, though, not truly suitable as a companion for a lady of your stature."

Emma accepted the compliment with a bored smile. "Well, since I must make do with your Ivetta—"

"Did Lord John tell you that I am one of the gentlewomen in attendance upon Queen Eleanor? Since you are my lady queen's sister by marriage, I cannot in good conscience allow you to be treated with less than your just due. I am suggesting, therefore, that I accompany you as I have so often accompanied my queen."

There was an abrupt silence. Emma looked dubious, John amused, and Durand and Justin appalled. "No!" they both cried out in unison, in what was the first and probably the only moment in which they were in such utter and perfect accord.

Emma's finely arched brows rose even higher. "I do believe that Sir Durand and Master de Quincy would rather you do not come with us, Lady Claudine." Her gaze moved from Claudine to the men, back to the girl again, and then she smiled, a smile that was almost feline in its detachment, its charm, and its silky malice. "My dear, I am delighted to accept your kind offer."

Justin and Durand were speechless, but John was no longer able to stifle his mirth. "When I draw my last breath," he said, his voice husky with laughter, "I daresay I will have many regrets. And one of them is sure to be that I had to miss this pilgrimage to Hell and back!"

CHAPTER VIII

January 1194
Laval, Maine

As Laval came into view, Emma drew rein. Her face was impassive as she gazed upon her late husband's lands, but Claudine noticed the shadow of a smile in the corners of her mouth. "It must feel good to be home," she said softly. Emma gave her a look of surprise, and then nodded.

Justin observed their quiet exchange with a sense of unease, for he'd not expected this to happen. Women did not like Emma, and she did not seem to like them; again and again he'd seen evidence of that. He never imagined that this odd alliance would develop between Emma and Claudine. He was not even sure if "alliance" was the right word. But by the time they'd reached Laval, the two women had obviously reached some sort of understanding, and he was not at all comfortable with their unlikely rapport.

He was not happy, either, with what they found at Laval. Emma's son Guy was absent, and no one seemed to know where he had gone. His steward thought he might be in Rennes, and Justin and Durand wanted to forge ahead into

Brittany, arguing that they could look for Guy at the same time that they sought Arzhela. But Emma wanted to wait at Laval for her son to return. After much acrimonious bickering, she agreed to continue on to Rennes, although she flatly refused to depart on the morrow. And so the next day found them still at Laval, glumly watching Emma entertain a steady stream of neighbors as word spread of her return.

Justin was bored and restless, until a chance conversation with the abbot of Clermont set his temper ablaze. Stalking away in anger, he went to look for Durand. He found the knight in a window seat with Emma's borrowed maid, Ivetta, murmuring in the girl's ear and making her blush prettily and giggle behind her hand. "Meet me in the village tavern," Justin said tersely, turning on his heel before Durand could object.

THE CASTLE AT LAVAL HAD LOOMED over the River Mayenne for almost two hundred years, a village nesting in its shelter. Justin knew there would be at least one tavern and located it in an alley off the market square. It was crowded, for Laval was on the main road from Paris to Brittany, and locals vied with merchants, pilgrims, and rough-hewn mercenaries for the attention of the harried serving maids and a bevy of perfumed and rouged prostitutes. Justin got himself a drink and eventually laid claim to a newly vacant table, where he settled down to await Durand.

He soon spied a familiar face. Morgan smiled in recognition and meandered over to join him. "Who are you hiding from, Justin, Lady Emma or Lady Claudine?"

"Both of them," Justin admitted with a wry smile, for when he'd not been dealing with Emma's complaints and demands on their journey, he'd been avoiding Claudine's overtures.

Nothing explicit; Claudine was too worldly for that. A sidelong smile that liberated her dimples, a flutter of long, silky lashes, a sudden, smoky glance from dark, doe eyes. Justin had not been sleeping well at night.

"She is a beautiful woman, the Lady Claudine," Morgan observed blandly. When Justin merely shrugged, he took the hint and began enthusing about the fine quality of the horses he'd found in Lord Guy de Laval's stables. He was telling Justin about a jewel of a roan mare when one of the prostitutes sauntered over.

"I am called Honorine," she announced without preamble, "and if you seek value for your money, you need look no further."

Justin was amused, both by her bluntness and her name. Whores usually chose fancy names like Christelle or Mirabelle or the ever-popular Eve. This girl had a sense of humor, for Honorine was a form of Honoria, a derivative of the Latin word for "honor." Instead of giving a flat refusal, therefore, he offered her a friendly smile and a diplomatic "Mayhap later."

Morgan looked offended when Honorine drifted away without propositioning him, too. "Well, damnation, did I become invisible of a sudden? What do you have that I lack, de Quincy?"

"A sword?" Justin suggested, recognizing a golden opportunity when he saw one, a chance to tease Morgan while at the same time engaging him in a discreet interrogation. Morgan shot him a look of such exaggerated indignation that he had to laugh. "No, you dolt, not that sword; this one," he said, slapping the scabbard at his hip. "A girl in her trade looks for evidence that a man can afford her services, and a sword is usually a good indication that he can." He paused before adding casually, "It would not hurt to have another armed man along. Can you wield a sword, Morgan?"

"Me?" Morgan sounded surprised. "Now how would a stable groom learn a skill like that?"

How, indeed, Justin thought, remembering Morgan's instinctive movement during his confrontation with the carter in Shrewsbury's Wyle. He liked Morgan. He also owed Morgan a huge debt. He was just not sure he could trust Morgan. But before he could continue with his indirect inquiry, the door swung open and Durand strode into the tavern.

"I want to talk to you," he said brusquely to Justin, and then looked pointedly at Morgan, who got to his feet, although without any haste. Making a comic grimace behind Durand's back, the groom strolled off, and Durand claimed his seat. "Do not summon me like that again, de Quincy. I do not like it."

His anger notwithstanding, he still remembered to keep his voice pitched low. So did Justin. "And of course I live to please you. Stop your posturing, Durand, and hear me out. I had an interesting conversation this eve with the abbot of Clermont Abbey. He'd been in Paris recently and was well versed in the doings at the French court. It seems that whilst I was chasing around Shropshire like a fool, the French king and Lord John were making one last attempt to foil King Richard's release. They dispatched messengers to the Roman Emperor's court, offering him a variety of bribes to delay Richard's release. If Richard were held until this coming Michaelmas, they'd pay Heinrich eighty thousand marks. Or they'd pay him a thousand pounds a month for as long as he kept Richard in captivity. Or they'd give him one hundred fifty thousand marks if he'd either hold Richard for another full year or turn Richard over to them."

Durand showed no reaction. "What of it? You are not going to tell me that you were disappointed by this, I hope? If you are still harboring illusions about John's conscience or his—"

"I am not," Justin said through gritted teeth. "What I want to know is when you planned to tell me about this."

"I'd have got around to it eventually. I sent word to those who matter."

Justin started to push back from the table, but Durand moved faster, intercepting a passing serving maid and ordering a flagon and two cups. "If it will stop your complaining, I'll buy the drinks," he declared magnanimously, and Justin reluctantly retook his seat. For a time, they actually managed to conduct a civil conversation, discussing Guy de Laval's likely whereabouts and how much trust they ought to place in Emma. Not much, they agreed. It occurred to Justin that the most trustworthy of his traveling companions was probably Emma's pampered little lapdog, but he refrained from sharing this thought with Durand.

Durand reached for the flagon and poured the last of the wine into his cup; Justin's was still half full. "I do not suppose we'll be getting an early start on the morrow. Her ladyship will be lying abed till noon if left to her own devices. I'm beginning to have some sympathy for you, de Quincy. How did you ever survive a summer in Wales with the Lady Emma?"

Justin was taken aback, for Durand had sounded almost friendly. But when the other man smiled, he went on the alert, for he'd seen that smile in the past—just before Durand pounced.

"To prove my goodwill, de Quincy, I am going to offer some advice of the heart. I'll not deny it has been amusing, watching Claudine stalk you like a vixen closing in on an unwary rabbit. But for Christ's sake, man, enough is enough. If you do not bed her soon, she's likely to start casting her pearls before swine," he drawled, aiming a significant look across the tavern where Morgan was flirting with one of the serving maids.

Justin knew he was being goaded; Durand had used Claudine as bait before. He also knew that what he was about to do was childish; he did not care. As he got to his feet, he reached for his cup, as if to finish it, and overturned it in Durand's lap. Durand was cat-quick, though, and twisted sideways to avoid most of the liquid. But enough of the wine splashed onto his mantle to satisfy Justin. "Sorry," he said cheerfully. "How could I have been so clumsy?"

Durand had the pale-sky eyes of a Viking; like most Normans, he had his share of Norse blood. As Justin gazed into their glittering blue-white depths, he was reminded that ice could burn. Heads were turning in their direction; they'd attracted the attention of the burly tavern owner, who started to lumber over.

A woman with flaxen hair was quicker, though. Moving to Justin's side, she said, with the aplomb of one accustomed to diverting tavern brawlers, "You said 'later,' sweet. Well, later is now. If you come abovestairs with me, I'll make it worth your while."

Before Justin could respond, Durand's hand shot out, catching Honorine's wrist. "Make it worth *my* while, love."

She gave Durand a practiced appraisal, liked what she saw, and let him pull her down onto his lap, giving Justin a "You missed your chance" smile. Durand, too, was smiling now, his a victor's smile.

But Justin did not begrudge him the prize. Leaning over, he murmured in Honorine's ear, "He is rich, lass. Make him pay dear for it."

* * *

THEY HEADED WEST ON THE MORROW, expecting to find Arzhela with the Lady Constance at Rennes. Their first stop was the castle of Vitré, where Emma insisted upon accepting the hospitality of its lord, André de Vitré, much to the annoyance of both Justin and Durand, for they'd covered only twelve miles. But they were in for a pleasant surprise. They were not Lord André's only guests. He was proudly playing host to his duchess, too.

LORD ANDRÉ ESCORTED EMMA AND CLAUDINE across the great hall to present them to Duchess Constance. Justin and Durand were trailing behind, not being of sufficient importance to warrant an introduction. Justin was curious to see the duchess, for if anyone could block John's march to the throne, it would be Constance. He'd cast her in the same mold as Queen Eleanor, a woman about whom legends were spun, and his first glimpse was disappointing. Unlike the English queen, Constance was no great beauty. She was a small-boned, almost painfully slender woman in her thirties, petite and surprisingly fragile in appearance. Her hair was covered by a veil and wimple, but it was not likely that her coloring was fashionably fair, for her eyes were dark. If she were not so richly dressed in brocaded silk and an ermine-lined pelisse, Justin thought strangers might have guessed Emma or even Claudine to be the Breton duchess.

As he got closer, though, Justin changed his opinion. Constance radiated energy and authority. There was an intensity about her that put him in mind of a high-strung and highborn mare, but he frowned when Durand murmured that she was a filly to give a man a wild ride, for he did not like finding out that his thoughts and Durand's could overlap like that.

Lord André had ushered Emma and Claudine toward the duchess and they were making graceful curtsies. But no one was expecting what happened next. Constance gave the women a cold, scornful stare and turned away without saying a word. Claudine looked stunned, Emma outraged, and Lord André flustered. The snub had not gone unnoticed and a buzz swept the hall.

"Did you see?" Durand jabbed Justin with his elbow. "I've seen street beggars get warmer receptions than that!"

Justin was equally baffled. Emma had been living in Wales for nigh on twenty years. So how likely was it that she'd offended a thirteen-year-old Constance so grievously that she was nursing a grudge two decades later? "It makes no sense. I know that Claudine has never met Constance and I doubt that Emma has, either."

"Use your eyes, man," Durand said impatiently. "If you were born a duck, would you have any liking for swans?"

That seemed too simple a solution to Justin. Before he could express his doubts, however, a low, throaty chuckle sounded behind them. "I've never understood how men can know so much about war and statecraft and the natural laws of Almighty God, but be so damnably stupid about women!"

They spun around to confront a stranger. Tall enough to laugh up at them without having to tilt her head, stylishly flat-chested, lithe and limber, glowing with good health and good humor. She had a determined chin, pale skin gilded with golden freckles, a wide, mobile mouth shaped for smiles, and eyes the sultry, caressing color of a summer sea.

"The duchess is too clever to be so petty, too ambitious to be so vain. You think there was a man ever born who'd trade power for white teeth and muscles? The lot of you would gladly look like misbegotten dwarves if only you could be crowned dwarves. Whatever makes you think that women do not have the same hungers?"

Justin and Durand exchanged quizzical glances. "Suppose you tell us, then," Durand challenged, "why the duchess was so rude to the Lady Emma if it has naught to do with mirrors and vainglory."

"It had nothing to do with Lady Emma's pretty face and everything to do with the blood that flows in her veins. The duchess would sooner embrace the Devil's daughter than a kinswoman of Eleanor, Richard, and John."

"The last I heard," Durand objected, "Duchess Constance is their kinswoman, too."

"By marriage, not by choice. She has good reason to resent the Angevins. King Henry dethroned her father and married her off to his son Geoffrey. Then, after Geoffrey's death, Richard forced her to wed the Earl of Chester, who was all of fifteen at the time, and thus more than ten years her junior. And I doubt that the happy couple have exchanged a civil word since."

Justin was startled into laughter, taken aback by such brash candor. "Are you always so fiercely outspoken, Lady Arzhela?"

She grinned. "Alas, I have been cursed since childhood with a runaway tongue... Master de Quincy." Her gaze flicked from Justin to Durand, but the knight's face was inscrutable; she could not tell if he'd guessed her identity as Justin had. "I had the advantage of you," she acknowledged, "for I needed only to pick you out amongst the Lady Emma's men, whereas you could not even be certain that I was in attendance upon the duchess. It helped, too, that our mutual friend sent me such a good description of you both. You, Sir Durand, he said looked like a 'pirate in search of a wench to ravish,' and you, Master de Quincy, like a 'young man accursed with a conscience.'"

She grinned again, as gleefully as a little girl, and Justin could not help responding to her warmth, her utter lack of pretense; she was not at all as he had imagined her to be. When he glanced around the hall to make sure they were attracting no attention, she smiled reassuringly. "None will think it strange that we are together. I'm known to have an eye for a well-formed male, and people will assume we're flirting. Clearly we cannot talk seriously here. I'd wanted to point out my likeliest suspect, but he has suddenly disappeared."

Justin and Durand traded looks again. "And who would this suspect be?"

"Meet me in the gardens on the morrow," she said, "and I might tell you." She winked, and glided away before they could stop her.

Durand was scowling. "The fool woman thinks this is a game," he said. Justin said nothing. He was troubled, too, by Arzhela's insouciance, but he saw no reason to admit that to Durand. If they were choosing sides, he was on Arzhela's.

THEY FOUND ARZHELA IN THE GARDENS the next day, holding out her fists to an urchin. The boy was very young, with a round face streaked with dirt, an untidy cap of curly hair, and much-mended clothes, which identified him as a servant's child. He hesitated and then chose a hand. Arzhela opened it to reveal an empty palm. He swiftly pointed to her other hand and his eyes opened wide when it, too, was empty. He burst into giggles, though, when Arzhela found the missing coin behind his ear. She flipped the coin to the boy and he caught it deftly, running off as Justin and Durand approached.

"With fingers that nimble, you'd have made a fine cutpurse, Lady Arzhela," Justin observed as they drew near and she glanced over her shoulder, smiling.

101

"A conjurer's trick, but it never fails to amaze the little ones. Johnny taught me; he always did have a gift for sleight of hand."

It was a moment before the men realized that her Johnny and their Lord John were one and the same. They digested this startling fact in silence, following as she beckoned them farther into the gardens. In summer it would be a small Eden, but now it was barren and desolate, the ground frozen, trees naked to the wind. Arzhela led the way to an arbor that would be lushly canopied in honeysuckle vines in another six months; till then, though, the latticework was skeletal, open to the pale winter sky. Feeling equally exposed, the men joined her upon a narrow wooden bench.

Noticing their unease, she gave an exaggerated sigh. "The two of you are as jumpy as treed cats. As I told you last night, no one will think twice about seeing me with a couple of handsome men!"

"You seem to think this is one great joke, Lady Arzhela," Durand said sternly. "You need to remember how much is at stake."

Arzhela refrained from rolling her eyes, but made her attitude quite clear by batting her lashes and simpering, "Yes, Sir Durand," with mock docility. Although he did not look happy, he showed he knew when to push and when to back off by saying nothing. Once she was sure she'd made her point, Arzhela leaned over and picked up a stick. Smoothing the ground in front of the bench with her foot, she drew a circle in the dirt.

"Think of this circle as the conspiracy against Johnny. I made it so large because we have to fit quite a few people into it. My cousin Constance. André de Vitré. The Bishops of St-Malo and Rennes. Raoul de Fougères. Alain and Pierre de

Dinan. Geoffroi de Chateaubriant. Canon Robert, of St Étienne's at Toulouse. Guy de Laval and Hugh de Gournay and most likely others whose names I have not yet learned."

Arzhela paused, looking pleased with herself. "You were right, Master de Quincy... Justin. I could have been a good cutpurse. But I'd have made an even better spy." Gesturing toward her scrawled circle, she continued. "I'd not call it a conspiracy, though, in the strictest sense of the word, for some of the men I named seem to believe that the letter is genuine, that Johnny was truly plotting to murder his brother."

"And your cousin Constance?" Justin asked carefully. "Does she believe that?"

Arzhela hesitated. "I am not sure," she admitted. "I think Constance and most of the men were more than willing to ignore any doubts. They wanted to believe in the validity of the letter, you see." Her smile was rueful. "And Johnny's history made that so easy for them."

"But we know the letter was forged." Durand was regarding Arzhela reflectively. "So if Constance did not forge it, who did? Where did she get it?"

"From the aforementioned canon of Toulouse. He is too clever by half, that one. He gives the impression of being forthcoming and affable, yet when you try to pin him down, he slithers away, as slick as you please. I have always read men as easily as a monk reads his Psalter," Arzhela boasted, with what she felt was pardonable pride, "and my reading of Canon Robert tells me that he has the answers we seek."

Justin felt a twinge of disappointment. He agreed that Canon Robert was a natural suspect, but he'd hoped that Arzhela would have more to offer than intuition. Durand seemed to share his disappointment, for he asked if that was all she had.

"Well, I did coax a confession from him, did I forget to mention that?" Arzhela's sarcasm was good-natured. "When Canon Robert is revealed to be as guilty as Cain, I shall expect apologies from the pair of you."

"Is he the one who vanished from the great hall last night, my lady?"

She nodded. "He fled the hall like a man pursued by demons, slipping out a servant's entrance, and if that is not cause for suspicion, what is? When I looked for him today, he was nowhere to be found. I eventually learned that he'd taken to his bed, claiming to be ailing!"

Neither Justin nor Durand thought that sounded particularly damning, but Justin was tactful enough to keep his doubts to himself. Durand was not. Before he could further irritate Arzhela by expressing his skepticism, though, they were interrupted by the arrival of a newcomer to the garden.

He was tall and blond and stylishly dressed in the newest fashion— an unbelted sleeveless tabard, visible because he'd draped his mantle casually around his shoulders in defiance of the winter weather. Durand stared at the tabard like a man mentally making notes for his tailor, but Justin took more notice of the milky-opaque toadstone that the stranger wore prominently on his mantle, for toadstones were used as a protection against poisons. There was something about his demeanor—the jut of his chin, the swagger in his step—that made it easy for Justin to believe this man did not lack for enemies.

"There you are, Lady Arzhela." He sounded aggrieved, as if she'd deliberately disappeared, and when he bent over her hand, he put Justin more in mind of a man marking a brand than bestowing a kiss.

Arzhela had already shown them that she did not suffer

fools gladly. But she was regarding the youth with an indulgent smile, introducing him fondly as Simon de Lusignan, a name that resonated harshly with both Justin and Durand. The de Lusignans were a powerful clan ensconced in the hills of Queen Eleanor's Poitou, blessed with high birth and cursed with hungers beyond satisfying. Their family tree had produced more than its share of adventurers, rebels, and brigands. If several had managed to lay claims to distant crowns, far more had cheated the hangman, and it was a common belief that if there was trouble to be found, a de Lusignan was likely to be in the very midst of it.

This de Lusignan acknowledged the introductions with a terseness that bordered upon outright rudeness, and insisted upon escorting Arzhela indoors. Durand and Justin stood watching them go. "She does like them young," Durand commented after a long silence. From sheer force of habit, Justin started to object, but he could not really fault the other man's cynical observation. Arzhela was in her late thirties and Simon looked to be barely beyond his majority. Moreover, now that he thought about it, he realized that she was at least ten years older than John, too. John and one of the de Lusignans. Passing strange, that a woman with so much mother wit should have such bad taste in men.

"I've heard the gossip about the de Lusignans," Justin said thoughtfully, "those tales told over a wine flagon that grow worse with each telling. How they feud with their neighbors and prey upon travelers and dare to defy both Church and Crown. You think it is coincidence that one of their lot has shown up at the Duchess Constance's court?"

"That same thought crossed my mind," Durand admitted. "God smite them, de Lusignans take to conspiracies like pigs to mud. But why would Constance and her Breton barons confide in a stripling like Simon? No, I'd say he is Arzhela's stud, no more than that."

Justin was inclined to agree. He still had a suspicion, though, that Arzhela was not being completely honest with them.

"*ITE, MISSA EST*." WITH THOSE WORDS, the Mass was ended and the castle chapel began to empty. Justin was one of the last to leave.

As he stepped out into the wan sunlight, he heard his name hissed, and turned to see Arzhela beckoning imperiously to him.

"Hurry," she insisted, pulling him in the direction of the stables. As soon as they'd passed into the gloomy shadows of the barn, she thrust a bundle at him. "Here," she said, "put this on. I have had an inspired idea, know how to get you in to see our reclusive canon!"

Justin unwrapped a man's tunic of coarse kersey wool, the undyed murky shade known as hodden grey, of such shabby quality that most servants would have balked at wearing it. Ignoring his questions, Arzhela was already tugging at his mantle. "Make haste," she urged. "Better we do this whilst Father Herve is still busy in the chapel."

She was not to be denied and Justin pulled the garment over his head, hoping it was not as flea-infested as it looked. As soon as he unbuckled his scabbard, Arzhela placed it on top of his folded mantle and instructed a wide-eyed young groom to guard it well. The youth vowed that he would and Justin did not doubt it; he was learning that Arzhela was one for getting her own way.

Returning to the castle bailey, he followed her toward the kitchens, where a platter with soup, bread, and wine was waiting for them. Trying to keep the soup from slopping out of the bowl, he hastened to keep pace with her as they headed toward a corner tower. As they walked, she finally deigned to offer an explanation for the masquerade.

"Canon Robert is still keeping to his bed, but I've come up with a clever way for you to get a look at him. Father Herve offered to share his own chamber as a courtesy and I am about to pay a sickbed visit to our ailing canon. Whilst I ply him with flattery and onion soup, you can study him to your heart's content," she concluded triumphantly. "A pity I could not think how to get Durand in with you, but he'd not have made a convincing servant!"

"But I would?" Justin said dryly.

Arzhela's grin showed she was not as oblivious as her words might indicate. "Dear heart, you are a spy, after all. So it is to the good that you can blend into the background when needed!"

By now they'd climbed the narrow stairs to the chaplain's top-floor chamber. Arzhela rapped sharply on the door and then, without waiting for a response, barged in. The lone occupant whirled away from the window in surprise. He was fully dressed, wearing the white rochet common to clerics. Justin was not surprised that he was garbed in such fine linen, for unlike their monastic brethren, canons took no vows of poverty. He was tonsured and clean-shaven, with features that were attractive but not memorable. He looked exactly like what he claimed to be—a man of God who was also at home in the secular world. But he did not look like a man too ill to rise from his sickbed.

"Canon Robert," Arzhela purred, "how wonderful to see you up and about! If I may say so, you seem in the very bloom of health. Dare I hope that you'll honor us with your presence at dinner this day?"

"Alas, my lady, I fear not. Lord André's physician advised me to walk for brief periods, lest I become too weak lying abed." The canon seated himself upon the bed, relieved by his illness of the demands of courtesy, and regarded them calmly. "What may I do for you, Lady Arzhela?"

"Nay, Canon Robert," she said sweetly, "what may I do for you?" With a flourish, she gestured toward Justin, standing inconspicuously behind her, as any well-trained servant would. "I've brought you some soup, very good for catarrh or a queasy stomach. And wine, good for almost any ailment!"

As the canon thanked her profusely for her kindness, Justin set his burden upon a coffer by the bed. While he welcomed this opportunity to scrutinize Canon Robert, he was not sure how much could be learned in such a brief encounter. The man was as urbane and polished as would be expected of one who served a bishop, not the sort to blurt out indiscretions if caught off guard. It seemed most likely that he was what he appeared to be—a conduit, a messenger. He might even believe that the letter was genuine.

Arzhela's attempts to engage the canon in conversation had been unsuccessful. His responses were polite, but so increasingly wan that she at last conceded defeat and bade him farewell. Once she and Justin were out in the stairwell, she said sarcastically, "I feared that if I stayed any longer, he was going to swoon dead away. Did you notice how halting his speech became, as if the poor soul did not even have the strength to finish a sentence!"

"How does he explain his possession of the letter?"

"He claims it was entrusted to him by the archdeacon of Toulouse, whilst hinting that the archdeacon was acting upon Bishop Fulcrand's behalf." Emerging again into the bailey, they headed back to the stables to retrieve Justin's belongings,

Arzhela speculating all the while about Canon Robert's reasons for keeping out of sight. "All I can think is that he recognized you or Durand. You are the queen's man, after all, and Durand serves Johnny."

"Trust me, my lady. I am not so well-known that a canon from Toulouse would have heard of me!" Justin could see that Arzhela was not convinced, loath to surrender her suspicions, and he did not argue further. Instead, he told her that Lady Emma had got word that morn of her son's return to Laval. "She insists that we leave for Laval on the morrow, for she is eager to speak to her son as soon as possible."

Arzhela was not pleased by that, but admitted that they had no choice; she'd met the Lady Emma. "Well, you must return to Vitré straightaway once you've questioned her son. Whilst you are gone, I will see what else I can discover. Who knows, I might have solved the mystery by the time you get back," she teased, but Justin did not share her amusement.

"Lady Arzhela, I urge you to keep your distance until we return. At first I saw nothing suspect about Canon Robert. But as we made ready to leave, I caught something odd. He was staring intently at me, my lady, or to be more precise, at my boots."

Arzhela followed his eyes, gazing down at the cowhide boots protruding from the hem of his threadbare woolen garment. She was quick-witted, understanding the significance at once. "Of course! No servant would have boots of such good leather! So he knows you are not who you pretended to be."

Justin nodded. "More than that, my lady. Canons are rarely, if ever, men of humble birth. He ought not to have even glanced at me, for men of rank do not pay heed to those who serve them. But he did pay heed to me, and I wonder why."

"Is that not obvious? The man has something to hide!"

"Be that as it may, will you promise me that you'll do nothing rash until we return?"

Arzhela frowned and sighed and argued. Justin persevered, though, until she reluctantly agreed to take no further action. But his relief was tempered by a few lingering misgivings, for he understood now why John had been alarmed on her behalf.

CHAPTER IX

February 1194
Laval, Maine

Guy de Laval's years were twenty and four, but he looked younger than that. He was pleasing enough to the eye, with flaxen hair and the easy smile of one who'd never gone hungry or questioned the good fortune that had been his from birth. From his father, he'd inherited the barony of Laval; from his mother, the blood of the Royal House of England and a taste for intrigue. But he had none of Emma's steely resolve, her coolness under fire, or her gambler's nerves.

"I... I know naught of this letter," he stammered. "Truly, I do not." Gaining confidence when no one contradicted him, he mustered up the sunlit smile that had long been the coin of his realm, able to buy whatever favors his lordship did not.

But his genial, shallow charm was wasted upon this particular audience. Durand and Justin eyed him skeptically, with none of the deference he'd come to expect as his just due. Nor did his lady mother appear impressed by his declaration of innocence. She'd not been a physical presence in his life, for they'd been parted when he was only four and he'd seen her but rarely since her marriage to a Welsh prince. He remembered a woman of heartbreaking beauty, as ethereal as one of God's own angels, memories of gossamer and magic nurtured by his imagination and her absence. He was both awed and intimidated by the flesh-and-blood Emma now standing before him, a handsome woman in her forties who was regarding him with very little maternal solicitude.

"We know that you're in this muck up to your neck," Durand said brusquely and Guy started to bridle. His pride demanded as much although, in truth, he was even more intimidated by Durand than he was by this stranger, his mother.

"I told you to let me handle this," Emma said, aiming her rebuke at Durand but keeping her eyes upon her son all the while. "Guy, do not waste your breath and my time in false denials. Use the meager common sense that God gave you. Would I be here if your youthful folly had not been exposed?"

Her scorn stung. "I do not see it as folly to oblige great lords, to be a kingmaker!" As soon as the words were out of his mouth, Guy realized how easily he'd fallen into his mother's trap, and his fair skin mottled with hot color. His confession hung in the air like wood smoke, impossible to ignore.

"Well, I for one am impressed," Durand drawled. "You held out for four whole heartbeats, mayhap even five."

"At least he dared to gamble for the highest stakes," Justin objected, picking up his cue as if the gambit had been rehearsed between them. "How many men have the courage to risk offending a king?"

Guy's flush had darkened at Durand's gibe, but now he swung around to stare at Justin. "John is not my king," he said indignantly. "I am not disloyal to my liege lord!"

Justin shook his head regretfully. "The French king might well think otherwise."

Guy frowned, an expression of defiance undercut by his darting, anxious eyes. "All know he is no true friend to John. Theirs is an alliance of expediency, one held together by cobwebs and spit. Why should he care what befalls John?"

"You do not know about their latest pact?" Justin feigned surprise, beginning to enjoy the playacting. "Lord John and King Philippe struck a devil's bargain soon after Christmas. In return for Philippe's continued support against Richard, John agreed to cede to Philippe all of Normandy northeast of the River Seine, save only Rouen, and to yield to the French a number of strategic border castles. It is now very much in Philippe's interest that John become England's next king. How do you think he'll react once he learns that his liege man, the Lord of Laval, is conniving to put a Breton child on the English throne?"

"I... I did not know about this." Guy was stammering again. "I was told that John and Philippe were at odds, each blaming the other for his failure to keep Richard imprisoned—"

"They were," Emma interrupted, "but their mutual fear of Richard is far stronger than their petty vanities. You ought to have known that, Guy. And you would have, if you'd given this scheme some serious thought. Why in Heaven's Name did you not consult with me first?"

For a moment, Justin thought Emma was making an oddly timed jest. But when he glanced toward her, he saw that she was in deadly earnest. The expression upon Durand's face mirrored his own astonishment. Guy looked no less nonplussed.

"Madame... Mother, I do not need your permission to enter into a conspiracy," he said, and as ludicrous as his words were, he managed to invest them with a doleful sort of dignity.

"Well, you should!" Emma snapped, confirming all Justin's suspicions about her utter lack of humor. "I'd have made sure that this foolishness ended then and there!"

"Why was it so foolish?" Realizing how feeble his protest sounded, Guy cleared his throat and said, with more conviction, "If Constance's little lad becomes king, she'll not forget the men who stood by her side!"

"Neither will John! How can I make you understand how badly you've blundered?" Emma glared at her son. "Constance and Arthur versus Eleanor and John. Do you truly see those scales as balanced? You might as well wager that a rabbit will devour a wolf!"

Guy had never learned how to hold his own against a stronger, more forceful personality. His surrender was abrupt, total, and abject. Slumping down upon the nearest seat, a rickety wooden bench, he muttered, "Oh, God... John knows about me, doesn't he? What can I do?"

Emma sat beside him on the bench. "You can tell us all you know about this plot."

Guy did, haltingly, keeping his gaze locked upon the floor rushes at his feet. His the mournful demeanor of a sinner seeking absolution, he described the December meeting in the pirate citadel of St-Malo, the dramatic revelation of the letter's existence, and the gleeful reaction of the Breton lords. They questioned him closely about Canon Robert of Toulouse, but he claimed to know little about the man. Nor did he know who was the master puppeteer in this political puppet show.

He did not think Duchess Constance was the instigator. Since he was not one of her confidants, though, that was merely an opinion, not actual evidence. So far, what he'd told them was not particularly helpful. But then he said, almost as an afterthought, "I think some of the Breton lords truly believed that the letter was genuine."

Emma's head came up sharply and she signaled to Justin

114

for wine. "How were you so sure that it was not, Guy?"

Guy gratefully accepted the brimming cup. "Simon told me."

Unlike Emma, Justin and Durand understood the enormous significance of those three simple words. Before Emma could reveal her ignorance, Justin said casually to Guy, "You and Simon de Lusignan are mates, are you?"

Guy nodded innocently. "We were squires together in the Viscount of Thouars's household. Simon is a good lad, a good friend. He is one for borrowing money and not one for repaying it, but that is not his fault, what with him being a younger son. He only gets crumbs from his father's table, so he must make do however he can. A reliable man to have beside you in a tavern brawl, though."

Justin and Durand's eyes caught and held briefly and in that moment, Justin knew exactly what the other man was thinking, for he was thinking it, too—that Guy had probably never been in a tavern brawl in his life.

Emma was occupied trying to place Simon in the de Lusignan hierarchy "He's one of the sons of William, who holds the lordship of Lezay," she said at last, in a dismissive tone that told Justin volumes about the lower social status of this branch of the de Lusignan clan.

Guy nodded again and, at his mother's prodding, admitted that Simon de Lusignan had been the one to ensnare him in the Breton conspiracy. No, he did not know how Simon had got involved in it. He'd been surprised, though, to see how much respect Simon seemed to command amongst the Breton lords, who treated him like a man of some importance rather than a stripling of two and twenty, a fourth son with little hope of advancement.

By now, Emma had realized that Guy had just given them a valuable clue. Her eyes went questioningly to Justin and he nodded imperceptibly, conveying the message that he would enlighten her at the first opportunity. Once again, his gaze crossed that of Durand, and once again, the same thought was in both their minds: it was time to have a long talk with the Lady Arzhela.

EMMA CHOSE TO REMAIN AT LAVAL with her son. Since Claudine's rationale for accompanying them was to act as Emma's companion, she could muster no convincing argument when Justin and Durand insisted that she remain at Laval, too. Emma refused to spare the young knight Lionel, although she grudgingly agreed to let them take Morgan and her men-at-arms. Guy would have liked to ride with them, for he was eager to escape his mother's chastisement, but he was not given that option.

The day was cold, yet clear, the road in decent shape for midwinter, and they covered the twelve miles to Vitré in two hours. Upon their arrival at the castle, however, they discovered that their journey was not over. The Duchess Constance had decided to accept the hospitality of Raoul de Fougéres, and the Lady Arzhela de Dinan had accompanied her.

FOUGÈRES WAS LESS THAN TWENTY MILES to the northeast of Vitré and by pushing their horses, they reached it just before dusk. At first glimpse, the castle appeared to be one of the most formidable strongholds Justin had ever seen, a rock-hewn fortress surrounded by miles of marshland and moated by the serpentine winding of the River Nançon. But as they approached, something struck him as odd about those massive defenses. Durand, with a more experienced eye, needed but one look.

"What sort of dolt would build a castle down in the valley instead of up on the heights?" he said incredulously, and Justin realized he was right; he'd never before seen a castle located on low ground. Drawing rein, they were marveling at the incongruity of it when Morgan pulled up beside them and burst out laughing.

"They must have been blind-drunk when they laid out these plans!" he chortled. "You'd think they'd have learned their lesson when King Henry, may God assoil him, took the castle in one day's time. But no, damned if they did not rebuild it in the exact same spot!"

"You're uncommonly knowledgeable about castles and royal military campaigns," Durand said, before adding snidely, "for a stable groom."

"A man need not be a baker to enjoy eating bread," Morgan pointed out amiably. "By your logic, Sir Durand, only a nun would know about virtue and only a whore would know about sin. We have a saying back home, that if—"

"Spare me your countrymen's homilies," Durand said, and spurred his stallion ahead until he attracted the attention of the castle guards. Allowed to advance within shouting range, he demanded entry with an arrogance that caused Justin and Morgan to wince, both expecting the gates to be slammed in Durand's face. But after a brief delay, they heard the creaking of a windlass and the drawbridge slowly began to lower.

FOUGÈRES MAY HAVE BEEN POORLY SITUATED, but it boasted a highly sophisticated water defense system. When Raoul de Fougères rebuilt the castle after the English king Henry burned it to the ground nigh on thirty years ago, he'd replaced the wooden structures with stone, and constructed an ingenious tower that was equipped with a mechanism for flooding the entrance area in the event of attack. Even Durand was impressed.

A removable footbridge spanned the water-filled inner

ditch, and the men led their mounts across it into the bailey, glancing up at the iron-barred double portcullis looming over their heads as they passed through. By the time they'd penetrated the heart of the castle, they'd all revised their initial view that Fougères could be easily taken, and were thankful that none of them would be asked to lay siege to this Breton border stronghold.

Justin made sure that he, not Durand, was the one to request a night's lodging from the castellan, for the village huddled outside the castle battlements had not looked promising. Once permission was granted, they sent their horses off to the stable and followed the castellan's servant into the great hall nestled along the south wall. There, the Duchess Constance, Lord Raoul, and other Breton lords were seated at the high table, enjoying a pre-Lenten feast of beef stew, marrow tarts, and stuffed capon. Places were found for Durand and Justin at one of the lower tables; Morgan and the men-at-arms would be fed, too, but they'd have to wait until their betters were served. In their haste to reach Fougères before dark, they had eaten nothing on the road, and the enticing aromas of freshly baked bread and roasted meat reminded them of how empty their stomachs were. They pitched into their food with enthusiasm, and only afterward did they roam the smoky, dimly lit hall in search of Lady Arzhela... and failed to find her.

The person most likely to know of her whereabouts was the Duchess Constance, but they knew better than to approach her unbidden. She was holding court upon the dais, surrounded by her barons and household knights and the abbot of Trinity Abbey. Justin and Durand lurked inconspicuously at the outer edges of the royal circle, watching in growing frustration as Constance demonstrated how much she liked center stage, accepting the attention, deference, and flattery as naturally as she did the air she breathed. Justin was not as sure as Emma that this woman would be no match for John, and neither was Durand, who murmured a rude jest in Justin's ear, declaring it must be devilishly difficult to lay with a woman who had her own set of ballocks.

As more time passed, Justin's anxieties about Arzhela multiplied, and he seized the first opportunity to intercept Raoul de Fougères as he descended the dais steps. "My lord, may I have a word with you?" he asked, politely enough to please the highborn lord, who paused and allowed that he could spare a moment or two. Raoul was stocky and well fed, with a surprisingly thick thatch of hair for a man his age, which Justin guessed to be mid-sixties. He had been doting noticeably upon a youngster of fourteen or so, his grandson and heir, but beneath the affable, avuncular air was a will of iron, a shrewd intelligence, and the chilling confidence of one who never doubted his own judgments or his right to enforce them.

"My lord, I was asked by Lord Guy de Laval to deliver a letter to Lady Arzhela de Dinan, but I have been unable to locate her and those I've asked disavow any knowledge of her whereabouts. I was hoping that you might be better informed..."

Raoul's brow puckered as he jogged his memory. "What did I hear about Lady Arzhela? Ah, yes, now I remember. The duchess told me that Lady Arzhela asked her for permission to make a pilgrimage to Mont St Michel."

He turned away, then, as someone else sought his attention, leaving Justin standing there, trying to make sense of what he'd just been told. A moment later, Durand was at his side. "Well?" he demanded, in a low voice. "Did you find out where that fool woman has gone? From the look on your face, I don't think I am going to like the answer much."

"No," Justin said slowly, "you are not going to like it at all."

CHAPTER X

February 1194
Mont St Michel, Normandy

Despite the raw winter weather, pilgrims continued to come to Mont St Michel. From her vantage point at a window in the abbey guesthouse, Arzhela watched as they trudged across the wet sands from Genêts, following single file in the footsteps of a local guide, for even at low tide, there was still the danger of quicksand bogs. From the abbey heights, they seemed as small and insignificant as carved toy figures, playthings to be scattered at a child's whim or at God's Will.

Wind rattled the shutters, causing Arzhela to shiver, but she did not close the window, mesmerized by the sight of those struggling pilgrims. What had driven them to make such a difficult journey, to bear so heavy a burden? She had made pilgrimages herself, of course, to Chartres and to the shrine of Our Lady at Rocamadour, proudly bringing back an oval pilgrim badge inscribed with the words *"Sigillum Beatae Mariae de Rocamadour."* But her pilgrimages had always been made in the glory of high summer, and had entailed no danger and little discomfort. More like pleasure excursions than true testings of the soul. She had visited the Mont on numerous occasions, but always as an honored guest, never as one of Christ's Faithful. And as she leaned from the window of the abbey's guesthouse, a hostel for the highborn, looking down at those distant men and women wading through the icy waters of the bay, she was shamed by the contrast between their barefoot, heartfelt piety and her sinful, luxury-loving past.

ARZHELA DINED WITH ABBOT JOURDAIN IN his private chambers in late-morning, along with several other guests deemed worthy of gracing the abbot's table: two merchants from Rouen who were bountiful patrons of St Michael, their generosity compensating for any defects of lineage; a distant cousin of Arzhela's first husband; the archdeacon of Rennes; a boastful Norman baron and his subdued, long-suffering wife. Arzhela found neither the company nor the conversation to be especially entertaining, and was thankful when the meal was over. As she emerged from the abbot's lodging, she encountered a flock of pilgrims being shepherded by monks up the great gallery stairs, and instead of returning to the guesthouse, she joined them.

THE PILGRIMS AND ARZHELA REVERENTLY CROSSED the central nave of the church, where they were given time to pray at the altar of Saint-Michel-en-la-Nef. Arzhela knelt when it was her turn, and as she offered up her prayers and her heart to Blessed St Michael, she was filled with a sudden sense of peace. How glad she was to be here! It had been an impulse, not fully thought out. When she'd realized she was in danger, realized her need to find a refuge, the abbey had been the first place to come to mind. She could wait there in safety for Justin and Durand.

She wasn't sure what would happen after that, but she felt confident that all would be resolved to her satisfaction. If need be, she could go to Paris, go to Johnny. He would protect her. He would also take a swift and terrible vengeance. A pity she could not simply tell Justin and Durand all that she'd discovered, leave the sorting out to them. Why must life be so damnably complicated?

Usually the monks were strict taskmasters, quickly ushering the pilgrims out so the next group could be given admittance. But these February wayfarers were but a trickle in the flood of the faithful that inundated the abbey every year, and the hosteller was willing to indulge such hardy souls, allowing them to tarry in the nave, breathing in the sanctity of St Michael, basking in God's Grace. Arzhela lingered, too, wondering whether she could charm Brother Gervaise into taking her down into the crypt of Notre Dame des Trente Cierges, where holy relics of the Virgin Mary were kept. Since the crypt was within the abbey enclosure—the area prohibited to all but the monks—she knew her chances were not promising. Still, she'd never know unless she tried. She was strolling about the nave, looking for the hosteller, when she saw *him*.

She froze, not fully trusting her senses, and when she mustered up the courage to look again, he was gone. Had she truly seen him? He'd been clad in the black habit of a Benedictine. The abbey had more monks than Johnny had concubines, nigh on sixty. And then there were visiting monks from the Mont's Norman priories, even monks on pilgrimage. How did she know her nerves were not playing her false? But her heart had begun pounding against her ribs, and she was finding it difficult to catch her breath.

Once she was back in the guest quarters, she did her best to convince herself that her imagination had conjured up a ghost. But when she asked herself the only questions that truly mattered—if he would dare to come after her and if his need to silence her was so great as that—she knew the only answers could be "yes," and "yes" again. Once she admitted that, she realized she dared not dismiss this sighting as fanciful, not when the stakes truly were life or death.

Fool that she was, she'd been sure she would be safe here, far safer than at her cousin's court. She paced the confines of the chamber as if it were a cage, her thoughts darting to and fro as rapidly as the gulls swooping outside the window. Could she feign illness, keep to this chamber until Durand and Justin found her? But if he'd dared to follow her onto the blessed soil of St Michael, into God's House itself, how long would a mere wooden door keep him out? No, she must find a hiding place. Where, though? She strode to a window and thrust open the shutters. Below, a black-clad monk was staring up at the guesthouse, his face hidden by his cowled hood.

Her first instinct was to recoil, but instead she stood her ground, staring down defiantly at the spectral figure who might or might not be her executioner. Her fear was giving way to a surging anger. Like the tides of the bay, it was all-engulfing, sparing no one, not even herself. She'd handled this poorly, making misjudgments and mistakes, but no more. Loyalty to a lover might be admirable; stupidity was not. She knew her enemy now, knew how ruthless and cunning he could be. But he did not know his enemy. He did not truly know her.

She stayed at the window long after the monk had gone, gazing across the bay. Pilgrims still straggled toward shore, their russet cloaks splotches of muted color against the endless grey of the sand and sky. A cormorant flew by, heading for the distant sea. The stark islet of Tombelaine rose out of the muddy flats that stretched between the Mont and Genêts, a bleak slab of rock that housed a small, forlorn-looking priory. It was a desolate scene, but to Arzhela it was beautiful, for it gave her the answer she sought. What better way to hide than in plain sight?

BROTHER ANDREV WAS STARING AT ARZHELA in horror. "My lady, you cannot do this. It is sheer madness!"

"I know. That is why it cannot fail!" When Brother Andrev did not return her smile, Arzhela sighed, wishing he could share her excitement, her sense of triumph. She was deeply fond of this man, but why must monks be so besotted with propriety, with doing what was "right"? She had to stifle a giggle, then, at her own foolishness. That was why monks became monks, after all, to serve God and to do good. Well, not all monks. That little weasel, Bernard, cared only about making mischief. She'd forgotten her plan to ask Abbot Jourdain to banish him to one of their Yorkshire priories until she'd seen him skulking around the church, like a cutpurse on the prowl for unwary victims.

"Lady Arzhela, are you even listening to me?"

Caught out, she flashed a quick smile. "I am sorry; I did let my thoughts wander for a moment. Brother Andrev, it warms my heart that you worry so on my behalf. But my plan is... well, it is downright brilliant. At first I thought about disguising myself as a nun," she confided, and grinned at his dumbstruck expression. "I realized that would not do, though, for nuns cannot wander freely about the countryside all by themselves, even for worthy purposes like pilgrimages. Then I thought, why not a monk?"

"Why not, indeed?" Brother Andrev echoed weakly.

"I soon saw that would not work, either. Even muffled in a monk's habit, I doubt that I'd be a very convincing man, if I do say so myself. But as I watched those poor pilgrims plodding across the sand, it came to me. Who notices one sheep in an entire flock?"

"Surely there must be another way. I understand why you cannot turn to the Duchess Constance for help. Well, truthfully, I do not, but—"

"You must take my word for that, Brother Andrev. The less you know, the better for you. I can tell you that the duchess would not be happy to learn of my recent activities. It would be awkward, to say the least."

"Well, then, why not appeal to the authorities in Normandy? There is a royal provost right here in Genêts—"

"I wish I could," she admitted, with such obvious sincerity that he was at a loss for words. "But you see, dearest friend, that provost answers to the wrong man." She could not turn for help to King Richard's provost, not without exposing the plot against Johnny. Nor could she explain this to Brother Andrev, for ignorance was his only protection. "I will tell you this much," she said with a smile that managed to be both arch and wistful. "I've learned that the worst thing about dealing with untrustworthy people is that they cannot be trusted!"

He didn't understand, of course, which was for the best.

"I WANT YOU TO GO TO the stables and check on my mare. After that, Alar, you can go to the tavern, for I'll have no further need of you till the morrow. I've decided to pass the night at the priory. There'll be a bed there for you."

"Yes, my lady!" As delighted as Alar was to be given a free evening, he was positively euphoric when she gave him a coin, too. Arzhela watched as he trotted off toward the stables, pleased that she could make him so happy with so little effort. In her present mellow mood, even a servant's pleasure was cause for contentment. She could not remember the last time she'd felt so sure of the right path, at one with the Almighty and her world.

This marvelous feeling lasted as long as it took to reach the church of Notre Dame and Saint-Sebastien, where she was intercepted by Brother Bernard. "My lady," he said, eyeing her coldly, "what may I do for you?"

"You may go away," she said rudely, eager to get rid of him, for he could thwart her plan if he were to follow her into the church.

"As you wish." He bit the words off, flinging them at her like weapons, but she had dealt with far more imposing men than this disgruntled Benedictine monk. Brushing past him as if he did not exist, she entered the church. He continued to stand there, staring after her, but she never looked back.

THE CHURCH WAS EMPTY AT THIS time of day, for it was between the canonical hours of None and Vespers. Arzhela crossed the nave, heading for the tower. She'd stored her disguise in the sacristy before seeking out Brother Andrev, for she could think of no safer hiding place. She was relieved, nonetheless, to find it lying undisturbed in the coffer of vestments. Closing the sacristy door, she undressed with some difficulty, for she was accustomed to having help from her maids. She decided to retain her own linen shift after feeling the scratchy coarse cloth against her soft skin. Stripping off her gown, silk stockings, pelisson, and riding boots, she hid them at the bottom of the vestment coffer, hastily pulling on a russet robe of such poor quality that she'd not have used it for a dog's bed. Her hair hidden under a veil and broad-brimmed hat, she thrust her feet into shabby sandals, wishing that there were a mirror in the sacristy so she could admire her astonishing transformation.

She was not concerned about the authenticity of her costume, for she'd purchased it right off the back of a departing pilgrim. The man had been eager to accept her odd offer. The coins she'd given him in exchange for his tattered garb had assuaged any qualms, and while he seemed convinced she was demented, he was willing to profit from her lunacy. She'd even thought to take clothes for him from the abbey's almonry so he need not attract attention in Genêts by buying new garments. In the morning, he'd be gone long before she'd be missed. It was foolproof.

Cracking open the church door, she peered cautiously around the churchyard. Seeing no one in the immediate vicinity, she stepped outside, self-conscious in her new identity as a poor but godly pilgrim. No one even glanced at her, though, and she soon regained confidence, making her way hastily down to the shore. A small cluster of pilgrims were milling about, the last group to go that day. An ice-edged wind had chased all others from the beach, and Arzhela found it easy to escape notice. She'd rolled her mantle up and tucked it under her arm. Unfolding it now, she looked around cautiously, and then dropped the mantle at her feet, kicking until it was half buried in the sand. A pity; it was one of her favorites. Johnny would owe her a new Parisian cloak for this. But it had to be done. No pilgrim would be wearing a mantle lined with fox fur. And if it was found and identified as hers, that would be one more red herring dragged across her trail, leading the hounds astray.

The last pilgrims were getting ready to cross. Two balked

abruptly, deciding that they'd wait until the morrow. Their unease proved contagious and several of their companions began to reconsider, too. Seeing his fees slipping away, the guide hastily assured them that the crossing was safe, that it was nigh on five hours until the next high tide and they'd be able to reach the Mont ere dark descended on the bay. Insisting that the monks believed Blessed St Michael looked with especial favor upon those who made a dusk crossing, he collected his flock before any others could stray, and passed out candles.

Clutching a candle in one hand and her sandals in the other, Arzhela joined the others. The mud was cold against the bare soles of her feet, the water even colder, but as she raised her eyes to the distant Mont, she forgot about her physical discomfort. The church spires seemed to be scraping the clouds and the last rays of the dying sun bathed the abbey in a golden glow. It was like gazing upon the glory of God, and Arzhela stared up at it in wonder, as if seeing it for the first time. The sense of peace that she'd experienced at St Michael's shrine came flooding back. Some of the other pilgrims had begun to weep and Arzhela wept, too, for sheer joy. Why had she been so slow to understand what the Almighty wanted of her?

Upon the beach at Genêts, a lone figure stood at the water's edge. The wind whipped Brother Bernard's cowl back, blew sand into his face, and chilled his body and soul. He did not move, though, never taking his eyes from the pilgrims wading toward the Mont.

CHAPTER XI

February 1194
Antrain, Brittany

THE FLAT TOMBSTONES WERE OVERGROWN WITH moss, and white with hoarfrost, as cold as ice, offering little comfort to aching bodies and weary bones. But Morgan and the men-at-arms sprawled upon them as if they were cushions, glad for a respite, however brief, from too many hours in the saddle. The churchyard was empty, save for them and the dead. The church itself was not welcoming, small, shuttered, and precariously perched on the heights above a wooded valley where two rivers merged. There was no castle, just the church and a scattering of dilapidated, unsightly cottages. Poverty stalked this Breton village, where suspicion of strangers was a lesson learned in the cradle, and hope always rode on by, never even dismounting.

The men were not fanciful. With the exception of Morgan, their imaginations were not so much underused as undiscovered. Still, they dimly sensed the isolation and the melancholy of these unseen, reclusive villagers, and they kept their hands upon their weapons, kept casting glances over their shoulders.

They did not like this Bretagne, this land of fog and legends and sunless, tangled woods where demons and bandits lurked. This was not a good place to be, not a good place to die.

"How much longer, you think?" Jaspaer's English was serviceable, although the echoes of his native Flanders were never far from the surface. He was more comfortable speaking Flemish or French, but his companions were English and he used their tongue as a courtesy.

Unlike Jaspaer, whose sword was for hire to any lord with money to pay, be he French, Danish, or Swabian, Rufus and Crispin were English lads, born and bred in Shropshire, and not happy to be so far from home. So Morgan responded in English, too, although French was his first language. "Soon, I'd expect," he said reassuringly. "How long does it take to replace a shoe, after all?"

"In this godforsaken land, who knows?" Rufus muttered darkly, his thoughts bleak enough to warrant making a quick sign of the Cross.

"We could wager whilst we wait," Morgan suggested, and succeeded in stirring a flicker of interest.

"On what?" Crispin asked, patting the scrip that dangled from his belt. "I lost the dice at Laval."

"See those two birds in that yew tree yonder? We could wager which one will fly away first. Or... when our good lords will get back from the farrier's. Or if they'll make it to Mont St Michel ere they kill each other."

They all grinned at that, even the morose Rufus, for Durand and Justin had been quarreling like tomcats ever since they'd left Fougères—clashing over which road to take, how fast a pace to set, whose fault it was that they'd not been able to ride out as early as they'd hoped, who was to blame for this latest delay.

"I'd best go see if the farrier has got bone-sick of their yammering and tossed them both into his horse trough," Morgan said, and they all grinned again, for the Breton blacksmith was the biggest man any of them had ever seen, with legs like tree trunks and hands like hams. Rising stiffly, Morgan stretched and winced and then halted, gazing toward the north. "Riders," he said, and the other men scrambled to their feet, too, wary and watchful.

AT THE FARRIER'S SHED, DURAND HAD made such a pest of himself, hovering close at hand and peering over the blacksmith's shoulder, that the Breton at last rose to his full, formidable height, pointed to the door and told him to get out. Durand spoke no Breton, but the man's gesture did not need translation.

Outside, Justin was pacing back and forth, unable to stand still for more than a heartbeat. He turned swiftly as Durand emerged from the shed. "How much longer?"

"You speak this accursed tongue of theirs," Durand snapped. "Ask him yourself."

"I've already told you that I do not speak Breton," Justin snapped back. "I understand a bit because I know some Welsh."

"Well, you still get more than I do." Durand glowered at Justin, as if his language lack were the younger man's fault. "Go ask him, not me!"

Justin silently counted to ten. It did not help. "If you'd checked your horse's hooves ere we left Fougères, you might have noticed that a shoe was loose. But of course you could not be bothered—"

Justin stopped for Durand was no longer listening, staring over Justin's shoulder with such intensity that he spun about. Morgan and their men-at-arms were hastening toward them, and now he and Durand could see it, too—the rising dust of approaching riders, coming from the north, from Mont St Michel.

"I KNOW HIM!" DURAND EXCLAIMED AS the newcomers rode into the village. Stepping quickly into the road, he called out, "My lord abbot! A moment, if you please!"

The abbot reined in, gazing down impassively at Durand. His guards urged their mounts closer, but Durand did not appear threatening. At his most courtly, he bowed gracefully. "We met in Paris last year, at the court of the king of the French. I am Sir Durand de Curzon."

The name meant nothing to Abbot Jourdain, but the man before him was well-dressed, well-spoken, and well-armed, clearly a member of the gentry. "Ah, yes," he said politely. "Sir... Durand, God's blessings upon you... and your traveling companions," he added, glancing toward Justin, Morgan, and the men-at-arms.

"They are my servants," Durand said dismissively. "A man would be foolish to ride alone in these dangerous times. It is indeed fortuitous that we've met on the road like this, my lord abbot, for I am heading to Mont St Michel. I would not have wanted to miss the opportunity to pay my respects to you."

The abbot responded with a courtesy of his own. He'd had much practice at extricating himself from tiresome social situations, and he said, kindly but firmly, "Alas, I cannot tarry, much as I would enjoy renewing acquaintance with you, Sir Durand. We must reach Fougères by dark."

Durand did not move from the center of the road. "Indeed? I have just come from Fougères myself, where I had the honor of performing a service for the Duchess Constance and Lord Raoul, her liege man."

Influenced, perhaps, by the names Durand was dropping with such abandon, the abbot curbed his impatience and mustered up a polite smile. Before he could make another attempt to end the conversation, Durand stepped closer. "I believe that a lady dear to my heart is currently enjoying the hospitality of your abbey, my lord. Not that I would imply there is anything improper between us," he said with a smile that suggested just that, "for she is of the blood royal of Brittany. Lady Arzhela de Dinan... I trust she is well?"

The abbot bit his lip, hesitated, and then said, "I assume so," with such obvious discomfort that Justin felt a chill of foreboding.

Shouldering his way forward, he demanded, "Has evil befallen her?"

The abbot looked annoyed now, as well as uneasy. "Your servant could do with a lesson in manners, Sir Durand."

"He is not my servant," Durand said grudgingly, glaring at Justin.

"I could be his baseborn son for all it matters! My lord, what of Lady Arzhela?"

"I do not know you," the abbot responded icily, "and I am not in the habit of being accosted by strangers." He included Durand in that rebuke, glancing from one to the other suspiciously, and Justin hastily knelt in the road.

"Forgive me, my lord abbot," he said humbly. "I did indeed misspeak myself. But we have reason to fear for Lady Arzhela's safety. Can you at least assure us that she has come to no harm?"

Mollified somewhat by Justin's penitent demeanor, the abbot was silent for a moment, considering. "I need to know your identity," he said at last.

Justin's brain was racing, weighing his options. They dare

not mention Lord John's name, not in Brittany. But the abbey lay within King Richard's domains, within Normandy. Why, though, would King Richard's men be seeking the Lady Arzhela? If that got back to Constance, there'd be hell to pay.

"I am Sir Luke de Marston," he said, going with the first name to pop into his head. "I am foster brother to Simon de Lusignan." He was gambling now that Arzhela's liaison with de Lusignan was an open secret, and gambling, too, that she'd much rather be called to account for her sexual sins than for her political ones. "Simon and Lady Arzhela... they quarreled a fortnight ago. She has refused to see Simon since then, and he hoped that if we told her how very sorry he was, her heart might soften toward him..."

"That is the truth, my lord abbot," Durand chimed in, shooting Justin a glance of surprised approval. "We are on a mission of mercy, if you will. We promised Simon that we'd put in a good word for him with his lady. The poor sod has been so lovesick that we could endure his lamenting and moaning for not another day!"

The abbot was regarding them with an odd expression, not easy to decipher. Justin was trying to come up with a plausible answer for the question he was dreading: Why is the Lady Arzhela in danger? To his astonishment, it was not asked. Instead, Abbot Jourdain said, choosing his words with conspicuous care, "Is it possible that Simon could not wait, that he acted on his own to mend this breach between them?"

"I suppose so," Durand acknowledged cautiously, and both he and Justin were taken aback by the abbot's emotional reaction. He closed his eyes for a moment, embracing hope like a drowning man might grab for a lifeline.

"That would explain it," he cried. "Thanks be to the Almighty and Blessed St Michael! She must have gone off with de Lusignan!"

"Are you saying she is missing?"

The abbot was so relieved that he did not even notice the terseness of the question. "So we thought. She rode over to Genêts yesterday and told her servant that she'd be staying the night. But when he went to the priory guesthouse this morn, she was not there. Her mare was still in the stable, and a search turned up a mantle that her man claimed as hers. None had seen her, though, since yesterday, none knew where she might have gone... I felt I had no choice but to inform the duchess, for the Lady Arzhela is her cousin. But now there is no need, for if it was a lover's quarrel... We all know how foolish women can be at such times..."

He got no further, his words trailing off and his smile fading, for Simon de Lusignan's friends had whirled and were running for their horses. As the blacksmith led a grey stallion out, the man who called himself Durand de Curzon vaulted up onto the animal's back and spurred after the others. The blacksmith was shouting that they owed him money, village dogs had begun to bark, and the abbot's escort milled about in confusion, uncertain what was expected of them.

"My lord abbot? Shall we go after them?"

Abbot Jourdain's shoulders slumped and he rubbed his fingers gingerly against his temples, like a man stricken with a sudden, sharp headache. By now the riders were already out of sight, the dust beginning to settle. "No," he said slowly. "I shall have to continue on to Fougères, after all."

THEY REACHED MONT ST MICHEL AS the late-afternoon shadows were lengthening. In spite of his fear for Arzhela, Justin was awestruck at sight of the abbey. At first glance, it looked to be a castle carved from the very rocks of the isle, its towering spires reaching halfway to Heaven, the last bastion of Christian faith in a world of denial and disbelief. A fragment of religious lore came back to him, that St Michael was known as the guardian of the threshold between life and eternity, and that seemed the perfect description for his abbey, too, a bridge between the land of the living and the sea of the dead.

Durand had reined in beside him, revealing by a muttered exclamation that was both involuntary and irreverent that this was his first sight of Mont St Michel, too: "Holy Lucifer!"

By now their men had caught up with them. Justin turned in the saddle as a local Breton approached and offered to guide them across the mudflats. Durand did not wait, though, and spurred his stallion out onto the wet sand. Justin called Durand an uncomplimentary name and then plunged after him. Much more reluctantly, so did the others.

WHILE JUSTIN AND DURAND CLIMBED UP the cliff to the abbey, Morgan went about finding lodgings for them in the village on the slope below. It was an easy task, for virtually every house offered bed and food; fishing was the primary occupation of the Montois, and more fished for pilgrims than for mullet or shrimp. They were soon settled in an ancient hostel called La Sirène, flirting with a sarcastic serving maid who claimed the unlikely name of Salomé. Yearning for their daily ration of English ale, Crispin and Rufus had been thirsty enough in Paris to try cervoise, a French beer, but they hadn't been able to get even that once they'd left the Île de France. Now they stared dubiously at the cups of hard cider brought by Salomé, but she brooked no refusals, pausing only long enough to slap Crispin's hand away from her hip.

They were dunking bread in steaming bowls of soup when Justin and Durand returned, looking so somber that Morgan pushed back from the table and moved to meet them. Unlike the men-at-arms, who were surprisingly incurious about their mission, Morgan had done some judicious eavesdropping and he knew at once that they'd not found the lady they sought.

"We've ordered food," he said, "and a Norman cider strong enough to peel paint off a wall. Would you eat?"

Justin shook his head. "It is a madhouse up there. No rumor is too ridiculous to be believed. The monks are like dogs chasing their tails, all going in different directions. They could tell us little more than we learned from Abbot Jourdain. But since she was last seen in Genêts, that is where we go next."

"Now?" Morgan blinked, unable to conceal his dismay. The men-at-arms had heard enough to alarm them, too, and they were staring at Justin and Durand as if they had suddenly revealed themselves to have horns and forked tails.

"Yes, now," Durand said curtly, reaching down to help himself to one of the ciders while Justin beckoned to Salomé. After a brief exchange, Justin turned toward a customer at a nearby table, a sparse, shriveled man of indeterminate years, with the deeply creased wrinkles and pale eyes of one who'd spent most of his life exposed to nature at its worst.

Morgan seized the opportunity to argue, even though he suspected that Durand was about as flexible as the granite stones of St Michel. "Sir Durand, we've been talking to some of the villagers and they say the tides are as treacherous here as anywhere in Christendom. Salomé told us that they've lost count of the unwary souls drowned as they tried to cross the bay, and the Genêts crossing is much longer than the one we made, nigh on three miles—"

"That is why we are hiring a guide," Durand cut in. Justin was coming back to their table, and Durand raised his eyebrows in a wordless question. When Justin nodded, he jerked his thumb toward their men-at-arms, saying, "We may have a rebellion on our hands. These stouthearted cocks are loath to get their feet wet."

That did not endear him to either Morgan or the men-at-arms, but his gibe was wasted upon Justin, who had thoughts only for the missing Arzhela. "Let them await us here, then," he said impatiently. "I've found us a guide, but he does not come cheap, not for a crossing at this time of day."

Durand shrugged; they were spending John's money, after all. Draining the last of the cider, he started toward the door. When Justin would have followed, Morgan stepped forward. "Godspeed, Justin. I hope you find her."

"So do I, Morgan." As their eyes met, though, Justin could see that they both feared it was too late.

THERE WERE NO PILGRIMS CROSSING TO the Mont that late in the day, and those already at the abbey were spending the night there. So Justin, Durand, and their guide had the bay to themselves, encountering only a large seal napping on a flat rock. Dusk was dimming the sky and blurring the horizon as they reached the beach at Genêts.

They knew at once that something was very wrong. People were gathered in clots before the priory walls, strangely subdued and silent. The priory gate was shut, and there was no response when they banged on the door. Vespers was being rung from somewhere in the town, but oddly enough, the bells of Notre Dame and Saint-Sebastien were not pealing out the hour. An unnatural stillness overhung the priory, and they knew instinctively that it had nothing to do with the disappearance of a Breton noblewoman.

They continued to pound upon the gate until footsteps

sounded on the other side and the door slowly creaked open. They glimpsed hollow eyes and blanched skin before a tremulous voice instructed them to come back later. Durand lunged forward to wedge his boot in the door, but it was already swinging shut. "Wait," Justin cried out. "Wait! We come from the abbey—"

The door opened so fast that Durand was caught off balance and stumbled against the post. With a choked cry of *"Deo gratias,"* the gatekeeper grabbed their arms and pulled them inside. He was tonsured and clad in a monk's habit, but they decided he was most likely a novice, for he looked barely old enough to shave, much less take final vows. "I am Brother Briag." His French was flavored with a strong Breton accent. His eyes darted from one to the other. "But you are not brethren. Who are you? Why did you lie?"

"We did not lie. We never said we were monks. We are friends of Lady Arzhela de Dinan and we need to speak with Brother Andrev, for we were told he was the last one to see her..." Justin stopped, for the young monk's eyes were filling with tears. "What is it? What has happened here?"

"There has been..." Brother Briag swallowed and then continued, his voice so low that they could hardly hear him. "... murder done."

THE PRIORY CELL AT GENÊTS WAS a very small one, with only four monks. Now one was dead, one lay near death, and the only two left were overwhelmed. The elderly Brother Martin was ostensibly in charge, but he was half blind and so dazed by the tragedy that all responsibility had fallen upon the novice, Brother Briag. Moving like one in a trance, Brother Briag pointed toward the infirmary. "Master Laurence is in there now, doing what he can." Swiping the back of his hand

139

across his cheek, he explained that Master Laurence was the town physician. He'd already revealed the identity of the victim—the man they'd come to Genêts to find, Brother Andrev.

"We summoned the provost's deputy. But by the time he came, whoever did this evil was long gone." Brother Briag's steps lagged as they approached the church porch. "Are you sure you want to see?"

"You need not come in," Justin said, and the young monk slowly shook his head.

"I'll be seeing it in my sleep for the rest of my life," he said softly. "One more time will not matter."

They followed him into the nave of the church. Almost at once they were assailed by the smell of blood. "There," Brother Briag gasped, pointing toward one of the transepts. "It happened there."

It was easy to see where the murder had been committed, for the floor was pooled in congealed blood. They stood staring down at the splattered tiles. The lantern light had begun to sway wildly, so badly was the monk's hand shaking. Taking the lantern from him, Justin urged quietly, "Tell us all that you can remember."

"The monk came in the afternoon. We know now that he was not truly a monk, for no man of God could commit such sacrilege. To kill in God's House..." Brother Briag shuddered. "He claimed to be here on Duchess Constance's behalf and he asked many questions about Lady Arzhela. We knew, of course, that she'd gone missing, but we had naught to tell him. After he spoke with Brother Andrev, I thought he went away. He did not, though, for later I saw him with Brother Bernard. They talked together for a few moments and entered the church. It was then that I went to find Brother Andrev."

"Why?"

Durand's question was so abrupt, so pointed, that the young monk flinched. "I... I'd rather not say," he whispered.

"Because you do not want to speak ill of the dead?" Justin's voice was soothing, nonjudgmental, and after a moment, Brother Briag gave a ragged sigh, almost like a sob.

"How did you guess? I did not like Brother Bernard. No one did. He took pleasure in causing trouble. I knew he'd sneaked off to see the provost's deputy once Lady Arzhela was reported missing. I knew, too, that he was no friend to her, and so I went to alert Brother Andrev that he was likely up to no good. If only I had kept my mouth shut, he'd not have been hurt!"

"Brother Andrev went into the church after them?"

The novice monk nodded miserably. "I was on the porch when I heard him cry out. I rushed inside and—" He shuddered again. "Brother Andrev was fighting with the monk, clinging to his arm. As I got closer, I saw the knife. I did not see him stab Brother Andrev, though, he was that fast. Brother Andrev staggered back and collapsed and the killer ran out. I tried to stop him, I swear I did, but he just shoved me aside." He glanced down at the bandage swathed around his forearm. "It was only later that I even realized I'd been cut."

"When did you find Brother Bernard's body?" Justin asked, for Durand seemed willing to concede the interrogation to him.

"Afterward..." He swallowed convulsively. "I was yelling for help once I discovered that Brother Andrev had been stabbed. I remember kneeling beside him, trying to staunch the blood, and then I saw—I saw Brother Bernard. He was crumpled in that corner, and there was blood, so much blood. Master Laurence later told me that his throat had been cut."

After that, there was no more to be said. No one spoke until they emerged into the fading light. Brother Briag was cradling his injured arm, in obvious discomfort. He looked from Justin to Durand, back to Justin again. "Do you know why this happened?"

They both answered him in the same breath, Justin admitting, "No, we do not," and Durand saying grimly, "Not yet."

JUSTIN AND DURAND HAD NO TROUBLE finding the house of the provost's deputy; Brother Briag had given them clear directions: off the marketplace, on the same street as the bakery. Genêts was a prosperous market town with several thousand inhabitants, a hospital, a salt works, and a shipyard. The fact that the town was located on a major pilgrim route made their task all the more difficult. It would have been much harder for the killer to escape notice in a small, inbred village where every stranger's arrival was fodder for gossip.

Thanks to Brother Briag, Justin and Durand were well armed with useful information about the provost's deputy, Master Benoit, a mild-mannered, diffident widower who had the good luck to be a cousin of the provost's wife. The positions of provost and deputy provost were political plums, unusual in that those who held them were the abbot's men first, and only secondly the king's, for the abbey had been given the privilege of appointing its own candidates. The provost had ridden out in search of the Lady Arzhela, Brother Briag had confided, his absence a misfortune for all concerned, including Master Benoit, who was no more qualified to handle a murder investigation than he was to lead a crusade to the Holy Land.

Justin and Durand already harbored suspicions about Master Benoit's capabilities, for why had he not been to investigate the murder scene yet? When their incessant knocking finally got him to open his door, one glance was enough to tell them what he'd been doing in the hours since the killing. His eyes were glazed and bloodshot, his clothing rumpled and stained, and he stank of wine, urine, and vomit.

Benoit seemed reluctant to admit them, but mustered up only a weak protest when they pushed their way inside. Stumbling after them like a guest in his own house, he asked what they wanted, his faltering, hesitant words sounding more like a plaintive lament than a forceful demand.

"Sit down ere you fall down," Durand ordered, shoving a chair toward him. He did, blinking up at them blearily as they circled him like large, hungry cats, shrinking the circle until he had to tilt his head to look into their faces. He sensed that they had him at a disadvantage, but when he tried to rise, Durand's hand closed on his upper arm, fingers digging into his flesh like iron hooks, and he decided to stay put.

"Who... who are you? If you've come to rob me, you've... you've made a great mistake." He licked his lips, sought to keep his voice steady as he told them he was the deputy provost of the barony of Genêts, but neither man seemed impressed.

"We know that, Master Benoit." Justin had to resist the urge to grab the man by those quaking shoulders and shake the truth out of him, so sure was he that Benoit had the answers they needed. "That is why we are here."

"I... I do not understand."

"The murder," Durand snapped, angrier than even he could have explained, for weakness and cowardice brought out the worst in his own nature; he was cruelest to those he scorned. "You do remember the murder, sousepot?"

Benoit shrank back in the chair. "Are you... are you the killers?"

Durand swore and would have dragged the man to his feet if Justin had not stopped him. "You're scaring him out of his wits. That is not the way."

"No? Given your vast experience, suppose you show me how it is done!"

Justin grabbed the knight by the arm and pulled him aside. "Look at him, Durand," he insisted, low-voiced. "He is terrified. Ask yourself why. I grant you that was no pretty scene in the church, but there has to be more to this than squeamishness. What is he drinking to forget?"

"I could use a drink myself," Durand growled. "I know I am way too sober when you start to make sense, de Quincy." With a mocking gesture, he indicated that Justin had the field.

"Benoit!" Justin said sharply, and the deputy sat upright, flinching as Durand snatched up a candle and brought it close to his face. "We are seeking the Lady Arzhela de Dinan and I think you can help us find her."

Benoit's gaze slid toward the table and the wine flagon. "How?" he mumbled, and then, "I am right thirsty..."

Justin picked up the flagon, holding it just out of reach. "You can drink yourself sodden if that is your wish. But first you must tell us what Brother Bernard told you about Lady Arzhela."

Benoit bowed his head. "I cannot..."

Justin flipped the lid on the flagon, letting Benoit see the sloshing liquid inside. His own stomach tightened at the sight, for it was dark red in the subdued light, the color of drying blood. "Yes, you can, and you must. You know that, Benoit."

"It was not my fault—" The deputy looked up suddenly, briefly, his eyes desperately seeking Justin's. "It was not my fault!"

"No one said it was your fault. What did he say?"

"It was a daft tale, made no sense." Benoit's words were slurred with wine and self-pity; he was no longer meeting Justin's gaze. "No one would have believed it, no one!"

Justin thrust the flagon into the man's hands, keeping his own hand clamped upon Benoit's wrist. "Tell us!"

"He... he claimed that Lady Arzhela had sneaked into the church and then come back out dressed like a needy pilgrim. Naturally I did not credit it, for who would? She is a lady of high rank and royal blood, one who likes her comforts. Why would she put on stinking, coarse sackcloth and mingle with the lowborn and poor, with beggars and rabble? And all know Brother Bernard was... odd. I thanked him and promptly forgot about it, as any sensible man would. And then... then he was slain in the church—"

His voice thickened, but he was so thoroughly cowed that he dared not drink until these fearsome strangers said he could. He was no longer being held and he glanced up imploringly, seeking their understanding, their mercy. But he was alone. The door stood ajar and the men were gone.

CHAPTER XII

February 1194
Mont St Michel, Normandy

While pilgrims and travelers of the upper classes would find a welcome in the abbey's guesthouse and the abbot's own lodgings, Christ's poor were admitted to the almonry. It provided protection from the rain, but it lacked fireplaces, and because it was exposed to the Aquilon, the name locals gave to those merciless winter winds that swept in from the north, it was a stark, frigid refuge. To people unfamiliar with luxury or comfort, though, it was enough.

It was different for Arzhela. Her first night at the almonry had been the longest of her life. She'd been sure they'd find her body come morning, frozen so solid that they'd have to thaw her out before burying her. The blankets provided by the monks were as thin as wafers, and the icy tiled floor was a martyr's bed of pain. She didn't doubt that she'd have slept better, and been warmer for certes, burrowing into the straw in the abbey stables.

But her shivering and chattering teeth finally awakened her nearest neighbors. "I am Juvette," a woman whispered, "and this is my daughter, Mikaela. Come huddle with us. Three bodies are warmer than one."

Arzhela hesitated, but she could no longer feel her feet, and she edged closer, discovering that the woman was right. When she awakened in the morning, she was snug against Juvette's back, and Mikaela's head was pillowed in her lap. Stirring as soon as Arzhela did, Juvette sat up sleepily. "We are stacked like pancakes," she laughed, and Arzhela's stomach rumbled, reminding her how long it had been since she'd eaten.

"Do the monks feed us?" she ventured.

"Of course, and right well. There'll be ample helpings of bread and cheese." Juvette easily recognized the notes of hunger in Arzhela's voice; that was a song she knew well. "We saved a bit of bread from yesterday's meal," she said. "Here, take some."

Arzhela looked at the stale pieces of bread wrapped in a scrap of cloth and quickly shook her head. "I could not, for you have so little!"

"We have enough to share," Juvette insisted, giving Arzhela no choice but to accept a small crust.

As the day advanced, Arzhela was astonished by the goodwill of these impoverished pilgrims. She'd expected that they would be pious, for a pilgrimage in winter, especially one as dangerous as this, was proof of serious intent. She'd not expected, though, that they would be so generous, so willing to share their meager belongings, their stories, and their laughter. There was a communal atmosphere in the almonry unlike anything she'd ever experienced on her own pilgrimages, and again and again she saw small examples of kindness and good humor.

Most were Breton or French, although there was one dour Englishman. While pilgrimages were lauded as acts of spiritual renewal, most pilgrims had more pragmatic, mundane reasons for making them. People sought out saints to beg for healing, to pray for forgiveness, and sometimes to die in a state of grace. Other pilgrimages were penitential in nature, for the Church often ordered caught-out or repentant sinners to atone for their transgressions at distant holy shrines. One of their company had already confessed cheerfully that he was there for habitual fornication, although he did not put it as delicately as that. Another admitted that his offense had been poaching on his bishop's lands. If any were expiating the sin of adultery, they prudently kept that to themselves.

Most of these February pilgrims were at Mont St Michel for obvious reasons. There was a man who coughed blood into stained rags. Mikaela had been born at Michaelmas, named in honor of the Archangel, and now that she was ailing, her mother had brought her to the Mont to plead for his intercession. One woman was there to pray that her hearing be restored. A man crippled by the joint evil was tended lovingly by his wife, but Arzhela could not imagine how—even with her help—he'd managed to climb the hill and the steep steps to the almonry. A young couple seemed in the bloom of health, but they'd wept together in the night.

Miquelots they were called, those who dared to brave the tides for the sake of blessed St Michael. With a dart of pride, Arzhela realized that she was one of them; she was a miquelot, too. She was amazed by the feelings that her fellow pilgrims had stirred in her. They were strangers, after all, lowborn, most of them, the sort of people she'd seen but never truly noticed before. But after just one night and one day, they'd begun to matter to her. When they'd been allowed to visit the shrine in the nave, she'd spent almost as much time praying for them as for herself. She winced every time she heard that strangled

148

death rattle of a cough. She'd got two of the able-bodied men to assist the cripple and his wife up the great staircase into the church. She'd surreptitiously hidden a pouchful of coins in Juvette's bundle, confident that when she eventually discovered it, Juvette would joyfully conclude that this was the Archangel's bounty. And she'd taken charge of Yann.

She still wasn't sure what she was going to do with him. She guessed his age to be between eleven and thirteen; he claimed to remember eleven winters, but truth telling was not one of his virtues, and she thought him quite capable of making himself younger than he truly was to appear more sympathetic. He said he was an orphan and she had no reason to doubt him. He was cunning in the way of children and young animals left to fend for themselves at an early age. He was also cheeky and quick to take advantage of an opportunity, qualities that she should deplore but found amusing instead.

While she'd lain wakeful and miserable late into the night, she'd seen him creeping cat-like among the sleeping pilgrims, deftly removing some of the coins from the self-confessed poacher's scrip. Clever lad, she'd thought, not to take it all, for the theft was less likely to be discovered that way. And the next morning she cornered him out in the north–south stairwell.

"You need a new trade, my boy, for you are a pitiful cutpurse," she announced, and waited until he'd run through his litany of impassioned denials. It was then that she pried his name out of him, as well as a grudging confession that he'd followed the pilgrims like a seagull followed fishing sloops. She made him promise that he'd do no more thieving whilst he was at the abbey, but she knew hunger would always win out over promises, especially those given under duress, and she insisted upon keeping him close for the remainder of the day. He protested at length, but she did not think he truly minded once he was sure she'd not turn him in, for attention was as rare as hen's teeth in an orphan's world.

He was as sharp as a Fleming's blade, though, the only one to notice that she did not talk like the others. As he put it, she sounded "like you've just eaten a marrow tart." She explained away the telltale echoes of education and privilege in her voice by telling him she'd been taught by nuns, and he seemed to accept that. She found it sad, though, that food was his tally stick, his only means of measurement.

Arzhela was thoroughly enjoying her incursion into this alien world, so much so that she wondered idly if she ought to consider giving over her life to God. A pity nuns had to live such cloistered lives. If only she could do good on a wider stage than a secluded convent. Though if she were to be honest, vows of poverty and obedience might begin to chafe after a while. And then there was that irksome vow of chastity. By now Arzhela was laughing at herself, realizing how ludicrous it was for her to even contemplate a religious vocation. She liked her comfort too much, liked feather beds and good food and Saint Pourçain wine from the Auvergne. She liked getting her own way and for certes, she liked men.

That had proven to be an expensive vice, she acknowledged ironically. The priests preached that wanton, fallen women risked ruination, scandal, and mortal sin. But none had ever warned her she could end up in an unheated almonry, sleeping on a bare floor, sharing her bed with good-hearted companions who were, nonetheless, much in need of baths, keeping an eye peeled for a killer.

Actually, she'd given *him* surprisingly little thought since arriving at the almonry. In part, she was distracted by the novelty of her surroundings, in part she was fascinated by the drama provided by the other pilgrims. But she also felt secure, confident that she had outwitted her enemy. This was one fox who had eluded the hounds. And she meant to make the most of it. She would prove to the Almighty and His Archangel that she deserved to be a miquelot. She would convince Constance to help her found a nunnery, where the nuns would pray for her immortal soul and the souls of her dead husbands and even her lovers. Well, at least most of them. And she would begin her good deeds by saving Yann from the gallows and eternal damnation, whether he wanted to be saved or not.

Because their numbers were small, the February miquelots were allowed to visit the Archangel's shrine again that afternoon. They were also permitted into the nave for the Vespers service that evening, and after being fed supper, they settled down in the almonry for the night. It was early by Arzhela's reckoning. But as the candles provided by the monks began to burn down, the drone of conversation gave way to drowsy murmuring, and eventually to silence.

An hour later, Arzhela was wide awake and very bored. Beside her, Juvette was snoring softly. On her other side, Yann had begun to squirm and she leaned over to whisper, "Do not even think about it, lad." She'd finally figured out what do to with the boy. She wouldn't be in a position to aid him herself until she'd got out of this snare, which, God Willing, would be soon; Johnny's men ought to be arriving any day now. Once the trouble was over, she'd find a place for him on one of her manors. Until then, she'd send him to Brother Andrev for safekeeping.

She couldn't tell Yann about her long-range plans for him, but she had confided her intent to entrust him to Brother Andrev. He'd objected vehemently, of course. She was confident, though, that Brother Andrev would be able to keep the sly imp under control until she could reclaim him. Mayhap by then she'd have thought of a suitable trade for him. With those nimble fingers of his, he might make a weaver one day. Or even a silversmith. Well, no, that might not be the best apprenticeship for a lad with larceny in his heart. She laughed soundlessly, imagining Yann stealing spoons right under his master's nose, and warned him to stay put when he started wriggling again.

The silence of the night was not really silent. The Aquilon wind was howling at the shutters. Pilgrims were snoring and muttering in their sleep. One of the remaining candles was sputtering. And over all, like the distant sound of the sea, was the coughing of the pilgrim with consumption. Arzhela was so accustomed to that throttled hacking that it had become background noise. It was a while before she realized that it had changed timbre.

Rising, she groped her way over to him. As soon as she touched his face, she jerked her hand back, for his skin was burning. It took her only a moment to decide what to do. "Get that candle, Yann," she murmured, as she stooped and maneuvered the man to his feet. He was so pitifully light and frail that it was not difficult at all. He gave her a feverish, bewildered look, but did not resist when she began to guide him toward the door. Yann had picked up the candle, although he'd yet to move. "Come on," she prompted. "You do not think I'm going to let you loose on these poor sleeping sheep, do you?"

It was too dark to see for certain, but she thought she caught the glimmer of a grin as he followed. "Where are we going?" he asked as soon as they were out in the portico. "The monks will have our hides for roaming around like this." He sounded more excited than alarmed at the prospect, and did not protest when she instructed him to help her support the man's weight.

152

"We have to get him down those steps," she said, jerking her head toward the great gallery stairs. "That will not be too hard. But then we have to get up a second flight of stairs."

Yann's expression clearly said that he thought she'd lost all her wits. "How? The last I looked, none of us have archangels' wings."

"Are you saying you cannot keep pace with an ailing man and a woman past her prime?" Arzhela gibed. "We are going up to the abbey guesthouse."

"As if they'd let the likes of us in there!"

"Oh, ye of little faith. Above the guest hall is the abbey infirmary."

"Oh," Yann said, somewhat deflated. "But what makes you think they'll treat him there?"

"Because the Almighty and I would have it so."

Yann shook his head. "You are daft, woman." He stopped complaining, though, and did his part as they began their laborious climb. It seemed to take forever, for they had to stop and rest repeatedly. The stricken pilgrim asked no questions, obediently shuffling forward in response to Arzhela's coaxing. His coughing had eased, but he seemed in a daze, only dimly aware of his companions and his surroundings. Arzhela knew there was little to be done for him, not unless the Archangel chose to bestow one of his miracles. But at least he'd get to die in a bed, she vowed. Every man deserved that much.

When they finally reached the infirmary, she did not bother seeking admittance, simply shoved the door open. Within, a flickering lamp cast eerie shadows, but it gave off enough light for her to make out several beds, simple structures little better than pallets. In two of them, ailing monks snatched at broken sleep, turning and tossing restively. Upon the third, the infirmarian was napping, still fully dressed for in a few hours he'd have to rise for Matins. Attuned to his patients' needs, he awakened at once.

"What is it?" he whispered. As his eyes fell upon the man sagging between Arzhela and Yann, he came swiftly to his feet. He was only of middling height and the sparse hair crowning his tonsure was as white as newly skimmed milk. But his appearance was deceptive, for he lifted the pilgrim without apparent effort and deposited the man upon his own bed. He asked no questions, for the patient's condition was self-evident, and hastened over to a table holding vials and powders. Arzhela and Yann watched with interest as he blended several herbs in a small mortar. He seemed quite competent, but Arzhela could not resist offering her help, suggesting softly that lungwort was good for consumption, as was wood betony. Her assistance was unappreciated, and within moments, she and Yann found themselves banished from the infirmary.

They stood there in the gloomy south stairwell, momentarily at a loss, for this seemed to be an anticlimactic end to their rescue mission. "Will he die, do you think?" Yann asked at last and Arzhela shook her head emphatically.

"Indeed not," she lied, with such assurance that Yann's face brightened, reminding her that for all his worldly, cynical posturing, he was still a child. "I'd go so far as to say your good deed tonight cancels out your theft last night, at least in the Almighty's account book. Mind you, another such lapse and you'll find yourself in Abbot Jourdain's dungeon, alone with the rats."

His eyes widened. He summoned up his usual bravado, though, saying skeptically, "Why would they need dungeons in an abbey? How many evil-doers go to church, after all?"

"You'd be surprised, Yann," she said dryly. "Moreover, the abbot is a lord as well, for he holds the barony of Genêts." She regretted having to scare him into hewing to the straight and narrow, but thieving was both crime and sin. "Now, are you sleepy yet?'

"No," he admitted, and added hopefully, "Have you some mischief in mind?"

"In a manner of speaking," she said, and there in the dimly lit stairwell they grinned at each other in a moment of comfortable and cheerful complicity.

CHAPTER XIII

February 1194
Genêts, Normandy

Genêts had many small, shabby taverns. Justin and Durand had been making the rounds after their guide refused to escort them back across the bay, seeking another local man to take the defector's place. Until the third tavern, they'd had no luck. Again and again the tavern patrons heard them out with interest, only to balk once they were told the crossing must be made now. Again and again Justin and Durand were warned about the treacherous tides and quicksand bogs. Again and again they were reminded that high tide that night would be soon after Compline, and Compline was not that far off. Finally, they offered a sum so large that the tavern fell silent.

One of the loudest nay-sayers, a cocky youth with snapping dark eyes and a birthmark upon his cheek, stood up abruptly. "I am Baldric," he said, "though some of these jesters call me Cain for reasons anyone with eyes can see. For what you are going to pay me, you can call me by either name."

The other tavern regulars had chuckled at the mention of Baldric's ironic nickname, but by the time he finished speaking, most of them were regarding him in dismay, and one of Baldric's companions seemed to speak for them all when he asked, "What will you use the money for, cousin, the fanciest funeral Genêts has ever seen?"

Baldric grinned. "No, I mean to spend it in St-Malo on Cock's Lane!" Snatching up his cousin's drink, he drained it dry, then swaggered over to Durand and Justin. "I want payment now, in case you do not make it to shore."

"Payment when we reach the shore," Durand countered coolly. "That will give you incentive to see that we do 'make it.'"

They settled upon half now, half when they reached Mont St Michel, and before Baldric's friends could seriously try to dissuade him, he led his new employers out into the night.

THE MONT WAS STILL SHARPLY ETCHED against the darkening sky and seemed to have a halo of stars. The horses were edgy, sensing the mood of their riders, and Baldric had difficulty getting his mount under control. "I usually do this on foot during the day," he admitted. "Any advice about keeping on this nag's good side?"

"Just do not fall off," Durand said laconically, and the young Norman laughed mirthlessly.

"Passing strange that you should say that, for I was about to warn you that we do not stop, not for anything or anyone. If one of you blunders off course into a bog, a pity, but we'll not be riding back to your rescue. Understood?"

Justin and Durand traded smiles like unsheathed daggers. "Understood."

Baldric was studying the clouds scudding across the sky. "At least the wind is from the north. The tide comes in faster if it's driven by a westerly wind. Given a choice, I'd rather be crossing at least two hours before the next high tide. But we still ought to have enough time. Just follow after me, and hope that the Archangel is in a benevolent mood tonight."

Justin was quite willing to put his fate in St Michael's hands. He was not as sure about Baldric. They dared not wait, though. If the murderous "monk" had crossed over after learning of Arzhela's masquerade, her chances of living to see the dawn were not good. The killer had several hours' head start on them, and a knife still wet with the blood of Brothers Bernard and Andrev.

The wind was cold and wet and carried the scent of seaweed and salt. The muted roar of the unseen sea echoed in Justin's ears, as rhythmic as a heartbeat. Seagulls screeched overhead, their shrill cries eerily plaintive. His stallion had an odd gait, picking up its hooves so high that it was obviously not comfortable with the footing. One of the tavern customers had told Justin that walking on the sand was like treading upon a tightly stretched drum; he very much hoped that he'd not have the opportunity to test that observation for himself. Behind him, he could hear Durand cursing. Justin kept his eyes upon the glow of Baldric's swaying lantern, doing his best to convince himself that, as St Michael led Christian souls into the holy light, so would this Norman youth lead them to safety upon the shore.

THE SOUND OF THE SURGING SEA was louder now. Along the horizon they could see the starlit froth of whitecaps. Despite all they'd been told about the tides of St Michel, they were amazed by the speed of those encroaching waters, and it was with vast relief that they splashed onto the sands of the Mont. Baldric did not slow his pace, though, urging them off the beach and on toward the steep rocks that sheltered the village.

They soon saw why he'd been in such haste. The water was rising at an incredibly rapid rate. By the time the tide hit the isle of Tombelaine, it had merged into a single white wave. It was soon swallowing up the beaches of the Mont, a wall of water slamming against the rocks with such force that spume was flung high into the air, and for the first time, Justin and Durand fully understood why it had been so difficult to find a guide.

MORGAN AND JASPAER TOOK THE REINS of the horses and led them off. Neither man seemed very sober to Justin, and he could only hope that there'd be a stable groom on hand. They could spare no more time, though, for Baldric was already some distance away and beckoning to them.

"Come on," he called, "and I'll show you the fastest way to get up to the abbey. If you go through the village and then up and around, you'll not get there for days! This is much quicker."

Baldric's shortcut was indeed that, although it also required the agility of a mountain goat. They scrambled up the slope after him, were breathing heavily by the time they reached the narthex, a vast arched porch that stretched along the west side of the abbey. "There you go," Baldric said, with an expectant pause that lasted until Justin added some extra coins to the pile already jangling in his money pouch. "You ought to have no trouble with old Devi. He's been the gatekeeper for the abbey since before the Great Flood, and is well nigh as ancient as God. Nine out of ten nights he forgets to latch the door, and since he sleeps like the dead, you ought to be able to sneak right past him. We outran the tides, so you seem to be on a lucky streak."

Durand grunted and headed for the porch. Justin paused long enough to throw a "Thank you" over his shoulder. "Our men have rented lodgings in the village. You can sleep there if you like."

"Not needed. I know a lass here who'll be happy to share her bed with me." Baldric had already started down the slope toward the village. "I do not know what you're up to, and better that I do not. Good luck, though," he said, before disappearing into the darkness.

It worked out as Baldric had predicted. The great wooden door was unlatched and they were able to creep past the elderly servant into the abbey's portico. Conferring in whispers, they agreed that the door to their left was most likely the entrance to the almonry. Creaking the door open, they slipped inside.

They found themselves in a vaulted stone chamber filled with slumbering pilgrims. Raising their lanterns, they began to walk among the sleepers, pausing before each muffled female form. The search proved futile. None of the faces revealed by the candle flames was Arzhela's, and the inevitable soon happened. A woman sat up, saw them, and screamed.

The hall erupted into chaos. People struggled to free themselves from their blankets, most of them talking at once. Justin did his best to calm them down, saying loudly that nothing was wrong, that there was no cause for alarm. His words went utterly unheeded. It was Durand who silenced them, shouting "Quiet!" in a voice like thunder.

They subsided, watching Durand warily as he stalked among them, mantle flaring, hand on sword hilt, a figure to intimidate anyone leery of authority. Once he'd quelled the clamor, he began to demand answers. "We are seeking a woman pilgrim, garbed like most of you, past her first youth, tall for a female and slim, with bright blue eyes, prideful, and a talker."

His words echoed into a void. They regarded him blankly, faces shuttered and eyes veiled. He'd bullied them into submission with no difficulty, for the poor were always

160

vulnerable to coercion of that kind. Justin could see, though, that these people would tell them nothing. Suspicion of the powerful, self-protection, a sense of solidarity with one of their own, fear: They had any number of reasons to keep silent.

"We mean this lady no harm," Justin said, with all the conviction he could muster. "She is very dear to me and I fear for her safety." As he'd expected, his sincerity was no more productive than Durand's belligerence. It occurred to him that some of the Bretons might not understand French, and he tried again, this time in his slow, careful Welsh. And because he was watching their faces so intently, he saw a young girl open her mouth, then shut it quickly when the woman beside her clamped a hand on her arm.

Crossing to her, he knelt beside the child. "Do you know this lady, lass? You can do her no greater kindness than to speak up."

The girl hesitated. But then the woman, rake-thin and careworn, hissed, "Mikaela, *roit peoc'h*!" Putting her arm protectively around her daughter's shoulders, she looked defiantly up at Justin and he knew he'd get nothing from either of them.

Getting to his feet, he made one final attempt. "We will give twenty silver deniers to the person who can tell us of her whereabouts." That was no small sum, would buy a man four chickens. But there were no takers, and when Durand swore and strode toward the door, Justin followed reluctantly.

Out in the portico, they communicated again in whispers, keeping an eye upon the sleeping gatekeeper. "We'll have to start searching," Justin said softly, but even as he spoke, he realized that would be an impossible undertaking. The abbey was the size of a small city, honeycombed with crypts, chapels, narrow corridors, and unlit stairwells.

Durand was gazing back at the almonry. "Wait," he counseled, refusing to say more. Justin fidgeted at his side for what seemed like an eternity. He was about to leave Durand and begin searching on his own when the almonry door hinges squeaked. A moment later, a shadowy form emerged and headed for the circle of light cast by their lanterns.

He looked surprisingly sleek and well fed for a pilgrim, and wasted no time with preliminaries. "Three sous," he said, "for what I know about the woman."

That was nearly twice what Justin had offered, but he was not about to haggle. Reaching for his money pouch, he said, "Tell us."

"And if you're lying," Durand warned, "I'll come back and cut out your tongue."

The man smiled faintly. "I've been threatened by a bishop, friend, so your threats scare me not. Anyway, I am not lying." Holding out his palm for the payment, he said, "There are three people missing from the hall. The woman you seek, a poor, doomed soul, and a bothersome whelp. Your woman took the cub under her wing, God knows why, and she was hovering over the ailing man earlier in the day. My guess is that you'll find them all up in the infirmary."

AFTER KNOCKING LIGHTLY UPON THE INFIRMARY door, Justin pushed it open. The scent of herbs was heavy in the air, mingling with the fetid odors of the sickroom. The infirmarian was leaning over a bed, tending to a man racked with convulsive coughing spasms. At the sound of the opening door, the monk glanced over his shoulder, barking out a brusque "What?"

"May I have a word with you, Brother?"

The infirmarian took note of Justin's demeanor and clothing, concluded that this was not one of the poor pilgrims from the almonry, but a higher-status guest, and said, more politely, "Unless you are deathly sick, it would be best if you come back later. As you can see, this patient's needs cannot wait."

Justin's eyes were roaming the infirmary, his hopes and heart plummeting when he failed to find Arzhela. "I am not ill," he assured the monk. "I am seeking a woman who came to you earlier this eve."

The infirmarian helped the dying man turn so that he could vomit into a small basin. "That one... she's gone."

"Where did she go?"

"How would I know? Make yourself useful and hand me those clean towels."

Justin did as he was bidden. "When did she leave? Was a youth with her?"

"A while ago," the monk muttered, so distractedly that Justin saw further interrogation was useless.

The infirmarian wiped his patient's face, frowning at the streaks of blood in the basin. Almost as an afterthought, he said, "Why do you want this woman? Need I remind you where you are? Any man who'd sin with a wench in God's House is courting eternal damnation." When Justin did not answer, he glanced over his shoulder again, just in time to see the door quietly closing.

"Where would she have gone, if not back to the almonry? Surely she'd not wander about with a killer on the loose!"

Durand snorted. "If you're offering a wager, I'll take it. I'd not put anything past that fool woman." Fairness forced him to add grudgingly, "She did not know Brother Bernard had betrayed her, so she may have thought the danger was past."

"And she is not alone, after all." Justin was doing his best to sound positive and optimistic. "It seems likely the lad is still with—" He checked himself, catching a glimpse of Durand's expression. "What? Why do you look so sour?"

"It just seems very convenient for this stripling to turn up with Arzhela at the almonry. We know nothing about him, do we? How do we know the killer does not have a partner?"

Justin stared at him. "Thank you for that comforting thought," he said at last. "We're accomplishing nothing standing here, arguing. Since she did not go back down to the almonry, she must have gone that way."

With Durand on his heels, he opened the door. His lantern's flame illuminated a small chamber, stark and simple, with an exposed timber beam ceiling and sparse furnishings: an altar, a long trestle table, several coffers, and, under an archway, a large stone bath.

"Bloody Hell," Durand muttered. "This is where they prepare their dead for burial."

Justin agreed with him, and since Arzhela was clearly not there, he continued on into the adjoining building, a central nave flanked by smaller bays on each side. Bitterly cold and austere, it looked sepulchral in the blanched moonlight filtering through the high windows of the nave. The men knew at once what it was—the abbey cemetery and charnel house. Here the monks would be buried until the cemetery was too full for any more graves, and then their bones would be dug up and stored in the charnel house. Some ossuaries were constructed to display skulls and skeletons as a reminder to all of man's mortality. The charnel house at Mont St Michel was partially walled up, much to their relief. They were not squeamish about death, but the sight of bleached human bones would have been ominous under the circumstances. Justin spoke for them both when he said, "Let's get out of here."

The corridor led them past the huge stone cistern, on into another chapel. By now they'd figured out where they were, agreeing that this must be the crypt of St Martin. Their guess was confirmed when they discovered they could go no farther, for St Martin's chapel was not within the monks' enclosure. Here, wealthy benefactors of the abbey would have the honor of being buried under the protection and sanctity of the holy relics preserved above them in the south transept of the church. This beautiful stone sanctuary did not have the same oppressive atmosphere as the funeral chapel and the charnel house, but Durand and Justin did not linger, hastily retracing their steps.

When they'd got back to the funeral chapel, they paused to plan their next move. "Damned if I know where she's gone," Durand confessed. "I do not see how she could have got entry into the abbey enclosure. Laypeople are not welcome in the cloistered areas, and the mere sight of a woman in their sanctum would have sent the monks into a frenzy of horror. I suppose this is neither the time nor the place to discuss the madness that drives a man to renounce the pleasures of the female flesh..."

His shrug said it all, as did the bemused shake of his head. "I admit I am confounded, de Quincy. All I can think to do is go back to the almonry, see if we can scare some of those good folk into being more forthright."

Justin had no intention of letting Durand terrorize the pilgrims, but he was at a loss, too. "Mayhap we ought to start looking for—" He stopped, seized with a superstitious belief that to say it would make it so.

Durand read his thoughts easily enough, for they were his, too. Where was the best place to dispose of a body? The cistern? What of the charnel house? There would be a diabolic brilliance in that, hiding a murder victim under a mound of bones.

They descended into the stairwell in silence, their spurs striking sparks on the steps. How many thousands of pilgrims must have passed this way, their feet gradually wearing deep grooves in the stones. Arzhela herself had climbed these stairs; Justin was sure of it. So where had she gone? He stopped so abruptly that Durand bumped into him.

"I think I know where she is," he said, cutting off Durand's complaint in mid-sentence. "We went down a great flight of stairs, then up another to reach the infirmary."

"I was there, de Quincy. I remember. What of it?"

"We were sure we'd find her abovestairs in the infirmary, so we passed it by. The chapel of Notre-Dame-sous-Terre— the holiest part of the abbey. It makes sense, does it not?"

It made enough sense to Durand that he was annoyed he had not thought of it himself. Women were partial to the Blessed Mary, all knew that. Besides, where else could she have gone? They reached the bottom of the stairs at the same time, elbowing each other for space in the narrow corridor. But they halted at the foot of the great gallery steps, their eyes drawn to the door on their right, standing slightly ajar. Now that the moment of truth was upon them, they hesitated.

The ancient chapel of Notre-Dame-sous-Terre was the very heart of the abbey. Although it had long since been replaced by the church above it, one of its two naves had been preserved. Their lantern light fell upon brick arches that had been old when Norse raiders were still plundering the Breton coast. Its original windows had been blocked up and shadows held sway, filling every corner, every cranny with the opaque darkness that knew neither sun nor stars.

Justin's disappointment was bitter beyond wormwood and gall. Too disheartened to speak, he stopped in the doorway, leaving it to Durand to voice the obvious. "She'd not venture into a cave like this. Not even Arzhela is that crazed."

He turned away and Justin slowly started to follow. But he'd taken only a step or two before a memory flickered. He stood very still, scarcely breathing until the image crystallized. When they'd passed the chapel on their way to the infirmary, there had been a glimmer of light coming from that open door. Raising his lantern, he scanned the wall until he located an alcove. It held an oil lamp. The wick was unlit, but when he reached out, it was warm to the touch.

"Lady Arzhela?" His words went unanswered, echoes on the wind. Moving deeper into the chapel, he felt an impending sense of dread with every step he took. "Lady Arzhela?"

He found her in a small sanctuary in the eastern end of the chapel, crumpled behind the stone altar. A thick tallow candle lay on the ground near her feet; he almost tripped over it. She was lying on her side, one arm outstretched. Her pilgrim hat had been knocked off and her veil was askew, revealing several reddish-blonde strands.

Until then he'd not known the color of her hair. He was close enough now to see the darkening stain across her breast, almost black against the russet of her robe.

"Christ on the Cross." The voice was Durand's. Justin himself said nothing, for his throat had closed up too tight for speech. He knew it made no sense to grieve so for a woman he'd known this briefly. But his sorrow was like a physical pain, as sharp-edged as the knife that had stabbed her. He'd not realized until now, looking down at her body, just how much he'd liked Arzhela de Dinan.

Kneeling beside her, he said huskily, "By this holy water and by His most tender Mercy, may the Lord forgive thee whatever thou hast sinned." That was all he knew of the sacrament of Extreme Unction. It was a meaningless gesture, anyway, for only a priest could absolve her of her sins. And then he caught his breath, for her lashes flickered and her eyes opened.

The blue of the sea was gone, drowned in blackness, for her pupils were dilated with the shadow of approaching death. She seemed to recognize him, though, for her lips parted and she gasped out one word. Her voice was as weak as a dying candle, and he leaned forward to be sure he'd heard her correctly. For a heartbeat, he felt her breath against his ear as her lips moved again. But when he looked into her face, the light was already fading from her eyes.

"Does she live?"

He swallowed, then shook his head. "No." The other man said nothing, but after a moment, he made the sign of the Cross. Justin continued to hold Arzhela in his arms, reluctant to let her down onto the cold stone floor. It was then that he saw it—a wet smear upon the tiles. He stared at the limp hand, the fingers stained with red. Had she tried to write her murderer's name in her own blood as her life bled away?

"Holy Mother of God!"

They whirled toward the sound. The infirmarian, flanked by two younger monks, was standing in the doorway of the chapel, staring at them in horror.

CHAPTER XIV

February 1194
Mont St Michel, Normandy

"Jesu," Durand said softly, "we knocked over the bleeding hive."

Justin was in no position at the moment to appreciate the metaphor, or he might have agreed it was unusually apt. The infirmarian had rushed into the chapel, a courageous act under the circumstances, but the other two monks fled and, within moments, they heard the muffled clanging of a fire bell. Kneeling by Arzhela, the elderly monk searched in vain for signs of life, shaking his head when Justin asked if he could adminster Extreme Unction.

"I am not a priest," he said, getting stiffly to his feet and beginning to edge away from them, as if only then becoming aware of his own danger.

"We did not do it," Justin said hastily. "We are not her killers!"

It was then that the chapel began to resemble an overturned hive. In one moment there were just the three of them standing over Arzhela's body. In the next, monks beyond counting were there, swarming into the crypt like angry bees making ready to defend their nest. Voices were raised, accusations flung, prayers mingled with expressions of dismay and revulsion, and chaos reigned. Justin and Durand found themselves backed against one of the granite pillars, surrounded by shouting, gesturing monks. They seemed more upset by the desecration of the church than they did by the killing of a woman, at least to judge by the epithets being hurled at the two men—"ungodly," "profane," and "accursed" outpacing the occasional cry of "Murderers!"

Justin's declarations of their innocence went unheeded, even unheard. By this time the male servants of the abbey were streaming into the crypt, too, as were some of the pilgrims, and Durand said, low-voiced, "It is now or never, de Quincy."

Justin stared at him incredulously, for escape was the one option not open to them. "Are you mad? You cannot slaughter monks in God's Church!"

"I've done worse," the other man said grimly, his hand tightening on the hilt of his sword. "They have no weapons but their tongues. You want to wait till they get the whole town up here, baying for our blood?"

Before Justin could respond, there was a sudden movement in the wall of bodies encircling them, men moving back, clearing a path. The newcomer was a man no longer young, tall and almost gaunt, with silvered hair that had once been flaxen. He was clad like the others in a simple, black habit, but upon him it had a certain stark elegance. Justin guessed at once that this was the prior, Abbot Jourdain's second-in-command. Everything about him proclaiming an authority sanctioned by God, he was the veritable embodiment of dispassion and the cool rationality of the intellect. But Justin could take meager

170

comfort in that, for the prior bore an unsettling resemblance to Aubrey de Quincy, Bishop of Chester, his father.

The prior lifted his hand and the noise stilled. "I am Clement de Roches," he declared, investing that popular papal name with prideful echoes of grandeur. "I am prior of the blessed abbey of St Michael. Who are you that have dared to defile the sacred altar of Our Lady?"

Justin's grief and fear gave way, then, to rage that Arzhela's death seemed of so little importance to these holy men of God. "A woman has also lost her life, my lord prior, a good woman. Why is that less offensive than bloodstains on a tiled floor?"

"Good going, man," Durand muttered. Justin ignored him, meeting the prior's piercing pale eyes without flinching.

"Because," the monk said coldly, "murder is a crime. Befouling a church is sacrilege."

"We are guilty of neither, my lord prior. We did not harm this woman, spilled none of her blood."

"I was told you were found kneeling beside her body."

"Yes, and does that sound like the action of a killer? The infirmarian can tell you that I was cradling her in my arms, seeking to comfort her in her last moments."

When the infirmarian tersely confirmed this, the prior turned his inscrutable gaze back upon Justin. "Men have been known to kill that which they love."

"But not with an unbloodied sword." The monks retreated a step when Justin slid his sword from its scabbard, only the prior standing his ground. "Look at the blade, my lord prior. Do you see even a droplet of blood? The same holds true for my eating knife and for the weapons of my companion." Turning, he demanded, "Show them, Durand," and the other man did.

"You could have hidden the murder knife," a voice from

the back of the crypt called out, and there were murmurings of agreement.

"Search the chapel," Justin challenged. "If it is not found, that proves our innocence. Unless you are claiming that we stabbed her and fled to dispose of the weapon, only then to return to the murder scene so we might be found with her body."

A number of the men had already begun to prowl the chapel, hunting for a dagger. When they failed to find one, some of them seemed willing to reconsider their certainty about Justin and Durand's guilt. The prior continued to regard them impassively, though, and raising a hand for silence again, he said, "The woman was one of God's poor— which you are not. Brother Nicolas told me that you came to the infirmary in search of her. Why? What did you want with her?"

Justin did not know how to answer this question, for neither the truth nor lies would serve them well. If he revealed Arzhela's true identity, the prior was likely to send an urgent message to the Duchess Constance, the last one in Christendom whom he wanted involved in this. But what lie could they devise that would seem plausible to the prior? What reason could they give for seeking out a needy female pilgrim that would not sound suspicious or immoral to the prior?

"She is my sister." All heads swung toward Durand, including Justin's. He stared at them defiantly, daring them to doubt him. "I do not know what name she was using at the almonry, but her real name is Felicia de Lacy; her husband holds lands of King Richard, south of Bayeux."

The prior looked down at the woman on the floor—truly looked at her for the first time. "Her coloring is similar to yours," he conceded. "But I find it difficult to believe that a

172

woman of gentle birth would be posing as an impoverished pilgrim."

"Look at her hands, her nails. Do you see any calluses or blisters on her palms?"

"No, I do not." The prior straightened up and stepped away from the body. "She has the hands of a lady," he admitted. "But why was she here in disguise?"

"She wanted to take holy vows. She'd been trying for a year to persuade her husband to give his consent, to no avail. She finally declared that the Almighty did not want her to wait any longer and ran away. Her husband has been looking for her and I thought it best to find her first; he has the Devil's own temper. So when I discovered that she'd gone on pilgrimage to the Mont, we came after her." Durand glanced at Arzhela's body, back at the prior. "We were not in time. Her husband must have found her first."

Durand's tale of a pious wife who'd wanted only to serve the Almighty found a receptive audience in this chapel filled with monks. But Justin kept his eyes upon the prior, knowing that he and he alone would be the arbiter of their fate.

Prior Clement took his time in passing his judgment. "There is logic in what you say," he said at last. "Mayhap things are not as they first seemed. But it is not for me to decide what ought to be done."

Durand cocked a brow. "Who, then? The provost in Genêts?"

"No. A murder committed upon abbey lands falls within our jurisdiction and this matter must be heard in our lord abbot's court."

"Well, then, we'll stay here at the abbey until the abbot returns and can question us," Justin offered cooperatively, and the prior inclined his head.

But then he said, "Alas, we will require more than your word. A woman has been cruelly murdered and a holy place polluted with blood. This church must be purified ere a Mass can be said here again. I intend no insult when I say that you must be held until Abbot Jourdain returns."

"Held how?" Durand's eyes narrowed. "And where?"

"It is not necessary under the circumstances to confine you in the abbot's dungeon. If you agree to surrender your weapons, you may await the lord abbot in more comfortable surroundings."

"We will surrender our weapons," Durand said, "when we see these 'comfortable surroundings' for ourselves."

The prior was not accustomed to being contradicted, and did not take it well. "My lord prior," Justin said, before he could respond, "can your monks see that Lady Felicia is treated with the honor she deserves?"

Again that proud head inclined. "She will be taken to the chapel of St Étienne, where our own brothers are prepared for their final journey."

"Thank you, Prior Clement. Will your brethren pray for her, too?" Justin asked, and the emotion in his voice earned him an approving glance from Durand, for the monks murmured sympathetically and even the prior seemed to thaw somewhat. But Justin's grieving was raw and real, and he could only hope that prayers for Lady Felicia de Lacy would count toward the salvation of Arzhela's immortal soul.

THE PRIOR'S "COMFORTABLE SURROUNDINGS" TURNED OUT to be the porter's lodge, a small, sparsely furnished hall underneath the abbot's private chambers. It was still vastly preferable to the dungeons that lay below the lodge, accessible only through a trapdoor in the vaulting. That trapdoor served as an unwelcome reminder to the men of how narrowly they had avoided those subterranean accommodations... for now.

The hall was deep in shadows and filled with the damp, bone-chilling cold of the tides laying siege to the Mont. To Justin's astonishment, Durand rolled up in one of the blankets provided by the monks, remarked that lying awake would do them no good, and went to sleep. Justin did not have such icy control over his nerves, and he tossed and turned for hours, listening to the even rhythm of the other man's breathing and the sound of the surf beating against the rocks. But he'd been in the saddle for hours in a day of turmoil and trauma, and finally he, too, fell into an uneasy doze.

When he awakened, Durand was standing over him, holding out a cup. "The monks brought us a loaf of bread and a flagon of wine to break our fast," he said. "I suppose it is a good sign that they are feeding us. But when they opened the door, I saw they are relying upon more than our honor or goodwill to keep us here. There are armed guards outside."

Justin took the cup, sat up, and winced, for even the body of a twenty-one-year-old was not immune to the physical abuses of the past day and night. Grimacing, he sought to wash away the foul taste in his mouth with several swallows of wine. Durand was pacing, looking as rumpled and edgy as Justin felt. When he stopped and glanced toward Justin, the younger man said sharply, "Do not say it, Durand. I do not want to hear that this is my fault for not agreeing to hack our way free. Even if we'd somehow got out of the chapel and then the abbey, where could we have gone? We'd still have been trapped on an island and we'd no longer be able to claim we were innocent of murder."

"Innocence is a greatly overrated defense." Durand sat down on the floor beside Justin and leaned back against the wall. "Actually, I was going to say you handled yourself well last night. That was quick thinking about the unbloodied weapons. It helps, too, that you can so convincingly act humble and servile. With men like the prior, a little arse-licking can never hurt."

Justin was too weary to summon up any anger. "You bought us some time with that sister-of-yours story. That was quick thinking, too. But, then, it's truth telling you have a problem with, not lying. You realize, though, that we are going to have to tell Abbot Jourdain the truth, or at least a good portion of it?"

He'd been half expecting Durand to argue, was surprised when he did not. "I know," Durand admitted. "The good abbot is not likely to have forgotten his encounter with us at Antrain. And it is only a matter of time ere Arzhela's true identity becomes known. Luckily, that monk over in Genêts is on his deathbed, for he'd have recognized her in a heartbeat. I got the sense that there was something going on between them."

"Not so lucky for him," Justin pointed out, but Durand was oblivious to sarcasm when it served his purposes.

"I assume you have one of those royal letters you like to flaunt, identifying you as the queen's man? Thank God they did not search us, but they are not quite sure how to treat us, are they? Not exactly guests, not yet murder suspects."

"Yes, I have a letter from the queen," Justin confirmed. "I can see we are in agreement about which fork in the road to take. The abbot is King Richard's man, so the less said about John, the better. I suppose I can always explain to the abbot that you are one of my hirelings or lackeys."

The corner of Durand's mouth twitched in acknowledgment of that payback jab. "If the abbot proves to be a skeptical sort, we might end up in some kind of confinement until the queen returns from Germany. But as long as it is in Normandy and not Brittany, I'll not complain."

Justin doubted that exceedingly; he'd met few men who complained as frequently or as vociferously as Durand did. It seemed foolish, though, to continue their usual squabbling when they were caught in the same trap. He began to speak, instead, about the tale they must stitch together for the abbot, and they spent the remainder of the morning deciding how much of the truth he should be told. At least they were no longer bound by the need to shield Arzhela; it mattered naught to her now if her plotting came to light. But that was a dubious comfort to Justin. He'd had little time yet to mourn Arzhela, but mourn her he would. She was a brave, charming, reckless woman who'd deserved a far better end, and he would regret to his last breath that he had not been able to save her.

He and Durand both felt that Simon de Lusignan was the prime suspect in her murder. She'd tried to protect him, not giving up his name to them, a lover's folly that had cost her dearly. The most likely scenario, they agreed, was that she'd learned something else from Simon, something of such significance that she'd no longer felt safe at Constance's court. Proof that Constance knew the letter was a forgery? Or that de Lusignan was much more deeply involved in the conspiracy than she'd first realized? Guy de Laval's testimony had put Simon in that shadowy inner circle, which was mysterious in and of itself. How had a younger son of a minor Poitevin lord gained such influence at the Breton court? And what secret was so dangerous that he'd kill to keep it quiet?

They speculated, too, about the missing youngster, the boy Arzhela had "taken under her wing." Had he been present when she was slain? Was fear keeping him quiet? Or something more sinister? For all they knew, Durand reminded Justin, he'd wielded the dagger himself. Arzhela had trusted the boy; she'd not have been on her guard with him.

"You'd suspect a babe in its cradle," Justin scoffed, and then jumped to his feet. So did Durand. But the footsteps they'd heard passed by the door. They assumed that the provost would cross over from Genêts sooner or later, hopefully later. He'd be occupied upon his return with the brutal attacks upon Brothers Andrev and Bernard, and then, of course, he'd have to wait for low tide.

The provost could pose a problem if he wanted to interrogate them straightaway, not waiting for Abbot Jourdain to return. He'd know about their visit to Genêts, know about their confrontation with his drunken deputy and, for certes, he'd want to know why they'd been so interested in the missing Lady Arzhela, They'd just have to play for time if it came to that, hint to the prior that the provost was infringing upon the abbey's jurisdiction. A hint ought to be more than enough. Men of God were as territorial as wolves, Durand gibed, and Justin agreed with him, thinking of that superb politician, his lord bishop father. But so were lords and queens and Welsh princes and even cocky Norman guides.

When their isolation was finally ended, it did not happen in the way they'd expected. The door opened and two men were ushered into the lodge, then the door closed again. Justin and Durand were on their feet, staring in surprise at Crispin and Rufus. They had been relieved of their weapons, but they seemed to be in good shape, showed no bruises or scratches. As soon as they saw Justin and Durand, they both began to talk at once and it took a few moments to settle them down.

"We told the monks we'd done nothing wrong," Crispin said plaintively, "but they said we'd be set free once you'd proved your innocence of a murder. My lords, you will be able to do that soon, I hope?"

"From your mouth to God's Ear," Durand said sourly. "How did Morgan and Jaspaer escape the net? And how did they net you in the first place? Who told them that you were our men?"

They exchanged sheepish looks before Crispin confessed, "We told them. The village was overrun with rumors and gossip. Something had happened up at the abbey in the night, but no one seemed to know what, so Rufus and I... we decided to go look for you." When Durand called him a blundering lack-wit, he flushed but protested with some spirit, "That is not fair, Sir Durand! We did not know you were murder suspects, not until it was too late!"

Justin had an unpleasant thought. "You did not tell them the woman was not Durand's sister, did you?"

Crispin shook his head emphatically. "When they began to ask us questions, Rufus whispered that we should 'be dumb' and we were. We kept saying we knew nothing about your business, that you'd not told us why we were going to the abbey—"

"And we spoke mostly English," the usually taciturn Rufus interrupted, "which seemed to vex them enormously."

"I assume Morgan and Jaspaer had the common sense to keep their distance, then?" Durand said caustically, and looked thoroughly disgusted when Crispin admitted that they'd tried to talk them out of going up to the abbey and wished mournfully that he'd listened.

THE REST OF THE DAY PASSED without incident. The porter's lodge was lit with small, narrow windows little bigger than arrow slits, and as daylight faded away, they were left in

179

darkness, lacking lamps or even candles. At Vespers, an abbey servant was sent in to empty the chamber pot, but he said nothing about the bloodshed over in Genêts and claimed none knew when Abbot Jourdain might return. He was willing to be bribed, though, agreeing to bring them an extra flagon of wine with their meal and more blankets. The bells of Compline were still echoing on the wind when the men settled down for another endless, uncomfortable night.

They'd been sleeping for several hours when the door was thrust open. Crispin slept on, but the other three jerked upright, blinking up blindly into a ring of blazing torches. It was like looking straight into the sun and as they squinted, trying to make out the dark, faceless forms behind the torches, a voice said, "Well?" and a second voice answered, "Yes, they are the ones." By now they were stumbling to their feet, but the light was already retreating. The door slammed shut and they were left alone.

PALLID, GREY LIGHT WAS SEEPING INTO the hall when they were roused again. Men bearing torches advanced into the chamber, followed by others. The former were obviously abbey servants, the latter just as obviously were not; they were armed and on the alert, putting Justin in mind of well-trained sheepdogs, confident of their ability to control the flock. The prior entered next, accompanied by two men in their middle years.

"This is Jocelin de Curcy, the provost of Genêts," he said. "And this is Sir Reynaud Boterel." A third man had entered, younger than the others, wearing an expensive mantle fastened with a large gold brooch, and the prior introduced him as the Lord of Château-Gontier, Yves de la Jaille. Before either Justin or Durand could respond, the prior raised his hand in an imperious demand for silence.

"There is nothing you could say that I want to hear," he said coolly. "The time for talking is past. I am here to tell you that you are to be handed over to the Lord of Château-Gontier. You are no longer the responsibility of our abbey and we waive any and all rights to prosecute you in our jurisdiction."

Justin stared at the prior, baffled. During their stay at Laval, Emma had made casual mention of the lordship of Château-Gontier, and so Justin knew it was a barony in Maine. This made no sense to him. Why would an Angevin lord take them into custody? He glanced over at Durand, was not reassured to notice Durand had lost color. "I do not follow this, Prior Clement," Justin said cautiously. "It was my understanding that we were awaiting the return of Abbot Jourdain."

"And it was my understanding," the prior said scathingly, "that the dead woman was Felicia de Lacy, whereas in truth, she is Lady Arzhela de Dinan, the missing cousin of Duchess Constance."

Neither Justin nor Durand spoke, for what was there to say to that? Justin was getting a very bad feeling about this, and that was before the door was shoved open again. The man stalking into the hall was young, fair-haired, and all too familiar. Striding forward, Simon de Lusignan regarded them in silence for a very long moment. The last time a man had looked at Justin with that much hostility, he'd been fighting for his life with a godless outlaw called Gilbert the Fleming. Simon had blue eyes, almost as brilliantly blue as Arzhela's, narrowed to smoldering slits, and his mouth was contorted, his lips peeled back from his teeth in a feral, ferocious grin.

"You thought you would get away with it," he said, "and you might have, if not for me. But I reached the abbey in time to identify that sweet lady you murdered, in time to see justice done!"

Durand tensed, deciding he had nothing left to lose, and Justin might well have followed his lead. He was never to know for sure, though. De la Jaille's men-at-arms had been moving closer while Simon de Lusignan claimed center stage, and, at an unseen signal from Yves de la Jaille, they sprang into action, flinging themselves upon the prisoners.

Outnumbered and unarmed, they were quickly subdued. Crispin and Rufus offered no resistance, holding up their hands like innocent bystanders in the wrong place at the wrong time. Justin struggled briefly, before his brain overrode his body's panic, and once he no longer fought them, his attackers stopped hitting him. Durand continued to kick and curse even after he'd been immobilized, not yielding until Simon de Lusignan stepped toward him and kneed him brutally in the groin.

Durand sank to his knees, his teeth tearing into his lower lip to stifle any cry, and Simon would have kicked him again had the prior not protested. Yves de la Jaille stepped between Simon and the grey-faced Durand, saying, "Back off, Simon." And though his words were given as a censure, his tone was casual, almost nonchalant.

Yves signaled again and his men dragged Durand to his feet, set about roping his hands behind his back. Justin was bound next. But when they started toward Crispin and Rufus, Yves stopped them.

"We've got the hawks, need not bother with the fledglings. Leave them for the provost to deal with."

The provost did not look pleased by that offhand dismissal, but he nodded to his own men, who took Crispin and Rufus into custody. They submitted meekly enough, but when de la Jaille's men-at-arms began pushing Justin and Durand toward the door, Crispin blurted out an involuntary protest. "Wait!

Where are you taking them?"

To their surprise, they actually got an answer. Yves looked back over his shoulder. "To the court of the Duchess of Brittany, so they may answer for the murder of her kinswoman."

CHAPTER XV

February 1194
Road to Fougères, Brittany

The sky was a pale, silvery blue, and the few clouds drifting by were white and fleecy. The wind was erratic, almost playful, a sheathed dagger instead of a gusting February blade. Bare beech and chestnut trees stood sentinel along the road, dappled by sunlight. For winter-weary Bretons, a day like this was a gift from God. To Justin, it seemed especially cruel that he should be given a bittersweet, beguiling glimpse of the spring he was not likely to see.

He was making a sincere effort not to surrender to despair; after all, he did not have a hangman's noose around his neck yet. Optimism did not come easily to a foundling, though. Nor was it in his nature to lie to himself, and he could envision nothing but trouble at the court of the Breton duchess.

His mount suddenly veered to the right. With his hands bound behind his back, he could only guide the stallion with the pressure of his knees, and he was unable to keep the horse from swerving to the end of its tether. The rider leading it glanced over his shoulder and swore, first at the animal and then at Justin. Another stallion shied, too, and its unease proved contagious. For several moments, men and horses milled about in the road, as the former sought to get the latter under control. By the time order was restored, it was decided they should take a break and Lord Yves ordered them to dismount.

This was the second time they'd halted since leaving Mont St Michel. They seemed in no hurry to reach Fougères, and that was fine with Justin, who would have been content to ride on into infinity. He did not think that was true, though, for Durand. He could only imagine how painful this ride must be for a man who'd been kicked in the ballocks a few hours ago. Durand's face was a mask of silent suffering, sweat trickling down into his beard, his jaw so tightly clenched that not even a breath could escape that taut slash of a mouth. The guards got them off their horses quite simply by pulling them from the saddle, pushing them down upon the ground, and warning them to "move only if you want to lose a body part."

Wineskins were passed around. The Lord Yves and Reynaud Boterel walked a few feet away and began to talk quietly, glancing occasionally toward their prisoners. Simon de Lusignan was tightening his stallion's saddle girth, but he, too, watched the prisoners, with an unblinking intensity that did not bode well for their future. The horses were led down to the river to drink, but Justin and Durand did without until one of the guards walked by and Justin asked for water.

He'd chosen this particular guard with care—a cheerful, garrulous redhead called Thierry, by the others, who'd been chattering like a magpie since they departed the abbey. As he'd hoped, Thierry could not resist any audience, even if it consisted of doomed men, and the guard paused, considered, and then shrugged.

"Why not?" Walking over to one of the tethered horses, he pulled a small metal cup from a saddlebag and filled it with river water. Leaning over, he held the cup to Justin's mouth, letting him drink his fill. When he turned toward Durand, Justin willed the other man not to do anything stupid, and for once, Durand did not, gulping the water as fast as Thierry could pour it into his mouth.

"Are you one of the Lord Yves's men?" Justin asked casually as Thierry straightened up. Taking the bait, the guard confirmed that he was, adding that he was Angevin, like his lord, not one of those stiff-necked Bretons.

"Why is your lord serving the Breton duchess?" Justin queried, trying to keep the man talking.

Thierry stepped back and stretched, but did not move away. "My lord is betrothed to Lord André de Vitré's daughter. He was at the duchess's court when she got word that her cousin had gone missing, and she selected him to investigate her disappearance. Also Sir Reynaud." With a toss of his head toward Yves's companion. "He is a former seneschal of Rennes or mayhap it is Nantes. I cannot tell one Breton town from another, if truth be told."

"How did Simon de Lusignan get picked?"

"Him?" Thierry glanced over at the glowering de Lusignan, and lowered his voice like someone about to share a ribald bit of gossip. "The duchess did not send that one. He showed up at the abbey on his own, was already there when we arrived." Dropping his voice even further, he confided that Simon and the Lady Arzhela were "having at it, if you know what I mean. The way I heard it, they had a hot quarrel and he went storming off, whilst she headed for the abbey. That is why the duchess was not too alarmed by Abbot Jourdain's news. Everyone seemed to think she was off making peace with the lad."

He contorted his face waggishly, as if implying there was no accounting for female tastes. "I'd think the Lady Arzhela could do better than de Lusignan," Justin prompted, and Thierry grinned.

"You'll get no argument from me, friend. The Lady Arzhela was a good mistress," he declared, winking in case Justin missed the double entendre, "and a sight to gladden the eye, for all that she was no longer young. As for her laddie over there, he may have a ready cock, but he also has a hot head and as many enemies as he has debts, or so I've been told. No, the lady could have done much better for herself."

Thierry seemed to remember, then, that he was speaking to the men accused of her murder, for he scowled and snatched his cup back. "Why did you kill her? She was a good soul, kindhearted for all that she was highborn, never did harm to man or beast—"

"I did not," Justin said quietly. "As God Almighty is my witness, I did not."

Thierry regarded him for a moment. "Damned if I do not almost believe you. A pity, for no one else will, friend." Throwing a glance over his shoulder toward Simon de Lusignan, he said confidentially, "That one pitched a firking fit when he identified the body, carried on something fierce. Took us by surprise, he did; who knew she was more to him than a fine piece of tail? He's been ranting ever since that death is too good for the likes of you, and if he'd had his way, you'd have been hanged then and there. The prior would have none of that, but my Lord Yves and Sir Reynaud might be easier to convince. Our men think so, for they are wagering that you'll not reach Fougères alive."

THE VILLAGE OF ANTRAIN LOOKED NO less desolate and forlorn at second sight than it had when they'd first passed through. It seemed bereft of life; the villagers knew enough to hide when men-at-arms rode by. They continued on, and the cottages soon vanished in the distance. The countryside was deserted. An occasional hawk soared overhead, and once, a brown flash that may have been a weasel ran across the road, spooking the horses. After they forded the River Loisance, they did not stop again until they reached the tiny hamlet of Tremblay.

Like Antrain, it seemed abandoned, for the inhabitants had run off at the approach of armed men. The elderly priest hovered anxiously in the doorway of his ancient church as they reined in. He did not appear much relieved when they told him they were halting only to rest their horses. Gathering up a small dog that looked as old as he was, he retreated into the church and bolted the door.

Justin was as apprehensive as the priest when they began to dismount, for Thierry's warning had been echoing in his ears like a funeral dirge. Once they'd been dragged off their horses, he and Durand were herded toward the small cemetery and told to stay put against a crumbling stone wall. As they watched, wineskins were shared and men wandered off to find places to urinate. The Lord Yves and Reynaud Boterel stretched their legs and laughed together, laughter that stilled as they approached their prisoners. They stood for a moment, looking over at Justin and Durand with a detached animosity that was somehow more chilling than outright anger would have been.

"I am not looking forward to telling the duchess about this killing of her cousin," Lord Yves said soberly. "I was never sure how much fondness there was between them, for they could not have been more unlike. But they are blood-kin and the duchess takes that very seriously, indeed."

"At least we can deliver up her killers. That may provide some small measure of comfort."

"Yes, it was lucky that Simon got to the abbey when he did. If he had not been able to identify her body, she might have been buried as this one's runaway sister." Yves glared at Durand. "Does it seem to you, though, that Simon is somewhat evasive about their reasons for the killing? I know he told us she had trouble with them at Vitré, but he really has not explained why they'd follow her all the way to Mont St Michel."

"Does it matter? Sometimes, the less a man knows, the better off he is."

Justin had been eavesdropping intently, but he'd learned little from this conversation that could benefit them. Durand was leaning against the wall, his eyes closed, but Justin knew he'd been listening, too. On impulse, Justin raised his voice, calling out, "My lords! If you want to know more about the murder, why not ask me?"

They exchanged skeptical glances, and Lord Yves jeered, "As if we could believe a word that came out of your mouth!" They'd moved closer, though, and Justin dared to hope that he might get his first chance to defend himself. But Simon de Lusignan was already striding toward them, coming so fast that heads were turning in his direction, men looking around to see what had alarmed him.

"Do not waste your time talking to these craven killers, my lord Yves. These are men of the worst sort, men who murdered a defenseless woman, attacked monks, and profaned two of God's Houses. How could you trust anything they'd say?"

Justin and Durand stared at him in disbelief. Even Lord

Yves looked startled. "What are you saying, that they are the ones who did the killings in Genêts, too? I thought the provost and the prior said the attacks took place in the afternoon, ere these two arrived at the Mont?"

"They were fooled. Think about it, my lord. What are the chances of two different murderers striking on the same day? Nay, they silenced the monks, then came back to the abbey and made a show of crossing over to Genêts to deflect suspicion from themselves. They never expected, after all, to be caught bloody-handed over Lady Arzhela's body!"

"That is an arrant lie!" Justin protested, too outraged for caution. "We can prove that we were nowhere near Genêts when—" He got no further, for Simon lunged forward, slammed him into the wall and backhanded him across the face. Justin stumbled and almost fell. His head swam and he tasted blood in his mouth. When his vision cleared, the first thing he saw was the glint of sunlight upon the blade of Simon's sword. He tensed, fully expecting to feel that steel thrust into his belly, for the expression on the other man's face was murderous.

"Easy, Simon." Yves was speaking soothingly, like one talking to a drunk or a madman. "You do not need that, lad. He's not going anywhere."

"Is he not? It looks to me like he's trying to escape." Simon took a backward step, but as he swung, Reynaud Boterel grabbed his arm and the blade sliced through air instead of Justin's flesh. De Lusignan spun around with a snarl, balancing on the balls of his feet like a cat about to pounce. "They deserve death! The bastards killed Arzhela!"

"And they'll answer for it to the duchess," Yves pointed out, still using that patient, patronizing tone, and Simon shook his head vehemently.

"I want them to answer to me!" he spat. "I want the pleasure of killing them myself!" He seemed about to renew his attack when a sudden shout echoed from the road.

"My lords! Riders approach!"

Simon hesitated, but the moment was past and he knew it. Sheathing his sword, he turned away with a curse that would have caused a sailor to blink. Lord Yves and Reynaud Boterel were moving toward the newcomers, waving to attract their attention.

Justin sagged back against the wall. He could hear Durand's heavy breathing and he wondered if his own breath sounded that ragged. "Jesu," he whispered, and spat blood onto the ground.

"I did warn you." The voice was Thierry's. Sidling closer, he murmured out of the side of his mouth, "I do not know whether you got a reprieve or not. That lord riding up is Alain de Dinan. He is Seneschal of Brittany, which is in your favor. But he is also the Lady Arzhela's nephew."

ALAIN DE DINAN WAS A PALE, balding man approaching his fourth decade. He was not particularly prepossessing in appearance, looking more like a mild-mannered Church clerk than one of Brittany's greatest barons. But within moments of his arrival, he took complete charge of the situation and the prisoners. He was on his way to Mont St Michel, having learned of Arzhela's disappearance, and it was obvious that he was not expecting such a tragic end to his mission. When told of Arzhela's murder, he seemed staggered by the news, waving the others away and turning his back until he'd got his emotions under control. Those few moments of grace gave Justin and Durand time to brace themselves, for he was soon stalking toward them, flanked by Simon and the other lords.

"The Lady Arzhela was my uncle Roland's widow," he said in a voice like a rasp, "the wife of his winter years. She was not my blood-kin, but she made my uncle happy during their marriage and she became very dear to me. She will be avenged, I promise you that. You will die for what you have done."

"We are not guilty," Justin said wearily, "if that matters at all. From what I've seen so far of Breton justice, it does not."

"You have not yet begun to taste Breton justice." Alain de Dinan folded his arms across his chest, regarding them disdainfully. "But if you have something to say, say it, then. I warn you, though, that if you seek to besmirch a great lady's name—"

"My lord!" Simon de Lusignan interrupted hastily. "This was not a lover's crime. It was far more foul."

Alain de Dinan frowned, and it occurred to Justin that he might be the only man in Brittany who did not know of Arzhela's liaison with Simon de Lusignan. "What do you mean?" he demanded, stiffening indignantly when Simon sought to draw him aside. His distaste for Simon was so evident that Justin dared to indulge himself in a moment of hope. Durand, older and wiser, knew better. Reluctantly allowing Simon to lead him away from the others, Alain conferred privately with the younger man for a few moments, and when he turned back to the prisoners, his demeanor had changed. Gone was the grieving kinsman seeking justice for his aunt. His face was utterly impassive, his eyes shuttered, his guard up.

"Get these men onto their horses," he said curtly. "We have a long ride to Fougères."

FOUGÈRES WAS THIRTY MILES FROM MONT ST MICHEL, an easy one-day's ride in summer, a more problematic undertaking in

192

winter. Favored by the mild weather and dry roads, driven by Alain de Dinan's implacable will, they pushed on into the gathering dusk. Several hours later, they were riding slowly along the street known as the Bourg Vieil, heading for the castle.

Night had long since fallen and the townspeople were abed. The air had cooled rapidly after losing the sun, and the wind carried to them the smoke of hearth fires and the sodden scent of the marshes and then the pungent, sickening stink of the tanner's quarter: the fetid stench of dog dung, tallow and fish oil, urine, slaked lime, and fermenting barley. A dog barked and then another, followed by some sleepy cursing. Lanterns gleamed along the castle battlements and as they approached, they were quickly challenged and, as quickly, given admittance.

JUSTIN AND DURAND WERE TRAPPED IN a circle of fire, surrounded by smoking torches. They'd been shoved into the great hall, which was emptying of drowsy servants and men-at-arms, who'd been rudely told to seek beds elsewhere. There was a low buzz of noise; it sounded as if the entire castle had been roused from sleep. Raoul de Fougères soon entered the hall. He'd obviously dressed in haste, and looked thoroughly annoyed. But after a brief colloquy with Alain de Dinan, his anger dissipated and he stared at the prisoners with an odd expression, one that seemed both suspicious and speculative.

The highborn guests had begun to stumble, disheveled and yawning, into the hall. André de Vitré, hair rumpled, reeking of wine. Abbot Jourdain, eyes puffy and swollen with sleep. The enigmatic canon from Toulouse, immaculately garbed even at that hour. Raoul's young grandson, who seemed as wide awake and alert as if it were midday. Others whom Justin did not recognize. Word was already spreading of Arzhela's murder, shock and grief and rage intermingling until they were indistinguishable, one from the other. But it was some time before the Duchess Constance made her appearance.

Her long, dark hair spilled down her back, inadequately covered by a carelessly pinned veil. She wore a fur-trimmed mantle that flared open as she walked, giving her audience a glimpse of a lace-edged chemise, and soft bed slippers peeked out from under the hem. Her fingers were barren of rings, her throat bare to the night air. Stripped of the elaborate accoutrements of power, she still dominated by sheer force of will, at once becoming the center of attention, the focal point of all eyes.

"What nonsense is this?" she demanded. "Why was I awakened? Who has—" Her head swiveled, her eyes darting from one man to another. "It is not Arthur? It is not my son?"

"No, Madame, no. No evil has befallen the young lord. That I swear to you upon the surety of my soul."

Alain de Dinan came forward from the crowd and made the formal obeisance of subject to sovereign. It might have appeared incongruous or even comical, coming from a man in such travel-stained disarray to a woman in a state of undress. But his gravity conferred a somber dignity upon his act, and as she gazed down at his bowed head, Constance sensed that there was tragedy in the making. As long as it spared her sunlight and joy, her only-begotten son, she could cope with it, whatever it may be, and she said swiftly, "Rise, my lord. What have you come to tell me?"

"Your cousin, the Lady Arzhela, is dead, Madame, cruelly slain in the holy shrine of St Michael."

***

Justin's memories of the ensuing events were never clear; blurred and random, like a half-forgotten dream or an unfinished puzzle, for bits and pieces were missing. He remembered the heat of the torches upon the skin of his face, the way the smoke spiraled upward toward the vaulted roof, as if seeking escape. The treacherous weakness of his body, which yearned only for sleep. The duchess's dark eyes filling with unshed tears. The hall resonating with prayers for the murdered woman's soul and, then, with the mindless cries of the mob, calling for vengeance.

Forced to his knees before the duchess, he looked up into a face as pale and unyielding as chiseled marble. This was a woman to demand every last portion of her just due, be it in coins, vassalage, deference, or blood. "Scriptures say, 'He shall have judgment without mercy, that hath showed no mercy,' " she said, enunciating each word as if it were carved from ice.

Justin swallowed with difficulty, for his throat was clogged with the dust of the road. But a bishop's son could quote from Scriptures, too, and he said, as evenly as he could, "Holy Writ also says that vengeance belongeth to God."

Raoul de Fougères's hand closed on his shoulder, fingers digging painfully into his flesh. "Watch your tongue when you speak to the duchess."

Constance did not need his intercession. "I spoke of judgment, not vengeance."

Justin raised his head and looked her full in the face. "There can be no justice, my lady, if we are not heard. And we've been given no chance to speak, to deny our guilt."

Constance showed no emotion. But after a moment, she said, "Speak, then."

The words were no sooner out of her mouth than the Abbot Jourdain gave a sudden, sharp cry. "I know these men!

I met them in the village of Antrain two days past, Your Grace. They were seeking the Lady Arzhela, and with great urgency—now I know why!"

"So do I." Simon de Lusignan shoved his way forward, saying loudly, "I know these men, too, Madame. They came to you at Vitré, escorting the Lady Emma, aunt to the English king."

"Indeed?" Constance's voice was dangerously dispassionate. "So they are King Richard's men?"

"Far worse, Your Grace." Simon turned toward the prisoners, his mouth curving into a twisted, triumphant smile. "They are agents of the Count of Mortain. They serve at the Devil's pleasure; they serve John!"

AFTER THAT, THERE WAS NOTHING MORE to be said. Simon de Lusignan claimed that they had murdered the Lady Arzhela at John's behest, weaving a tale with great gaping holes in it, for he offered no reason why John should order her assassination. No one seemed troubled by this, though, for no one tugged at the loose threads that would have unraveled his story. The mere mention of John was enough to seal their fate.

As they were restrained, none too gently, by the guards, a heavy trapdoor was raised. Dragged forward, Justin found himself staring down into a black abyss. A sudden slash of a knife blade and his hands were freed. He assumed that was to enable him to descend a rope ladder, but then he was roughly shoved and went tumbling down into the dark. It was not that great a fall, about ten feet or so, but the impact drove all the air from his lungs. He lay still for several moments, stunned, until Durand came plummeting after him. There was a thud as he hit the ground, then silence. Justin rolled over, was starting to sit up when the trapdoor was slammed shut, and they were left alone in the worst of Fougères Castle's underground dungeons.

The utter blackness disoriented; at first, Justin could not even see his hand in front of his face. That past summer, his investigation in Wales had led to an ancient Roman mine. He remembered peering down into its depths, thankful he need not descend into that bottomless shaft. That Welsh mine seemed almost benign now that he found himself buried alive in this netherworld hellhole.

He fought a desperate, silent struggle with panic, a battle that left him limp and drained. His eyes were slowly adjusting to the dark, and he was becoming aware now of the overwhelming stench of death and decay. Breathing this air was like inhaling in a cesspit. It was bitter cold and damp. When he touched one of the stone walls, he discovered that it was coated with some sort of slimy growth. Getting stiffly to his feet, he explored the dimensions of their prison; it did not take long. His boot knocked into something solid; one whiff told him he'd found the slop bucket. But as carefully as he searched, he did not find a water bucket.

He was so intent upon the search that Durand's continuing silence did not at once register with him. When it did, he cautiously retraced his steps and squatted down beside the shadowy form. "Durand?" he said, and then, with greater urgency, "Durand!"

"Who do you think they dumped in with you?" the other man said waspishly. "The Holy Roman Emperor?"

For once, the sarcasm was not unwelcome; Justin could imagine no better proof that Durand was not badly hurt. "Thank God," he said. "I feared I might be stuck down here with a dead man!"

"Give it time," Durand muttered, "give it time." Sitting up

with a groan, he leaned back against the wall. "What in damnation is that noise? It sounds like we're trapped underneath a waterfall!"

"Close enough." Justin had never thought he'd be glad to hear the sound of Durand's voice, but it was a great relief not to be entombed down here alone. "It must be the River Nançon we're hearing. Just our luck to have taken lodgings with a moat of running water. One with a stagnant moat would have been much quieter." It was a lame joke even to his own ears, and he was not surprised when Durand snorted.

"You're probably not in the mood for more bad news," Justin said, after a few moments of silence. "But they forgot to send down dinner. We've got a slop bucket and mayhap a rat or two. That is it, though."

"Are you going to talk all night, de Quincy? The one tolerable thing about you is that you usually keep your tiresome thoughts to yourself. So now you start jabbering like a popinjay when there's no escaping your babbling?"

"It gladdens me to be sharing a dungeon with you, too, Durand." Justin realized that Durand was right; he was talking more than usual. But as long as he was talking, he didn't have to think. "At least we flushed de Lusignan out into the open. He killed Arzhela and now he's trying to put the blame on us."

" 'Trying,' de Quincy? Look around you. I'd say he's damned well done it!"

"It was obvious in the hall who was in on the plot and who was not. Yves de la Jaille and Reynaud Boterel did not know about the forged letter. But Alain de Dinan did, for certes. So did André de Vitré, Raoul de Fougères, and the duchess, of course. Constance seemed willing to hear us out until John's name dropped like a hot rock into the middle of the conversation. De Lusignan offered no plausible motive for why John would want Arzhela dead. He did not need to, for his co-conspirators thought they knew what it was—that accursed letter! If he can—"

"For the love of God, enough! You think you're telling me anything I do not already know? What ails you, man? Are you scared? Is that it?"

Justin exhaled a very uneven breath. He was rubbing his arms to restore the flow of blood; they were numb after being pinned behind his back for so many hours. After another long silence, he heard his own voice saying defiantly, "What if I am?"

"Well, that is the first sensible thing you've said tonight. You ought to be scared half out of your wits."

"And I suppose you're not, Durand?"

Silence again. Durand was little more than a disembodied voice; they were both cloaked in a night darker than dark. When Justin could stand the stillness no longer, he said, "Morgan and Jaspaer were not taken. So they know what happened to us. If they get word to John..."

"What good will it do? In case you haven't noticed, John does not wield a great deal of influence on this side of the border."

Justin could not argue with that. But neither could he yield every last scrap of hope. "The queen and Richard could get us freed."

"Yes, they could. But there are two fatal flaws in that plan, de Quincy. First of all, you are assuming we would still be alive by the time the queen returns from Germany. Second, you are depending upon John to do the right thing, even at risk to himself, and tell the queen of our plight. You truly want your life to balance upon the head of a pin that passes for John's conscience?"

Justin tried to muster up anger; Durand deserved it and at least it might keep him warm. But the ashes of his temper were as cold as Durand's practiced cynicism. "So what you are saying," he said at last, "is that we can expect nothing but a quick trial and an even quicker execution."

"Trial?" Durand's laughter was brittle, unsteady. "We're not getting a trial. You know what they call these dungeons? Oubliettes. You know what that means? Oblivion, de Quincy, oblivion. They put us down here to rot."

CHAPTER XVI

February 1194
Fougères Castle, Brittany

When the trapdoor opened, Justin and Durand did not move, instinctively keeping very still. Justin now knew how a rabbit felt, frozen in fear as a predator approached. The light spilling into their black hole was painfully bright, forcing them to avert their eyes. A bucket was being lowered down to them; when it hit the ground, they heard a wonderful sound, the splash of liquid. A moment later, something else came through the opening, landing with a small thump, and then the trapdoor slammed shut again.

Time was impossible to track in a void. By Justin's best guess, they'd been in the dungeon for at least twelve hours. As thirsty as he'd ever been in his life, he dived for the bucket, and he and Durand took turns drinking their fill. Only then did he try to discover the reason for that other thud, fumbling around in the dark until he found the prize—a loaf of bread. It was stale, so hard it was difficult to break into halves, the gritty rye that was contemptuously known as "alms bread." It was delicious.

"At least they are feeding us," Justin ventured. "So they must want to keep us alive."

"For now," Durand mumbled, stuffing another chunk of bread into his mouth.

"You might want to slow down," Justin cautioned. "We do not know when we'll get another loaf."

"I'm not going to hoard my bread like a starveling mouse." After another silence without beginning or end, Durand said, "I've been thinking about it, and I realized I'm likely to outlive you, de Quincy. You're younger but I'm tougher. So, the way I figure it, if worst comes to worst, I can always gain myself some time by gnawing on your dead body."

"Mother of God!"

"Well, I'm willing to be fair about it. If perchance I do die first, you have my permission—nay, my blessing—to feast on my flesh."

"Thank you, Durand, for that remarkable generosity. But I think I'd rather make do with one of the rats we hear scuttling around in the shadows." Justin gave a shaken, incredulous laugh. "Jesu, listen to us! How can we jest about something like that?"

"How can we not?" Durand asked succinctly, and after that they lapsed into silence again, listening to the muffled roar of the river-moat, the occasional scraping of rodent feet, and the loudest sound of all, the pounding of their own heartbeats.

JUSTIN TRIED TO COUNT THE DAYS by keeping track of the number of times the trapdoor opened and they were given food and water. But he soon realized the flaws in that system. He had no way of knowing if this was done on a daily basis. Even more troubling, he discovered that his always-reliable memory was suddenly fitful, erratic. Had they been there for six days? Or was it five?

They passed the time by discussing Arzhela's murder and the forged letter, although their conclusions, speculations, and suspicions would remain immured with them. Justin confided what Arzhela had whispered in his ear with her dying breath, a single word—Roparzh. It might be a Breton name, he suggested, but he did not know enough of the language to be sure of that, and Durand was quick to point out that it could as easily have been a Breton prayer or even a curse. Unable to decipher the word's meaning, they moved on to those facts that were not in dispute.

They were in agreement that Arzhela had died because she'd learned too much. They also agreed that it was unlikely her murder was part of the conspiracy. Constance might well wink at the authenticity of the letter implicating John. Neither man could see her agreeing to the killing of her own cousin. It was logical, then, to assume they were dealing with two crimes: forgery and murder. Since Simon de Lusignan was their favorite suspect in Arzhela's slaying, it seemed plausible that he was behind the forgery, too.

"Let's suppose, then," Justin said pensively, "that Simon came to the duchess with the letter. Or that he offered to 'obtain' it for a fee. Say that Arzhela found out the letter was a forgery. Would he have killed her for that?"

"He might," Durand mused, "if he'd convinced Constance and her barons that the letter was genuine."

The more Justin thought about that, the more tenable it seemed. The duchess might well have been furious to find she'd been cheated, tricked by a forgery that John could prove to be false. "Arzhela let us think that she had learned of the letter from Constance. It seems more likely that she learned of it in bed, Simon de Lusignan's bed."

"And then she tried to have it both ways, God love her." Durand laughed harshly. "She warned her old lover whilst trying to shield her current lover. If she'd been honest with us from the first, she'd still be alive. Fool woman."

"She made an error in judgment," Justin conceded. "But she does not deserve to be blamed for her own murder."

"I forgot—you had a fondness for the lady. You might have had a chance with her, too. After all, you're even younger than de Lusignan!"

"Let it lie, Durand," Justin said, almost absently, for he'd resolved early on to shrug off the other man's sarcasms; it was either that or kill him. And although he knew Durand would never admit it, he'd not been as unaffected by Arzhela's death as he claimed.

"Well, we solved John's mystery." Durand helped himself to another piece of bread. "We discovered the identity of the mastermind behind the plot. Of course he'll never know that. But as we go to our graves, we'll have the satisfaction of knowing we did not fail him. Will that give you much comfort, de Quincy?"

"About as much as it gives you." Justin broke off a small crust, chewed it slowly. "God damn de Lusignan! How could we let him outwit us again and again? What did you call him—Arzhela's 'stud'?"

"Blaming me, are you? What a surprise."

"I am not blaming you, Durand. I misjudged the man, too. He seemed to be such a hothead, not capable of cold-blooded calculation like this."

"A truly cunning wolf would pretend to be a sheepdog, at least until it was in the midst of the flock." Durand slumped back against the icy, wet wall. "And from the bottom of this oubliette, he's looking like a very cunning wolf, indeed."

As Justin's view was from the bottom of the oubliette, too, he was not inclined to argue, and so he let Durand have the last word. They stopped talking after that, each man alone with thoughts as bleak and bitter as their underground prison.

JUSTIN MOANED, TURNING HIS HEAD FROM side to side. Durand crouched over him, his fingers knotting in the cloth of the younger man's tunic. "Wake up!" he said sharply. "De Quincy, wake up!" Justin jerked upright, staring around him with glazed, unfocused eyes, and Durand loosened his hold, settled back on his haunches. "You were having a bad dream, man, no more than that."

"I am living a bad dream," Justin muttered. He did not remember the details of his dream, but his pulse was racing, his temples were damp with sweat, and his chest felt constricted with the weight of his dread. His waking hours were hurtful enough without dragging demons into his sleep, too.

"You were yelling like a man about to get gutted with a dull knife," Durand shared, telling Justin more than he cared to know about his nightmare. "By the way, who is Aline?"

Justin's breath stopped as memory of the nightmare came flooding back: *He was trapped here in the dungeon, only now he was manacled to the wall, too. The trapdoor opened slowly and he saw a faceless figure laughing down at him. This unknown enemy was holding a small bundle. When he dangled the object above the opening, Justin realized it was his daughter; it was Aline. He lunged to the end of his chains, shouting. But it was too late. The man dropped her and she came plummeting down into the abyss, into the never ending dark.*

"Christ Almighty..." he whispered, closing his eyes to blot out the terrifying vision.

"Well?" Durand prodded. "Who is Aline? Some peasant girl you ploughed and cropped? A fancy whore? A Southwark slut? Or did I mishear and you were really calling out for Claudine?"

"Rot in Hell!" Justin snarled, with such fury that Durand stared at him in surprise, seeking in vain to penetrate those cloaking shadows.

"I hit a sore spot, did I? I just thought you'd like to talk about your women for a while. I've already unburdened my conscience, told you about Barbe, my first, and Cristina, the mercer's wife, and Adela, the runaway nun."

"Do not forget Jacquetta and Richenda and Rosamund Clifford and Maid Marian and the Queen of Jerusalem," Justin said caustically.

Once the initial shock of confinement had worn off, their role reversal had ended. Justin had retreated into the sanctuary of his silences while Durand launched sardonic monologues about John's multitude of vices, old enemies who'd met unfortunate ends, and women he'd lain with. He either had a vivid imagination or more bedmates than any man since Adam, for to hear him tell it, he could not even cross the street without being accosted by a lustful wanton. He described some of these encounters in such loving detail that Justin began to regret having refused Claudine's overtures, and he'd had a few feverish dreams about Molly.

"You sound downright jealous, de Quincy. Is it my fault that I've had more women in a fortnight than you have in your entire, pitiful life?"

"And how many of them did you pay for, Durand?" Justin stood up, moving away until he reached the wall. "Tell me this," he said. "Is there anyone who'll mourn you? Anyone at all?"

Durand was quiet for so long that Justin began to think

he'd hit a sore spot, too. "There might be one," he said at last. "Violette."

"Who is she?"

"It is a long story, de Quincy."

"I am not going anywhere, am I?"

"No, I suppose you're not." Durand rose, groped his way to the water bucket, where he stooped and drank. "This is the tale of a younger son, a father who loathed him, and an older half brother—a brother who did his utmost to make the lad's life Hell on earth."

Justin's curiosity was stirred in spite of himself. "Why did they despise him?"

"The brother hated him because their father had put his first wife aside for the lad's mother. The father hated him because his alluring young wife died in childbirth, leaving him with an unwanted, spare son, his mother's murderer."

"So what happened to him?"

"What do you think happened? The lad grew up nursing his bruises and blackened eyes and grudges of his own. You might say he bided his time. And then Elder Brother took a bride."

"Violette?"

"Yes, Violette. Seventeen years old, sweet as a ripe strawberry, with skin like milk and three fat manors as her marriage portion."

Justin waited, and then prompted, "Well?"

"Well what? Ah, you want to know about the lad and little Violette. He seduced her. Rather easily, too, or so I've been told."

"So what are you saying, Durand? That you were the younger brother?"

"Not necessarily. How do you know I was not the elder

brother? Or an interested neighbor, watching from afar. Or Violette's kinsman. Nothing is as it seems, de Quincy, nothing."

"That will make a fine epitaph for our gravestones," Justin said darkly, vexed with himself for walking right into one of Durand's webs, and this time the last word was to be his.

IN THE DAYS THAT FOLLOWED, DURAND offered up other versions of his past. In one, he was estranged from his family because he'd balked at taking holy vows like a dutiful younger son. In another, he boasted of having lived as an outlaw. Once he even claimed to be a bastard son of the old king, Henry, and thus a half brother to John and Richard. But he never spoke of how he had entered the service of the queen.

JUSTIN HAD GIVEN UP TRYING TO keep track of their days in confinement; what was the point? He had no way of even knowing when it was day and when it was night, and for some reason, that bothered him greatly. Sleep was becoming the enemy now, too. When it came at all, it brought troubled dreams. He'd lie awake for hours, listening to Durand's cough, wondering how long they could survive under these conditions, wondering how long ere they went mad.

"Have you heard of St-Malo, de Quincy?"

It still startled him, the sudden sound of a human voice echoing from the surrounding dark. "Yes, it is a Breton port and an infamous pirate's den. Why?"

"Did I ever tell you about a kinsman of mine, a notorious sea wolf?"

"So now you are a pirate's whelp? You must think that the damp down here is rotting my brain, Durand. You do not speak a word of Breton."

"Do you ever look before you leap? I did not say the pirate

208

was my sire, nor did I say we lived in St-Malo. As it happens, he was my uncle and it was another well-known pirate's nest—Granville in Normandy."

Sometimes Justin welcomed Durand's flights of fancy. They were usually more entertaining than the other pastimes available to them: fending off the bolder of the dungeon's rats, cursing John and Simon de Lusignan and the Bretons, trying not to freeze to death. But on this day—or night—Justin's head was throbbing, his stomach so hollow that it hurt, and his gorge threatened to rise with every breath of this foul, tainted air.

"Spare me another one of your fables, Durand," he said morosely, and the other man laughed mockingly, an effect spoiled somewhat when it ended in a coughing fit.

"Fair enough, de Quincy. Let's hear from you, then. You are so closemouthed about your past that naturally I suspect the worst. But since we're both going to die, why take your secrets and your sins with you to the grave? Think of this as the confessional with me as your priest."

"I'd rather not."

"Aha!" Durand exclaimed, managing to sound both triumphant and accusing. "Do you know why you're clinging to your wretched little secrets? Because you have not abandoned all hope! Admit it, de Quincy, you still believe that the Almighty is going to work a miracle on your behalf and free you with a celestial thunderbolt. You poor fool!"

Justin actually felt a twinge of shame, as if hope was one of the Seven Deadly Sins. Mayhap for prisoners, it was. But he knew that he could never surrender unconditionally, not until he drew his last mortal breath. He owed that much to Aline, even if she'd never know it.

Durand heard it first, the creaking of wood. That was the

most important sound in their world, for it meant the trapdoor was opening. But they'd already got their water and bread a few hours ago, and it was only yesterday that a guard had descended into the dungeon to empty the slop bucket. This break with routine was ominous, alarming, and they watched tensely as a sliver of light spread across the ceiling, spilling into the dark.

The trapdoor opening was a blaze of brightness. Above them, a man knelt, peering over the edge. "Justin? Durand? Are you down there?"

Justin's first fear was that his wits were wandering. But Durand's audible gasp indicated that he'd heard it, too. "Yes, we're here!"

With a loud thud, a wooden ladder was dropped into the dungeon. Moments later, a man was scrambling down, nimbly using one hand for the rungs, the other holding a swaying lantern. Landing with a solid thump, he turned toward them with a grin as dazzling as an Easter sunrise, and that square, freckled face was one of the most beautiful sights Justin had ever seen.

"Morgan!"

"Aye, it's me!" Beaming, he raised the lantern, whistling softly at what its light revealed. "No offense, lads, but your own mothers would shrink from the likes of you! Can you climb the ladder without help? We can haul you up if need be—"

He got no further, for Durand was already halfway up the ladder, with Justin close behind. Morgan glanced around at the encroaching fetid blackness and hastily headed for the ladder, too.

Justin had no idea what to expect when he clambered up into the storeroom under the great hall. He knew only that it could not be worse than where he'd been. A man was holding out his hand and Justin grabbed for it. As he regained his footing, he was assailed by a fragrance that seemed intoxicatingly sweet after the stench of the oubliette, and then a soft female body was in his arms, her breath warm against his throat.

Almost at once, Claudine recoiled, clasping her hand to her mouth. "Justin, thank God!" she cried, though she made no further attempts to embrace him, edging away as unobtrusively as possible. "I'd despaired of ever seeing you again," she confided. "But oh, my love, you do need a bath!"

"What are you doing here, Claudine?" Durand sounded as baffled as Justin felt. "What is happening, Morgan? No, tell us later. Let's just get out of here!"

"There is no hurry," Morgan said cheerfully. "Our men hold the castle."

Blinking like barn owls even in the subdued light of the storeroom, Justin and Durand exchanged glances, the only two rational souls in a world of lunatics. "What men?" Justin demanded. "*Whose* men?"

"I'll let him tell you that." Morgan raised his lantern, pointing toward the corner stairwell. "He is awaiting you abovestairs in the great hall."

As impatient as they were to get answers, Justin and Durand mounted the stairs at a measured pace, uneasy about what they might find. They could think of only one man who might have ridden to their rescue, and neither of them could imagine circumstances under which John had got control of Fougères Castle. Even if he'd been willing or able to raise an army on their behalf, Paris was almost two hundred miles away. None of this made any sense.

The last time they'd been in the great hall, it had been a

scene of torch-lit tragedy. Now it looked peaceful and welcoming. Men-at-arms were seated at trestle tables, drinking and eating. A fire burned in the hearth, giving off bursts of blessed heat, hot enough to banish even the harsh, piercing cold of a subterranean dungeon. Two high-backed chairs had been positioned close to those dancing flames, where a man and woman were making conversation between sips of wine.

"Master de Quincy. Sir Durand." The Lady Emma's smile was coolly complacent; she was almost purring. But the men barely glanced at her, their gaze riveted upon the man beside her. He was quite young, not much older than Justin, dark complexioned and of small stature, well dressed but somewhat untidy in appearance, wearing his clothes as he did his command, with the nonchalance of one who wielded so much power he could afford to take it for granted. "There is no need for introductions," Emma said archly, "for you know His Grace, the Earl of Chester... and husband to the Duchess Constance, the Duke of Brittany."

Both men sank to their knees, looking so stunned that Emma, Claudine, and Morgan burst out laughing, and even Chester smiled faintly. "I am sure you have questions," he said amiably. "But they can wait. The Lady Emma, a woman of great practicality, has ordered baths for you in the kitchen, so you can eat whilst you soak off some of that grime. Afterward, we'll talk."

They did as he bade, as he expected they would. Following Morgan from the hall, Justin halted in the doorway, glancing back over his shoulder at his unlikely saviour. "My lord earl... How long were we imprisoned?"

Chester conferred briefly with Emma. "I'm told," he said, "that it was twelve days."

* * *

Two wooden tubs had been dragged close to the huge kitchen hearth and filled with hot water. They were soon so dirty that they had to be refilled. Justin had never enjoyed a bath so much and when he glanced over at Durand, he saw the same blissful expression on his face. It was hard to believe that less than an hour ago, they had been entombed alive, even harder to believe that their lifetime of imprisonment had numbered only twelve days on the Church calendar.

"You want more?" Morgan was leaning over the bathing tub with a platter of roasted chicken. He grinned as Justin snatched another drumstick. "You've probably lost track of time, so you do not realize how lucky you are. If you'd been freed one day later, you'd have had to make do with fish. The morrow is the start of Lent."

Now that he was warm and clean and fed, Justin could concentrate upon his next urgent need: his desire for answers. Unable to wait for the Earl of Chester's explanation, he sat up with a splash and smiled at Morgan. "Take pity on us, man, and tell us how this came about!"

Morgan was happy to oblige. "We were watching as they rode off with you, and it was easy enough to learn you were being taken to Fougères Castle. When we heard that Rufus and Crispin were under arrest, too, Jaspaer decided that there was a 'time to fish and a time to cut bait,' as he put it. He said he'd have no trouble finding a lord wanting to hire his sword, and we parted company at Pontorson, with him heading into Normandy and me riding for Laval. I pushed my horse and got there by dusk on Friday, so you owe me for a fine crop of saddle blisters and sores!"

"I owe you for a lot more than that, my friend," Justin declared, overcome with gratitude as he realized what a narrow escape they'd had. If Morgan had not proved more loyal than

213

Jaspaer, they'd never have been freed. No one would even have known of their plight.

"When I told the Ladies Claudine and Emma what had happened, Lady Claudine was sorely distressed and insisted upon seeking aid from Lord John. The Lady Emma agreed to let her son send a man to Paris, but she said it would do no good. After thinking about it for another day, she announced that there was only one man who might be able to help, and she ordered me to ride for the Earl of Chester's castle at St James de Beuvron. She said all knew he and the Duchess Constance had no fondness for each other, but he was still her lawful husband, still Duke of Brittany and that had to count for something. The fact that he was on this side of the Channel and not back in Cheshire, well, that most likely played a part in her thinking, too. St James de Beuvron is a lot closer than Paris!"

"Emma's been accused of many things," Durand observed, "but no one has ever called her a fool. There'll be no living with her after this, de Quincy. Not only was it a clever idea, but she actually coaxed Chester into agreeing to it!"

That amazed Justin, too. He did not know the Earl of Chester that well. They'd worked together that past summer to recover the portion of King Richard's ransom that had gone missing in Wales, and he'd been favorably impressed by the man. But he'd never have expected Chester to be the one to throw him a lifeline. He was about to ask Morgan to tell them more when the kitchen doors swung open and the earl himself strolled in.

"The Lady Emma insisted that every stitch you were wearing be burned, but she is sending in some garments for you to wear, courtesy of the lord of the manor. Raoul is providing you with swords, too, even if he does not know it yet. But he can well afford it."

Justin was unable to restrain his curiosity any longer. "Where is Lord Raoul, my lord earl?"

"Fortunately for you, Constance wanted to give her cousin a noble funeral. She and Raoul and the rest of her court are at Mont St Michel, burying the Lady Arzhela. That gave me the opportunity I needed. I knew the garrison would not dare deny me entry in my wife's absence. If any of them harbored suspicions, the presence of the Lady Emma and the Lady Claudine assuaged them, and we were made welcome. Once my men were admitted, it was easy enough to overcome the garrison and take control. We'll free them when we leave, and if Raoul de Fougères or my lady wife have any complaints, they can take them up with me."

Justin was regarding Chester with something approaching awe. "You make it sound so simple, my lord earl. I shall never forget what you have done here this day. I doubt that I can ever repay you, but it will be an honor to try."

Chester nodded graciously, then glanced over at Durand, so pointedly that Durand hastily expressed his own thanks. "De Quincy is too polite to ask," he continued audaciously, "but I am not. Why did you agree to help us, my lord?"

The earl could easily have taken offense. But Durand's luck held, for Chester prided himself on his own forthrightness and was confident enough to appreciate it in others. "Just as the ingredients in a rissole vary according to the tastes of the cook, so did our little alliance contain its share of differing motives. The lovely Lady Claudine seems to fancy Justin. The Lady Emma appears to be trying to curry favor with the queen. As for your man Morgan, you'll have to let him speak for himself; I have no idea what is motivating him. But for myself, I've come to respect Justin de Quincy. He proved his worth in Wales last summer, is too good a man to rot in a Breton gaol."

"Thank you, my lord," Justin said, startled. Durand's smile was more skeptical.

"It could not hurt, either," he said cynically, "to do a good deed for the man who might be England's next king."

"Durand, can you never control that loose tongue of yours?" Justin growled, but the Earl of Chester looked wryly amused.

"He is right, de Quincy. Unless King Richard sires a son, it is inevitable that men will look to John as his heir. I know you to be the queen's man, body and soul. You'd never act against her interests. So if you are involved in this, it can only be because the queen wants it so—reason enough for me to offer my assistance."

Chester helped himself to a portion of roast chicken. "Are you two up to riding? It would probably be wiser to return to my castle at St James rather than tarry the night here. I doubt that Lord Raoul will be pleased by my abuse of his hospitality. Nor will my lady wife," he added, with a sudden, malicious grin that revealed he had another motive for interceding. He could not resist this God-given chance to make mischief for Constance.

CHAPTER XVII

February 1194
St James de Beuvron, Brittany

Watching a new life come into the world was the perfect restorative after living so intimately with death for twelve days. The foal's first steps were wobbly, like those of a sailor stranded on dry land. Its legs seemed too long for its little body, and Justin marveled that this tottering baby would one day run a hole in the wind.

"He's a handsome lad," the Earl of Chester said, sounding more like a proud father than a master. "I think he'll be a good one."

Justin thought so, too. "A pity Morgan was not here to see the birth. He has a way with horses like no man I've ever known."

"Has he come back from the Mont yet?" When Justin shook his head, Chester gave him a contemplative look. "Spying on Lord Raoul and my lady wife, is he? Why do I think there is more involved in his mission than that?"

"Most likely because there is," Justin conceded. He should have known Chester's sharp eye would not miss much. He hadn't been trying to keep anything from the earl, but reticence was a natural habit with him. "We were held in the porter's lodge for two nights," he explained, "and whilst I was there, I hid a letter under a coffer. Morgan thought he'd be able to retrieve it without arousing suspicion."

"I can guess what this letter said. Lucky you thought of that. You'd not have wanted to be found with a letter proclaiming you to be Queen Eleanor's man—not in my wife's court—and they would have been sure to search you right thoroughly ere they threw you into that Breton dungeon."

"They did that," Justin said, grimacing at the memory.

"They took all of your money, too, of course. A shame, for you'll never see a sou of it again."

Justin ducked his head to hide a smile, amused that the earl offered only sympathy. Back in Cheshire, he'd had a reputation for being frugal, not an admired trait in a man of such high rank. "The Lady Emma has agreed to lend us what money we need, or rather, she says her son will, contingent upon being paid back by Lord John when we reach Paris."

"Repayment from John? That I'd truly like to see," Chester said with a chuckle.

Justin grinned, for he agreed with Chester. Guy de Laval had a better chance of sprouting wings than he did of collecting any money from John, and Emma, of all women, would know that. But the more costly she made her son's foray into conspiracy, the less likely he was to repeat it.

Justin was relieved, although not surprised, when Chester asked no further questions. The earl had a finely developed sense of what he needed to know and what he did not when dealing with royal intrigues, and seemed content knowing only that Justin and Emma had been attempting to expose a Breton plot against John. Justin wasn't sure how much Emma had confided in Chester to gain his assistance, but he felt confident that her son's involvement would not be among the secrets she'd shared.

A shout from outside drew their attention away from the mare and her nursing newborn, and they emerged from the stables in time to see Morgan dismounting in the bailey. At the sight of Justin, he broke into a wide grin. "I've got it," he announced. "It was almost too easy, not a challenge at all." Handing over the queen's letter, he said, "And I am bringing back some interesting news, too. Yesterday Lord Raoul got an urgent message from his castle garrison and the whole lot of them went galloping off, including your lady duchess, my lord of Chester!"

"I'll be expecting company, then, in a few days," Chester predicted placidly. "I expect you'll be gone by that time, though. Where to—back to Paris?"

Justin nodded. "But first we must go to Genêts, where two of our men are being held. The Bretons turned them over to the local provost, and since he answers to King Richard, not Duchess Constance, I hope that we can persuade him to free them."

"Even after a summer amongst the Welsh, you remain remarkably trusting, Justin." Chester's tone was dry, but his black eyes held a gleam of amusement. "The queen's letter would serve you better if the provost did not think you guilty of murder. I think I'd best give you a letter of my own, explaining that you and Sir Durand were unjustly accused by those rash, reckless Bretons, and avowing your innocence upon my honor as a Norman baron."

"That would be most welcome, my lord," Justin said gratefully. He'd planned to ask Chester for just such a letter, for the earl was the only man he knew who exercised power on both sides of the Breton-Norman border. He was pleased now that he did not have to ask, though, for he was already so deeply in Chester's debt that it seemed greedy to seek any more favors.

"I'll send some of my men with you to Genêts," Chester said. "After that, you'll be on your own."

THEY WAITED FOR MORGAN IN A grove of trees about half a mile from the town of Genêts. He was not gone long, and when he came into view, his smile communicated the success of his mission before he said a word. "The provost is on his way to the abbey. As soon as I told him Abbot Jourdain had need of him, he was off. By my reckoning, he'll be gone for hours. First he has to cross the bay, then seek out the abbot, who'll doubtless make him wait. By the time he discovers that the abbot sent no message, he'll not want to venture out into the bay at dusk and he'll—"

As usual, Morgan took the roundabout route; he was never one to use ten words when he could use twice as many. That was fine with Justin, who thought Morgan had earned the right to talk from now till Judgment Day if it made him happy. Durand was not as indulgent and cut him off brusquely, saying, "Let's look for the gaol, then. Are you still set upon coming, Lady Emma?"

"Of course," she said, no less brusquely. "They are my men, are they not?"

Justin wasn't sure if Emma had any genuine concern for Rufus and Crispin, or if it was simply that her sense of possession was offended by their gaoling, but he welcomed her presence, for she'd prove to be a formidable distraction.

And she did. As soon as she flounced into the gaol, lifting her skirts and curling her lip, she had the provost's deputy off balance, so flustered that Justin could almost feel sorry for him. Identifying herself as the Lady Emma Plantagenet, consort of the Prince of Gwynedd, sister of King Henry of blessed memory, aunt to King Richard Coeur de Lion, she demanded that he free her men at once, and for a moment they thought she was going to prevail by the sheer audacity of her performance. Master Benoit stammered and stumbled, visibly wilting under that haughty stare. But then his eyes moved past her to Justin and Durand, widening in horrified recognition.

"We are not escaped murderers," Justin said hastily. "We had nothing to do with the slaying of the Lady Arzhela de Dinan. But I do not expect you to take our word for that. I have here a letter from the Earl of Chester, attesting to our innocence."

Master Benoit reached for the letter as gingerly as if it might burst into flames at his touch. After reading it, he said hesitantly, "The earl argues most persuasively on your behalf. But I do not have the authority to release your men, Madame. The provost has been called away, but I will discuss the matter with him straightaway upon his return."

Justin and Durand had been expecting this; their brief experience with the deputy provost had shown them that he suffered from a malady detrimental to officers of the law: a total absence of backbone. "Have it your own way," Durand said nonchalantly. "So... the provost has forgiven you, then? I must say you're a lucky man, for an argument could be made that your blunder brought about the Lady Arzhela's death."

The deputy's Adam's apple bobbed. "What... what do you mean?"

"Well, if you'd told him what Brother Bernard had confided in you—that the lady was disguised as a humble pilgrim— he'd have sought her out at the abbey and the killer would not

221

have had his chance to corner her in the crypt."

"You look very pale of a sudden." Justin did his best to sound solicitous. "Are you ailing? Surely you told the provost about that conversation with Brother Bernard?"

Master Benoit swallowed again, inhaling air in a convulsive gulp. "Of course I did!" He looked down at the earl's letter. "I suppose it would do no harm if I release them now. They'd be freed as soon as the provost returns, after all. It would be a pity to make a fine lady such as yourself delay your journey, Madame. You are planning to depart Genêts today?"

Emma nodded coolly and as the deputy scurried off to fetch the prisoners, she gave Justin and Durand an approving glance and a rare compliment: "Well done."

"Thank you," Justin said dryly, thinking that the Lady Emma was the only woman he knew who viewed extortion as a social skill. Durand leaned against the wall, arms folded, looking bored. But Justin knew how deceptive that familiar pose was; Durand could move as swiftly as a panther if the need arose—if the deputy decided to double-cross them.

Master Benoit kept faith, though, soon emerging with Rufus and Crispin in tow. They were deliriously happy to be freed, almost embarrassingly grateful, and Justin realized that men-at-arms were too often viewed as expendable by their masters. Emma waved aside their thankfulness, wrinkling her nose at their ripe odor. "I suppose it is too much to hope there is a bathhouse in town?" she queried.

"Of course there is!" Master Benoit sounded offended, as if she'd insulted his civic pride. "It is close by the shipyard and a fine one it is, too—" Belatedly remembering that it was in his best interest to get them out of Genêts as soon as possible, he added lamely, "But it might not be open today. In fact, I am sure it is not."

Emma paid him no heed and instructed her men-at-arms to go off and scrub themselves clean. Doling out coins sparingly, she warned them not to spend the money on wine, on anything but the baths. "Then meet us at the priory," she said, "and if you tarry over-long, you'll be left behind." When Crispin reminded her that they were "right famished," she grudgingly agreed that they could also stop at a cook-shop.

Master Benoit had snatched up the earl's letter and was holding it close to his chest. "You're going to the priory, too? Do you not want to leave whilst there is still light?"

He blanched when Durand said blandly that they might want to pass the night in Genêts, looking so miserable that Justin took pity on him. "We'll not be staying. After we arrange to have Masses said for Lady Arzhela and the two slain monks, we'll be on our way."

Master Benoit blinked. "Two? But Brother Andrev is still alive!"

THE TOWN PHYSICIAN HAD THE GRUFF, no-nonsense demeanor of a man overworked and underappreciated. Brother Andrev was still grievously ill, he warned, and although he was expected to recover, God Willing, he was very weak and tired easily. Only after they'd promised to keep their visit brief were Justin and Durand allowed to enter the sickroom.

The infirmary was much smaller than the one at the abbey and Brother Andrev was the sole patient. He had a sallow sickbed pallor, his eyes hollowed and sunken in, giving him an almost cadaver-like appearance. Justin had been nervous about this meeting, worried about agitating a man who'd come so close to death, and wondering how they were going to convince him that they'd played no part in Arzhela's murder. But as soon as Justin said their names, Brother Andrev became much more animated, insisting that they come closer, and with his first words, it was obvious that he needed no persuasion to trust them.

"Justin and Durand? You are the men Arzhela was awaiting? But I thought you'd been dragged off to Fougères Castle. How did you escape?"

"It is a long, strange story. You know we are innocent, then?"

"Of course. Arzhela would not tell me the name of the man she feared. But she did tell me your names, said she'd be safe once you reached the abbey." Brother Andrev's spurt of energy was already ebbing away. He had no pillow, for truly devout monks scorned such comforts. He did not object, though, when Justin rolled up a spare blanket and placed it under his head. "I tried to tell the provost once I'd regained my wits, saying I was sure you were not the ones. He did not seem to believe me..." He closed his eyes and Justin wondered if the interview was over. This man's spirit burned like a lone spark in a cold hearth, all too easy to extinguish.

After a time, Brother Andrev opened his eyes again. "She always wanted to be buried here," he said sadly, "at our church... But it must be reconsecrated, and... and the duchess would not wait..."

What followed was a patchwork quilt of silences and sighs and laborious, strained utterances. Brother Andrev could tell them nothing that would be of use in solving Arzhela's murder, for all he remembered of his brief struggle with his would-be assassin was the terrifying image of an upraised, bloodied blade. But as he painstakingly recounted his last conversation with the Lady Arzhela, it seemed to Justin that there were four now in this room that had held only three. A lively ghost with laughing eyes lingered for a moment in their midst, an elusive, caressing breath of summer on a day of grey skies and frigid sorrows.

"There is something you can do for me, for the Lady Arzhela..." Brother Andrev was obviously tiring, but his will overrode his failing body. "She took a lad under her wing at the abbey... Yann. He was with her that night. He told me she'd taken him into the chapel of Notre-Dame-sous-Terre to offer up a prayer to the Blessed Lady Mary for a dying pilgrim, promising that they'd sneak into the monks' enclosure afterward and raid the kitchen. She took so long at her prayers, though, that he got bored and he crept away, left her alone..."

Justin nodded grimly, remembering the feel of that lamp's still-warm wick against his fingers. She'd entered a well-lit chapel, secure in God's Grace and her pilgrim's armor, unaware that she was still being stalked by a killer. If only she'd stayed in the almonry. If only. "The boy—he saw nothing, then?"

"He says not, and I believe him. He says he returned to the almonry, expecting her to return soon and scold him for running off. I suspect he may have had some mischief in mind, mayhap a bit of thieving... When the fire bell sounded and word spread of her death, he was terrified and guilt-stricken, too. He will not talk of it, but I think he blames himself for leaving her..."

"How did you find this out, Brother Andrev?"

"Yann was too fearful to stay at the abbey. Arzhela had told him about me, and so he fled to Genêts, having nowhere else to go. He'd become right fond of her, I think. She had a way about her..."

His voice had thickened and he gestured toward a nearby table, toward a clay cup filled with a greenish liquid. Propping his head up, Justin held the cup to his lips. "We will want to talk to the lad. What can we do for you, Brother Andrev?"

"It is a great favor, but I hope you'll do it for her, for Arzhela. She told me she planned to settle Yann on one of her manors, see that he learned a trade. I'll do what I can for the lad, but he's not one to be taking holy vows..." A faint smile twitched one corner of his mouth. "Moreover, I do not know how safe he is here. What if the killer decides to make sure he saw nothing that night? There was talk at the abbey about a boy being with her in the infirmary—"

"You cannot be asking that we take this tadpole with us?" Durand interrupted incredulously, turning to glower at Justin when the latter agreed to consider it. "Why is it, de Quincy, that I can always rely upon you to make my life even more wretched than it already is? What are we going to do with a light-fingered Breton whelp?"

Justin didn't know, but he agreed with Brother Andrev about the boy's possible danger. "We'll talk to the Lady Emma," he said. "Mayhap her son can find a place for the lad at Laval." He tilted the cup so the monk could drink again. "Brother Andrev, there may be something you can help us with, too. Lady Arzhela whispered something to me with her dying breath. I thought it might be a name, but I cannot be sure. Neither Durand nor I speak Breton."

Brother Andrev's eyes focused intently upon Justin's face. "What did she say?"

"One word—Roparzh."

If he'd hoped for a sudden illumination, he was to be disappointed. The monk frowned, slowly shook his head. "It is indeed a name, a man's name. Very common amongst the Bretons. But I know no one called Roparzh... I am sorry."

So was Justin. "We've kept you too long. Rest now. We'll return later, once you've talked to the lad. Better he hear it from you, for he has no reason to trust us."

At the sound of the opening door, Brother Andrev raised himself feebly on his elbows. "That may be Yann now," he said. "He went out to get me some soup from the cook-shop."

"Blood of Christ!" That stunned bit of swearing spun both Justin and Durand toward the door. Simon de Lusignan was standing there, obviously as astonished to see them as they were to see him. "How did you escape?" he cried, with such amazement that they knew he'd not been at the Mont when Raoul de Fougères had got word of the Earl of Chester's tour de force. He recovered quickly, though, for the next sound they heard was the metallic whisper of his sword clearing its scabbard. "You'll not get away again," he snarled, "not from me!"

Durand's sword was unsheathed in the blink of an eye, or so it seemed to Justin, and there was something chilling about his smile. "We need him alive, Durand!" Justin said swiftly, even as he drew his own weapon.

"Tell him to yield, then!" With a shiver of steel, the two blades came together, setting off sparks. Simon parried Durand's next blow with such ease that the knight's smile faded, eyes narrowing as he realized he was facing a superior swordsman. Justin was surprised, too, by de Lusignan's skill, for like many people, he had a naïve tendency to equate evil with inadequacy. But there was nothing inept about the way Simon handled a sword; he looked to be more than a match for Justin and possibly even as good as Durand.

Simon's next maneuver was a classic move; he feinted high and then struck low. Durand anticipated him and stepped in, parrying the cut with the flat of his sword. Since neither man had chain mail or a shield, they circled each other warily, so intent upon their lethal duel that Justin was, for the moment, forgotten. Seeking to take advantage of that, he darted around the monk's bed, but Simon caught the blur of Justin's movement and swung about in time to deflect the blow.

"Did she beg?" Simon panted. "Did she entreat you whoresons to spare her life?"

"Spare *us*!" Durand spat. "This is not the great hall at Fougères Castle, and you've got no audience! We know what happened!"

"So do I!" Simon lunged forward with a downward thrust that would have eviscerated Durand had he not blocked it. "You killed her!"

Realization hit Justin like a blow. "You believe that," he gasped. "You truly believe we killed her!"

Simon backed up a step, his chest heaving as he sought to catch his breath. "You did kill her, you bastards!"

"No, we did not!" Justin overturned the table with a sweep of his arm, forcing Simon to take another backward step. "We thought you did!"

"You've got to do better than that," Simon jeered, swinging his sword in a tight circle to keep them both at bay. "I would never harm Arzhela!"

"I am beginning to believe you," Justin admitted. "You were so set upon accusing us that we could not see past that. But Arzhela whispered a name to me ere she died, and I think mayhap it was her killer's name."

"How simple do you think I am? Only a half-wit would believe a fable like that!"

"Hear me out! It was a Breton name, a man's name, and she said it twice! You think she'd waste her dying breath on a lie? She said 'Roparzh,' and if he is not her killer, who is he, then?"

"Roparzh?" Simon echoed the name blankly at first, as if it meant nothing to him. But then his sword wavered slightly. "She said 'Roparzh' as she died?"

"It is true." This confirmation came from an unexpected source, from the bed where Brother Andrev had been watching helplessly as they fought. "He confided in me, not sure what it meant. I was the one who told him it was a Christian name, a Breton name."

Simon expelled his breath in an audible hiss, his pupils shrinking to pinpoints like the eyes of a man suddenly exposed to a blinding flash of light. It was at that moment that the door opened and a youngster entered, a dark imp of a lad who could only be Yann. He froze at the sight of the drawn swords, and then whirled to flee. But Claudine was close behind him and she barred his escape, the partially opened door blocking her view of the room.

"Easy, lad," she said in a good-natured rebuke. "You'll spill the soup for certes leaping around like a grasshopper!" She screamed then, for as she advanced into the room, Simon de Lusignan pounced, pulling her roughly against him and crooking his free arm around her throat.

"No," he warned as Justin and Durand tensed. "I can snap her neck like a twig ere either of you can reach us. You, boy, over there with them! Do as I say and I'll not hurt her. Drop your swords on the ground and kick them into the corner. Do it!"

When Justin hesitated, Simon must have tightened his hold, for Claudine gave a soft, involuntary cry, almost like the squeak of a rabbit in a snare. Justin dropped the sword with a clatter, and Simon looked over at Durand. "You, too," he ordered. "If you do not, I'll kill her."

Durand didn't blink. "I can live with that," he said, but before he could act upon his words, Justin tackled him, sending them both sprawling. By the time they'd untangled themselves, Simon had backed out the door, dragging Claudine with him. Passersby stopped, staring at the sudden drama spilling into the street.

By now Justin and Durand had recovered their swords, trading curses as they tried to shoulder their way through the doorway. They reached the street as Simon snatched the reins from a rider who'd just dismounted from a big-boned grey gelding. The man cried out in astonished protest, but when he tried to get the reins back, Simon shoved Claudine into him, with enough force to knock them both to the ground. Vaulting up into the saddle, he spurred off down the street, kicking up clouds of dirt as people scattered to get out of his way.

Kneeling by Claudine, Justin lifted her up and carried her into the infirmary. She was pale and shaken, wrapped her arms so tightly around his neck that he had trouble disengaging her hold once they were inside. "Stay here," he said. "You're safe now."

"Wait! Where are you going?"

"After him." She called out his name but he did not heed her, plunging back out into the street. There all was chaos. People were milling about, dogs barking, someone shouting for the provost. Justin ran for the priory stables. Durand was already there, lugging a saddle toward his stallion's stall while he tongue-lashed a cowering groom for having unsaddled their horses. "Stop berating the man," Justin snapped, hastening toward his own mount. "This is not his fault!"

"No, it's yours!" Durand shot back, glaring over his shoulder as he fumbled with the cinches. "If you had not been such a fool, he'd not have got away!"

"At the cost of Claudine's life!"

"He'd not have hurt her!"

"You do not know that!"

They were shouting at each other so angrily that the stable

groom shrank back into the shadows, convinced that they were both lunatics. Other men were entering the stables, drawn by the uproar, but they dispersed hastily as Durand spurred his stallion through the doorway. The other men had just regained their footing when Justin's horse came shooting by, sending them scrambling for safety again.

Morgan was outside, shouting something unintelligible at Justin as he galloped past. Justin did not have time to explain, but as he glanced over his shoulder, he saw Morgan running toward the stables. Wheeling his mount, he raced after Durand.

CHAPTER XVIII

February 1194
Road to Fougères, Brittany

Justin knew from the first that their chase was likely to be futile; Simon had too much of a head start to be overtaken if he was willing to abuse his mount. But his horse could always throw a shoe or pull up lame, and so they pushed on in pursuit. A man racing by at full speed attracted attention and they had no trouble following his trail; he left numerous gaping bystanders in his wake. Once they'd left the Norman town of Avranches behind, they slowed down, pacing their horses, for the hunt was no longer a mad dash; it had become a grim endurance test.

Simon was riding south. The road ahead beckoned them on, but neither man wanted to advance too deep into Brittany. They slowed down again, eventually pulling up to rest their horses and plot their strategy. "How far do you think we are from Chester's castle?" Justin asked. "Five miles or so?"

Durand grunted an assent, swearing when he realized that he'd left his wineskin back in Genêts. "I see some alder trees over there," he said. "There ought to be a spring close by."

Leading his lathered mount toward a pond of murky water, he let the horse drink and then knelt and drank himself, cupping the water in his hands and splashing it onto his hot, dusty face. "What—you think to ask Chester for help?"

Justin was drinking, too, ignoring the brackish taste of the water. "I am not eager to ride on to Fougères alone," he confessed. "I do not fancy the lodgings they offer there."

"Nor do I. But I doubt that Chester is going to give us men enough to launch an assault upon the castle." Durand sat down tiredly in the withered grass. "Are you so sure that is where he's heading?"

Justin shrugged, no less wearily. "Your guess is as good as mine. But this is the road to Fougères and he's likely to be looking for a safe burrow."

"I suppose..." Durand stretched out in the grass. "Christ Jesus, but I hate Brittany. Nothing about this accursed country makes sense. If that poxy hellspawn de Lusignan did not kill the woman, who did?"

"We might be able to get that answer from Simon de Lusignan. But we have to catch him first." Justin rose reluctantly to his feet, and then cocked his head, listening intently. "Riders coming," he said, "from the south."

Durand was on his feet, too, now. "A goodly number, by the sound of them. I do not much like this, de Quincy."

Neither did Justin. "I think we ought to pay the Earl of Chester a visit," he said and they both made haste to mount. The riders were within sight now, detouring off the road in their direction. Justin was about to spur his stallion into an urgent race for Chester's castle when Durand gave a startled profanity.

"They are not Bretons!"

"Are you sure?"

"Aye." Durand's voice was flat and cold. "I know that

whoreson in the lead. They call him Lupescar—the wolf."

Even in England, Justin had heard of Lupescar, a notorious mercenary whose sword was always for hire to the highest bidder, a man with such a foul reputation that his name was used to scare small children into going to sleep at night. *Stay abed or Lupescar will come for you.* "How can you be so sure he is not in the pay of the Bretons?"

"Because," Durand said harshly, "he's been working of late for John."

LUPESCAR HAD THE DARK HAIR AND eyes of his native Provence, a surprisingly pleasant voice flavored with the soft accent of langue d'oc, the language of the south. He also had a raw, jagged scar across his forehead, and another around his throat that looked suspiciously like rope burns. "Well, Durand," he said in a mellow, melodious tone that was utterly at variance with those cold, empty eyes. "Are you not gladdened to see me?"

"Beyond words. What are you doing here, Lupescar?"

"Why, coming to your rescue, of course. When John got word that you'd been clumsy enough to get yourself caught, bloody-handed, over some poor pilgrim's body, he sent me to pull your chestnuts from the fire—assuming they were not burnt to a crisp, of course. We did a bit of spying around Fougères, learned that you'd managed to get free, and we were on our way to Mont St Michel to see if we could pick up your trail." Those unsettling eyes drifted over toward Justin. "You must be John's other lost lamb. De Quincy, is it?"

Justin nodded tersely. "What would you have done if we'd still been imprisoned at Fougères?"

Lupescar smiled. "We'll never know, will we?" And then he and his men turned back toward the road, where riders had appeared in the distance. They were coming from the north, and Justin breathed a sigh of relief when he recognized Morgan.

Drawing rein, Morgan looked from one to the other, aware of the tension but not understanding it. "My lords? You were not easy to catch. We left Sir Lionel and some of my lord Chester's men at Genêts to protect Lady Emma and Lady Claudine, but the rest of us decided to join the hunt." His gaze kept flicking toward Lupescar. He was obviously curious about this scarred stranger, but he asked no questions, waiting to follow Justin and Durand's lead.

Lupescar returned Morgan's appraisal, noted he wore no sword, and decided he was not worthy of further attention. "So, Durand, what are you hunting? Any quarry that might interest me?"

Durand took his time in replying. "If you came from the south, you may have seen him. Young, fair-haired, on a grey gelding, riding as if he were trying to outrun his sins."

"We did see a man like that," Lupescar acknowledged. "He swerved off the road into the woods when he saw us, but we saw no reason to follow. A man with money would not have been riding a nag like that. Who is he and why are you chasing him?"

Justin could feel the hairs prickling on the back of his neck every time he glanced at Lupescar, and he was glad when Durand balked at answering, saying only that it was nothing Lupescar need concern himself with.

"I expect you'll be going back to Paris now," Durand continued, his voice toneless, utterly without inflection, although Justin was close enough to see that his hand had tightened upon the hilt of his sword. "If John sent you to find out what had befallen us, you did. Since we freed ourselves, we are not in need of your aid, are we?"

The two men stared at each other, the silence stretching out until it threatened to become smothering. Lupescar was the first to blink. "I do not think we want to return to Paris just yet. We'll let you get on with your hunt, though. I promised my men they'd have a town to sleep in tonight, with real beds, wine, and wenches—not necessarily in that order. If my memory serves, that would be Avranches. Look for us there; mayhap we can ride back to Paris together."

Durand said nothing. No one spoke until Lupescar and his wolves were on their way, disappearing into the gathering mist, for one of those mysterious Breton fogs had rolled in without warning, cloaking the countryside in a damp, grey cloud that smelled of the sea.

"John never fails to surprise me," Durand said at last. "Who'd have thought he'd take our plight seriously?"

"You think he did?" Justin queried, and Durand laughed, a sound like shattering glass.

"He sent Lupescar, did he not?"

THEY PASSED THE NIGHT AT CHESTER'S castle of St James, for it was too far to return to Genêts. The next afternoon, they were fed in the great hall, amidst men-at-arms, several well-to-do merchants, household servants, and a few pilgrims bound for the Mont. Chester himself was not present. He'd made them welcome, but his hospitality seemed perfunctory this time. Chester had not been pleased to learn that Lupescar and his mercenaries were on the prowl so close to his own lands. It was evident that the earl was tiring of being dragged into their never-ending troubles, and Justin felt like a dinner guest who'd overstayed his visit.

"So we are in agreement, then?" Durand had propped his elbows on the trestle table, staring down glumly at a trencher of Lenten fare: salted herring seasoned with mustard. "We head back to Genêts, collect the women, and return to Paris."

Justin nodded, toying listlessly with his own fish. Only Morgan seemed to have an appetite; popping a Lenten fritter into his mouth, he looked at them in surprise. "We are not going to follow de Lusignan to Fougères?"

"For what purpose?" Durand shoved his trencher away with a grimace. "What would you have us do, Morgan—ride up to the gatehouse and ask if Simon can come out to play?"

"No, I'd suggest you send me." Morgan reached over, helping himself to Durand's discarded fish. "Let me go in on a scouting expedition, make sure that de Lusignan is indeed there."

"Are you eager to put your neck in a noose?" Justin scowled. "You were there with Chester barely four days ago. You truly want to wager that none of the garrison would remember you?"

"I've thought of that," Morgan said, with a blithe wave of his hand. "The solution is simple. I need only take a page from the Lady Arzhela's book." Spearing another chunk of fish on his knife, he gestured with it toward a table of russet-clad pilgrims. "A man becomes well nigh invisible once he dons a monk's habit or a pilgrim's robe. I'd be in, fed, and out ere anyone even looked twice at me."

"You know," Durand said slowly, "he might be right. What do you say, de Quincy? Shall we go over and barter for one of those cloaks marked with a red cross?"

Justin nodded again and started to push back from the table. "This is the plan, then, Morgan. We'll await you with the horses in the woods east of the castle. You put on the pilgrim's garb, and go try your luck. Just be sure you truly want to risk this."

"Why not? It sounds like good sport." Morgan rose, claiming

one last fritter. But as Justin started after him, Durand grabbed his arm.

"How about asking *me* if I want to risk that? Why cannot we wait for Morgan here?"

That had not even occurred to Justin. "It is only fair that we share the risk, Durand."

Durand looked at him balefully. "Whenever I hear words like 'fair' and 'honorable' coming out of your mouth, de Quincy, I start saying the paternoster."

"I'm glad to hear you're keeping up with your prayers. But if you are truly loath to take the risk, wait for us here."

Durand responded with an obscenity so profane that even John would have been impressed. Justin turned away, biting back a smile. As he expected, Durand followed.

THE WOODS WERE THICKLY GROWN WITH beech trees, spruce, and pine. With but one day to go, February seemed intent upon inflicting its full measure of misery and the weather was wretched, the cold so damp and penetrating that Justin and Durand were huddled in their mantles like turtles in their shells, clutching their hoods with frozen fingers as the wind gusted, sending dead leaves swirling into the sky like skeletal butterflies. They dared not build a fire and their smoldering tempers provided the only source of heat. Both men's nerves were raw, all the more so because they were not willing to admit it, and they tensed every time they heard the slightest sound. When it began to rain sometime after noon, Durand started calling Justin every foul name he could think of, and Justin was too miserable to argue with him. As the afternoon dragged on, the great hall back at Chester's castle was looking better and better.

It didn't help that they'd camped in such an eerie,

otherworldly setting. Ancient stones rose up around them, arranged in strange patterns that could only have been done by man... or demons. Their spectral shapes reminded Justin of gravestones, and he made the sign of the Cross every time he glanced over at those mossy, ageless rocks, wondering what bloody pagan rites had taken place under those craggy silhouettes. He very much wanted to move, but he was not about to admit his unease to Durand. Durand shared his edginess, but as he also shared Justin's stubborn pride, they remained where they were, listening intently for approaching footsteps and watching for ghostly apparitions from the corners of their eyes.

Despite their vigilance, they still did not hear Morgan's quiet footfalls on the sodden ground, were alerted only when their stallions began to nicker in welcome. Emerging through the trees, he looked odiously cheerful for a man dripping wet and muddied. "Wait till you hear what I have to tell you!" he exclaimed. "Every man, woman, and child in the castle was talking about it, about what happened yesterday—"

Afraid that Morgan was about to go off on one of his digressions, Durand cut in hastily. "First things first, man. What of de Lusignan? Was he there?"

"He was, but no longer. He arrived yesterday on a horse half dead, with him looking little better. When he was admitted to the castle, he rode that horse right into the great hall ere anyone could stop him. It was the dinner hour and the hall was filled with highborn guests. Simon's entrance caused quite an uproar."

Morgan paused for dramatic effect. "But that was nothing compared to what he did next. He flung himself from the saddle, leaped over one of the trestle tables, and tried to throttle a man of God!"

CHAPTER XIX

March 1194
Laval, Maine

By the time Laval's great stronghold came into view, the men were tired, hungry, and still angry with the women they hoped to find behind those castle walls. Their anger could be measured in miles, more than ninety of them. After retrieving their men at the Earl of Chester's castle of St James, Justin and Durand had ridden north to Genêts, only to learn that the Ladies Emma and Claudine were no longer there.

Brother Andrev could tell them only that he thought they were heading for Laval. The Earl of Chester's men had been instructed to escort them to Genêts, no farther, and so they were traveling with a meager escort, especially in light of Lupescar's presence at Avranches. Nor had the Lady Emma taken Yann with them. Brother Andrev recounted sorrowfully that she'd dismissed the suggestion out of hand and he'd had no luck in changing her mind. He did have better luck with Justin, for when they rode out of Genêts, Yann was perched upon the back of Morgan's horse, clinging tightly to the man's belt, looking both fearful and excited.

Three days later they'd reached Laval, having failed to overtake the women on the road. They were admitted at once into the castle bailey, and Durand was soon stalking into the great hall with Justin on his heels. There they found the objects of their wrath seated at the high table enjoying a Lenten supper made tolerable by the free-flowing wine. Guy de Laval welcomed them nervously, looking like a man in need of allies, and Claudine's smile was dazzling, but Justin and Durand had eyes for no one but the Lady Emma, who greeted them with a nonchalance they found infuriating.

"Into the solar," Durand rasped. "Now!" When Emma stiffened in outrage at that peremptory tone, he leaned across the table and jerked her to her feet, looking over then at Guy, as if daring him to object. Guy did not. Emma was made of sterner stuff than her son, and her hand closed upon the eating knife she'd been using to fillet her pike. But Justin now echoed Durand's command with no less heat and she decided that submitting to their high-handedness was a lesser evil than making a scene in front of the servants. Flinging down her napkin as if it were a gauntlet, she marched across the hall toward the stairwell. Claudine followed her, and after a very conspicuous hesitation, so did Guy.

As soon as they reached the privacy of the solar, Emma turned on the men in fury. "How dare you put hands on me like that! I am not one of your kitchen wenches to be ordered about at your pleasure, Durand de Curzon! You're fortunate I did not have my men flail you till your back was bloody."

"First of all, Your Queenship, they are your son's men, not yours, and I'd have liked to see them try! But if you think Sir Stoutheart there has the ballocks to give a command like that, you must believe in unicorns and barnacle geese and winged griffins!"

"I—I resent that," Guy said, sounding more unhappy than

indignant, and his flush deepened when Durand did not even deign to respond to his feeble protest.

Emma's breath hissed through her teeth. Before she could lash out, Claudine stepped between them, speaking with an authority that reminded Justin of what he'd too often forgotten—that she was Queen Eleanor's kinswoman. "Stop this! It serves for naught to be hurling insults at each other like brawling alewives. Why are you so wroth? No, not you, Durand. Let Justin speak; he has a far cooler head than yours."

"By all means," Durand said nastily, with a mocking bow toward Justin. "Go to it, de Quincy."

"How could we not be wroth?" Justin demanded. "We reached Genêts on Monday and found you gone!"

Emma blinked in surprise. "Is that what this is all about? We waited Friday night and all of Saturday, with nary a word from you, I might add. For all I knew, you'd be gone for a fortnight! How did I know how long it would take to catch de Lusignan? I made the sensible decision to await you in comfort back at Laval."

"And of course you did not think to send us word of this decision."

"How was I supposed to reach you, Durand?"

"The way anyone with the sense God gave a sheep would have done, by dispatching a man to Chester's castle," Durand said scornfully, provoking Emma into using her royal brother's favorite oath.

"By God's Liver, I've heard enough of your whinging! What difference does it make now?"

"About sixty miles," Durand snapped. "That is how much farther we had to travel, thanks to your foolish, female whims!"

"Not to mention," Justin said sardonically, "the pleasure of fearing that we'd be finding your bloodied bodies by the side of the road."

Claudine deflected Emma's angry retort. "I would never fault a man for caring about my welfare or safety, but we had an escort, Justin. Surely Brother Andrev told you that?"

"As if Rufus and Crispin would have been a match for Lupescar's cutthroats!"

Claudine lost color. "Lupescar was nigh?" When Justin nodded grimly, she made the sign of the Cross. "We did not know."

Emma was not cowed. "The Wolf is presently in John's hire, so I rather doubt I had anything to fear from him. He'd not dare to molest his lord's aunt."

"There is a reason why shepherds use dogs and not tame wolves to guard their flocks," Durand sneered. "A wolf is a wild creature, impossible to trust, for it can slip its leash at any time."

"Moreover," Justin said grimly, "the men riding with Lupescar are Hell's dregs. If he'd sent some of them out scouting and they ran across two beautiful, rich, poorly guarded women, you truly think they'd humbly wish you 'Good morrow' and ride on by?"

Emma scowled, for she sensed that she was being outmaneuvered. "You exaggerate the risk. We had three good men with us. If we were in such danger, we'd have been in danger, too, when we first left Paris, for we had only seven then. Four more men could not make that much of a difference!"

"They could as long as I'm one of them," Durand drawled, and Emma tartly called him an "insufferable, preening peacock." But she tacitly conceded defeat by abruptly changing the subject, demanding to know the whereabouts of Simon de Lusignan.

"I did not see him being dragged in shackles into the great hall. So I assume he got away from the both of you, then."

Neither Justin nor Durand cared for that implicit accusation, that they'd been bested by de Lusignan. "We tracked him to Fougères Castle," Justin said coolly. "But I'll let Morgan be the one to tell you." He half expected Emma to object, but she'd obviously done some reassessment of her hired man, who was constantly revealing talents above and beyond a groom's skills at mucking out stalls or soothing spooked horses, and she said nothing as Justin moved toward the door.

Morgan responded so swiftly that Justin wondered if he'd been eavesdropping out in the stairwell. He showed no nervousness at being summoned into his lady's solar, acting as comfortable as if they'd been meeting in the stables, and when Emma sent for a servant to fetch wine, Morgan took it for granted that one of the cups was for him. "You want me to tell them about Fougères?" he asked Justin, and needed no further encouragement to launch into a vivid account that was quite polished by now, after much repetition.

"Simon de Lusignan rode his horse right into the great hall, just like King Henry used to do when he came to dine with Thomas Becket ere he became God's man instead of the king's. But Simon had murder in mind, not feasting. He leapt from his mount onto that canon from Toulouse and was making good progress toward strangling him ere they dragged him off."

Guy gasped. "Why would Simon try to kill Canon Robert?" He was about to make an ill-advised defense of his friend, but he caught his mother's eye and thought better of it.

"From what I was told," Morgan resumed smoothly, "the people in the hall did not understand that, either, and concluded

244

that Simon was roaring drunk. That was not unreasonable, as Simon had bloodshot eyes, slurred speech, and was stinking of wine. But we know he'd been awake for nigh on a day and a night, most likely had nothing to eat, and I'd guess he was drenched in wine from diving across that table. They decided to put him where he'd do no harm till he sobered up and so they confined him to a storeroom out in the bailey. Interesting that they did not toss him into the dungeon, is it not?"

Emma regarded him thoughtfully. "You are saying, then," she said, "that Simon de Lusignan was accorded special treatment?"

Morgan beamed approvingly. "Exactly, my lady. It was like a signed confession from the duchess and her barons that they were up to their necks in this plot with Simon. Canon Robert insisted he had no idea why Simon had attacked him, and adroitly played the role of injured innocent. Apparently the others honestly did not know what had provoked Simon's attack. We do, of course."

"What—that the canon killed the Lady Arzhela?"

Morgan nodded so vigorously that Justin felt the need to interject a cautionary note. "Well, all we can say for certes is that Simon thinks he did."

"I'm with Simon," Morgan insisted. "That canon was always too slick for a man of God. And you told me yourself, Justin, that the Lady Arzhela never trusted him a whit."

"And we know both Simon and Arzhela had judgment as infallible as the Holy Father's."

This acerbic comment came from Durand, and earned him no favor with Morgan, who showed a rare flash of irritation. But Emma was losing patience and she moved to take control of the conversation, saying swiftly, "Be that as it may, we are still waiting to hear what happened after that."

"The next morning, they discovered the lock on the storeroom had been broken; inside there were signs of a struggle and blood, but Simon was gone."

Morgan found the reaction of his audience quite gratifying. Guy and Claudine cried out, and even Emma looked startled. "There is more... Canon Robert was missing, too!"

MORGAN WAS HAPPY TO PROVIDE ADDITIONAL details: Simon had stolen a horse in the village and when last seen, was heading into the sunrise. The duchess and Breton lords seemed relieved to have him gone, for none of them showed any enthusiasm for pursuing the fugitive. There was some concern about the missing canon, especially after the discovery of a bloodstained rochet on the outskirts of the village. Gossip had it that Simon must have escaped and slain the cleric, although no one could explain the lack of a body.

"No one could explain, either, how Simon got himself out of a room locked from the outside," Morgan observed. "The castle servants seemed to think he'd called upon his master, Lucifer, who cast a spell that allowed him to walk through the wall. If I were wagering, I'd put my money on one of the Breton barons sneaking down in the night and setting him free."

"But what of the missing canon?" Emma said skeptically. "I never met the man; he was taken ill upon our arrival at Vitré. So I am not the one to pass judgment upon him. But Simon did, or at least he tried to when he attempted to throttle the man. If he were so set upon murder, would he have fled upon being freed by one of Constance's barons, as meek as a lamb? Or would he seek to finish what he'd begun?"

"That seemed more likely to me, too," Justin admitted. "I can see Simon being freed by one of Constance's conspirators. And I can see Simon then going in search of the canon, determined to avenge Arzhela. What I cannot understand, though, is why he would hide the body afterward, nor do I know where he'd hide it. Fougères is a vast place, but he would not have had much time ere the castle servants would be up and about."

"In other words," Durand said morosely, "what we have are even more questions and few answers. Jesu, how I hate Brittany!"

"What of the canon's horse?" Claudine asked hopefully. "Was it gone, too?" She looked deflated when Morgan said it had been found in the stables. "Well, then, I am at a loss," she confessed. "None of this makes sense."

"Not to me, either," Guy ventured, but no one paid him any mind and he lapsed back into a sulky silence.

"It seems to me," Emma commented, "that Simon de Lusignan has the answers you are seeking. Do you have any idea where he'd go? Back to Poitou, to his family's manor in Lezay?"

Justin and Durand exchanged glances, in agreement for once that Morgan deserved to be the one to tell her. Morgan thought so, too. With an actor's fine sense of timing, he drew a deep breath as if to speak, waiting until all eyes were upon him.

"As a matter of fact, we do know where he's heading. He was seen riding away from the village, toward the east."

Emma nodded. "Yes, I remember your saying that. But what of it? Half of Christendom lies to the east of Fougères, including Laval."

"We know that, my lady," Morgan said patiently. "But he was not heading southeast toward Laval. He was heading due east toward Mayenne, and that is a toll road. So we detoured on our way to Laval, asked the toll collectors if they remembered a man like him, looking much the worse for wear and in a great hurry. Eventually we found one who did. He remembered Simon because he had bloodstains on his clothes, and because he'd asked a question." Morgan paused again, theatrically. "He wanted to be sure this was the road to Paris!"

THEY SET SUCH A FAST PACE, pushing themselves and their horses to the limits of exhaustion, that they covered the 188 miles to Paris in just six days, reaching the city after dark on the ninth of March. It would have been difficult to say who was happiest as that forest of church spires came into view, for Emma and Claudine were not accustomed to hardships and the men were thoroughly sick of hearing their complaints after six demanding days on the road.

The one most affected by the sight of the city walls was Yann. Justin had told him that Paris was home to more than forty thousand souls. The boy could neither count nor even imagine numbers that high. He would never have admitted it, but his first view of the French capital was thoroughly intimidating: a maze of narrow streets and crooked alleys, most unpaved and muddy, crowded with loud, brash city folk hurrying home before curfew rang; imposing, overhanging, whitewashed houses of wood and stone towering above his head, blocking out all but the puniest slivers of moonlight; and more noise than his country-bred ears could bear.

Church bells chimed. Chains rattled as the bailiffs made ready to close the west end of the River Seine. Boatmen offered cheap passage. Street vendors shouted out their wares and often exchanged taunts as they fought over the day's last customers. Dogs barked and geese honked and beggars cried out for alms, and from darkened doorways rouged and powdered women boldly accosted male passersby. Even the air filling his lungs seemed foreign to him. He felt as if he were inhaling smoke. Sickening stenches rose from the streets, the cesspits, the river, overwhelming the occasional appealing odor of baking bread or eel pie. Clinging to the back of Morgan's belt, his thighs and buttocks blistered from endless hours on horseback, Yann blinked fiercely, keeping tears at bay.

He'd learned long ago that tears served for naught. But in just a month, his life had been turned topsy-turvy. The Lady Arzhela had been as close as he'd ever expected to get to a miracle. She'd teased him with winks and hints, whispering that all was not as it seemed and offering the promise of better tomorrows. He'd not understood half of what she'd said, nor had he fully believed it. It had been enough for him that this odd, fey woman had given him what he'd never got before: attention and even affection. And then she was dead and his dreams were drenched in blood, his peace slashed to shreds at night by a killer's knife. Desperate to get away from Genêts, for he did not believe that a sickly, kindly monk could protect him against such evil, he'd agreed to accompany these strangers back to their world, clutching his only thread of faith—that the monk had said they were the Lady's friends.

At Laval, he'd learned that none of them truly wanted him, not like the Lady did. The woman the others called Lady Emma and he privately called the She-wolf had made it quite clear that she would not be burdened with a Breton cub, and the Weakling, her son, had only agreed because the Lady's friends bullied him into it. Yann knew that as soon as they'd gone, he'd be cast out to beg his bread again, and so he'd stolen food from the kitchen, making sure that he was caught in the act. The Weakling had been indignant and balked at taking him in, backed by the She-wolf.

It was then that the other woman intervened, the Lady Claudine. To Yann, she was the Plum, for he still remembered his one taste of that sweet fruit. The Plum had taken the one called Justin aside, and Yann had crept closer to eavesdrop. The lad could go with them to Paris, Plum said, where her cousin would find a place for him on her estates. Justin had seemed surprised and grateful, and Plum had laughed and said they could not leave the lad to starve, after all. Yann could see no humor in that, for his whole life had been a battle against starvation.

And so he'd heeded his fear and his hunger, thinking that he might be striking a deal with the Devil, but at least the Devil was feeding him well. He'd tried to keep away from the She-wolf and the Knight, for that was how he'd christened Durand, staying close to the ones he instinctively recognized as his protectors—Justin and Morgan, the Groom. Gradually the terror knotting his stomach had begun to ease and the death dreams no longer came each night without fail. He'd even relaxed enough to admit that he knew more of their French tongue than they'd first thought, and because of the Plum's careless kindness, he dared to hope that she really would keep to her word. But now that they were in Paris, a hive from Hell aswarm with alien bees, he was afraid that he'd made a great mistake.

THEY ESCORTED THE WOMEN TO THE town house of Claudine's cousin Petronilla, planning to spend the night there themselves, for curfew had rung. Justin had been hoping to delay his meeting with John for one more night, but it was not to be. Petronilla had invited John to be her guest, ostensibly because his lodgings with the Templars lay beyond the city walls and a residence within the city would be more convenient, as well as more comfortable. Petronilla did not seem pleased with her coup, though, and Claudine felt a flicker of relief, for she'd warned her cousin that a dalliance with the Devil was a walk on the wild side. This prince was best left to his own dark domains. Seeing Petronilla's discontent, Claudine was thankful that nothing had come of her cousin's high-risk flirtation, although she was very curious why that was so. She was wondering how to find out what had gone wrong when she saw her answer framed in the doorway of the stairwell.

Claudine recognized the other woman at once, for John's continuing involvement with Ursula had been a source of much court gossip. Ursula had lasted far longer than most of his bedmates, and Claudine did not understand why. She was a spectacularly beautiful, lush creature, but Claudine thought she was also a selfish, slow-witted bitch and John could do better. She was very glad, though, that it wouldn't be with her cousin. Amused in spite of herself by John's sheer audacity in bringing his mistress along when he accepted Petronilla's misguided invitation, Claudine greeted Ursula with one of those brittle, fake smiles that women use to convey a social snub. Much to her annoyance, Ursula did not even seem to notice.

John had entered the hall with Ursula, and he hastened in their direction. "How did Lupescar get you out? I did not really think he'd be able to do it."

"He did not," Durand said, very emphatically. "We freed ourselves." Glancing sideways at Justin, he added grudgingly, "With some help from the Earl of Chester."

But Justin had other matters in mind than giving credit where credit was due. On the ride to Paris, he'd remembered Lupescar's mocking words: *You'd been clumsy enough to get yourself caught, bloody-handed, over some poor pilgrim's body*. It was possible that John, for whatever reason, had chosen to mislead Lupescar about the identity of the murder victim. It was also possible that the message sent by Guy de Laval had been mangled and that John himself did not know Arzhela had been slain.

"My lord John," he said, "I think it best that we continue this conversation in a more private place."

John agreed, but at that moment, Emma sauntered over. "Aunt Emma, what a delightful surprise. I thought you might have stayed in Laval with my cousin Guy." John smiled, and only those in the know would have recognized his pleasantry as a sarcastic reminder of her son's plight.

Emma parried his thrust with a sharp smile of her own. "I was sorely tempted, John, but we still have so much to discuss, do we not?" Linking her arm in his, she suggested that they retire to Petronilla's solar. "We have much to tell you. There have been some unexpected developments since the Lady Arzhela's death." John stopped so abruptly that she glanced at him in surprise. "John—?"

John's face was very still, as rigid and impassive as a sculpted death mask; only his eyes showed life. "The Lady Arzhela is dead?"

Emma nodded. "She was the pilgrim slain at the abbey. Did Guy's messenger not tell you that?" Getting her answer when John turned away without a word.

JUSTIN HAD FALLEN ASLEEP ALMOST AS soon as he'd stretched out on his blankets. When he was awakened a few hours later, he fought his return to reality, had to be shaken before he could clear the cobwebs from his head. Durand was leaning over him. "Come on," he said. "John wants you."

All around Justin, men were rolled up in blankets, sleeping

peacefully, and he yearned to be one of them. With a sigh, he sat up and tugged on his boots. He followed Durand from the hall, the two of them threading their way through the sleepers, and up into the stairwell. He had not even asked where they were going; he'd find out soon enough.

It was John's bedchamber, so lavishly furnished that he decided Petronilla must have given him her absent lord husband's room. Which John was now sharing with his concubine. Too tired to marvel at the morals of the highborn, Justin looked around, then saw John sitting in the shadows beyond the light cast by the hearth. He was still dressed, a wine cup in his hand, a flagon at his feet. Two other flagons had already been discarded in the floor rushes.

"Sit down. But keep your voice low lest you awaken Ursula," John said, gesturing toward the canopied bed. "I want you to tell me what you found out in Brittany."

"I thought we were to do this in the morning, my lord."

"I decided I did not want to wait." John drained his cup, refilled it with an unsteady hand. "There is wine over there. Help yourself."

Justin made one final try to get back to his bed in the great hall. "Durand is here, my lord. He must have already told you what we learned."

"He did. But now I want to hear it from you."

Durand shoved a drink into Justin's hand, saying in a low voice, "Do what the man says or we'll be trapped here all night."

Justin did, dropping down onto the cushions scattered about the floor, and taking a long swallow of what turned out to be a very good Gascon wine. "We confronted the Lady Emma's son at Laval," he began.

* * *

253

THE HEARTH FLAMES HAD BURNED LOW and a distinct chill had crept into the chamber, but the men were warding it off with wine. Durand was sprawled out in the floor rushes, a wine cup balanced on his chest, which rose and fell so evenly that Justin suspected he slept. John remained in the shadows. He'd killed two more flagons, adding them to the other empties, stacked, one upon the other, like a funeral bier for wine gone but not forgotten.

This was such a fanciful thought that it occurred to Justin that he was not entirely sober. He'd been trying to limit his own wine intake, for John was the last man in Christendom with whom he'd want to get drunk. But he was bone-tired and there was something oddly lulling about the dying fire. If he stared into it long enough, he could make out all sorts of strange shapes, putting him in mind of summer days when he'd lain out in Cheshire meadows with Bennet and Molly, finding castles and ships under full sail and swans in the clouds floating over their heads.

"So... you truly do not think that swine Simon killed her?"

Justin started and glanced toward the sound of that voice. John remained well camouflaged in shadows, preferring the obscuring gloom to the warmth of the waning hearth. What had Claudine liked to call him—Prince of Darkness. To Justin, that seemed unusually profound, although he was not exactly sure why. He groped for this understanding but his thoughts were as elusive as minnows, impossible to catch.

"Wake up, man!" John tossed an empty flagon in his direction. "I asked you if you thought that hellspawn killed her."

"I already told you, my lord," Justin said testily, "that I do not. We did at first, but not now. Now I think it was that canon, though God knows why..."

"God knows why," John repeated solemnly, and then laughed suddenly. "Indeed He does." There was a clatter in the darkness as he fumbled for another flagon. "The last one," he announced, in the grave tones of a man on a sinking ship, watching the spare boat drift out of reach. "I'd send you to the buttery for more, but I do not trust you to come back."

"Send Durand," Justin suggested, and John laughed again.

"Tell you what, I'll share it with you," he offered. "But you'll have to wait till the room stops moving."

"I do not want to share with you, my lord," Justin said, slowly and distinctly, while the image of Claudine's face formed behind his closed eyelids.

"All the more for me then." John swore as he spilled some of the wine onto his tunic. "I loved her, you know," he said softly, and Justin sat up straight, for a moment thinking he meant Claudine.

"She was my first love," John said. "I was sixteen when she took me to her bed. It was a revelation..."

Justin thought that over. It did not seem very likely to him. "You are not saying she was the first woman you bedded, are you?"

"No, of course not." John sounded mildly offended. "But she was the first one who showed me what sinning is like if it is done right. She taught me a lot, did that lady. She claimed that most men could pleasure a woman about as well as a dog could read."

Justin laughed, for he could hear Arzhela saying exactly that. "She deserved better than Simon de Lusignan," he said, not drunk enough to say that she'd deserved better than John, too.

"She always did say she had bad taste in men." John sounded wryly amused, but he sounded sad, too, and Justin decided he'd definitely had too much to drink if he was starting to feel sorry for the queen's son.

"To the Lady Arzhela," he said, raising his wine cup high.

"To Arzhela," John echoed, leaning out of the shadows to clink his cup against Justin's. "*Requiescat in pace.* But not the whoreson who killed her, de Quincy. Not in this lifetime nor the next."

THE FOLLOWING DAY, JUSTIN WAS SUFFERING the aftereffects of their bizarre, drunken wake for Arzhela. It was some consolation that John was, too, but he was irked that Durand seemed to have been spared. The knight's trencher was piled with pasties stuffed with trout and he was eating with gusto, whereas the mere sight of them was enough to chase away Justin's appetite.

John was faring no better with his meal, and when a messenger arrived for him, he pushed away from the table with no noticeable regret. Justin made do with almond milk and bread, refusing to watch as Durand devoured yet another fish-filled pasty. Even Claudine's good news—that she'd coaxed Petronilla into taking Yann into her household—did not raise his spirits all that much.

John soon returned, beckoning abruptly to Justin and Durand as he strode toward the stairwell. By the time they reached the solar abovestairs, he was pacing back and forth impatiently, a rolled parchment in his hand. "It seems," he said, "that I'd have done better to keep you both here in Paris. For certes, it would have saved me a fair sum of money!"

"It is early in the day for riddles, my lord," Durand said. "I assume yours has something to do with that letter you hold."

"Indeed it does." John brandished the parchment like a processional torch. "I've finally heard from the one man I've always been able to depend upon. The Breton got the last message I sent, thanks to Emma's assistance. Not surprisingly, he took action straightaway, learning more in a fortnight than the two of you could in a twelvemonth. And," John said, triumphantly, "he has obtained what you two could not—proof that it is a forgery!"

CHAPTER XX

March 1194
Paris, France

Petronilla's great hall was a scene of superficial domestic tranquility. Most of the trestle tables had been taken down after supper. A fire burned in the central hearth. John was absent, having gone off soon after dusk to meet the Breton at the cemetery of the Holy Innocents. Petronilla and Claudine were listening to a harpist while chatting and doing the needlework that was the lot even of women of rank. Emma was reading. Her young knight Lionel was playing chess with a knight of Petronilla's household. Rufus and Crispin were hunched over a game of queek, others occupied with merels, but most of the men in the hall were wagering on a raucous dicing game of raffle. Ursula was reclining in a cushioned window seat, idly petting the small lapdog that was a recent gift from John, apparently oblivious to the admiring male glances being cast her way. Morgan had disappeared after supper, but Justin and Durand were seated at a table, gazing gloomily into half-filled wine cups, looking as frustrated as they felt.

They were not in John's favor at the moment, as he'd made

abundantly clear by not taking them as part of his escort that evening. Now that he no longer needed their services in proving his innocence, he'd felt free to berate them for their failure to prove the letter was a forgery, complaining that he'd paid Lupescar "enough to ransom the Pope," and had got little to show for it. While he'd exercised enough restraint not to blame them for Arzhela's death, they knew he did. Anger was an easier emotion to deal with than grief, and the hunt for scapegoats was a favorite pastime of the highborn.

Justin should have been pleased with the turn of events, for if John could produce proof of the conspiracy, he ought to be free, then, to return to England. But as much as he yearned to see Aline, as much as he detested being yoked to Durand, and as much as he'd disliked taking orders from John, he felt oddly unsettled and dissatisfied with this outcome. He knew John would do all in his power to find and punish Arzhela's killer. He'd hoped, though, to play a part in that reckoning. He owed it to Arzhela.

Pushing his chair back from the table, he encountered resistance. He'd befriended one of Petronilla's pampered greyhounds and as he glanced down, he expected to see its sleek brindle body stretched out behind him. But it was Yann, curled up in a ball like a cat, sound asleep. Justin looked pensively at the boy, who'd been trailing after him all day as faithfully as his absent dog, Shadow. Shadow was motivated by affection, though, Yann by fear. The Breton orphan was the proverbial fish out of water, stranded on unforgiving Parisian shores.

After making sure that Yann was sleeping, Justin said quietly, "I would to God I'd thought to leave the lad with the Earl of Chester at St James. The Welsh do not do well when they are uprooted from their native soil. I fear that the same may be true for the Bretons."

"Well, you can always wed the Lady Claudine and adopt the boy." But Durand's mockery was habitual, not heartfelt; he had too much on his mind to enjoy tormenting Justin. "No man could be as good as the Breton claims to be. I know the stories told about him—that he comes and goes like a phantom in the night, that few men have even seen his face, that he is as elusive as a fox and twice as sly. Mayhap he did find proof positive that the letter is forged, but I'll need to see it with my own eyes ere I'll believe it."

"It sounds as if your nose is out of joint, Durand," Justin said, mildly amused. "For all we know, he has blood-kin at the Breton court, spying on his behalf. If he were able to tunnel under the walls whilst we had to assault the outer bailey, that would give him a huge advantage."

Durand grunted. "No one knows for sure if he is even a Breton."

"If he's not, that would play havoc with my theory," Justin conceded. "He might well be the bastard spawn of a Granville pirate, for all we know."

The corner of Durand's mouth twitched in what was almost a smile. "I've never laid eyes upon the whoreson. That is a select brotherhood. John has met him. So has the queen. I am not sure if Richard has. Emma did, years ago with her brother, the old king, who knew him well, mayhap the only one who did. We can probably add the French king to the list and the Counts of Toulouse and Champagne and Flanders. Our master spy travels in rarefied circles, does not care to deal with underlings."

"Underlings like us." Justin took a swallow and made a face, wondering how long it would take his taste for wine to return. "We are still confronted with two crimes, the plot against John and Lady Arzhela's murder. The Breton may have found out who is behind the forgery, but what of her killing?"

"I thought Simon settled that with his grand dive over the table at Fougères. Damn, I wish I'd seen that!"

"Something about this still does not fit," Justin insisted. "We assumed that Canon Robert is the killer because of Simon's action. But why, then, did she say 'Roparzh' with her dying breath?"

Durand shrugged. "Mayhap she was no longer lucid. Mayhap she was back in time and Roparzh was the name of the squire who'd taken her maidenhead twenty-some years ago. Or a fond name for her second husband. Or her favorite dog."

"No. I saw her eyes, you did not. She knew she was dying and she was trying very hard to tell me her killer's identity. I am as sure of that as I've ever been of anything."

Durand shrugged again. "So who is Roparzh? We've been over this again and again, de Quincy. We met no one at the Breton court with that name."

Before Justin could respond, a small voice piped up behind his chair. "Yes, you did."

They both swung about to stare down at Yann. "What do you mean, lad?"

Yann sat up, yawning. "I was half asleep, heard you talking..." His words trailed off, for he was becoming aware of their tension. "I was not eavesdropping on purpose!"

"That does not matter, Yann. You said we knew someone named Roparzh. Who?"

"That canon you were talking about," Yann said warily, still not sure he wasn't in trouble. "Robert and Roparzh... They are the same name."

Durand let out his breath. "You are saying that Roparzh is Breton for Robert?"

Yann grinned, gaining enough confidence to add impishly, "No, Robert is French for Roparzh!"

There was a long silence as they took this in. "This still does not make sense," Justin said slowly. "She was trying to tell me who her killer was. Why did she not say 'Robert,' then? Why the Breton form of his name? If she'd called him Robert, we'd have thought of the canon straightaway. Why Roparzh?"

"She was dying, de Quincy. She was Breton-born, so why would she not be thinking in Breton at the last?"

"I suppose it is possible," Justin said, not convinced. "She was so intent upon telling me—what? If she used the name Roparzh, it must mean something."

"Let me know if you figure it out." Durand picked up his cup, saw that it was empty, and reached over to claim Justin's. "I think I'll stop torturing myself with riddles and go win some money at raffle." But although he glanced across the hall toward the dice game, he did not move, no more able than Justin to let go.

Yann looked from one to the other, yearning to help. If only he'd not left the Lady alone. She'd paid with her life for his greed, for those few coins he'd filched from the sleeping poacher. "If the Lady called him Roparzh," he ventured, "mayhap he was Breton."

"No, lad," Justin said, as kindly as he could. "He was from Toulouse, though that was likely a lie, too. But even if he were Breton-born, why would it matter? Why would Lady Arzhela have wanted me to know that?" He had no answer, and neither did Durand.

Rising, Justin coaxed Yann to his feet, and started to lead him toward a corner where he could sleep without fear of being stepped upon. He stopped almost at once, struck as if by lightning by an improbable idea. "Durand, this is going to sound crazed. Hear me out, though. What if Arzhela were trying to tell us that Robert was the Breton?"

"You said yourself it would not matter if he were Breton."

"Not *a* Breton. *The* Breton."

"That is preposterous!"

"Is it? Think about it. If Constance and her barons wanted to entrap John in a web not of his making, who better to do it than a legendary spy?"

"I'll grant you that much. But we need more to go on than your sixth sense, de Quincy!"

"Why else would Arzhela have called him Roparzh? She was telling us his true identity. She was suspicious of him from the first, was convinced he was feigning illness at Vitré to avoid us. And she was right, Durand. But it was not you or me he was evading, it was Emma—Emma who could recognize him!"

They looked at each other and then turned as one, a perfectly coordinated movement in Emma's direction. She glanced up, startled, as they bore down upon her, but once she understood what they wanted of her, she could not give them the certainty they craved. "I did meet him," she confirmed. "But I do not remember anything that distinctive about him, nothing like a scar or red hair or even freckles. He was attractive in a subdued sort of way, and well spoken. His hair was brown, I think. He was neither uncommonly tall nor unusually short. In other words, he was a man who'd not call undue attention to himself, a useful attribute for a spy. You truly think this Canon Robert is the Breton?"

They could not blame her for sounding dubious. "We are exploring the possibility," Durand said dryly. "Let us assume that you are right, de Quincy. Arzhela learns through pillow talk with her lover who Canon Robert really is. He then learns of Simon's slip of the tongue. He knows that Arzhela has a past with John. So he kills her to keep her from telling John of his double-dealing. But then he has a new problem: Simon de Lusignan."

"And not one he'd anticipated," Justin said. "He did not realize that Simon truly cared about Arzhela. So now he has Simon set upon collecting a blood debt, awkward at best, dangerous at worst. We've been approaching this from the wrong end. Everyone assumed that Simon had broken out and then gone in search of Canon Robert. What if it were the other way around? If Canon Robert had come in the night to silence Simon?"

Durand nodded thoughtfully, accepting that premise. "So he enters the storeroom, intending to make sure Simon does not blurt out any inconvenient accusations on the morrow. But he finds that Simon is not as easy to kill as Arzhela; we can testify to that. They fight and... what then?"

"The toll collector said Simon had blood on his clothes. Let's assume he was the one wounded. But he got away, stole a horse, and fled. I can understand that if he had the Breton on his tail. Once he had escaped, though, why did he not return and seek out the duchess for help? Why ride for Paris?"

Durand saw where Justin was going, for his thoughts were heading along that same sinister path. "John is here," he said flatly, and Emma turned to stare at him in astonishment.

"You think he came to Paris to tell John how and why Arzhela died?"

"If I were the Breton," Justin said, "I'd be wondering that, too."

Emma was shaking her head. "How could he betray the Breton without betraying his own involvement in the plot? What man would willingly put himself at John's mercy?"

"A desperate man. A man wanting vengeance and seeing no other way to get it," Justin said without hesitation, for he was becoming increasingly convinced of the Breton's guilt. "But even if de Lusignan was not coming to Paris to seek John out, the Breton would fear he was. He could not take that chance, would have to follow Simon and stop him, whatever the cost."

"That would not be easy," Emma pointed out, "not in a city the size of Paris."

"No, it would not," Durand agreed. "It would be easy enough, though, to find John."

It took a moment for Emma to realize the full implication of his words. "No, he would not dare!"

"Then why," Justin said, "did he send John that message? A message we know to be untrue."

"But all of this is based upon supposition," she objected. "You are assuming that Canon Robert and the Breton are one and the same. What if they are not?"

"If we are wrong," Durand said grimly, "it does not matter much. But if we are right, John has been lured into a trap."

THE CEMETERY OF THE HOLY INNOCENTS was the primary burial ground for Paris. Situated on the right bank of the Seine, in the area known as Champeaux, it was close to Les Halles, the large indoor market of the weavers and drapers. Until a few years ago, the cemetery had been an open, marshy field. But the French king had got so many complaints about the unsanitary conditions and the brazen behavior of the prostitutes, thieves, and beggars who congregated in the graveyard that he had ordered it to be surrounded by walls and closed at night.

As John and his escort rode along the rue de la Ferronnerie, several of the men grinned when they passed a narrow, adjoining alley, for one of the city's more notorious brothels was to be found in that dark, winding lane. Listening to their ribald bantering, John grinned, too, thinking he might let them stop there or at the equally infamous bawdy house in rue Pute-y-Muce, Whore-in-Hiding Street, on their way back. If the Breton's information proved accurate, he'd have good reason to celebrate.

When they reached the first of the cemetery gates, he called a halt and ordered the men to dismount. "You will await me here," he instructed Garnier, the household knight he'd chosen to command his men. "I'll not be long."

Garnier was young and eager and not happy at being excluded from his lord's mysterious graveyard meeting. "Are you sure you do not want some of us to accompany you, my lord? Would it not be better to have us there in case some mishap should befall you?"

"What sort of mishap, Garnier? You think I might fall into an open grave? Or be snatched away by a demon on the prowl?"

Garnier did not think it was wise to jest about evil spirits, especially so close to a burial ground. Unable to remonstrate with his lord, he contented himself with a dutiful "As you will," and John relented enough to offer an explanation.

"You need not fret on my behalf, Garnier. I agree that a graveyard is an odd place for a meeting, but the man I am meeting is rather odd himself. He shuns the daylight more than a bat does, prefers to skulk about in the shadows where none will notice his passing. This is not the first time I've met him at Holy Innocents, nor will it be the last."

Approaching the gate, John smiled at the sight of the broken lock. "I see he got here first." Reaching for Garnier's lantern, he shoved the gate back and stepped inside. Holy

Innocents, like most urban cemeteries, was laid out like a monastery cloister, with the church and charnel houses enclosing an inner expanse of open ground. There the poor were buried in common grave pits; the affluent sought their final resting places under the charnel house galleries or within the church itself. By daylight, the cemetery would offer an ironic affirmation of life, for many activities besides funerals were conducted here. People came to gossip, to flirt, to strike bargains with peddlers, to rejoice that they were not yet one with the bones piled in the spaces above the charnel house arches. But by night, Holy Innocents was the realm of the dead.

The sky was splattered with clouds and very little moonlight was trickling through into the cemetery. Light did glow from the *Lanterne des Morts,* the Lantern of Death that was a common feature of French graveyards. A stone column shaped like a little lighthouse, its lamp had been lit at dusk, but its feeble illumination was no match for the encroaching dark. John was not sure of its purpose, whether it was intended to protect the dead from the Devil or the living from ghosts, but as he cautiously made his way across the marshy, uneven ground, he hoped it was the latter.

For all his bravado, John was not happy to be meeting the Breton in a burial ground. He was willing to indulge the spy's whim because so much was at stake, but he was not as indifferent to his spectral surroundings as he'd have Garnier believe. One of the more unpleasant experiences of his childhood had taken place in a cemetery. He'd been about four or five years old. It had been one of those rare occasions when most of his family had gathered under the same roof, probably a Christmas court, and he'd been tagging after his older brothers Richard and Geoffrey, much to their annoyance.

When they'd attempted to lose him by detouring into a graveyard, he'd doggedly followed and fallen into an open grave. He wasn't sure how long he'd been trapped, but for months afterward he awakened screaming, and he never believed his brothers' avowals that they'd not heard him crying out for help.

He took care now to steer clear of the common graves, for they were open, too. Christ's poor were interred in these deep ditches, laid to rest on top of others who'd gone to God, and then covered with only a foot or two of dirt. When the grave was filled to capacity, their skeletons were dug up and carted off to the charnel house, and it was not unusual to stumble over stray skulls or forgotten bones on a stroll through the cemetery. But such grisly evidence of man's mortality was not as troubling in the full light of day. After dark, it was all too easy to conjure up phantom fears and to shy at shadows, and whatever his other faults, no one had ever accused John of lacking imagination.

Raising his lantern, John saw no corresponding gleam of light. In the past, he'd met the Breton by the oldest charnel house and he started in that direction. It was slow going for not all the graves had markers or wooden crosses. He'd covered half the distance when he caught movement from the corner of his eye. He spun around as figures began to emerge from the darkness.

There were three of them, spreading out as they approached him, cutting off his avenues of escape. Swearing under his breath, John unfastened the money pouch from his belt, and flung it onto the ground. "Have it and be damned," he said, for he was not foolish enough to take on three opponents. They were close enough now for him to see they were armed, one with a sword, the other two with knives and a nasty-looking club. John made an effort to convince himself that this was just foul luck, but he knew better; why would it profit outlaws to be lurking around Holy Innocents now that the cemetery was closed at night?

He felt no surprise when they ignored the money pouch, continuing to advance. That could be picked up afterward, once they'd done what they had been paid to do. With chilling certainty, John realized he was facing men hired to kill him. He'd already drawn his sword. Now he unfastened his mantle, dropped his lantern, and shouted, "Garnier, to me!"

The man in the lead smirked. "I'd not count on his help," he said, as a fourth shadow took shape, this man coming from the direction of the rue de la Ferronnerie. At the same time, there was a loud pounding, curses, and Garnier yelled that the gate had been barred from the inside. His heart thudding, John began to back up slowly. Eventually his men-at-arms would either break through the gate or scale the wall. But he was not sure they'd be in time. He'd seen knaves like these before, scarred and battered by life, with only one marketable skill, at which they excelled—killing.

Like wolves stalking a deer, they were herding him toward the charnel house gallery, where he'd have little room to maneuver. Knowing he had to break free of this deadly circle, John feinted at the man with the sword and then pivoted upon the one with the club, such a high-risk gambit that it often worked. It almost did. His target yelped as his sword found flesh, and recoiled, but the wound was not lethal, nor even incapacitating. John may have drawn first blood, but he was still outnumbered, four to one.

It was then that another man materialized from the darkness, swinging a cudgel. He took the assassins by surprise, had struck one down before they even knew he was there.

John took advantage of the confusion to impale the closest of his attackers. The man screamed, and when John jerked his blade free, both of them were sprayed with blood. His new ally was grappling with the club-wielder. A sudden splintering sound, followed by cries of jubilation, signaled that the tide was turning in John's favor and the third killer whirled and fled. The outlaw with the club broke free and brought his weapon down upon the head of the Good Samaritan, who staggered and fell to the ground. Leaping over his body, the man disappeared into the darkness just as Garnier and John's men came panting upon the scene.

When his lantern illuminated the blood smearing John's face and hair, Garnier gasped. "My lord! Where are you hurt?"

"Go after them!" At that moment, John wanted nothing so much as to see his assailants suffer, preferably through all eternity. "Each one of those whoresons is worth twenty silver sous!" His men found that to be powerful motivation and gave chase, yelling as if they were on the hunting field. Raising his lantern, Garnier gasped again at what its light revealed: three crumpled bodies and a veritable sea of blood.

Ignoring two of them, John crossed to the third. "This one saved my life," he told Garnier. "If not for him, you'd have stumbled over my body."

"Who is he, my lord?"

"I have no earthly idea," John said, although when the lantern's glow fell upon the man's face, he did look familiar. Feeling for a pulse, he said, "At least he still breathes. We'll need a litter to get him back to the house—"

"Lord John!" The wind carried the cries to them before the ground began to quiver under the impact of horses being ridden at full gallop. Torches flared in the dark as riders burst through the shattered gate and into the cemetery. Durand and

Justin slid from their saddles even as they reined in, hastily drawing their swords at the sight of the bodies and blood. Justin got his breath back first. "You were lured into a trap, my lord. The man you know as the Breton wanted you dead!"

"You really think so?" John's sarcasm was all the more savage because he knew just how close he'd come to dying here in the cemetery of the Holy Innocents. "Good of you to warn me, de Quincy, but you're just a bit late!"

Some of Justin and Durand's men had dismounted; the others were spurring their horses toward the sounds of pursuit. John stalked over to the man he'd run through, grasped his hair, and jerked him into a sitting position. He groaned, eyelids fluttering, and then cried out when John shook him roughly.

"Hurts, does it? You tell me what I want to know and you'll die quick. If you do not, I swear by every saint that you'll be begging to die! Who hired you?"

"Never knew... name." A bubble of blood had formed in the corner of his mouth. "Paid us goodly sum to kill..."

"To kill who?"

"Some rich fop who'd be alone in graveyard... easy money, he—" He gave a muted scream as John slammed him back onto the ground, then began to choke.

John got to his feet, stood staring down at the convulsing man. "Murder is one thing," he said coolly, "but calling me a 'fop' is quite unmerited. That's an insult I'll not be forgiving."

Neither Justin nor Durand was fooled by the flippancy. They could see he'd been badly shaken by this attempt on his life. So were they, for they could imagine nothing worse than having to face their queen and tell her that her son had died in their care. They did not blame themselves, though, for being slow to suspect the Breton's treachery. It still seemed incredible that he'd have dared to kill a would-be king. But the evidence of his demented audacity was all around them.

"My lord!" Their men were coming back, triumphantly dragging a bedraggled prisoner. "One got away, but we caught this gutter rat going over the wall!" Shoving the man to his knees before John, they crowded around expectantly. Now that the hunt was over, they wanted to be in on the kill.

The man's face resembled a slab of raw meat, both eyes swollen to slits, bloodied gaps where teeth had been. All the fight had been beaten out of him. He answered their questions numbly, confirming what they'd got from his dying partner. They'd been offered a vast sum of money to murder a man in the cemetery. They neither knew nor cared who they'd be killing. It was enough that they'd be well paid for their deed, and had been promised, too, that they could keep whatever valuables their victim had on him.

"Lord John!" Garnier pushed his way through to John's side. "The man who came to your aid—he needs a doctor straightaway. His eyes are rolling back in his head."

John nodded, suddenly realizing how much he wanted to get out of the cemetery himself. Looking toward the cowering outlaw, he said tersely, "Take care of him, Durand," and turned away to retrieve his money pouch.

"As your lordship commands," Durand said, and with almost casual violence, drove his sword up under the man's ribs, deftly stepping back in time to avoid being splashed with blood. Justin was the only one startled by such summary justice. He stood for a moment gazing down at the body, but he could not summon up any pity for the dead man. Hoping that he was not learning to value life as cheaply as the queen's son did, he hastened after John.

"Are you sure you were not hurt, my lord?" he asked, his

eyes flicking to those profuse bloodstains. "Thank God you had a man with you in the cemetery! We feared you'd go in alone."

"I did." John paused in the act of mounting. "He is not one of mine, is one of yours. I do not know his name, but I recognized him after, assumed you'd sent him to follow me."

"No," Justin said, "we did not." His eyes met Durand's, but the knight seemed just as baffled. Looking no less perplexed now, John led them over to the wounded man. As the torch flames fell upon that ashen, familiar face, Justin caught his breath. "My God, it is Morgan!"

CHAPTER XXI

March 1194
Paris, France

Morgan had probably never got so much attention and coddling in his life. Unfortunately, he was in no condition to enjoy it. Petronilla provided a private bedchamber for the injured man, and she and Claudine hovered around his bed like benevolent butterflies as they waited for the doctor to arrive. Women were expected to have some knowledge of the healing arts, but Justin was touched by their solicitude, for it seemed genuine. He was not surprised when Emma showed no inclination to visit the sickroom, for it took more imagination than he possessed to envision her nursing the poor, the maimed, the halt, and the blind. Nor was he surprised by Ursula's indifference; she did not even appear all that troubled by John's close brush with death.

Justin was very surprised, though, by John's obvious concern, for gratitude had never been one of his more conspicuous virtues. But he'd sent at once for the French king's own physician and insisted upon seeing for himself that

Morgan was comfortably settled. Only then had he gone to clean off a dead man's blood.

As soon as he'd bathed and changed, John had summoned Durand and Justin and banished a pouting Ursula from his bedchamber. Servants had brought wine and a fire burned in the hearth but that richly furnished room was still as cold and forbidding as a crypt.

"Tell me," John had commanded, and they did, taking turns as they laid out their reasons for believing the Breton was Arzhela's killer. John listened without interruption, but they were not expecting his response. "No," he said, "I think not."

"So, by purest chance, those hired killers just happened to be lurking in the graveyard instead of the man you were to meet?"

"No, Durand, I do not believe that. I am not a fool, as you'd do well to remember."

"What, then, are you saying?" Justin interposed. "Why would the Breton have tried to murder you if he'd not slain the Lady Arzhela?"

"I am saying I do not think he killed Arzhela to keep her quiet. You do not cut off your toe to treat a blister."

Seeing that they did not understand, John said impatiently, "The Breton was not guilty of a personal betrayal. All know his services are available to the highest bidder. Would I have been wroth to find out he'd offered his skills to Constance? Of course. Would I have done whatever I could to make him regret it? You could safely say that. But I would not have declared a blood feud against the man and he was shrewd enough to know that. I might even have made use of his talents again should the need arise. Killing Arzhela would have changed all the rules of the game."

"You do not believe he killed her, then?"

"Do not fret, de Quincy. I am not finding fault with your logic or your conclusions. I do think the Breton killed Arzhela, for nothing else explains his mad attack upon me tonight. But there is a piece missing from the puzzle, his real motive for the murder."

At that moment, there was a knock on the door and Claudine popped her head inside. "My lord John, the doctor wants to talk to you about Morgan."

Justin would have liked to accompany him, but John offered no invitation, and he sank back in his seat. While John was gone, he and Durand speculated about his reasoning. They still thought the need to silence Arzhela was a sufficient motive for murder, but they conceded that John knew the Breton better than they did. John returned before they could pursue this subject at length, and the news he brought was not good.

"The doctor cannot say if he'll recover, claiming it is too early to tell. If you ask me, physicians have found the perfect way to fleece their flock. The patient will live or die. No way they can be wrong, is there? Rather like a soothsayer telling a woman with child that she'll give birth to either a boy or a girl." John flung himself down upon his bed. " 'Wounds to the head are difficult to heal,' " he mimicked. "Fool doctors. We do not need them for the injuries that are easy to heal."

"What does he say we should do for Morgan?"

"He promises to be back on the morrow with more potions and herbs. But for all his fine talk, I'd say Morgan's best chances rest with the Almighty." Reaching for his wine cup, John drank, frowned, and drank again. "So if neither of you sent Morgan to the cemetery, why was he there? Why would he have followed me?"

Justin shook his head. "My lord, those are questions only

Morgan can answer."

John grimaced. "It seems to me that we have an abundance of questions and a dearth of answers, and I am getting heartily sick of it. As far as we know, there are two men with the answers we need. I doubt that either of you are capable of running the Breton to ground, but you ought to be a match for Arzhela's hotheaded lover. Find Simon de Lusignan even if you have to search every hovel and tavern and bawdy house in Paris. Find him!"

SECURITY WAS INCREASED AT PETRONILLA'S TOWN house, and while she did her best in her role as gracious hostess, she had the bemused expression of a woman aware that she'd utterly lost control of events. John instructed Garnier to take men and prowl the city's taverns in search of Simon de Lusignan, a task they embraced with commendable enthusiasm. Claudine volunteered to sit by Morgan's bedside in case he regained consciousness. And Justin and Durand left the house unnoticed and unheralded, pursuing a hunch.

They walked along the rue de la Draperie, heading for the Grand Pont that linked the Right Bank to the Île de la Cité. This river island, anchored in the middle of the Seine, was the beating heart of Paris, the left ventricle ruled by the Crown, the right ventricle by the Church. In a domain divided between the French king and the Bishop of Paris, here were located both the royal palace and the cathedral of Notre-Dame, only partially completed but already giving promise of the magnificence it would eventually obtain. And here, too, was their destination, the Hôtel-Dieu.

"I hope you are right, de Quincy. Without some luck, we do not have a prayer in Hell of finding de Lusignan. What's one fish in a sea of forty thousand?"

"What made me think of this," Justin said, "was a similar hunt back in London. You remember Gilbert the Fleming. Well, we were trying to track down his mad dog of a partner, and it finally occurred to me that a man like that was bound to run afoul of the law. So we went to Newgate Gaol and there he was, already facing the hangman's noose. Sometimes the most obvious answer is the one overlooked."

"So you're guessing that Simon might be in need of a doctor's care."

"All that blood was convincing evidence that someone had been hurt, and we know Simon had bloodstains on his clothing. We also know he did not die on the way to Paris. So why has he not contacted John? Changed his mind? Not likely after riding nigh on two hundred miles."

By now they'd reached the Grand Pont. Justin was very impressed, for unlike the old London bridge, this one was of stone, almost twenty feet wide, and so well fortified that the moneychangers and even some goldsmiths chose to operate their businesses from the small stalls and booths lining both sides of the span. It was so thronged with people and carts and horses that it took them a quarter hour to cross over to the island. It was slow going there as well, for the streets were barely as wide as a sword's length in places. Justin was content to follow Durand's lead, as he'd boasted there was not one of Paris's three hundred streets he couldn't find blindfolded.

The Hôtel-Dieu was the oldest hospital in Paris, under the supervision of the canons of nearby Notre-Dame. When they were ushered into the great *salle,* they halted in astonishment, for it was enormous, more than three hundred feet long and filled with beds. Not only was every bed occupied, many held two patients and a few even held three. To the men, it looked as if half of Paris was ailing. Splitting up, they began walking along those crowded aisles, but they searched in vain for a patient with blue eyes, golden beard and hair, and bloody hands.

They did not give up, though, primarily because they had no other viable leads, and from the Hôtel-Dieu, they returned to the Right Bank and visited the Hôpital des Pauvres de Sainte Opportune, and the Hôpital de la Trinité. Justin even girded himself to check the leper hospital of Saint-Lazare north of the city gates; Durand balked and waited outside the wattle-and-daub fence. After that, they ran out of hospitals.

UPON THEIR RETURN TO PETRONILLA'S, THEY found John in a foul mood, Morgan still unconscious, and Garnier's men in need of sobering up, for Paris seemed to have an inexhaustible supply of taverns to search. The weather had turned on them, too, and a cold, sleeting rain poured from lead-colored clouds, a last gasp of winter that plunged their spirits even lower. But as they shivered around the hearth in John's bedchamber, they received aid from an utterly unexpected and unlikely source.

They'd been relating the day's futile hunt to John, doing their best to shrug off his sarcastic asides, when his beautiful bedmate drifted over to complain of their presence. Neither Justin nor Durand was surprised, for they'd been around Ursula long enough to realize that nothing ever pierced her cocoon of self-absorption. She displayed so little interest in the rest of the world that they'd sometimes wondered why John put up with her; they could only conclude that in bed she must set the sheets on fire.

John brushed off her objections with the unconcern born of long practice. "If you need a task to occupy yourself, Ursula, you can fetch us wine from the table over there." Glancing back at the men, he said, "I understand why you think de

Lusignan may have been wounded. Why are you so sure, though, that he did not sicken and die on the road to Paris?"

"Every time we stopped to water the horses, to eat, or to pass the night, we asked about a flaxen-haired stranger riding through in a tearing hurry. Twice we found people who remembered Simon. But we found no one who'd nursed him and no one who'd buried him."

"Your wine, my lord," Ursula said sulkily. When she returned with wine for the other men, she made no attempt to hide her resentment, shoving the cups at them with such calculated carelessness that liquid slopped over the rims and would have splashed their clothes had they not anticipated her bad behavior.

"Thank you, darling," Durand said, smiling at Ursula with poisonous politeness, and she looked sorry she'd not overturned the cup in his lap. The men returned to their discussion of Simon de Lusignan's whereabouts, and John paid Justin a barbed compliment, saying his idea had been a good one, if only it had worked. It was then that Ursula made her contribution to the conversation.

"If I were hurting," she said, "I'd not wait till I reached Paris. If I were sick enough to need a doctor's care, I'd find one as soon as my pain worsened, even if it meant veering off the main road. And if I thought I was being chased, I'd be all the more likely to seek a safe burrow to lick my wounds."

They all turned to stare at her, surprised both by the sense of her statement and the realization that she paid more heed to her surroundings—and their conversations—than they'd thought. After a moment to reflect, though, Justin shook his head doubtfully. "We know he did not seek help on the Paris road. And how many hospitals would he be likely to find out in the countryside? Other than the lazar houses, they are always located in towns."

John sat upright in his chair, his eyes gleaming in the lamplight. "I can think of one," he said.

FOR MORE THAN SIX CENTURIES, THE Benedictine abbey of Saint-Germain-des-Prés had reigned over the open country south of Paris. Within twenty years, it would be absorbed by the encroaching city suburbs. But on this March morning, the abbey rose above the meadows in isolated, fortified splendor, a citadel of God keeping the world at bay with the walled, moated defenses of a secular stronghold.

The church was surrounded by the abbey buildings: two cloisters, the refectory and dormitory, the abbot's lodgings, the kitchen, the barns and stables, the gaol, a chapel devoted to the Virgin Mary, and a large, well-equipped infirmary. Although not as spacious as the *salle* at Hôtel-Dieu, it was still a good-sized hall, with both an infirmarian and a physician in residence to treat ailing monks, pilgrims, and travelers. After Durand concocted a plausible story, they were allowed to enter in search of a missing cousin.

In the middle of the hall, people were clustered around a frail, gaunt figure lying on the bare floor. He was clothed in sackcloth, and ashes had been sprinkled over his emaciated body. At first, Justin thought he was looking at a corpse, but then he saw the feeble rise and fall of the man's chest, and realized they were witnessing the last hours of an aged brother of the Benedictine order. Such dramatic deathbed abasement was seen as atonement for past sins of pride and arrogance, although Justin wondered how many opportunities an elderly monk could have had for prideful fits of temper.

About a dozen beds were occupied by patients, several of them shielded by screens. It was in one of the latter that they found Simon de Lusignan, sleeping peacefully and so soundly that he had to be shaken awake. They were tense, anticipating resistance, but he merely gazed up at them, his face impassive, his thoughts masked.

"Are you going to come with us quietly?" Durand asked, low-voiced. "Or will I have the pleasure of dragging you behind my horse?"

"Still holding a grudge for that kick in the ballocks, are you?" With an effort, Simon propped himself up on his elbows, and as the blanket slipped, they saw the Breton's handiwork: his ribs were tightly bandaged. "Where are we going?"

"I think you can guess. Where are your clothes?"

Simon pointed to a nearby coffer, and when Justin tossed his clothes onto the bed, he struggled to pull his shirt over his head, wincing but offering no protests. "You're being very cooperative," Justin said suspiciously, and he smiled tightly.

"I hear that all the time." By now he'd got his tunic on, although the exertion had obviously taken its toll. "I'll need help with my boots," he said, and Justin reached for them with a sigh, knowing Durand would let him walk barefoot back to Paris before lending a hand. Once Simon was on his feet, he looked from one to the other. "I do not suppose you'll believe this, but I was planning to seek your lord out as soon as I was on the mend."

Justin did not care to hear John described as his "lord," and he felt a sudden nostalgic pang for those bygone days when he could identify himself as "the queen's man" and take pride in it. He knew nothing was likely to be so simple or straightforward once King Richard was free and back in England. For better or for worse, it would be a different world.

***

THEIR ARRIVAL WITH SIMON DE LUSIGNAN created a gratifying commotion, and Justin and Durand were both amused when Claudine strode over and slapped her abductor across the face. Justin was not so amused, though, when Simon gallantly kissed the hand that had struck him, vowing that he'd never have harmed one so beautiful. There was good news about Morgan; he'd awakened briefly and seemed lucid before falling asleep again. But John showed none of the jubilation they'd expected, tersely instructing them to join him abovestairs in the solar. Simon was exhausted after the ride back to the city. He knew better than to object, however, and did as he was bidden. The sangfroid he'd shown at the abbey infirmary was beginning to thaw and he was regarding John with the wariness of a small prey animal in the presence of a much larger predator.

Emma accompanied them, taking it as her just due, and when John did not object, so did Claudine. Simon asked meekly if he could sit down. Hotheaded or not, he had clearly taken John's measure. The queen's son gestured abruptly toward a stool, but chose not to sit himself, pacing back and forth with such smoldering, restless energy that he unsettled them all.

"I've seen corpses with better color," John said, studying Simon with a noticeable lack of sympathy. "So de Quincy was right, then, and you had a close encounter with the Breton's ever-handy dagger."

Simon blinked. "You know about the Breton?" His head swiveled toward Justin and Durand. "Ah... so you figured out what Roparzh meant. Clever, very clever," he said softly, and they were not sure if he meant Arzhela's stratagem or their deduction. Simon swallowed, glancing toward a nearby wine flagon, but no one took the hint. "My lord count, I am here for justice."

"Well, you're a bold son of a bitch; I'll give you that."

"Not for me, for the Lady Arzhela de Dinan. I tried to avenge her, but I failed. It is my hope that you can do better."

"I have no interest whatsoever in your hopes, de Lusignan. We know the Breton killed Lady Arzhela. What we do not know is how this pretty conspiracy of yours was hatched. Whose idea was it to hire the Breton?"

"It was his. He sought me out the first Sunday in Advent, told me he knew of a way for us to make a large sum of money. I was to go to Raoul de Fougères and say that I'd learned that there was a canon in Toulouse with evidence that would be your ruination, and ask if he was interested in pursuing it. Naturally he was, and in time I produced 'Canon Robert' and his incendiary letter. The Bretons were only too happy to buy it."

John could hide neither his surprise nor his skepticism. "You're saying they never knew they were dealing with the Breton? I would think his credentials would have been an asset, a means of validating the so-called proof."

"He was adamant from the first that his identity not be disclosed. I did not understand why myself," Simon acknowledged, "but I was not about to question my good fortune. He'd not have needed me as a go-between if he'd not been so set upon staying in the shadows. He provided me with the letter and the finest set of forged seals a man could hope to see." Forgetting, for the moment, the audience he was addressing, Simon sounded almost admiring of his partner's artistry. "He was never one to stint on quality and I daresay many at the Breton court believed the letter was genuine."

"Forgive me if I do not share your enthusiasm for a forgery meant to be my 'ruination,'" John said, and the tone of his voice raised the hairs on the back of Simon's neck.

"I know I've given you no reason to think kindly of me," he said hastily, "but I was not motivated by malice. It was just for the money, no more than that."

His listeners could only marvel at the most inept, awkward apology they'd ever heard. "That makes me feel so much better," John said caustically, "knowing it was never personal. If I go to the gallows for treason, at least I'll have the consolation of knowing you bear me no ill will!"

Simon swallowed again. "It was the Breton's doing. I came along for the ride but the hand on the reins was his."

John walked over to Simon, standing so close that the younger man shifted uneasily on the stool. "Tell me about the Breton and Arzhela."

"I'd had too much to drink, and she got it out of me about the Breton. She was good at that. I warned her to keep quiet, which was a mistake. She had a hellcat's temper." Simon smiled ruefully, glancing up at John as if they were allies in the eternal male-female wars. "So we fought and I went off to brood about women and their vexing ways and, to be honest with you, to drown my troubles in a river of wine. When I sobered up, I rode back to Fougères, but Arzhela had already gone on to Mont St Michel. So we never got to make our peace, and the next time I saw her, she was laid out on a bier in St Étienne's crypt..."

His voice thickened and he bowed his head. Justin watched the performance with apprehension. He did not doubt Simon's grieving for Arzhela was genuine, but neither did he doubt that the other man was quite capable of using that grief to his own advantage, just as he'd attempted to forge a sense of male camaraderie with John. He feared that Simon would try to retreat into the shadow world of loss whenever he was cornered, and he glanced over at John, hoping that he'd not allow it.

He need not have worried. "I think you are forgetting something, Simon," John said, the coolness of his voice belied by what they saw in his eyes. "When did you tell the Breton that you'd misspoken and Arzhela knew his true identity?"

Simon expelled a long-held breath. "I did tell him," he admitted, almost inaudibly, keeping his eyes fixed upon the floor rushes. "Arzhela could be as strong-willed as any man, as impulsive as a swallow on the wing. I thought I ought to warn him that there might be trouble brewing. But I never thought he'd harm her." He looked up then, his eyes glistening with unshed tears. "I swear by all that's holy that I did not!"

"So why then," Justin asked, "did you go racing off to the abbey as you did?"

"I wanted to mend our quarrel. I did not suspect him, even after he disappeared from Fougères. He was always going off on mysterious errands of his own..." Simon's shoulders twitched in a half-shrug that quickly brought a spasm of pain to his face. Placing a hand to his bandaged ribs, he said earnestly, "I did not suspect he had killing in mind, I did not!"

"Of course you did not, lad," Durand said, his voice dripping icicles and disbelief. "After all, this was the Breton, a man of known integrity and honor. Jesu forfend that he'd ever resort to murder!"

Simon showed his temper was not truly tamed, then, by glaring at Durand. "Of course he's killed men," he snapped. "But not a woman, not one so highborn, so dear to me. I tell you it never occurred to me that he could be guilty, not until that day at the Genêts priory when you told me she'd whispered 'Roparzh' ere she died. Then I knew; too late, I knew what I'd done!"

It was Emma who gave voice to the query in all their minds. " 'So dear to me,' " she echoed incredulously. "Why should the Breton give a flying fig for your passing fancies? For that matter, why should he have entrusted you with so much? Even if he needed a go-between, as you claim, why you?" She did not need to finish the rest of that disdainful thought; the tone of her voice said it all.

Simon's head jerked as his eyes cut sharply from Emma to John. "You do not know, then?"

"Know what?"

"The Breton and I—we are kinsmen."

If he'd been hoping for a dramatic response to his revelation, Simon was to be disappointed. There was a long silence, although over his head, their eyes met in mutual amazement. "Do not stop now," John said sardonically, "not when we are hanging upon your every word."

"It is true," Simon insisted. "His mother and mine were sisters, albeit born twenty years apart. This was the first time I'd had any business dealings with him, but I've known him all my life and his identity as the Breton was an open family secret. He chose me because of my involvement with Arzhela— ironic, is it not? He said I was already familiar with the lords of the Breton court, and he knew for certes that I'd jump at his offer like a starving trout. He'd been an impoverished younger son, too... once."

Although none of them would give Simon the satisfaction of acknowledging it, he'd just established his bona fides beyond doubt, for the weak link in his story had been the one that forged a bond between him and the Breton. "Assuming for the moment that we believe you," John said, "what happened at Fougères?"

"You know that already, my lord. The Breton tried to kill me. But he discovered that was not so easily done," Simon said, with a hint of smugness in his voice. "He had the weapon and thought he had the element of surprise. I was waiting for him, though, and I was younger and faster, if not fast enough." His hand slid, unbidden, to his side. "I knew he'd try again, so I stole a horse and rode for my life."

Glancing toward Justin, Simon added, "Your men told me that the Breton tried to make it seem as if I'd killed him, leaving behind a bloodstained garment. He then stole a horse, too, or bought one for all I know, and came after me."

"Why did you not tell the Duchess Constance of your suspicions?" Durand demanded, but this time Simon knew better than to shrug.

"I thought about it. But then it would have come out that the letter was a forgery and I was not sure if the duchess knew that. I was afraid, too, that the Breton would twist the truth, for I had no actual proof that he'd slain Arzhela. The duchess wanted to believe the letter was genuine. I thought they might decide to cast the both of us into one of Lord Raoul's oubliettes, let God sort out our guilt."

"So you were coming to me," John said, and Simon flashed a sheepish smile that was not quite as artless as he'd hoped.

"That sounds mad, I know. But I was wagering that you'd rather thwart the Breton and avenge Arzhela's murder than punish me for my lesser sins. Is this... is this a wager I'll win, my lord count?"

"It is too early to tell. Where is the Breton now?"

"I would to God I knew. I am sure he is in Paris, though. I am willing to be the bait, my lord, if that will draw him out of hiding."

"How kind of you. As it happens, he has already made a move. He paid to have me slain."

Simon's shock seemed genuine; his jaw dropped. "He would dare? That does not sound like him, for he's never been one to panic. It was a family joke that if he were cut, he'd bleed ice water. I can see him trying to silence me now, but to strike at you, my lord... ?" His words trailed off dubiously.

This was the second time that the Breton's motives had been questioned, and Justin was beginning to wonder if John and Simon were right, and there was more at stake here than they knew. He looked from Simon to John and then over at Durand, realizing that Simon's capture was not going to be the magic elixir, after all. Dross would not turn into gold on the words of Simon de Lusignan.

Simon had begun to sweat, and his complexion was now the color of chalk. Observing his obvious distress, John said dispassionately, "How did you ever get as far as Paris?"

"It was not so bad at first. But the day ere I reached the abbey at St Germain, the wound began to bleed again..."

"See that he gets medical care," John said to the room at large, brushing aside Simon's gratitude with a stark, simple truth: "It is in my interest to keep you alive... for now."

John halted at the door, glancing back over his shoulder. "What is the Breton's real name?"

If it was a test, Simon passed, saying without hesitation, "Saer de St Brieuc."

"So he is a Breton, after all." John's gaze lingered for a moment upon the master spy's rash young cousin. "I should have known," he said, "that the whoreson would turn out to be a de Lusignan."

Simon was long accustomed to hearing defamatory remarks about his more notorious kinsmen. He objected only halfheartedly, reminding John that the Breton was kin on his mother's side of the family. But John had already gone.

Simon's shoulders slumped with the easing of tension. Looking around at the others, he confided, "Well, that was not so bad. In truth, I expected far worse."

Justin had been surprised, too, by John's lack of rage. He'd seemed aloof and somewhat distracted, as if part of his mind were mulling over matters far removed from this Paris solar and Simon de Lusignan. As he rose to follow Durand and Simon from the chamber, Claudine caught his sleeve.

"That wretch was luckier than he deserves," she said quietly. "John got news this noon that chased Simon and even the Breton from the forefront of his cares."

Justin stopped. "What news?"

"Richard," she said. "He learned that Richard has reached Antwerp and is making ready to sail for England."

CHAPTER XXII

March 1194
Paris, France

Morgan was drowning. His lungs were laboring, and he could not shake off the ghostly fingers clutching at him from the depths, dragging him down. He kept fighting, though, lunging toward the light, and at last he broke the surface, gulping in air sweeter than wine.

"You are safe now," a female voice murmured soothingly. "It was a bad dream, no more than that."

The chamber was lit by oil lamps, but they seemed to burn with unnatural brightness to Morgan, and he did his best to filter the glare through his lashes. The woman smiling at him was very pretty, but not familiar, not at first. She brought a cup to his lips, held it steady as he drank, and his memory unclouded, identifying her as Ivetta, Lady Emma's borrowed maid.

"About time you decided to rejoin the living." This was a male voice, belonging to a youth in a nearby bed. Propped up by pillows, he was smiling at Morgan affably. "I've been lonely with no one to talk to."

"No one to talk to, indeed," Ivetta said tartly. "My lady

says no work is getting done because half the women in the household keep coming in to see if you are in need of drink or food or comfort, Master Simon."

"But you're the one I yearn to see, Mistress Ivetta," Simon insisted, and she tossed her head, partially placated, and said she'd let the others know that Morgan was awake.

As she departed, Morgan struggled to sit upright, alarmed that he felt so weak. He still was not sure where he was, although he guessed it was the Lady Petronilla's residence. But he had no idea who his cheerful chambermate was, nor did he know why he was bedridden. "What happened to me?" he asked, and even his voice sounded odd to his ears, hoarse and raspy.

"You do not remember? I can only tell you what I've heard from Ivetta and the others; Lord love them, but women do like to gossip! They say you're the hero of the hour, that you saved John from a hired killer's dagger. I'd think a skirmish in a cemetery would not be easy to forget!"

Morgan's memories were still blurred and too slippery to handle. "I do remember a graveyard," he said uncertainly. "At least I think I do." In truth, though, the memory that was most vivid, disturbingly so, was his dream of drowning. His head was aching and he lay back against his pillow. "Do I know you?"

"Well, we've never been introduced, but you know of me, for certes. I am Simon de Lusignan." Simon watched mischievously as Morgan processed that information, as his face registered first puzzlement and then realization and then horror. "Ah," he said complacently, "I see your memory has come back."

MORGAN'S BED WAS SURROUNDED BY WELL-WISHERS, beaming

at him with such heartfelt pleasure in his recovery that he was both touched and taken aback. "I was not going to die," he protested, "not with money owed me from that last game of raffle."

That evoked laughter, and Crispin blushed, mumbling that he'd settle up as soon as he got paid. A tray of hot soup had been placed on the table by the bed, and Claudine coaxed Morgan into swallowing a few spoonfuls, ignoring Simon's plaintive plea that he was hungry, too. Morgan still did not understand why he was sharing a bedchamber with the chief suspect in the Lady Arzhela's murder. He'd been told that Simon was on their side now, but there was so much to absorb that not all of it had sunk in yet.

Justin was teasing him about his graveyard gallantry, wanting to know why he hadn't single-handedly broken them out of that Fougères dungeon, when the door opened and John strode in. "I am glad," he said, "to have the chance to thank you at long last."

"There is no need for thanks, my lord." Morgan returned John's smile, but he did not seem comfortable and Justin noticed, for he usually gave the impression of being utterly at home in his own skin.

"Yes," John said, "there is. Consider it a matter of courtesy if nothing else, but my lord father always said it was just good manners to thank a man for saving one's life. I admit I am curious, though, about your presence in the cemetery. What made you follow me?"

That was the question they all wanted to ask and the room fell silent as they waited for Morgan's reply. His lashes swept down, veiling those smoky grey eyes. "The truth is..." He seemed to sigh, and then said softly, "I do not know, my lord. That night is a muddle for me, my memories drifting in and

293

out. I remember the cemetery. I do not remember the fight or being hurt and... and I do not remember why I was there. I... I suppose I feared you were walking into a trap, but why..." He shrugged helplessly.

John's eyes narrowed. "Well, you might remember more later. Now you'd best get some rest." He smiled, but as he moved toward the door, his eyes caught Justin's. Leaving Morgan to be coddled by the women, Justin followed the queen's son from the chamber. As he expected, John was awaiting him in the stairwell.

"I cannot interrogate a man on his sickbed, but I do not believe a word of that blather about his failing memory."

Neither did Justin, but loyalty to Morgan kept him quiet. John did not even notice. "I wish I could say his motive for coming to my aid did not matter. But it does, de Quincy, as we both well know. Find out what he is hiding."

Justin opened his mouth to object, but John was already turning away.

JUSTIN HAD RIDDEN OUT TO THE Pré aux Clercs, the open field west of the city walls where Parisians gathered to play games of camp-ball and bandy-ball, to watch tourneys and impromptu horse races. On this sun-blest afternoon, it was crowded with truant students, for Paris was becoming celebrated for its schools at Notre-Dame and Sainte-Geneviève and St-Victor, and the mild weather had lured large numbers from their classes. Justin was playing truant, too. He had no intention of spying on Morgan for John, and he needed time to himself, time to decide what he should do next.

Now that King Richard and the queen were back in England, he felt he had a duty to return, too. But he was reluctant to leave until he was sure Morgan was truly on the mend. And his desire to catch the Breton still burned with a white-hot flame. He'd failed to save Arzhela. He did not want to fail her again. At the least, she deserved justice.

The noisy crowd at Pré aux Clercs put him in mind of London's Smithfield, where he'd entrapped Gilbert the Fleming, and he could not help studying the faces of the men jostling around him, hunting for the Breton. It was an exercise in futility, of course. They'd had no luck in their search of the city, even though John had been lavish with his offers of bribes and bounties. Arzhela's killer seemed to have disappeared from the face of the earth.

After watching a rousing game of camp-ball, Justin reluctantly remounted and headed his horse back into the city, stopping to buy a whipping top for Yann from a street vendor. When he rode into the courtyard of the Lady Petronilla's residence, he found it crowded with men and horses. Some had dismounted and were lounging on the steps and mounting blocks; the rest were still in the saddle, passing around wineskins. Justin did not like the looks of them, and he pushed past them into the house with a sense of foreboding.

The great hall was unnaturally still. People were standing around awkwardly, most of them watching Durand, who was stalking back and forth, scattering floor rushes with every angry stride. Garnier was closest to the door, and at the sight of Justin, he edged over.

"What is amiss?"

"Lupescar. He is up in the solar with Lord John."

Justin immediately understood why there were no women in the hall, not even scullery maids. "Did he quarrel with Durand?" he asked quietly, and the young knight nodded.

"There is bad blood between them, and I thought it was about to flow in earnest. I'm glad you're here to help me keep the peace. We would ill repay Lady Petronilla's hospitality by turning her hall into a battlefield."

By now Justin was accustomed to being dragged into other people's problems. "I'll see if I can get Durand out of here," he agreed, and crossed the hall. "Garnier says Lupescar is abovestairs. Was John expecting him?"

"How would I know?" Durand said curtly, and then, "No, I think not. He said nothing to me about—" He stopped abruptly, and then Justin heard it too, the jangle of spurs in the stairwell.

When Lupescar emerged, Justin moved swiftly to intercept him, hoping to deflect another confrontation with Durand. Lupescar paused, recognition flickering across his face. "Ah, the lost lamb, is it not?"

"The lamb and the wolf. That sounds like an ancient Roman fable. I am surprised to see you back in Paris. I'd have thought life would be more to your liking out in the Norman-Breton borderlands."

"Less law, you mean?" Lupescar sounded faintly amused. "You may tell your friend Durand that he has got a reprieve, for we'll not be working together, after all. Lord John has no need of me now."

"You do not sound very disappointed by that."

"I care not who hires me as long as his coin is good. I'll not be lacking for work."

"No, I do not suppose you will," Justin admitted grudgingly. Glancing over, he saw Garnier at Durand's side, talking with considerable animation, a restraining hand on the other knight's arm. Justin took several steps toward the door, attempting to shepherd Lupescar in that direction, a maneuver that did not escape the Wolf's notice.

"I am not going to mend Durand's bad manners, tempting

as that may be. I am not one for burning bridges if it can be avoided, and your lord is likely to need my services again," Lupescar said, still sounding amused.

Justin found his amusement more chilling than another man's enmity. He'd met few who took genuine pleasure in killing, but he did not doubt that Lupescar was one of them. By now they'd almost reached the door, and he looked over his shoulder, reassured to see Garnier still claiming Durand's attention. "I suppose you'll be leaving Paris, then," he said to Lupescar. "Godspeed."

Lupescar paused in the doorway, giving him a supercilious smile. "You truly do not see, do you? France is going to be for men like me what the Holy Land is for pilgrims. War is coming, as inevitable as spring and as full of promise."

"What do you mean?"

"Have you not heard that the English king has been set free? The highborn are not noted for paying their debts, but Richard always pays his blood debts, always. And by his reckoning, he owes the king of the French a blood debt. It may be true that vengeance is a dish best eaten cold, but Richard has never been one for waiting. I'll wager that he will soon descend upon France like the Wrath of God Almighty."

He sounded so pleased by that prospect that Justin's fingers twitched with the urge to make the sign of the Cross, an instinctive impulse to ward off evil. Watching as Lupescar sauntered down the steps toward his waiting men, Justin found himself thinking that this godless man could have ridden with the Horsemen of the Apocalypse. " 'And I saw and behold, a pale horse, and his name that sat on him was Death,' " he murmured, and this time he did sketch a Cross in the mild March air.

***

AFTER SUPPER THAT NIGHT, JUSTIN WAS playing a game of chess with Claudine. He usually sought to keep his distance, but she had asked him in front of Durand and Petronilla to play and he'd not wanted to shame her by a public refusal. So far it had not been as awkward as he'd feared. She soon had him laughing with her stories of Petronilla's vexation over her unwanted houseguest, Simon de Lusignan. According to Petronilla, he was making a nuisance of himself from dawn to dusk, flirting with the bedazzled serving maids who were fluttering around him like bees around the hive, upsetting her cook by demanding his favorite foods and then complaining that they weren't done to his liking, luring the men-at-arms into his chamber to throw dice, where they made enough noise to raise the dead.

Justin was sure she was exaggerating Simon's sins, although he had seen Simon's effect upon the female servants. He supposed Simon was easy enough on the eye, but he no more understood their partiality for Simon than he had Arzhela's. "I grant you that Simon is a pretty polecat," he said, "but he's a polecat all the same. Why are women so drawn to the darkness?" As soon as the words had left his mouth, he regretted them, for his question could easily have applied to Claudine and John.

She did not seem to take it that way, though, smiling and shrugging. "I could as easily ask you why men are so taken with simpering, biddable poppets."

"I hope you are not including me in that lot," he protested, laughing, thinking that he'd never known a biddable poppet in his entire life. Claudine's reply took him by surprise.

"Actually, I was thinking of the queen and her husband."

It never occurred to Justin that Claudine might be referring to Richard and his neglected consort, Berengaria. Whenever anyone spoke of "the queen," it was Eleanor of Aquitaine they had in mind. In the same way, he assumed that the husband in question was the late king of the English, Henry, and not Eleanor's first husband, the French king Louis, for Henry had been a living legend, a fit mate for the most beautiful heiress in Christendom, the only woman to ever wear the crowns of both England and France.

"What are they, the exception that proves the rule?" he joked. "Clearly all men do not fancy docile, gentle females, for none would ever call the queen 'biddable,' now, would they?"

"Jesu forfend!" she said, just as lightly, and he realized how long it had been since they'd been able to talk without constraints. "But you see, Justin, the old king did want a woman like that. Why else would he have turned from the queen to a meek little mouse like Rosamund Clifford?"

He found that to be an interesting question, and gave it some serious thought. "I am just guessing, but mayhap Rosamund was, well, restful. At times, marriage to Queen Eleanor must have been like riding the whirlwind."

She considered that. "I daresay she could have said the same of King Henry. What of you, Justin? Do you want a Rosamund Clifford or an Eleanor of Aquitaine?"

"Must I choose one or the other? I've never been drawn to extremes, am most comfortable riding in the middle of the road. What of you, Claudine? If you could spin the wheel of fortune, what would you ask for?"

"I no longer know," she admitted. "I was once so sure that I'd not want to marry again. That surprises you, does it?"

"Yes, I suppose it does. From what you'd told me, I thought your husband had treated you well."

"He did. He was kind and indulgent, in an almost paternal sort of way. I was young enough to have been his daughter, mayhap even his granddaughter, after all. I was contented enough as his wife. But widowhood offered me something more precious than contentment—freedom. For the first time in my life, I could do as I pleased. That was a heady draught, Justin, a brew few women get to drink."

"Not that many men get to taste it, either, lass." The chess game forgotten, he regarded her pensively, seeing neither John's spy nor the tempting siren who'd wrought such havoc in his life. "But you are no longer sure, you said, that you'd not want to wed again. What changed your mind?"

She glanced around, making sure none were within earshot. "Aline," she said softly. "I'd never conceived, believed I was barren. Now I know better. So it may be that one day I'll want more children. Not yet, though!" She smiled ruefully. "Not until my memories of the birthing chamber have got much dimmer."

Justin's memories of Aline's birth were traumatic, too, even from the other side of the birthing chamber door. "We've never talked like this, have we? You think we can be friends, Claudine, after being lovers?"

"Why not?" Her dimples flashed as she added impishly, "In the best of all worlds, we could be both. I had plenty of time during my pregnancy to learn which herbal potions are most effective in preventing conception!"

He shared her laughter, but he was wary of succumbing to her charms, for there was no potion for the restoration of trust. "I do not think I am ready to get my heart broken again, thank you," he said, mingling honesty with humor.

She pretended to pout. "Coward. Who knew the queen's man was so easily affrighted?" An odd expression crossed her face then, as she heard her own words. " 'The queen's man,' " she repeated slowly. "Jesu, could it be?"

"What is it, Claudine?" he asked, both puzzled and curious, and she leaned toward him, her dark eyes sparkling with excitement.

"Justin, I had the most outlandish idea! It makes perfect sense, though. I think I know why the Breton killed Arzhela."

JOHN HAD RETIRED EARLY TO BED, though not to sleep. He was dozing in the afterglow of his lovemaking with Ursula when there was a commotion in his bedchamber. Recognizing the voices of Justin, Durand, and his squire, he jerked the bed hangings aside.

"I am sorry, my lord," the squire cried. "I told them you were abed, but they paid me no heed!"

John's gaze flicked from Durand to Justin. He was irked by the intrusion, but he remembered that the last time Durand had burst into his bedchamber uninvited he'd been bearing an urgent warning from the French king. "What is it? What could not wait till the morrow?"

"We think we know why the Breton murdered the Lady Arzhela and tried to have you slain."

John was wide awake now and, knowing that he'd not be able to get back to sleep, decided he might as well be up and about. "Meet me in the solar," he directed the men, and then instructed his squire to fetch his clothes. Ursula was sleeping peacefully, and he felt a dart of envy, for his nights were never as restful as hers. Even as a boy, sleep had not come easily, a fickle bitch that teased and tantalized and hovered just out of reach.

By the time John entered the solar, a fire had been lit in the hearth and wine flagons set out. Dropping down into a high-backed chair, he regarded them with open skepticism. "Well? Enlighten me."

"You've been telling us all along that the Breton would not have silenced Arzhela out of fear of your retribution. I think you were right, my lord. The Breton was acting out of fear, but not of you. The man he feared was his master, the French king."

John blinked. He opened his mouth to dismiss Justin's claim as ludicrous, only to realize it wasn't. "Go on," he said tensely. "Tell me more."

"It was Claudine's idea. She called me 'the queen's man' and a spark flared in the back of her brain. What if the Breton was 'the king's man'? It would explain everything!"

John was already beginning to see flaws in that theory. "I grant you that the Breton could well be working for Philippe. But you are forgetting the pact Philippe and I made in January. In return for French support, I agreed to cede much of Normandy. That accord gave him a vested interest in my kingship. Philippe wants to see me on the English throne as much as I do. He'd not have forged that letter."

"I agree, my lord. The forgery was not Philippe's doing. It was the Breton's, and set in motion before your deal with the French king. Simon de Lusignan said as much, that the Breton came to him with the scheme months ago. When the Breton cast out the bait for Duchess Constance, you and Philippe were at odds, blaming each other for King Richard's impending release. Then you mended your rift and made that pact. But it was too late for the Breton to stop what he'd started. They already had the letter."

John's eyes cut from Justin to Durand. "You agree with this?"

"I do, my lord. The Breton could only hope that his part would never come to light. But then Cousin Simon blabbed to his bedmate, and the Breton found out about it. He seems to have panicked, which is interesting in and of itself, showing us how much he thought was at stake. He killed Arzhela to keep her quiet, fearing that she'd confide in you. And that you, in your rage, would confide in your ally, the French king."

"But it started to go wrong for him," Justin said, "for mayhap the first time ever. Suddenly he had a lunatic on his hands, intent upon avenging the Lady Arzhela. When he failed to kill Simon, he was driven to truly desperate straits. If he could not find Simon to silence him, he could seek to make sure that you never heard Simon's confession."

John was quiet, staring into the leaping hearth flames, which had taken on the shade of molten gold. "That would explain something else," he said at last. "If he is no longer offering his services to the highest bidder, has pledged himself as the French king's man, then his insistence upon concealing his identity from the Bretons makes sense."

They hadn't thought of that. "Would he agree to such an exclusive arrangement, my lord?" Justin asked, and John smiled mirthlessly.

"Philippe would have demanded no less. I do not find it easy to give my trust, but compared to Philippe, I am as simple and naïve as any country virgin. He would have expected the Breton to serve his interests and his alone."

"So, you agree with us, then?"

John nodded. "There has always been a piece missing from this puzzle. I never expected, though, that Claudine would be the one to find it!"

Rising, John began to pace the solar, moving from darkness to light and back to darkness again. They watched him in silence for a time, and then Justin asked quietly, "What would you have us do, my lord?"

John turned to face them. "It is time," he said, "to pay a visit to my dear friend, the French king."

CHAPTER XXIII

March 1194
Paris, France

The royal gardens of the French king jutted out into the River Seine like the prow of a ship. They would be magnificent in high summer, with raised flower beds of peonies, poppies, and Madonna lilies, trellised bowers of roses and honeysuckle, and well-pruned fruit trees. Now it was only mid-March. The day was mild, though, and it had seemed like a good place to await John's return.

Justin and Durand were seated on the stone wall overlooking the river, Emma and Claudine on a nearby turf bench. A few other people sauntered along the pebbled paths; several young women were gathered in a bower, listening to one of them read from a leather-bound book; a man in cleric's garb was playing ball with a spaniel. None of them were familiar to Justin, who'd never been to the French court before. He was disappointed that he'd not get to see the French king, for he was developing a healthy curiosity about Philippe.

He knew Philippe's age—twenty-eight—and his pedigree—only son of Queen Eleanor's first husband, Louis Capet. He knew Philippe had assumed power in his teens, had already lost one wife in childbirth, and had wed a Danish princess that past summer. And he knew Philippe had clashed bitterly with Richard in the Holy Land, returning to France as an avowed enemy of the Lionheart. But the man himself remained a mystery.

After learning that Claudine and Durand had met the French king, he'd begun fishing for insights into Philippe's character. Durand had not been overly impressed by Philippe, but Justin doubted that he'd have been impressed if the holy martyr St Thomas had risen up from his tomb at Canterbury. "Shrewd, pious, implacable, and fretful," was his concise verdict.

Claudine's observations were more detailed. "He does not ever curse," she reported, with the amazement of one coming from the profane court of the Plantagenets. "He has a liking for wine. He is not fond of horses and disapproves of tournaments. He is quick to anger, not as quick to forgive. He does not have John's perverse sense of humor, which is probably for the best! For certes, he does not possess Richard's fearlessness, but then, few men do. I would say he likes women. I agree with Durand, though; he is not sentimental. If I had to choose one word to describe him, it would be 'capable.'"

"I heard," Emma put in, "that he came back from the crusade a changed man. He was very ill whilst there, nigh unto death, and it left its mark. From what I've been told, he is more suspicious now, and his nerves are more ragged around the edges."

"That is true enough," Durand confirmed. "He goes nowhere without bodyguards. Wherever he was meeting with the Breton, you may be sure it was not at night in the cemetery of the Holy Innocents! John says he became convinced on crusade that Richard was plotting against his life. When his ally Conrad of Montferrat was slain by Assassins sent by the Old Man of the Mountain, Philippe suspected that Richard was behind it. Supposedly he was warned that Richard had connived with the Old Man, who'd dispatched four Assassins to kill him, too."

Justin was shocked to hear of such vicious infighting among the crusaders. He'd imagined that men would put aside their rivalries in their joint quest to free Jerusalem from the infidels. Durand's story made it sound as if they'd taken all their enmities and grudges with them to the Holy Land. "Who is the Old Man of the Mountain?"

"The leader of a Shi'ite sect who believe that murder is a legitimate tactic of war." Durand's mouth curved in a cynical smile. "In other words, they openly preach what other rulers merely practice."

Now it was Claudine's turn to be shocked. "No true Christian king would resort to murder, Durand!"

"I take it that means you do not believe Richard had a hand in Conrad's killing?" Durand asked sarcastically.

Claudine and Justin answered as one, she crying, "Of course not!" and he demanding, "Surely you are not saying he did, Durand?"

"No—Richard is not one for planning that far ahead."

Claudine seemed genuinely offended. "Richard is a man of extraordinary courage!"

"Courage is like charity," Emma said dryly. "It covers a multitude of sins. When the Emperor of Cyprus surrendered to Richard on condition he not be put in irons, Richard agreed and then had shackles made of silver."

Justin did not like the tone of this conversation any more than Claudine did. Richard was a celebrated crusader, whose deeds in the Holy Land had become the stuff of legend. He'd taken it as a matter of faith that Richard was a more honorable man than John, worthy of the sacrifices the English people had made to gain his freedom. He did not want to doubt his king, and he hastily changed the subject, calling their attention to the young woman just entering the garden, fair of face and clothed in costly silks.

"Is that the French queen?"

To his surprise, they all laughed. "What?" he asked, perplexed. "I do not see the humor in my question."

"You truly do not know?" Claudine marveled. "So great was the scandal that half of Christendom was talking of nothing else—ah, but you were in Wales last summer! That explains why you did not hear."

"Hear what?"

"The day after their wedding, Philippe disavowed Ingeborg and sent her off to a monastery, where she has been held ever since. Less than three months later, Philippe convened a council at Compiègne, where French bishops and lords dutifully declared the marriage was invalid because Ingeborg was related to Philippe's first wife within the prohibited fourth degree."

Justin was astonished. "If the marriage was dissolved, why is Ingeborg still being kept at the monastery? Why has she not been allowed to go back to Denmark?"

"Philippe would like nothing better than to rid himself of her," Durand said, grinning. "But she claims their marriage is valid in the eyes of God and man, and is appealing to the Pope. What I find truly odd about the whole matter is that men say she is a beauty: eighteen years of age, tall and golden-haired. Now if she'd been a hag, I could better understand his skittishness!"

"It is very sad for her," Claudine insisted, frowning at

Durand. "She is a captive in a foreign country, surrounded by people who speak no Danish whilst she speaks no French. She has been badly treated, indeed. But for the life of me, I do not understand why she is being so stubborn about clinging to this hollow shell of a marriage."

"Because," Emma said coolly, "this 'hollow shell of a marriage' has made her Queen of France."

Justin was too well-mannered to remind her that she did not value her own crown very highly, and Claudine shared Emma's view that life in a remote, alien land like Wales was a form of penance, but Durand relished rushing in where angels feared to tread. Before he could pounce, however, Garnier came into view, obviously searching for them. Justin signaled to catch his eye and he veered in their direction. "Lord John is ready to depart," he announced.

They were leaving the gardens when they encountered John himself, standing on the steps. At the sight of them, he waved his attendants aside and moved to meet them.

"Where the Devil have you been?" Not waiting for explanations, he continued on past them into the gardens. They looked at one another, shrugged, and followed after him. He'd stopped by the stone wall, was gazing out upon the river, silvered by sunlight. He did not turn as they approached, dropping pebbles down into the water.

"Well?" Durand blurted out, when they could stand the suspense no longer. "Did he admit the Breton is in his service?"

"No, but he did not deny it, either, and for Philippe, that qualifies as a confession. He acknowledged he has used the Breton in the past, and expressed dismay when I told him of the man's crimes."

"Is he willing to help us?" Justin asked, puzzled by John's demeanor; it was obvious something was troubling him.

John nodded, flinging a pebble out into the swirling current. "We've come up with a plan to lure him out into the open. It seems the Breton has made a practice of finding informers all over Paris. Philippe says he has sources at the provost's, at the hospitals, the gaols, even the Templars. It must have vexed him sorely when I moved out of the Temple into Petronilla's dwelling."

There was a faint splash as another stone broke the surface. "The provost is going to put the word out that an unknown man sought to enter the palace grounds. When he was stopped by the guards, he insisted he had to see 'the king or the Count of Mortain,' babbling wildly about plots and murder in an abbey. He was badly wounded, though, and died ere he could be questioned. It ought not to take long for word to reach the Breton. He is going to assume—to hope—it was Simon, but he'll need to be sure. I'm wagering that he will come out of hiding to identify the body. And when he does, we'll be waiting."

They exchanged glances, encouraged, for the plan sounded promising. Eager to set it into motion, they waited impatiently as John continued to watch the ripples stirred up by his pebbles. It was Claudine who ended the impasse, saying softly and with more sympathy than Justin liked, "My lord John? What is amiss? Are you not pleased that this will soon be resolved?"

"Delighted beyond measure." John threw away the last of the stones, just missing a low-flying bird. "Philippe told me," he said, "that Richard was welcomed into London by huge, enthusiastic crowds, who were rejoicing as if it were the Second Coming of the Lord Christ."

THE SKY WAS A MISTY PEARL color, the sun cloaked in morning

haze. Justin was standing on the porch of the parish church of the Holy Innocents, gazing out across the cemetery. It was early, but the gravediggers had already been busy; a body had been fished from the river the day before, and it was being buried in the common grave reserved for the poor and the unknown. Justin had seen few sights as sorrowful as this hasty, impromptu burial. The body had been sewn into a shroud and lowered into the grave, and the gravediggers were shoveling dirt over the remains, while trying to keep upwind, for the corpse was waterlogged and badly decomposed. Head bowed, a priest was uttering a prayer for the soul of this nameless, luckless stranger, unmourned but by God.

At the sound of a step behind him, Justin turned to see a Benedictine monk. Stifling a grin, he shook his head. "I never thought to see you in monk's garb, Durand, no more than I'd look for a whore in a nunnery."

"You do not exactly look like a lamb of God yourself, de Quincy. Let's face it, neither of us make good monks. But it will be dark enough to fool the Breton, assuming all goes as planned."

"You think it will not?"

"The Breton has the Devil's own luck. And it is not heartening to have to rely upon that lunatic de Lusignan. That scatter-brain of his seems able to entertain only two thoughts at a time—getting laid and getting vengeance."

Justin laughed and followed Durand back into the church. The parish priest scowled at them as they passed, outraged at their intrusion into God's House but unable to disobey a royal command. Crossing the nave, they entered the funerary chapel, where the dead were made ready for burial. Rush-lights in wall sconces illuminated two stone slabs. Crispin was stretched out on one, clad in a monk's habit, hands folded across his chest, snoring softly. The other "corpse" was not so content; Simon de Lusignan was squirming around on his bier, unable to get comfortable. "I do not see why I cannot have a pillow."

The third player in the drama looked glad to see them. "About time," Garnier grumbled. "If I have to listen to any more of his complaints, I'm going to fetch him that pillow and stuff it in his mouth."

Garnier made a surprisingly convincing priest, although he'd sworn that without a sword he felt as naked as a plucked chicken. Justin and Durand had the advantage of him there, for they could hide their weapons under their monastic robes.

"Are you absolutely sure, Sir Garnier, that the Breton has never laid eyes upon you?"

"I swear on my mother's soul," Garnier said patiently. "You and Durand are the only two he knows by sight."

"And the corpse, of course," Durand said, glancing over at Simon. "So help me, de Lusignan, if you sneeze or cough or fart and spoil this, I'll have your guts for dinner."

"I prefer a good beef stew myself," Simon said flippantly, and all three of the men glared at him. "You need not worry," he insisted. "I know my part. I even agreed to have my face powdered and painted so I'd look more like a dead body!"

"If I'd had my way," Durand warned, "there'd have been no need for pretense," and after that, Simon settled down, lapsing into silence as their vigil began.

THEY'D NOT EXPECTED SO MANY PEOPLE to turn out to view Simon's corpse. Several were seeking missing family or friends. But most were the curious, coming to gawk at the man who'd died in the palace grounds under such mysterious circumstances. This complicated matters for them and made it more difficult for Simon to be a convincing corpse. Finally, Garnier began to demand visitors make an offering to the church before looking at the body. That thinned the crowd out.

By mid-afternoon, the men's hopes had begun to flag. They stiffened, though, at the sudden sound of Garnier's voice in the nave, speaking loudly for their benefit, alerting them that the newcomer might be the man they were seeking. He was explaining that there were two Norman monks in the chapel, praying over the body of a comrade who'd fallen sick soon after their arrival in Paris. "So sad that he'll not be buried with his brethren," he said, keeping up a distracting flow of chatter as he ushered the man into the chapel.

Justin and Durand made sure their cowls hid their faces. Crispin's lashes fluttered, and then he shut his eyes again; he was taking his role seriously. Simon seemed to be lying very still, too.

"Here is the body," Garnier announced, adding a pious, "May God have mercy upon his soul."

The man stepped into the shadows of the chapel. He no longer wore a cleric's rochet, but Justin recognized him at once. Canon Robert. The Breton. Arzhela's killer.

The Breton stopped before Simon's bier, stood staring down at the body. His face showed none of the satisfaction and relief he must have been feeling. "Alas," he said, feigning disappointment, "this is not my friend. But I will pay for his funeral."

"Indeed? God will bless you for that," Garnier assured him, and he shrugged, saying modestly that it was the duty of all Christians to see to the burial of the less fortunate. Justin glanced toward Durand, both savoring the irony of the Breton's offer. It was a chilling glimpse of the warped way the Breton viewed the world; he could murder a cousin without

312

qualms but balked at a pauper's burial for him. Meeting Durand's eyes, Justin nodded and they began to move toward the door, still maintaining a monk's pose, a monk's sedate pace until they were within range.

It was then that Simon struck. Quick as a snake, he came off the bier, a concealed dagger suddenly in his hand, lunging at the Breton with murderous intent. Only the Breton's remarkable reflexes saved his life. He flung up his arm and the blade meant for his throat slashed from wrist to elbow. He reeled backward, blood spurting like a fountain. Simon's momentum carried him onward, and he crashed into Garnier, who was coming to his aid. Justin and Durand were already in motion, but they were momentarily halted by the entangled bodies on the floor, giving the Breton a chance to dart out the door, slamming it behind him.

Simon was gasping for breath, clutching his injured ribs, Garnier struggling to his feet. Justin reached the door first, with Durand but a step behind him. The nave of the church was empty, blood splattered on the floor and on the open door leading out to the porch. Almost at once they discovered a monk's habit was not meant for pursuit, and they lost precious time ripping the garments off. "If he gets away," Durand panted, "I swear I'll skin Simon alive with a dull knife!" Justin shared the sentiment, but he was saving his breath for the chase. Bolting out into the garth, he came upon an amazing scene.

Their men had emerged from their hiding places and were running after the Breton. Bystanders were gaping, a funeral interrupted by the uproar, a woman screaming unintelligibly. The Breton had left a trail of blood in his wake, but desperation had given wings to his heels and he'd outdistanced his pursuers. He'd done the unexpected, not heading for the closest exit, the one opening out onto rue Saint-Denis, once again proving he did have Lucifer's luck, for they'd locked that gate as a precaution. He risked a glance over his shoulder, sprinting toward the open gateway, the same one his hired killers had barred to entrap John within the cemetery.

But it was then that a band of horsemen galloped through the gates, onto the open field. To avoid being run down, the Breton dodged, first one way and then another, but he was like a fox trying to evade a pack of hounds; wherever he turned, he found his way blocked by a horse and rider. He was being herded away from the gate, back into the middle of the cemetery, and suddenly the ground gave way under his feet and he went tumbling down into one of the open grave pits meant for Christ's poor.

AN UNREPENTANT SIMON HAD BEEN SENT back to Petronilla's town house, newly in need of a doctor's care. Durand had been in favor of shoving him into the open grave with the Breton, but John overruled him, saying he'd deal with Simon later. As soon as he saw John, the Breton must have known he was doomed. He made a game try, though, claiming that he'd never sent John a message to meet him in the cemetery. He passionately denied that he'd slain Arzhela, insisting that Simon was the killer, and the one responsible for the attack upon John, too. Simon had murdered Arzhela in a lover's quarrel, and then sought to blame him for the crime. Simon had almost killed him at Fougères Castle. Why had he tried again in the funerary chapel? Because a dead man could offer no defense, could not prove his innocence. Justin found it disquieting that the Breton sounded so convincing.

It was not long before the French king rode into the cemetery. His arrival created chaos, for by now a large crowd of spectators had gathered and they surged forward in excitement, had to be pushed back by the royal bodyguards. Sliding from the saddle, Philippe strode over to John. "Well?" he demanded. "Where is he?"

John pointed toward the open grave. Philippe looked startled, then walked over to see for himself. The Breton had wrapped his mantle around his bleeding arm, was leaning against the loose earthen bank as if he needed support. At the sight of the French king, his already ashen face went even paler. "My lord king..."

For what must have seemed like infinity to the Breton, John and Philippe stood there in silence, staring down at him. Justin had edged closer to get a look at the French king, and he was struck by the contrast between the two men. Philippe was ruddy whereas John was dark, and more plainly dressed than the Plantagenet, who did not let betrayal and rebellion interfere with his pursuit of the newest fashions. He was taller than John, and although they were only about fifteen months apart in age, the French king looked considerably older for he'd lost his hair and nails during his near-fatal illness in the Holy Land; his nails had grown back, but his hair had not. The one trait the two men had in common was that they both made bad enemies, as the Breton soon would be able to attest, assuming he lived long enough to make a dying declaration.

The Breton was attempting to persuade Philippe of his innocence, just as he'd tried with John. Those listening had to give him credit for glibness; he had a tongue that could charm birds out of the trees and virgins out of their maidenheads. But his eloquence was wasted upon the only two members of the audience who mattered. When he at last ran out of breath—or hope—the French king turned to his provost.

"Arrest this man."

"I WANTED THE PLEASURE OF KILLING the whoreson myself!" Simon glowered defiantly at his interrogators. Only the fact that he was in bed, mother-naked and having his wounds re-bandaged, kept Durand and Justin from laying rough hands upon him. Simon did not seem to realize how narrow his margin of safety was, for he continued to insist that he'd been in the right. "If not for these sore ribs of mine, I'd have done it, too, skewered him like a Martinmas shoat!"

"You have no notion, do you, of how lucky you were?" Justin shook his head in disgust. "Lord John and the French king wanted the man taken alive. You think they'd have thanked you for sending him to Hell?"

That gave Simon pause—briefly. "I did not think about that," he admitted. "When I saw him, all I could think about was Arzhela, bleeding to death on that chapel floor."

"Good try, lad," Durand jeered. "But if it was not planned, why did you have that dagger?"

Simon considered the question. "For protection, of course. Better than you, I knew how dangerous the Breton was."

Morgan, an interested observer, could not help laughing. "Give it up, mates," he advised Justin and Durand. "The lad is always going to have an answer for you, no matter what you ask him."

"It is John he has to answer to," Durand said, sounding grimly gratified by the prospect. "I only hope he lets me watch!"

ON THE FOLLOWING DAY, PARISIANS AWAKENED to a chilly downpour. The skies were a drab wintry grey, a damp wind was gusting off the river, and spring seemed to have absconded under cover of darkness. John did not let the foul weather interrupt his plans, riding off to Philippe's palace to discuss the Breton's fate. But most of those in Petronilla's household chose to stay indoors, preferring boredom to getting soaked.

John did not return in time for dinner, and Justin noticed that the noonday meal was less lavish than in the past. For the first time, it occurred to him that entertaining a prince must be costing Petronilla a goodly sum of money. He hoped that she'd remember this lesson the next time she was tempted to flirt with a high-living lord like John. Fortunately for Petronilla, her cousin had provided her with a plausible reason for putting an end to her expensive hospitality. Claudine still wanted to travel into Poitou to visit her father and brothers, and Petronilla had jumped at the chance to accompany her. Emma, too, had accepted Claudine's invitation, although in her case, Justin suspected she was trying to keep as many miles as possible between herself and Queen Eleanor. Justin had agreed to speak on her behalf, feeling that he owed her after her intercession at Fougères Castle, but he did not know if the queen would heed him, and neither did Emma.

It was still raining several hours later, and the infamous black mud of Paris was turning the city into a quagmire; only those city streets that were paved were passable. When John entered the great hall, his boots were caked, his mantle so splattered that its original color was not easily determined. He shrugged out of it, let it puddle to the floor at his feet, and crossed to the hearth to warm himself. Only then did he beckon to Justin and Durand. "Come with me," he said, and headed toward the stairwell.

They obeyed, followed a few moments later by Emma and Claudine, expecting to be led to the solar. To their surprise, John continued to lead them on up the stairs until they'd reached the room up under the eaves of the roof where Morgan and Simon were lodged. They were both up and dressed, seated cross-legged on one of the beds as they played a game of draughts. Startled by the intrusion, they jumped to their feet, Morgan looking interested, Simon nervous, for he'd not yet had a reckoning with John.

It was obvious to them all that John had something of significance to report, and they fidgeted as they waited until he chose to share what he'd learned. The chamber was cramped, dimly lit, and had a musty, sickbed odor. John sat on Simon's bed, and then lounged back, his muddy boots doing some damage to the blanket. Justin was beginning to resent this strange game of cat and mouse John was playing with them, but he had decided he'd not be the one to blink first. Durand seemed to have made the same resolution, for he was leaning against the door, feigning indifference. But Emma had no patience for the games of men, and she said sharply, "Well, John? What did you find out? When will the Breton be brought to trial and, more important, what will he be charged with?"

"There will be no trial, Aunt Emma." John's face was in shadows and his voice was toneless, difficult to read. "Philippe told me that the Breton is dead. He'd been taken under guard to the dungeons at the Grand Châtelet, and was found this morning, hanged by his bedsheet."

There was a startled silence, but it didn't last long. They all began to talk at once, raising their voices to make themselves heard, and it was soon apparent that they were of one mind. No one believed the Breton had killed himself. Who ever heard of a prisoner being given bed linens? How convenient it was, that the Breton had taken so many men's secrets to his grave! Had he, by chance, left a confession behind, admitting his guilt in other crimes the provost and bailiffs had been unable to solve?

Simon finally cut through the sarcasm and skepticism by pointing out a salient fact: whether the Breton had died by his

318

own hand or he'd had help, he was dead and on his way to Hell. Justice had been done. "I feared that he'd weasel out of the charges at a trial. Could we truly have proved he murdered the Lady Arzhela? As much as I'd like to have seen that misbegotten hellspawn publicly shamed and pelted with mud and rotten eggs as he was dragged to the gallows, at least he has paid for his crimes with his life. I, for one, am going to celebrate. Who wants to join me in the great hall to drink to the Lady Arzhela's memory and the Breton's eternal damnation?"

They looked toward John, and when he did not object, Morgan and Simon started for the door. Glad to escape the room's stale atmosphere, Claudine and Emma followed. Justin and Durand would have liked to follow, too, but John had yet to move.

"Are you disappointed that there will be no trial, my lord?" Justin asked. "That would have been the most effective way to prove the letter was a forgery, but—"

"You are such an innocent, de Quincy," Durand scoffed. "Do you truly think that letter would ever have been mentioned in court? How would that benefit the French king? As little as he'd have liked that forgery to succeed, he is not about to make any accusations against the Duchess Constance. With war looming between France and England, Brittany may prove useful down the road. As a possible heir to the English throne, young Arthur is worth his weight in gold."

Justin had never thought of himself as an innocent, certainly not after more than a year as the queen's man. But he'd still clung to a few illusions about royal justice, illusions he was loath to surrender. As he glanced from Durand to John, he found himself hoping that he'd never become as jaded and distrustful as they were. The price of something and its value were not always one and the same.

"Do not mock de Quincy, Durand," John said. "This world of ours is one of sheep and wolves, and God made him a sheep, as simple as that. A man cannot fight his fate."

Justin was rankled enough to hit back. "And what was the Lady Arzhela, my lord? A lamb to the slaughter or a she-wolf?"

John looked at him, his expression giving away nothing of his thoughts. "I do not blame you for not wanting to be a sheep, de Quincy. But you are not ready to run with the wolves. For example, I daresay it never occurred to you that this forgery scheme of the Breton's most likely originated with Philippe. It was too well conceived for the Breton to have plucked it out of the air. My guess is that this was one of Philippe's contingency plans, to be used if and when needed. The Breton's great mistake was thinking that he was the puppeteer, not the puppet. My friend the French king does not like his hirelings to show so much enterprise. And then, he blundered even more badly by getting caught at it. Found-out sins are the only unforgivable kind."

Justin was momentarily at a loss, disquieted by a cynicism so corrosive, so soul-stifling. "If you are saying that the Breton would never have faced a reckoning over the forgery, my lord, at least he has not escaped punishment for the Lady Arzhela's murder. At least he has answered for that."

"Yes," John said, and then, "assuming that he is really dead."

CHAPTER XXIV

March 1194
Paris, France

"Master Justin, come quick!" Yann tumbled out of the stairwell into the great hall. "Hurry," he pleaded. "They are fighting!"

"Easy, lad." Justin grasped the boy by the shoulders. "Who?"

"Morgan and the other one—" For a confused moment, Yann could not recall the name of the man he privately called the Cock for the way he strutted around. "Simon," he gasped, "Simon!"

Justin plunged into the stairwell, as did Durand and Garnier. Other men would have followed, too, for a fight was always a popular form of entertainment, but Emma halted their rush. "They can deal with it," she said, and after the others dispersed in disappointment, she indulged her own curiosity and started up the stairs, with Claudine right behind her.

They heard the sounds of conflict before they reached Morgan and Simon's small chamber under the roof eaves. Bursting into the room, they halted in surprise. They'd taken it for granted that Simon was the instigator, but it was obvious from the first glance that he was defending himself. Blood trickling from a torn lip, he was trying to keep Morgan at bay. "Hell and furies," he insisted, "I do not want to fight with you!"

Morgan paid him no heed and drove his fist into Simon's stomach. He cried out in pain and fury and grabbed for the closest weapon at hand, a wine flagon, which he swung at Morgan's head. Morgan ducked under it and tackled Simon, who went crashing into one of the overturned pallets. Rolling around in the floor rushes, they were cursing and pummeling each other as Justin and Durand intervened.

"Stop it, you fools!" Durand bellowed, laboring to separate the two men. Morgan proved harder to convince than Simon, and continued to struggle until Justin and Garnier pinned him down. Shoving Simon into a corner, Durand glowered at Morgan. "If we let you up, will you cease acting like a crazy man?"

"Yes—" Morgan was breathing as heavily as a foundering horse, his face darkly flushed, but his fury had yet to diminish. "I found that hellspawn going through my belongings!"

Leaning against the wall, Simon daubed at his bleeding mouth with the sleeve of his tunic, clutching his bandaged ribs with his free hand. "You would not let me explain, you idiot," he complained. "I was not stealing!"

"The Devil you weren't! I caught you right in the act!"

"I am no thief!"

"Two Bretons who're missing horses might dispute that," Durand said, very dryly.

"That was different and you know it! Any man would take a horse if his life were in danger. Even you, Durand—especially you!"

"Suppose you tell us, then," Justin suggested, "what you

were doing, if not stealing."

Simon opened his mouth, shut it again as he considered his plight. "Ah, shit," he muttered. "I guess I have no choice now. I was merely doing Lord John's bidding."

Morgan looked shocked. "Lord John told you to steal from me?"

"No, he told me to find out what you were hiding, who you really were. He said if I did, he might take me into his service."

"Over my dead body!" Durand sputtered. Garnier was no less horrified. But Emma, standing in the doorway, burst out laughing, and so did Claudine. Justin could not help grinning, too, at the sight of the other men's consternation. Never one to miss an opportunity, Simon moved swiftly to take advantage of this one.

"That is all I was doing, I swear," he said earnestly. "And Lord John was right to be suspicious. I like you, Morgan, wish you no misfortune. But how do you explain those?" He pointed dramatically toward the floor rushes.

Justin stooped and picked up the items. Morgan stiffened, but he seemed to realize protest was useless, and he said nothing as Justin showed the others what he'd recovered: a handsome gold ring set with a glittering emerald, and a small leather-bound Psalter.

Emma had a good eye for the value of jewels, and her eyebrows rose as she studied the ring. "This is very costly, Morgan. How would a groom come by it?"

"I did not steal it," Morgan said hotly. "It was a gift!"

"You need to do better than that, Morgan," Simon said, with a smile that somehow managed to be both sympathetic and condescending. "And what about the book of prayers? How do you explain that?"

"I do not owe you any explanations!"

But Simon saw that the others were swinging over to his side. "How many grooms know how to read?"

"There are surely some," Justin objected, but even he sounded halfhearted, and Simon moved in for the kill.

"Grooms who read Latin?" he asked incredulously, and when Justin flipped the psalter open, he saw that the prayers were indeed inscribed in Latin.

Morgan scowled, feeling the weight of their eyes upon him. "You win," he said at last. "I'll tell you what you want to know. But I am only telling it once, so I'll not be saying a word until Lord John gets back."

By the time John returned to the house, darkness was obscuring the city skyline and curiosity was at fever pitch. At first John dismayed them by insisting that Morgan's revelations could wait until after supper, but he was joking, and soon led them abovestairs to the solar. Morgan faced a small, select audience; John permitted only Justin, Durand, Emma, and Claudine to join him, much to the disappointment of Simon and Garnier. Once a fire had been lit in the hearth and wine fetched, John regarded Morgan with narrowed, speculative eyes and then said bluntly, "Who are you?"

"I'd prefer to sit," Morgan said, "for this will take a while." With John's permission, he seated himself on a wooden bench. Usually he was one for lounging or sprawling, but now he sat bolt upright, arms tightly folded across his chest, a very defensive pose. "My name is Morgan Bloet; I did not lie about that. My father is Sir Ralph Bloet, Lord of Lackham. He is liegeman to the Earl of Pembroke, and holds lands in Gloucestershire, Hampshire, and Wiltshire. His brother is the Lord of Raglan—"

"There is no need to give us your family history since Adam," John cut in impatiently, but Morgan was not intimidated.

"I must do this my way, my lord," he said stubbornly, "or I'll not do it at all." After a pause to make sure he'd won this clash of wills, he continued. "My mother is the Lady Nesta, daughter of Iorwerth ab Owain, the Lord of Caerleon in Gwent. I am their firstborn son, but I was told as far back as I can remember that I was meant for the Church." His eyes flicked toward the others, coming to rest upon Emma. "So yes, my lady, I can read." Adding, *"Fronti nulla fides,"* warning her, in excellent Latin, that a book should not be judged by its cover, a gibe that was wasted upon Emma, whose Latin did not go beyond the responses to the Mass.

John had leaned back in his seat, his expression enigmatic. "I think I see where this road is going," he said softly. If so, he had the advantage over the others, who were listening in varying degrees of perplexity and amazement.

Emma was gazing at Morgan coldly, for an insult that was too cerebral to be understood was especially offensive. "So why is the son of the Earl of Pembroke's vassal disguised as my groom?"

Morgan returned the look; he'd shed his humble servant's demeanor when he'd walked through the solar doorway. "If you listen, my lady, you'll know. Last year I overheard something I was not meant to hear. My father and uncle were quarreling and my uncle said... He called me a..." It was the first time any of them had seen the loquacious Morgan fumbling for words. "He said I was not of my father's blood." Taking refuge again in Latin, he said, his voice barely audible, *"Nullius filius."*

Justin drew in his breath, for that cut too close to the bone.

Nullius filius meant "no man's son," and that was how he'd felt for his entire life. "Did you believe that, Morgan?"

"Oddly enough, I did. I had no reason to, for I'd never lacked for love. But somehow I knew that my uncle had spoken true. So, I went off and got drunk, and when I sobered up, I sought out my mother and asked for the truth. She did not deny it, saying that she'd wed my father whilst pregnant with another man's child." This was turning out to be more painful than Morgan had anticipated. Reaching blindly for his wine cup, he drank deeply. "She did not deceive Sir Ralph. He knew from the first, offering marriage to spare her shame."

Justin glanced involuntarily toward Claudine; she'd gone pale and one hand was clasping her throat. Durand and John were inscrutable, but Emma looked skeptical. "The Welsh have queer ideas of morality," she said. "To bear a child out of wedlock is not the shame it would be in a more Christian country."

"My mother had been a handmaiden to the Lady Gwenllian, the wife of the prince of South Wales, the Lord Rhys. She could not turn to her family, for the man was her father's sworn enemy. She loved her father, could not bear to hurt him so."

"That explains her reason for wanting the marriage," Durand said, and now he sounded no less skeptical than Emma. "But what of Sir Ralph... Bloet, was it? Why would he take on another man's whelp?"

Morgan bristled at the tone, but he held his temper. Looking toward John, he said succinctly, "My mother was highborn, and very beautiful."

"I do not doubt it." John sipped his wine, gestured for Morgan to continue. "Did your mother tell you the name of the man who'd sired you?"

"Yes, my lord, she did. The same man who sired you. Henry Fitz Empress, the English king."

Emma choked on her wine, seemed in danger of strangling for several moments. Claudine gasped and Justin's mouth dropped open. Even Durand looked startled. Only John seemed to take this amazing revelation with equanimity. "Indeed? When did they have this... tryst?"

"September of God's Year 1171. Lord Rhys came to the English king at Pembroke, where he was planning to sail for Ireland. He brought his court, and my mother was amongst them. She was young, and Henry was the king," Morgan said, with a slight shrug, as if that explained it all and, to his audience, it did. "She was flattered, bedazzled, easily seduced. But when she learned she was with child, she was panic-stricken. The king had taken Caerleon from her father that summer, and he'd declared war upon the English Crown. She feared her father would never have forgiven her had he known she'd lain with Henry. She knew Sir Ralph, and when he found her in tears, she confided in him. You know the rest of the story."

"Yes," John agreed, "we do. It is not that uncommon a tale, is it?"

"I suppose not. But this one ended better than most, I daresay. My mother and Sir Ralph have been very content in this marriage, and he always treated me as if I were his own."

"But you have brothers, do you not?" John said, with certainty. "That would explain why they steered you toward the Church, even though you were the firstborn. It is only natural that he'd want his demesnes to pass to his blood kindred."

Morgan nodded. His shoulders slumped, as if the truth had been a burden he'd carried too long. "So now you know."

"Why," John asked, "did my father not provide for you? Say what you will about him, he always took care of his own. Jesu, he even brought a few of his bastards to his court for my mother to raise!"

"My mother never told him. He'd sailed for Ireland by the time she realized her plight. After she wed Sir Ralph, they agreed that no one need know. People would assume that Sir Ralph had sampled the cream ere he bought it, and I daresay most did, for I remember no whispers, no sidelong looks from neighbors. My mother named me Morgan, after her favorite uncle, and Sir Ralph gave me his name, his protection, and his affection. I have no complaints. They did the best they could under the circumstances. Nor can I blame the English king. He did not reject me, never knew about me."

Justin flinched, wondering if Morgan realized how lucky he was to be able to say that. He started at the touch of a hand on his shoulder, for he'd not heard Claudine's soft footsteps in the rushes. She said nothing, merely squeezed his arm in silent understanding.

"So why did you come to me under false pretenses?" Emma was obviously having difficulty accepting that her stable groom might also be her nephew. "What did you want?"

"From you, nothing. After I learned the truth, I was confused," Morgan said, with a faint smile at such a vast understatement. "It took time for me to come to terms with it. I was angry at first, and I was no longer sure that I wanted a vocation in the Church. It is an unsettling thing, learning that your identity is false, your life a lie."

"And then you sought us out," John said.

"Yes. I am not truly sure why," Morgan admitted. "I suppose I was curious. To find I had another family..."

"A royal family," Emma said tartly, making it clear that she had no intention of welcoming this newfound kinsman with open arms. "You saw a chance to enrich yourself at my brother's expense, for Harry was no longer alive to deny your claims!"

"How did I enrich myself by grooming your horses and mucking out your stalls?" Morgan shot back. "I admit I was curious, and I have a right to be! The same blood that flows in your veins, Lady Emma, also flows in mine!"

"So you say. But you have no proof of any of this, do you?"

"No," Morgan said reluctantly. "I have the emerald ring that the king gave my mother and I have her word. I need no more than that, for she would not lie to me."

Emma found an unexpected ally now in Durand, who laughed. "Did I miss something? It was my understanding, lad, that she'd been lying to you since the day you were born!"

Morgan glared at Durand. "She had no choice, not whilst her father still lived. They agreed that they'd not lie to me should I ever ask, and they did not." When Durand did not respond, he swung back toward Emma. "That is why I came to you under 'false pretenses.' Had I come to you with the truth, you'd have turned me away at once. I knew I had no proof that would satisfy you."

"I disagree." All heads turned toward John. "You do have proof, Morgan. You showed it to me in the cemetery of the Holy Innocents."

Once again, Morgan seemed at a loss for words. Emma was not. "Since when have you become as trusting and guileless as a cloistered nun? I thought you had more sense, John!"

John shrugged. "A man," he said, "can never have too many brothers."

* * *

MORGAN ATE SUPPER THAT EVENING AT the high table, a magnet for all eyes. Petronilla looked bewildered by his sudden elevation from groom to high-ranking guest; Emma was smoldering; most of John's household avidly curious. Justin was astonished, but very pleased by the outcome. "I wish Morgan well," he said quietly to Claudine. "I never expected, though, that John would accept him so easily or so wholeheartedly."

"It does not surprise me," she confided. "What did John say, that his father looked after his own? Well, so does John. He is very good about acknowledging his bastard children, sees that they want for nothing. And of all his brothers, the only one he seems truly fond of is Will Longsword."

At the mention of John's baseborn half brother, Justin suddenly realized why Morgan had seemed vaguely familiar from their first meeting. "That is who he reminds me of— Will! They do not have the same coloring, but there is a resemblance for certes."

Claudine nodded. "You never met King Henry, did you? Well, as soon as Morgan's secret was out, I could see the father in the son. The same grey eyes, the same powerful build, the freckles, even the bowed legs. And if I can see it, you may be sure that John does, too. Who would not welcome the ghost of a lost loved one?"

"Emma," Justin countered. "Moreover, I thought John hated his father."

"No, Richard did. Everything was always so much easier for Richard. But John was his father's favorite."

"But he betrayed Henry, abandoned him on his deathbed and went over to Richard and the French king."

"Yes," she said sadly, "he did."

On the following day, Justin began making preparations to depart. He'd hoped to leave at cockcrow, but John had gone to see the French king, taking Morgan along to introduce him to Philippe, and Justin did not want to go without bidding farewell to the newest Plantagenet. He'd tried to coax Morgan into returning to London with him, offering to introduce him to the brother with whom he had the most in common, Will Longsword, but Morgan had declined, saying that John had asked him to stay so they could get to know each other. Justin was not happy about that, convinced that John was a corrupting influence upon everyone he encountered, but there was nothing to be done about it. It was some small consolation that Emma was so disgruntled by the turn of events.

"Are you still set upon leaving this afternoon?" Claudine gave him a sidelong, flirtatious glance, half serious, half in jest. "Are you not tempted to spend the night?"

"Good Lord, yes," he said, with enough emotion to take any sting out of his refusal. "But I vowed to forswear any and all temptations during Lent." Now that he and Claudine were back on friendly terms, he thought it wise to put some distance between them, for nothing had changed; he'd still be lusting after a woman he could not trust.

"Mayhap you ought to be the one considering a life in the Church, not Morgan," she said, with mockery but no malice. "Do you think he'll ever take vows, Justin? I know there can be no higher calling than to serve the Almighty, but it still seems a waste of a good man."

She giggled, looking both pleased and shocked by her own irreverence, and Justin laughed, too. "You ought to hear Durand on that subject," he said, remembering the knight's diatribe about "the madness that drives a man to renounce the pleasures of the female flesh." "And if I needed more proof

331

that it was time for me to leave, starting to quote Durand is surely it!"

"I think you showed great forbearance in not murdering the man and disposing of the body in some Breton bog. Care to wager how long it takes for Durand and Simon to be at each other's throats?" When he shook his head, grinning, she glanced around the hall before saying confidentially, "I hear that Yann asked you to take him with you to England, and you mustered up enough fortitude to refuse."

"How did you know that? Ah, Claudine, that was so hard to do. But I had no choice. I could not look after him, not as long as I serve the queen."

"Well, what about that tavern maid... Belle? She could keep him when you were away. Though I suppose she is not the motherly sort."

Justin was surprised by that sudden flash of claws. "You mean Nell, and I could not ask her to do that. She has enough on her plate, taking care of her daughter and running the alehouse. Why do you not like her, Claudine?"

"Are you going to claim that she speaks well of me?" she demanded, and he conceded defeat with a smile and a shrug. It was then that Yann appeared at his elbow, startling them both.

"I promise," he said, before Justin could say anything, "that I'd be no trouble. I do not eat much and I could take care of your dog and run errands—"

"Yann, we've been over this already. I am rarely in London, and that is not a city for a Breton lad to be roaming about on the loose. You'd not have to go looking for trouble. It would come looking for you."

Yann ducked his head, as if blinking back tears. "The Lady Arzhela would want you to take me," he said, so disingenuously that Justin and Claudine were both touched and amused, in equal measure.

"Yann, you scare me sometimes," Justin said wryly. "Lad, listen to me. A city like Paris or London is not where you belong. If only I knew someone who could find a place for you on a country manor, the way Lady Petronilla can—"

"Justin, you do," Claudine interrupted. Leaning over, she whispered a name in his ear. When he shook his head vehemently, she looked at him challengingly. "Why not? Who better to do a good deed than a man of God? Or are you too proud to ask him for a favor?"

"If you want to learn how to get people to do what you want, Yann, you need only watch the Lady Claudine in action," Justin said, more sharply than he'd intended. "This is what I can do, lad: I will ask the Bishop of Chester if he can take you into his household or find a place for you on one of his manors. It is likely he will agree, but you must remain here until I get word that he does. Then, I will come back for you. Agreed?"

"How do I know you are not just saying this? That you will come back for me?"

"You have my sworn word. If the bishop agrees, I will return and take you to Chester. But you must promise to stay here in Paris until you hear from me. Fair enough?"

Yann was not happy with the bargain they'd just struck. But at least it offered a glimmer of hope, and he'd learned to settle for much less. "I promise," he said, fingers crossed behind his back.

Within the hour, though, John and Morgan returned, and Morgan would have none of it. "You do not want to live in England, Yann. You'd be happier in Wales, for Welsh is much easier for a Breton lad to learn than English. Stay here with me and when I go home, you can come with me. I've cousins about your age at Raglan and my mother's brother Hywel is the Lord of Caerleon now, so you'll have your pick of places. Do we have a deal?"

"Deal," Yann said happily, and Justin, blinking at how quickly the boy switched allegiance from him to Morgan, gave his approval, not seeing what else he could do. He trusted Morgan, after all, could hardly blame the man for being John's brother. Sending Yann off on an errand to the kitchen, Morgan looked intently from Justin to Claudine, back to Justin again.

"John learned something from the French king that disquieted him greatly. He would not tell me what, and I did not feel free to press; after all, our relationship has lasted barely a day. He went out into Lady Petronilla's gardens, and is still there. I was hoping that you or Durand or mayhap you, Lady Claudine, might be able to find out what is troubling him. I suspect it concerns the Bretons and that damned letter."

Justin was not thrilled at the prospect; the last place he wanted to venture was into the murky terrain of John's mind. But Claudine and Morgan were looking expectantly at him. Getting to his feet, he started across the hall to find Durand.

JOHN WAS SEATED ON A WOODEN bench in the gardens, playing with one of Petronilla's greyhounds. Seeing the men and Claudine bearing down upon him, he showed no surprise. "Passing strange how quickly people are drawn to the site of a disaster."

"We want to help," Morgan said, so simply that not even John could doubt his sincerity. "Why not let us?"

"I would that you could," John conceded, "but there is naught to be done. One of Philippe's spies at the Breton court has sent him word that Constance plans to make use of that accursed letter. I was hoping that they'd decide it was too risky after Simon and the Breton both disappeared under such strange circumstances. I ought to have known better. My luck has always been rotten."

"But you can prove the letter is false," Claudine said, sounding puzzled. "The Breton is dead but Simon de Lusignan is not, and he can testify that it was a scheme to cheat the Bretons at your expense."

"And you think anyone in Christendom would give credence to a de Lusignan?" John looked at her in disbelief. "No one would believe anything he had to say. His evidence would either be dismissed out of hand because no de Lusignan has ever been on speaking terms with the truth or it would be assumed that I'd paid him to lie on my behalf."

"The French king knows the truth," Morgan suggested, and winced when John laughed harshly.

"God spare me, another innocent! Morgan, you have much to learn about our family. Brother Richard would sooner believe the Devil than the French king. Moreover, it is no longer in Philippe's interest to clear me of suspicion, now, is it?"

Only Durand seemed to follow John's thinking; the others looked so baffled that John sighed, struggling to hold onto the scraps of his patience. "Things have changed dramatically in the past fortnight, or have you not noticed? Richard is free, back in England, and most likely besieging my castles even as we speak. Once he reduces them to rubble, he'll be heading for the closest port, eager to wreak havoc and let loose the dogs of war upon Philippe. With Richard's fiery breath on the backs of our necks, we're going to be hard pressed to defend our own lands, much less strike into his domains. I'd say my chances of becoming England's king are about as good right now as yours are of becoming Pope, Morgan. And you may be sure that has not escaped Philippe's notice."

Morgan still did not see, but Justin did and he felt a strange pang of pity for John and Philippe and Richard, even for his queen, for all those wielding power whilst treading on shifting sands that were no less treacherous than those in the Bay of Mont St Michel. "He is saying, Morgan, that Philippe will fear he may be tempted to try to make his peace with Richard. So the more suspicion and rancor between the brothers, the better it now is for the French king."

"Good for you, de Quincy," John said, with a sardonic smile. "You might one day make it to wolfdom, after all."

That was incomprehensible to Morgan and Claudine, who'd not been present for John's little lecture about wolves and sheep. Morgan hesitated, sensing that he was stepping out onto thin ice. "What of Queen Eleanor? Could you not tell her that this letter was a forgery? She could convince Richard, then, surely?"

The others tensed, knowing from painful experience that John's tangled, tortured relationship with his mother was a bottomless swamp, from which few emerged unscathed. John surprised them, though, by not lashing out at Morgan, giving his newfound brother something he rarely gave to anyone— the benefit of the doubt.

"That tactic—truth telling—might work with you and the Lady Nesta," he said tersely, "but not in the bosom of our loving family. My lady mother would not believe me."

With that, Justin heard the jaws of the trap slam shut. "Mayhap she would not," he said wearily, "but she might believe me."

CHAPTER XXV

March 1194
London, England

JUSTIN AWAKENED WITH A GASP, FLEEING the darkness of a
Fougères dungeon. It was not the first disquieting dream he'd
had of his entombment, but this one had a happy ending: a
blazing surge of sunlight as the trapdoor was flung open and
freedom beckoned in the guise of Morgan Bloet. He lay back
upon the bed, heartened by his night escape, hoping it meant
that the dreams would come less and less often and, eventually,
not at all. He was drifting off to sleep again when there was a
sharp knocking on the cottage door.

He'd got to London just as curfew was sounding, and was
one of the last travelers allowed to pass through the city gates.
By the time he'd reached Gracechurch Street, the alehouse
was shuttered and still, and the houses were dark, oil lamps
and hearth fires doused for the night. He'd stabled his mount
in a stall next to his stallion, Copper, and stumbled off to his
cottage behind Gunter's black-smithy. Not even bothering to
remove his boots, he'd fallen into bed, asleep before he'd
taken half a dozen breaths.

The knocking continued. Swinging off the bed, he was starting toward the door when it opened and a black whirlwind burst into the cottage to fling itself upon him. He staggered backward under the assault, and was fending off a hysterical canine as Nell followed Shadow in. "Dogs," she said briskly, "are more loyal than men and not as much trouble. The mad beast has not forgotten you, I see."

"How did you know I was back?" Justin asked, going over to give her a hug.

"What—you think Gunter would not notice another horse in his stable? Come with me," she insisted, steering him toward the door. "Lord only knows the last time you ate, so I made you a meal over at the alehouse."

Justin would have liked to change his clothes, but he knew better than to argue with Nell, and followed her outside, where he was surprised to see a twilight dusk settling over the city. Nell confirmed that he'd slept for more than eighteen hours. "We let you stay abed all day like a sluggard" was how she put it as she hastened him across the street.

"Who are 'we'?" he asked, and had his answer as he pushed open the door of the alehouse. It was crowded with his neighbors and friends: Gunter the blacksmith; Odo the barber, his wife, Agnes, and their nephew, Daniel; Ulric the chandler and his wife, Cicily; Marcus the cartwright; Avice, the tanner's widow; Nell's helper Ellis and Nell's young daughter, Lucy; even Aldred and Jonas, the one-eyed sergeant who was the bane of London's lawless and Justin's mentor. With a shy grin, Justin stepped forward into the warmth of their welcome.

By now they knew the rules—he never talked about what he did for the queen—so no one asked about his sudden disappearance or his long absence from Gracechurch Street. Instead they caught him up on neighborhood gossip and local happenings, telling him that the cobbler's wife had run off with a peddler, that Humphrey the mercer had disgraced himself by turning up drunk as a sailor's whore for Candlemas Mass, that a woman over on Aldgate Street had given birth to twins, that a fire had damaged the cook-shop down by the river, and that King Richard's entry into the city had been a spectacle to dazzle all eyes.

"All the shops closed early," Nell explained. "Even the taverns and alehouses shut down, since they knew everyone would be out in the street, watching for the king's coming. And they were, too. So many people lined up that there was not space for a snake to slither by. They hung out of windows and perched in trees and some fools had even clambered onto rooftops to see!"

"And the streets were clean," Aldred reported in awe. "The rakyers had actually worked for their wages and swept away all the dung and mud and straw and rubbish. It was a sight to behold... like a great fair day, with banners strung across the streets and ribbons wrapped around ale-poles and people waving scarves from windows and doves set free in white clouds when the king reached Cheapside!

"Thank God no fires broke out," he added, "for no one would ever have heard the fire bells over the clamor of the church bells. I'm surprised you did not hear them as far away as France, Justin! It was a fine welcome we gave the Lionheart. We did ourselves proud for certes, and the king and queen seemed right pleased that we'd turned out in such great numbers."

"Bearing in mind," Jonas said dryly, "that Londoners will come out by the hundreds for a hanging."

Justin smiled fondly at Jonas, for the sergeant's habitual skepticism seemed like starry-eyed optimism when compared to John's lethal cynicism. "It is good to be home," he said. "You spoke of the 'queen,' Aldred. So Richard had Berengaria with him? I've never laid eyes on her; few have. Was she fair to look upon?"

Aldred blinked in confusion. "Beren... who? I meant Lady Eleanor. What other queen is there?"

At the mention of his royal mistress, Justin lost some of his cheer; he was not looking forward to pleading John's case with the queen. But it had to be done on the morrow, even before he rode to St Albans to see Aline. "Where is King Richard lodging?" he asked. "Are they at the Tower or at the palace at Westminster?"

"King Richard did not dally here in London. He's long gone, off to put down Lord John's rebellion."

"And the queen?"

"Why, she went with him, lad," Odo volunteered, "and all the court, too, streaming out of Westminster like a flock of peacocks. Those pampered lords will be earning their bread now, just trying to keep up with the king!"

It sounded to Justin as if he would be earning his bread, too, chasing over half of England after the Lionheart. "Where has he gone?"

By common consent, they looked toward Jonas, for he was the sheriff's man, would be likely to know. And he did. "You've got a long ride ahead of you," he told Justin, with more amusement than sympathy. "He went north to besiege Lord John's castle at Nottingham."

BABY ELLA WAS AWAKE IN HER cradle, utterly intent upon getting her foot into her mouth. In the other cradle, her milk-sister slept peacefully, oblivious to her audience. "You must be amazed by how big she's got," Rohese said, pointing out the obvious with a coquettish smile, and her brother Baldwin rolled his eyes. She'd been visiting when Justin de Quincy arrived and she'd been so charmed by his courtly manners that she'd been hovering close by, insisting upon playing a role in his reunion with his daughter. Now she was chattering nonstop as Justin leaned over the cradle, and Baldwin and Sarra exchanged the sort of amused, exasperated glances that Rohese so often provoked.

"Of course Ella is much larger, but then, she's older so she would be... bigger, I mean." Rohese said, giggling self-consciously as she realized how silly she was sounding. "But your little lass is doing right well for her age. When she's not swaddled, she squirms about like a baby eel, doesn't she, Sarra? If you lie her down on her belly, she can roll over onto her back now. And when she wakes up in the morning and sees Baldwin or Sarra, she greets them with the sweetest smile."

Baldwin wished his sister would stop gushing over the poor lad, and Sarra thought it was not tactful of Rohese to remind Justin de Quincy of all the milestones he'd missed in his daughter's life. But in truth, Justin was not even listening to Rohese. Aline was the only one in the cottage for him at that moment, the only one in the world. She had a surprisingly thick cap of dark hair and skin like flower petals; when he touched her cheek with his finger, it felt like the soft, downy feathers of a baby bird.

"Do you want to hold her?" Rohese murmured throatily and, reaching for Aline, placed the sleeping infant in his arms before Sarra could object.

Justin cradled his daughter with such exaggerated care that it was both touching and comical to those watching. "I am back, butterfly," he said, and those silky lashes fluttered, revealing eyes the color of ground cinnamon, Claudine's eyes.

For a heartbeat, they looked at each other, and then Aline's lower lip began to tremble. Before he could react, her mouth contorted and she started to cry. There was nothing gradual or tentative about it, either; she screamed loudly enough to set his ears ringing, color flooding her little face, tiny fists beating the air in distress.

Sarra came swiftly to his side and reclaimed the frightened child. For several moments, there was no sound but the baby's wailing and a soothing, wordless murmur from Sarra. Back in familiar arms, Aline soon quieted, her sobs subsiding into broken hiccups, and Sarra sat down in a chair, discreetly opened her bodice and offered Aline the comfort of her breast.

After an awkward silence, Rohese said, in some embarrassment, "She is usually such a calm, good-natured baby, skittish only with—" She caught herself, but not in time, and Justin finished the sentence for her.

"Only with strangers," he said softly.

WILLIAM THE BASTARD HAD CHOSEN NOTTINGHAM'S site for its strategic significance, on a red sandstone ridge high above the River Trent. A new settlement had quickly sprung up in its protective shadow, nestled between the castle and the old town, and more than a hundred years later, the partition persisted. Nottingham was separated into the Norman-French Borough and the Saxon Borough, each with its own sheriff and bailiff. Justin was both intrigued and unsettled by the dichotomy—two towns, two ethnic identities—for he rarely thought about the social consequences of the Conquest. While French was his mother tongue, he also spoke English, and felt equally at home with the Saxon Aldred or the Norman Luke de Marston. The two halves of Nottingham reminded him that England, too, was a country divided, with a king who spoke not a word of English.

While the castle still held out, the city had opened its gates to Richard at once. The streets were filled with men-at-arms, vendors, peddlers, beggars, the inevitable prostitutes drawn by an army's presence, and local curiosity-seekers, eager to watch as Christendom's most celebrated soldier lay siege to his brother John's stronghold. The atmosphere was almost festive—until Justin reached the castle.

Justin had been told that the fortress had been under siege for weeks, but it was obvious that there had been a recent assault. The timber palisades enclosing the outer bailey were still smoldering, and the acrid smell of smoke hung low over the site. The torn-up bloody ground testified to the cost of the onslaught, as did the newly dug grave pits. The king's men were now in control of the outer bailey, and were in the process of making ready for an attack upon the upper and middle baileys. Even with his limited siege experience, Justin could see this would be a much greater challenge, for Richard's soldiers would be charging uphill against men entrenched behind thick stone walls.

He was searching for Will Longsword, John's half brother. They'd established a good rapport and he could rely upon Will for an accurate account of the events that had occurred since Richard's return to English soil. He was sure, too, that Will would know where the queen was lodging. But finding Will in this turbulent, roiling sea of soldiers would not be easy.

He never did find Will but, much to his surprise, he soon saw a familiar figure, a small man astride a big bay stallion, well armored in chain mail and the authority of command. "My lord earl!" he cried, loudly enough to attract the Earl of Chester's attention. At the sight of Justin, he looked equally surprised, and urged his mount in the younger man's direction.

"What are you doing here?" Justin exclaimed, and then grimaced, for it was obvious what the earl was doing—laying siege to Nottingham Castle. He amended his query to "When did you get here, my lord?"

"A few weeks ago. Last month the Council authorized the seizure of Lord John's castles at Nottingham, Tickhill, Marlborough, Lancaster, and St Michael's Mount in Cornwall. The earls of Huntingdon and Derby and I were chosen to reduce Nottingham to a pile of rubble, so I made haste to return from Brittany. Marlborough and Lancaster were quickly taken, and the commander at St Michael's Mount died of fright upon hearing that King Richard was free." Chester's smile was mordant. "A pity all of the king's foes could not be so obliging."

"So that leaves only Tickhill and Nottingham?"

"Only Nottingham. We got word this morn that Tickhill has yielded to the Bishop of Durham. Unfortunately the stubborn sods behind these walls"—with a wave of his hand toward the castle keep—"have balked at surrendering. They are convinced that King Richard is dead and this is a clever trick to deceive them into giving up. The king did not take kindly to being dismissed as an impostor, as you can well imagine."

Justin looked over at the charred palisade walls. "So he ordered an assault upon the castle."

"He led it himself, de Quincy, and a bloody one it was, with fierce fighting and many deaths. But he did in one day what we'd failed to do in nigh on a month. He took the outer bailey, set fire to the barbican guarding the second gate, and only withdrew when night fell. Today he ordered his carpenters to build mangonels, and whilst we wait for them to be done, he has provided some entertainment for our men, and for those huddling within the castle."

"What do you mean, my lord?" Justin asked in perplexity and Chester smiled grimly.

"Come with me," he said, "and I'll show you."

THE SIEGE ENGINES WERE BEING CONSTRUCTED on the hill north of the castle, within sight of the garrison but out of range of their crossbows. And here, too, a gallows had been erected. Several bodies dangled slowly in the wind. As Justin and Chester reined in to watch, another prisoner was dragged up onto the gallows, hands tied behind his back. A noose was placed around his neck and then he was dispatched to God. Justin made the sign of the Cross over the strangling man, relieved when his legs finally stopped kicking.

"Some of John's men," Chester said, "taken in yesterday's assault. The king wanted these rebels to see what awaits those who defy him." Glancing toward approaching horsemen, he said, "Here he comes now."

Justin did not need to be told that. Richard Lionheart wore the light armor he'd become accustomed to in the heat of the Holy Land, a chain-mail hauberk and a helmet with nose guard. He was as fair as John was dark; the hair curling out of the back of his helmet was a burnished red-gold and the eyes narrowed upon the castle walls were a blazing blue. He was astride the most spectacular stallion Justin had ever seen, the shade of polished pearl, with a gait that was poetry in motion and a streaming silver tail that trailed almost to the ground. Gilded by sunlight, man and horse looked otherworldly, as if they'd ridden right out of a minstrel's tale of bygone glory, and as he looked upon the English king, Justin found himself thinking unexpectedly: *Poor John.*

* * *

THE QUEEN HAD CHOSEN TO AWAIT the resolution of the siege of Nottingham at a nearby royal manor. The next morning, Justin set out for Clipstone, deep in the heart of Sherwood Forest. He'd been told it was a hunting lodge built by Eleanor's husband, the late King Henry, and he half expected it to be a rustic, simple structure, for Henry had never been overly concerned about comfort, especially when he was pursuing his passion for the hunt. He discovered, though, that Clipstone was a residence of substance, with a large stone hall, a king's chamber, chapel, stables, fishpond, even a deer park, and Queen Eleanor was holding court as if she were back at Westminster.

Admitted into the great hall, Justin was startled to see so many princes of the Church. At first glance, it looked as if every bishop in England had come to do honor to the English king. He recognized the Archbishop of Canterbury and the Archbishop of York, who was—like Morgan Bloet and Will Longsword—a bastard son of King Henry. He recognized, too, the bishops of Hereford and Worcester, and did not know whether to be relieved or disappointed when he did not find his father's tall, stately figure among the others.

The queen was the center of attention, as she'd been for almost all of her seventy years on God's earth. Her face framed by a fine linen barbette, her hair covered by a delicate, gauzy veil held in place by a gold circlet, she was elegant and regal in damask silk the color of claret, and from a distance, she appeared to be defying time as boldly as she'd defied two royal husbands and the conventions that defined and circumscribed female behavior in their world. Up close, though, she looked far more fragile, a woman who'd lost as many battles as she'd won, relying upon an indomitable will to spur on an aging body.

Surrounded by prelates, she was relating a story of her son's experiences in the Holy Land, and, as always, Justin was startled to see John's greenish-gold eyes in her face. "It was my son's greatest sorrow that he was unable to recapture Jerusalem from Saladin. On one of his scouting expeditions, he rode to the top of the hill the crusaders called Montjoie, which offered a view of Jerusalem from its heights. But Richard refused to join the others, instead putting up his shield to block out the sight, saying that if he was not able to deliver the Holy City from the infidels, he was not worthy to behold it."

That was a story sure to win approbation from an audience of churchmen, and there were murmurings of admiration and approval. Eleanor's smile was one Justin would long remember, for he'd never seen her show such unguarded joy. He settled himself on the fringes of the crowd, content to wait until she took notice of him.

THE SUN WAS SLANTING TOWARD THE west as Justin walked beside the fishpond with his queen. Others were trailing after them—her ladies-in-waiting, chaplain, an earl, and several bishops—but they kept at a discreet distance, allowing Eleanor to converse in private with her agent. The fishpond was located in a southeast corner of the estate, some distance from the manor, and Justin was surprised by the queen's stamina; she'd set a brisk pace that had yet to falter. Approaching the water's edge, she halted, listening to the silence, breathing in the cool spring air, and then said, "Tell me more about this forged letter."

He did, to the best of his ability. It was a long story and he worried that she'd tire, but she brushed aside his concerns, and listened intently, without interruptions. Once he was done, she gazed for a time at the mirrored surface of the pond, her eyes following the drift of the reflected clouds. "Richard's release almost did not come to pass," she said. "The emperor had got letters from John and Philippe, pledging to pay him even more money for every month that he'd keep Richard captive. Heinrich was sorely tempted to accept their offer, and he even dared to show Richard the letters."

Her lip curled. "The man has no shame. Fortunately that was not true of his lords, who were horrified that he'd consider this eleventh-hour betrayal. Richard defended himself with the eloquence of outrage and when Heinrich realized that his barons were utterly on Richard's side, he agreed to honor our pact. But for two days, my son's fate hung in the balance, thanks to Heinrich's greed and their treachery. John is right to be fearful."

Justin wisely kept silent, for he admittedly did not understand the moral ambiguities that clouded the crimes of the highborn. In his judgment, John's treachery was reason enough to cast him out into darkness. But he knew that was not true for the queen. Apparently there were sins that could be forgiven and sins that could not, and those who wielded power seemed to know instinctively which were which. He had done his duty, giving his queen an honest account of her youngest son's troubles, and he felt he owed John no more than that.

"It would appear," Eleanor said, with a hint of dry humor, "that you got more than you bargained for in France, Justin. I do not imagine you enjoyed pulling in harness with Durand."

"No, Madame, not much."

"You have acquitted yourselves well. I am very pleased with you both."

"Thank you, my lady," he said, wishing he did not have to share her praise with Durand, and as if reading his mind, she smiled at him.

"Durand is comfortable exploring the netherworld; he would have to be in order to keep pace with John. But it was harder for you, I know. I will not forget the service you have done me." She'd resumed walking and he fell in step as she continued to skirt the edge of the pond. "I daresay you never expected to be pleading Emma's case with me."

Or John's, either, he thought. "Lord John called it my 'pilgrimage to Hell and back,' " he said ruefully.

"Yes, that sounds like John," she said, and he thought he heard her sigh. "Did you hear?" she asked, after another silence. "The garrison at Nottingham has agreed to surrender. The men in command—Ralph Murdac and William de Wenneval—sent out two knights under a flag of truce to ascertain for themselves if Richard had truly returned. Once they were satisfied that was indeed so, they lost all stomach for further resistance."

Thinking of those gallows set up north of the castle, Justin was not surprised. "So it is over, then."

"At least on this side of the Channel. My son has summoned a great council to meet at Nottingham in a few days. Amongst the matters to be dealt with will be John's treason. He will be given forty days to appear before the council to answer these charges. If he does not, he will be judged to have forfeited any and all rights to the English Crown, his lands already having been confiscated."

Again, Justin kept silent and they walked on. After a time, Eleanor said, "Richard means to have a reckoning with Philippe as soon as possible. I expect that we'll be in France ere the spring is done. But I will need you, Justin, to return sooner than that."

"What would you have me do, Madame?"

She smiled faintly, for his matter-of-fact tone did not

completely disguise his dismay. "You need not leave right away, lad. Take some time to visit with your daughter. And then I would have you go back to France, where you must do your best to convince John that his only chance of survival is to throw himself on Richard's mercy. It will be no easy task, and not one you'd choose of your own free will."

Eleanor paused, her eyes searching Justin's face. "May I rely upon you, Justin, to do my bidding?"

Justin's hesitation was barely noticeable. "I serve at the queen's pleasure," he said.

AUTHOR'S NOTE

I WOULD LIKE TO BEGIN THIS note with the remarkable saga of Morgan Bloet. Morgan was indeed the illegitimate son of Henry II. While it was known that Morgan's Welsh mother, Nesta, was wed to Sir Ralph Bloet, her family lineage remained a mystery. I wasn't willing to give up that easily, however, and began to search the Internet for clues. Eventually a Bloet family Web site pointed me in the right direction—to a biography of William Marshal written by an esteemed British historian, David Crouch. His research had identified Nesta as the daughter of Iorwerth ab Owain, Lord of Caerleon, and with that information in hand, it was easy to fill in the gaps in Nesta's pedigree. I was also intrigued to discover that once John became king, he was very generous to the entire Bloet family, which argues quite strongly for an affectionate bond between John and his half brother Morgan. I enjoyed "working" with Morgan, and am sure he'll be popping up in other story lines.

But the most interesting episode in Morgan's life occurred nineteen years after the events in *Prince of Darkness,* and since I don't think that I'll ever get to dramatize it, I want to share it with my readers here. Morgan subsequently took holy vows, and rose rapidly in the Church, doubtless due to John's favor. By 1213, he was Bishop-elect of the See of Durham. In that year he traveled to Rome to receive papal confirmation of his election, only to be told that his illegitimacy barred him from serving in such a high Church position. As Morgan's half brother Geoffrey had been recognized as Bishop of Lincoln and then as Archbishop of York, Morgan probably assumed that, like Geoffrey, he'd be able to obtain a papal dispensation waiving the issue of his bastardy. But he was facing a different Pope, Innocent III, who was less inclined than his predecessors to do a friendly favor for an English king, especially one who was currently embroiled in a bitter power struggle with the papacy.

Pope Innocent III was apparently touched by Morgan's plight, however, and offered to confirm him as Bishop of Durham if he would swear an oath that he was the son of Ralph Bloet and Nesta rather than the son of Henry II and Nesta. Faced with the choice between gaining a bishopric and repudiating his paternity, Morgan declared that he could not deny his father, the king.

I was quite interested to learn that Welsh and Breton were still so similar in the twelfth century that a Welsh speaker would be able to understand Breton speech and vice versa. This definitely worked to Justin's benefit. People sometimes forget that so many different languages flourished in medieval times, often in the same country. A contemporary of King Henry II said that he was conversant with all the languages "from the coast of France to the River Jordan." He appears to have had some understanding of English, although there is no evidence that he ever spoke it, and neither of his sons—Richard and John—had any knowledge of the native tongue of their island realm. They were Kings of England who never thought of themselves as English. They are often called the Angevins because Henry's father was the Count of Anjou. They are more familiarly known as the Plantagenets, the surname of the dynasty that ruled England from 1154 to 1485. I employed this surname in *Prince of Darkness* as a convenience, although Henry and his sons never made use of it themselves.

Readers with photographic memory may notice that Eleanor has grown younger, shedding two years since my earlier mysteries. This is a fascinating example of the way history is an ongoing process; we are always learning new facts or discovering that long-established facts are erroneous. Historians have always accepted Eleanor's birth date as occurring in the year 1122, and I followed their lead in my earlier novels, *When Christ and His Saints Slept* and *Time and Chance*. But in 2002, a wonderful book called *Eleanor of Aquitaine: Lord and Lady* was published, and Andrew Lewis, one of the contributors to this valuable study, makes a most convincing argument that Eleanor was actually born in 1124. Eight hundred years after her death, Eleanor is still surprising us!

Simon de Lusignan and Arzhela de Dinan are products of my imagination, engrafted upon actual family trees. I implanted Simon onto a cadet branch of the notorious de Lusignan clan who settled at Lezay. In Arzhela's case, I took the liberty of marrying her to an actual Breton lord, Roland de Dinan. As Roland had died without heirs of his body, he seemed an ideal candidate for matrimony with the much younger Lady Arzhela, and I like to think he would not be displeased to be given such a lively fictional wife.

Richard Lionheart's wet nurse was Hodierna Neckham, and her son, Alexander, proudly boasted of being Richard's milk-brother. I couldn't resist using that royal connection for Justin's daughter, Aline. Justin is, of course, a fictional character mingling with actual historical figures, as are Durand and Claudine. Emma is based upon a real woman, however, sister to one king, aunt to two others, wife to a Welsh prince—and a blessing to a novelist in need of a quickwitted sophisticate with very sharp claws. I suspect that we have not seen the last of Emma.

There was no forged letter implicating John in a plot to assassinate Richard. There was very bad blood, though, between Duchess Constance and the English Royal House, and John was later threatened by a similar ploy when the French king attempted to dupe Richard into believing that John had switched his loyalties again; fortunately for John, he won that particular credibility duel.

Henry and Eleanor and *Devil's Brood* are next on my agenda. But if I may borrow a line from Bernard Cornwell and his marvelous Sharpe series: Justin will march again.

S.K.P.

September 2004

www.sharonkaypenman.com

ACKNOWLEDGMENTS

In my last mystery, *Dragon's Lair,* I quoted my favorite line from *Casablanca:* "Round up the usual suspects." Well, nothing has changed and the same cast gets top billing again. I have been blessed with the editor of every writer's dreams— Marian Wood; may she never consider retirement. I've been blessed, as well, with two remarkable agents, Molly Friedrich and Mic Cheetham. They deserve my gratitude and appreciation, as do the friends who continue to support me in my times of doubt, even in my occasional "diva" moments: Earle Kotila, Jill Davies, Marilynn Summers, Peggy Barrett, and my computer guru, Lowell LaMont. I'd like to thank my brother Bill for proving to me that the camera does not really hate me, and my dad for passing on the Penman writing gene. And, of course, Valerie Ptak LaMont, who helped me navigate those lonely Breton roads; there is much to be said for a friend with excellent map-reading skills.

A letter from the publisher

We hope you enjoyed this book. We are an independent
publisher dedicated to discovering brilliant books,
new authors and great storytelling. Please join us at
www.headofzeus.com and become part of our
community of book-lovers.

We will keep you up to date with our latest books, author
blogs, special previews, tempting offers, chances to win
signed editions and much more.

If you have any questions, feedback or just want to say hi,
please drop us a line on hello@headofzeus.com

 @HoZ_Books

 HeadofZeusBooks

www.headofzeus.com

HEAD *of* ZEUS

The story starts here